THOMAS MANN

MARIO AND THE MAGICIAN

AND OTHER STORIES

Translated by
H. T. Lowe-Porter

PENGUIN BOOKS

PENGUIN BOOKS

Published by the Penguin Group
27 Wrights Lane, London W8 5TZ, England
Viking Penguin Inc., 40 West 23rd Street, New York, New York 10010, USA
Penguin Books Australia Ltd, Ringwood, Victoria, Australia
Penguin Books Canada Ltd, 2801 John Street, Markham, Ontario, Canada, L3R 1B4
Penguin Books (NZ) Ltd, 182–190 Wairau Road, Auckland 10, New Zealand

Penguin Books Ltd, Registered Offices: Harmondsworth, Middlesex, England

First published in Great Britain by Martin Secker & Warburg 1936
Published in Penguin Books 1975
Reprinted 1978, 1984, 1988

English translation copyright 1936 by Martin Secker & Warburg
All rights reserved

Made and printed in Great Britain by
Richard Clay Ltd, Bungay, Suffolk
Set in Monotype Plantin

CONTENTS

A MAN AND HIS DOG

(1918)

He Comes Round the Corner

WHEN spring, the fairest season of the year, does honour to its name, and when the trilling of the birds rouses me early because I have ended the day before at a seemly hour, I love to rise betimes and go for a half-hour's walk before breakfast. Strolling hatless in the broad avenue in front of my house, or through the parks beyond, I like to enjoy a few draughts of the young morning air and taste its blithe purity before I am claimed by the labours of the day. Standing on the front steps of my house, I give a whistle in two notes, tonic and lower fourth, like the beginning of the second phrase of Schubert's Unfinished Symphony; it might be considered the musical setting of a two-syllabled name. Next moment, and while I walk towards the garden gate, the faintest tinkle sounds from afar, at first scarcely audible, but growing rapidly louder and more distinct; such a sound as might be made by a metal licence-tag clicking against the trimmings of a leather collar. I face about, to see Bashan rounding the corner of the house at top speed and charging towards me as though he meant to knock me down. In the effort he is making he has dropped his lower lip, baring two white teeth that glitter in the morning sun.

He comes straight from his kennel, which stands at the back of the house, between the props of the veranda floor. Probably, until my two-toned call set him in this violent motion, he had been lying there snatching a nap after the adventures of the night. The kennel has curtains of sacking and is lined with straw; indeed, a straw or so may be clinging to Bashan's sleep-rumpled coat or even sticking between his toes – a comic sight, which reminds me of a painstakingly imagined production of Schiller's *Die Räuber* that I once saw, in which old Count Moor

7

came out of the Hunger Tower tricot-clad, with a straw sticking pathetically between his toes. Involuntarily I assume a defensive position to meet the charge, receiving it on my flank, for Bashan shows every sign of meaning to run between my legs and trip me up. However at the last minute, when a collision is imminent, he always puts on the brakes, executing a half-wheel which speaks for both his mental and his physical self-control. And then, without a sound – for he makes sparing use of his sonorous and expressive voice – he dances wildly round me by way of greeting, with immoderate plungings and waggings which are not confined to the appendage provided by nature for the purpose but bring his whole hind quarters as far as his ribs into play. He contracts his whole body into a curve, he hurtles into the air in a flying leap, he turns round and round on his own axis – and curiously enough, whichever way I turn, he always contrives to execute these manoeuvres behind my back. But the moment I stoop down and put out my hand he jumps to my side and stands like a statue, with his shoulder against my shin, in a slantwise posture, his strong paws braced against the ground, his face turned upwards so that he looks at me upside-down. And his utter immobility, as I pat his shoulder and murmur encouragement, is as concentrated and fiercely passionate as the frenzy before it had been.

Bashan is a short-haired German pointer – speaking by and large, that is, and not too literally. For he is probably not quite orthodox, as a pure matter of points. In the first place, he is a little too small. He is, I repeat, definitely undersized for a proper pointer. And then his forelegs are not absolutely straight, they have just the suggestion of an outward curve – which also detracts from his qualifications as a blood-dog. And he has a tendency to a dewlap, those folds of hanging skin under the muzzle, which in Bashan's case are admirably becoming but again would be frowned on by your fanatic for pure breeding, as I understand that a pointer should have taut skin round the neck. Bashan's colouring is very fine. His coat is a rusty brown with black stripes and a good deal of white on chest, paws, and under side. The whole of his snub nose seems to have been dipped in black paint. Over the broad top of his head and on his cool hanging ears the black and brown combine in a lovely velvety pattern. Quite the prettiest thing about him, however, is the whorl or stud or little tuft at the centre of the convolution of white hairs on his chest, which stands out like the boss on an ancient breastplate. Very likely even his splendid coloration is a little too marked and would be objected to by those who put the laws of breeding above the value of personality, for it would appear that the classic pointer type should have a coat of one colour or at most with spots of a different one, but never stripes. Worst of all, from the point of view of classification, is a hairy growth hanging from his muzzle and the corners of his mouth; it might with some justice be called a moustache and goatee, and when you concentrate on it, close at hand or even at a distance, you cannot help thinking of an airedale or a schnauzer.

But classifications aside, what a good and good-looking animal Bashan is, as he stands there straining against my knee, gazing up at me with all his devotion in his eyes! They are particularly fine eyes, too, both gentle and wise, if just a little too prominent and glassy. The iris is the same colour as his coat, a rusty brown; it is only a narrow rim, for the pupils are dilated into pools of blackness and the outer edge merges into the white of the eye wherein it swims. His whole head is expressive of honesty and intelligence, of manly qualities corresponding to his physical structure: his arched and swelling chest where the ribs stand out under the smooth and supple skin; the narrow haunches, the veined, sinewy legs, the strong, well-shaped paws. All these bespeak virility and a stout heart; they suggest hunting blood and peasant stock – yes, certainly the hunter and game dog do after all predominate in Bashan, he is genuine pointer, no matter if he does not owe his existence to a snobbish system of inbreeding. All this, probably, is what I am really telling him as I pat his shoulder-blade and address him with a few disjointed words of encouragement.

So he stands and looks and listens, gathering from what I say and the tone of it that I distinctly approve of his existence – the very thing which I am at pains to imply. And suddenly he thrusts out his head, opening and shutting his lips very fast, and

makes a snap at my face as though he meant to bite off my nose.
It is a gesture of response to my remarks, and it always makes me
recoil with a laugh, as Bashan knows beforehand that it will. It
is a kiss in the hair, half caress, half teasing, a trick he has had
since puppyhood, which I have never seen in any of his pre-
decessors. And he immediately begs pardon for the liberty,
crouching, wagging his tail, and behaving funnily embarrassed.
So we go out through the garden gate and into the open.

We are encompassed with a roaring like that of the sea; for
we live almost directly on the swift-flowing river that foams
over shallow ledges at no great distance from the poplar avenue.
In between lie a fenced-in grass plot planted with maples, and
a raised pathway skirted with huge aspen trees, bizarre and
willowlike of aspect. At the beginning of June their seed-pods
strew the ground far and wide with woolly snow. Upstream, in
the direction of the city, construction troops are building a pon-
toon bridge. Shouts of command and the thump of heavy boots
on the planks sound across the river; also, from the farther
bank, the noise of industrial activity, for there is a locomotive
foundry a little way downstream. Its premises have been lately
enlarged to meet increased demands, and light streams all night
long from its lofty windows. Beautiful glittering new engines
roll to and fro on trial runs; a steam whistle emits wailing head-
tones from time to time; muffled thunderings of unspecified
origin shatter the air, smoke pours out of the many chimneys to
be caught up by the wind and borne away over the wooded
country beyond the river, for it seldom or never blows over to
our side. Thus in our half-suburban, half-rural seclusion the
voice of nature mingles with that of man, and over all lies the
bright-eyed freshness of the new day.

It might be about half past seven by official time when I set
out; by sun-time, half past six. With my hands behind my back
I stroll in the tender sunshine down the avenue, cross-hatched
by the long shadows of the poplar trees. From where I am I
cannot see the river, but I hear its broad and even flow. The
trees whisper gently, song-birds fill the air with their penetrating chirps and warbles, twitters and trills; from the direction of
the sunrise a plane is flying under the humid blue sky, a rigid,

mechanical bird with a droning hum that rises and falls as it steers a free course above river and fields. And Bashan is delighting my eyes with the beautiful long leaps he is making across the low rail of the grass-plot on my left. Backwards and forwards he leaps – as a matter of fact he is doing it because he knows I like it; for I have often urged him on by shouting and striking the railing, praising him when he fell in with my whim. So now he comes up to me after nearly every jump to hear how intrepidly and elegantly he jumps. He even springs up into my face and slavers all over the arm I put out to protect it. But the jumping is also to be conceived as a sort of morning exercise, and morning toilet as well, for it smooths his ruffled coat and rids it of old Moor's straws.

It is good to walk like this in the early morning, with senses rejuvenated and spirit cleansed by the night's long healing draught of Lethe. You look confidently forward to the day, yet pleasantly hesitate to begin it, being master as you are of this little untroubled span of time between, which is your good reward for good behaviour. You indulge in the illusion that your life is habitually steady, simple, concentrated, and contemplative, that you belong entirely to yourself – and this illusion makes you quite happy. For a human being tends to believe that the mood of the moment, be it troubled or blithe, peaceful or stormy, is the true, native, and permanent tenor of his existence; and in particular he likes to exalt every happy chance into an inviolable rule and to regard it as the benign order of his life – whereas the truth is that he is condemned to improvisation and morally lives from hand to mouth all the time. So now, breathing the morning air, you stoutly believe that you are virtuous and free; while you ought to know – and at bottom do know – that the world is spreading its snares round your feet, and that most likely tomorrow you will be lying in your bed until nine, because you sought it at two in the morning hot and befogged with impassioned discussion. Never mind. Today you, a sober character, an early riser, you are the right master for that stout hunter who has just cleared the railings again out of sheer joy in the fact that today you apparently belong to him alone and not to the world.

We follow the avenue for about five minutes, to the point where it ceases to be an avenue and becomes a gravelly waste along the river-bank. From this we turn away to our right and strike into another covered with finer gravel, which has been laid out like the avenue and like it provided with a cycle-path, but is not yet built up. It runs between low-lying, wooded lots of land, towards the slope which is the eastern limit of our river neighbourhood and Bashan's theatre of action. On our way we cross another road, equally embryonic, running along between fields and meadows. Farther up, however, where the tram stops, it is quite built up with flats. We descend by a gravel path into a well-laid-out, park-like valley, quite deserted, as indeed the whole region is at this hour. Paths are laid out in curves and rondels, there are benches to rest on, tidy playgrounds, and wide plots of lawn with fine old trees whose boughs nearly sweep the grass, covering all but a glimpse of trunk. They are elms, beeches, limes, and silvery willows, in well-disposed groups. I enjoy to the full the well-landscaped quality of the scene, where I may walk no more disturbed than if it belonged to me alone. Nothing has been forgotten – there are even cement gutters in the gravel paths that lead down the grassy slopes. And the abundant greenery discloses here and there a charming distant vista of one of the villas that bound the spot on two sides.

Here for a while I stroll along the paths, and Bashan revels in the freedom of unlimited level space, galloping across and across the lawns like mad with his body inclined in a centrifugal plane; sometimes, barking with mingled pleasure and exasperation, he pursues a bird which flutters as though spellbound, but perhaps on purpose to tease him, along the ground just in front of his nose. But if I sit down on a bench he is at my side at once and takes up a position on one of my feet. For it is a law of his being that he only runs about when I am in motion too; that when I settle down he follows suit. There seems no obvious reason for this practice; but Bashan never fails to conform to it.

I get an odd, intimate, and amusing sensation from having him sit on my foot and warm it with the blood-heat of his body. A pervasive feeling of sympathy and good cheer fills me, as almost invariably when in his company and looking at things from his angle. He has a rather rustic slouch when he sits down; his shoulderblades stick out and his paws turn negligently in. He looks smaller and squatter than he really is, and the little white boss on his chest is advanced with comic effect. But all these faults are atoned for by the lofty and dignified carriage of the head, so full of concentration. All is quiet, and we two sit there absolutely still in our turn. The rushing of the water comes to us faint and subdued. And the senses become alert for all the tiny, mysterious little sounds that nature makes: the lizard's quick dart, the note of a bird, the burrowing of a mole in the earth. Bashan pricks up his ears – in so far as the muscles of naturally drooping ears will allow them to be pricked. He cocks his head to hear the better; and the nostrils of his moist black nose keep twitching sensitively as he sniffs.

Then he lies down, but always in contact with my foot. I see him in profile, in that age-old, conventionalized pose of the beast-god, the sphinx: head and chest held high, forelegs close to the body, paws extended in parallel lines. He has got overheated, so he opens his mouth, and at once all the intelligence of his face gives way to the merely animal, his eyes narrow and blink and his rosy tongue lolls out between his strong white pointed teeth.

How We Got Bashan

In the neighbourhood of Tölz there is a mountain inn, kept by a pleasingly buxom, black-eyed damsel, with the assistance of a growing daughter, equally buxom and black-eyed. This damsel it was who acted as go-between in our introduction to Bashan and our subsequent acquisition of him. Two years ago now that was; he was six months old at the time. Anastasia – for so the damsel was called – knew that we had had to have our last dog shot; Percy by name, a Scotch collie by breeding and a harmless, feeble-minded aristocrat who in his old age fell victim to a painful and disfiguring skin disease which obliged us to put him away. Since that time we had been without a guardian. She telephoned from her mountain height to say that she had taken to board a dog that was exactly what we wanted and that it might be inspected at any time. The children clamoured to see it, and our own curiosity was scarcely behind theirs; so the very next afternoon we climbed up to Anastasia's inn, and found her in her roomy kitchen full of warm and succulent steam, preparing her lodgers' supper. Her face was brick-red, her brow was wet, the sleeves were rolled back on her plump arms, and her frock was open at the throat. Her young daughter went to and fro, an industrious kitchen-maid. They were glad to see us and thoroughly approved of our having lost no time in coming. We looked about; whereupon Resi, the daughter, led us up to the kitchen table, and squatting with her hands on her knees, addressed a few encouraging words beneath it. Until then, in the flickering half-light, we had seen nothing; but now we perceived something standing there, tied by a bit of rope to the table-leg: an object that must have made any soul alive burst into half-pitying laughter.

Gaunt and knock-kneed he stood there with his tail between his hind legs, his four paws planted together, his back arched, shaking. He may have been frightened, but one had the feeling that he had not enough on his bones to keep him warm; for indeed the poor little animal was a skeleton, a mere rack of bones with a spinal column, covered with a rough fell and stuck up on four sticks. He had laid back his ears – which muscular contraction never fails to extinguish every sign of intelligence and cheer in the face of any dog. In him, who was still entirely puppy, the effect was so consummate that he stood there expressive of nothing but wretchedness, stupidity, and a mute appeal for our forbearance. And his hirsute appendages, which he has to this day, were then out of all proportion to his size and added a final touch of sour hypochondria to his appearance.

We all stooped down and began to coax and encourage this picture of misery. The children were delighted and sympathetic at once, and their shouts mingled with the voice of Anastasia as, standing by her cooking-stove, she began to furnish us with the particulars of her charge's origins and history. He was named, provisionally, Lux, she said, in her pleasant, level voice; and was the offspring of irreproachable parents. She had herself known the mother and of the father had heard nothing but good. Lux had seen the light on a farm in Hugelfing; and it was only due to a combination of circumstances that his owners were willing to part with him cheaply. They had brought him to her inn because there he might be seen by a good many people. They had come in a cart, Lux bravely running the whole twenty kilometres behind the wheels. She, Anastasia, had thought of us at once, knowing that we were on the look-out for a good dog and feeling certain that we should want him. If we so decided, it would be a good thing all around. She was sure we should have great joy of him, he in his turn would have found a good home and be no longer lonely in the world, and she, Anastasia, would know that he was well taken care of. We must not be prejudiced by the figure he cut at the moment; he was upset by his strange surroundings and uncertain of himself, but his good breeding would come out strong before long. His father and mother were of the best.

Ye-es – but perhaps not quite well matched?

On the contrary; that is, they were both of them good stock. He had excellent points – she, Anastasia, would vouch for that. He was not spoilt, either, his needs were modest – and that meant a great deal, nowadays. In fact, up to now he had had nothing to eat but potato-parings. She suggested that we take him home on trial; if we found that we did not take to him she would receive him back and refund the modest sum that was asked for him. She made free to say this, not minding at all if we took her up. Because, knowing the dog and knowing us, both parties, as it were, she was convinced that we should grow to love him, and never dream of giving him up.

All this she said and a great deal more in the same strain in her easy, comfortable, voluble way, working the while over her stove, where the flames shot up suddenly now and then as though we were in a witches' kitchen. She even came and opened Lux's jaws with both hands to show us his beautiful teeth and – for some reason or other – the pink grooves in the roof of his mouth. We asked knowingly if he had had distemper; she replied with a little impatience that she really could not say. Our next question – how large would he get – she answered more glibly: he would be about the size of our

15

departed Percy, she said. There were more questions and answers; a good deal of warm-hearted urging from Anastasia, prayers and pleas from the children, and on our side a feeble lack of resolution. At last we begged for a little time to think things over; she agreed, and we went thoughtfully valley-wards, changing impressions as we went.

But of course the children had lost their hearts to the wretched little quadruped under the table; in vain we affected to jeer at their lack of judgement and taste, feeling the pull at our own heartstrings. We saw that we should not be able to get him out of our heads; we asked ourselves what would become of him if we scorned him. Into what hands would he fall? The question called up a horrid memory, we saw again the knacker from whom we had rescued Percy with a few timely and merciful bullets and an honourable grave by the garden fence. If we wanted to abandon Lux to an uncertain and perhaps gruesome fate, then we should never have seen him at all, never cast eyes upon his infant whiskered face. We knew him now, we felt a responsibility which we could disclaim only by an arbitrary exercise of authority.

So it was that the third day found us climbing up those same gentle foothills of the Alps. Not that we had decided to buy – no, we only saw that, as things stood, the matter could hardly have any other outcome.

This time we found Frau Anastasia and her daughter drinking coffee, one at each end of the long kitchen table, while between them he sat who bore provisionally the name of Lux, in his very attitude as he sits today, slouching over with his shoulder-blades stuck out and his paws turned in. A bunch of wild flowers in his worn leather collar gave him a festive look, like a rustic bridegroom or a village lad in his Sunday best. The daughter, looking very trim herself in the tight bodice of her peasant costume, said that she had adorned him thus to celebrate his entry into his new home. Mother and daughter both told us they had never been more certain of anything in their lives than that we would come back to fetch him – they knew that we would come this very day.

So there was nothing more to say. Anastasia thanked us in

her pleasant way for the purchase price – ten marks – which we handed over. It was clear that she had asked it in our interest rather than in hers or that of the dog's owners; it was by way of giving Lux a positive value, in terms of money, in our eyes. We quite understood, and paid it gladly. Lux was untied from his table-leg and the end of the rope laid in my hand; we crossed Anastasia's door-step followed by the warmest, most cordial assurances and good wishes.

But the homeward way, which it took us an hour to cover, was scarcely a triumphal procession. The bridegroom soon lost his bouquet, while everybody we met either laughed or else jeered at his appearance – and we met a good many people, for our route lay through the length of the market town at the foot of the hill. The last straw was that Lux proved to be suffering from an apparently chronic diarrhoea, which obliged us to make frequent pauses under the villagers' eyes. At such times we formed a circle round him to shield his weakness from un-friendly eyes – asking ourselves whether this was not distemper already making its appearance. Our anxiety was uncalled-for: the future was to prove that we were dealing with a sound and cleanly constitution, which has been proof against distemper and all such ailments up to this day.

Directly we got home we summoned the maids to make acquaintance with the new member of the family and express their modest judgement of his worth. They had evidently been prepared to praise; but, reading our own insecurity in our eyes, they laughed loudly, turning their backs upon the appealing object and waving him off with their hands. We doubted whether they could understand the nature of our financial transaction with the benevolent Anastasia and in our weakness declared that we had had him as a present. Then we led Lux into the veranda and regaled him with a hearty meal of scraps.

He was too frightened to eat. He sniffed at the food we urged upon him, but was evidently, in his modesty, unable to believe that these cheese-parings and chicken-bones were meant for him. But he did not reject the sack stuffed with seaweed which we had prepared for him on the floor. He lay there with his paws drawn up under him, while within we took counsel and eventually came to a conclusion about the name he was to bear in the future.

On the following day he still refused to eat; then came a period when he gulped down everything that came within reach of his muzzle; but gradually he settled down to a regular and more fastidious regimen, this result roughly corresponding with his adjustment to his new life in general, so that I will not dwell further upon it. The process of adaptation suffered an interruption one day – Bashan disappeared. The children had taken him into the garden and let him off the lead for better freedom of action. In a momentary lapse of vigilance he had escaped through the hole under the garden gate and gained the outer world. We were grieved and upset at his loss – at least the masters of the house were, for the maids seemed inclined to take light-heartedly the loss of a dog which we had received as a gift; perhaps they did not even consider it a loss. We telephoned wildly to Anastasia's inn, hoping he might find his way thither. In vain, nobody had seen him; two days passed before we heard that Anastasia had word from Hugelfing that Lux had put in an appearance at his first home some hour and a half before. Yes, he was there, his native idealism had drawn him back to the world of his early potato-parings; through wind and weather he had trotted alone the twelve or fourteen miles which he had first covered between the hind wheels of the farmer's cart. His former owners had to use it again to deliver him into Anastasia's hands once more. On the second day after that we went up to reclaim the wanderer, whom we found as before, tied to the table-leg, jaded and dishevelled, bemired from the mud of the roads. He did show signs of being glad to see us again—but then, why had he gone away?

The time came when it was plain that he had forgotten the farm – yet without having quite struck root with us; so that he was a masterless soul and like a leaf carried by the wind. When we took him walking we had to keep close watch, for he tended to snap the frail bond of sympathy which was all that as yet united us and to lose himself unobtrusively in the woods, where, being quite on his own, he would certainly have reverted to the condition of his wild forebears. Our care preserved him from this dark fate, we held him fast upon his civilized height and to his position as the comrade of man, which his race in the course of millennia has achieved. And then a decisive event, our removal to the city – or a suburb of it – made him wholly dependent upon us and definitely a member of the family.

Notes on Bashan's Character and Manner of Life

A man in the Isar valley had told me that this kind of dog can become a nuisance, by always wanting to be with his master. Thus I was forewarned against taking too personally Bashan's persistent faithfulness to myself, and it was easier for me to discourage it a little and protect myself at need. It is a deep-lying patriarchal instinct in the dog which leads him – at least in the more manly, outdoor breeds – to recognize and honour in the man of the house and head of the family his absolute master and overlord, protector of the hearth; and to find in the relation of vassalage to him the basis and value of his own existence, whereas his attitude towards the rest of the family is much more independent. Almost from the very first day Bashan behaved in this spirit towards me, following me with his trustful eyes that seemed to be begging me to order him about – which I was chary of doing, for time soon showed that obedience was not one of his strong points – and dogging my footsteps in the obvious conviction that sticking to me was the natural order of things. In the family circle he always sat at my feet, never by any chance at anyone else's. And when we were walking, if I struck off on a path by myself, he invariably followed me and not the others. He insisted on being with me when I worked; if the garden door was closed he would disconcert me by jumping suddenly in at the window, bringing much gravel in his train and flinging himself down panting beneath my desk.

But the presence of any living thing – even a dog – is something of which we are very conscious; we attend to it in a way that is disturbing when we want to be alone. Thus Bashan could become a quite tangible nuisance. He would come up to me wagging his tail, look at me with devouring gaze, and prance provocatively. On the smallest encouragement he would put his fore-paws on the arm of my chair, lean against me, and make me laugh with his kisses in the air. Then he would examine the things on my desk, obviously under the impression that they must be good to eat since he so often found me stooped above them; and so doing would smudge my freshly written page with his broad, hairy hunter's paws. I would sharply call him to order and he would lie down on the floor and go to sleep. But when he slept he dreamed, making running motions with all four paws and barking in a subterranean but perfectly audible sort of way. I quite comprehensibly found this distracting; in the first place the sound was uncannily ventriloquistic, in the second it gave me a guilty feeling. For this dream life was obviously an artificial substitute for real running, hunting, and open-air activity; it was supplied to him by his own nature because his life with me did not give him as much of it as his blood and his senses required. I felt touched; but since there was nothing for it, I was constrained in the name of my higher interests to throw off the incubus, telling myself that Bashan brought altogether too much mud into the room and also that he damaged the carpet with his claws.

So then the fiat went forth that he might not be with me or in the house when I was there – though of course there might be exceptions to the rule. He was quick to understand and submit to the unnatural prohibition, as being the inscrutable will of his lord and master. The separation from me – which in winter often lasted the greater part of the day – was in his mind only a separation, not a divorce or severance of connections. He may not be with me, because I have so ordained. But the not being with me is a kind of negative being with me, just in that it is carrying out my command. Hence we can hardly speak of an independent existence carried on by Bashan during the hours when he is not by my side. Through the glass door of my study I can see him on the grass-plot in front of the house, playing with the children and putting on an absurd avuncular air. He repeatedly comes to the door and sniffs at the crack – he cannot see me through the muslin curtains – to assure himself of my presence within; then he sits down and mounts guard with his back to the door. Sometimes I see him from my window prosing along on the elevated path between the aspen trees; but this is only to pass the time, the excursion is void of all pride or joy in life; in fact it is unthinkable that Bashan should devote himself to the pleasures of the chase on his own account, though there is nothing to prevent him from doing so and my presence, as will be seen, is not always an unmixed advantage.

Life for him begins when I issue from the house – though, alas, it does not always begin even then! For the question is, when I do go out, which way am I going to turn: to the right, down the avenue, the road towards the open and our hunting-ground, or towards the left and the place where the trams stop, to ride into town? Only in the first case is there any sense in accompanying me. At first he used to follow me even when I turned left; when the tram thundered up he would look at it with amazement and then, suppressing his fears, land with one blind and devoted leap among the crowd on the platform. Thence being dislodged by the popular indignation, he would gallop along on the ground behind the roaring vehicle which so little resembled the cart he once knew. He would keep up with it as long as he could, his breath getting shorter and shorter. But the city traffic bewildered his rustic brains; he got between people's legs, strange dogs fell on his flank, he was confused by a volume and variety of smells, the like of which he had never imagined, irresistibly distracted by house-corners impregnated with lingering ancient scents of old adventures. He would fall behind; sometimes he would overtake the tram again, sometimes not; sometimes he overtook the wrong one, which looked just the same, ran blindly in the wrong direction, farther and farther into a mad, strange world. Once he only came home after two days' absence, limping and starved to death, and seeking the peace of the last house on the river-bank, found that his lord and master had been sensible enough to get there before him.

This happened two or three times. Then he gave it up and definitely declined to go with me when I turned to the left. He always knows instantly whether I have chosen the wild or the world, directly I get outside the door. He springs up from the mat in the entrance where he has been waiting for me and in that moment divines my intentions; my clothes betray me, the cane I carry, probably even my bearing: my cold and negligent glance or on the other hand the challenging eye I turn upon him. He understands. In the one case he tumbles over himself down the steps, he whirls round and round like a stone in a sling as in dumb rejoicing he runs before me to the gate. In the other he crouches, lays back his ears, the light goes out of his eyes, the fire I have kindled by my appearance dies down to ashes, and he puts on the guilty look which men and animals alike wear when they are unhappy.

Sometimes he cannot believe his eyes, even though they plainly tell him that there is no hope for the chase today. His yearning has been too strong. He refuses to see the signs, the urban walking-stick, the careful city clothes. He presses beside me through the gate, turns round like lightning, and tries to make me turn right, by running off at a gallop in that direction, twisting his head round and ignoring that fatal negative which I oppose to his efforts. When I actually turn to the left he comes back and walks with me along the hedge, with little snorts and head-tones which seem to emerge from the high tension of his interior. He takes to jumping to and fro over the park railings, although they are rather high for comfort, and he gives little moans as he leaps, being evidently afraid of hurting himself. He jumps with a sort of desperate gaiety which is bent on ignoring reality; also in the hope of beguiling me by his performance. For there is still a little – a very little – hope that I may still leave the highroad at the end of the park and turn left after all by the roundabout way past the pillarbox, as I do when I have letters to post. But I do that very seldom; so when that last hope has fled, then Bashan sits down and lets me go my way.

There he sits, in that clumsy rustic posture of his, in the middle of the road and looks after me as far as he can see me. If I turn my head he pricks up his ears, but he does not follow; even if I whistled he would not, for he knows it would be useless. When I turn out of the avenue I can still see him sitting there, a small, dark, clumsy figure in the road, and it goes to my heart, I have pangs of conscience as I mount the tram. He has waited so long – and we all know what torture waiting can be! His whole life is a waiting – waiting for the next walk in the

22

open, a waiting that begins as soon as he is rested from the last one. Even his night consists of waiting; for his sleep is distributed throughout the whole twenty-four hours of the day, with many a little nap on the grass in the garden, the sun shining down warm on his coat, or behind the curtains of his kennel, to break up and shorten the empty spaces of the day. Thus his night sleep is broken too, not continuous, and manifold instincts urge him abroad in the darkness; he dashes to and fro all over the garden — and he waits. He waits for the night watchman to come on his rounds with his lantern and when he hears the recurrent heavy tread heralds it, against his own better knowledge, with a terrific outburst of barking. He waits for the sky to grow pale, for the cocks to crow at the nursery-gardener's close by; for the morning breeze to rise among the tree-tops — and for the kitchen door to be opened, so that he may slip in and warm himself at the stove.

Still, the night-time martyrdom must be mild compared with what Bashan has to endure in the day. And particularly when the weather is fine, either winter or summer, when the sunshine lures one abroad and all the muscles twitch with the craving for violent motion — and the master, without whom it is impossible to conceive doing anything, simply will not leave his post behind the glass door. All that agile little body, feverishly alive with pulsating life, is rested through and through, is worn out with resting; sleep is not to be thought of. He comes up on the terrace outside my door, lets himself down with a sigh that seems to come from his very heart, and rests his head on his paws, rolling his eyes up patiently to heaven. That lasts but a few seconds, he cannot stand the position any more, he sickens of it. One other thing there is to do. He can go down again and lift his leg against one of the little formal arbor-vitae trees that flank the rose-bed — it is the one to the right that suffers from his attentions, wasting away so that it has to be replanted every year. He does go down, then, and performs this action, not because he needs to, but just to pass the time. He stands there a long time, with very little to show for it, however — so long that the hind leg in the air begins to tremble and he has to give a little hop to regain his balance. On four legs once more he is no better off than he was. He stares stupidly up into the boughs of the ash trees, where two birds are flitting and chirping; watches them dart off like arrows and turns away as though in contempt of such light-headedness. He stretches and stretches, fit to tear himself apart. The stretching is very thorough; it is done in two sections, thus: first the forelegs, lifting the hind ones into the air; second the rear quarters, by sprawling them out on the ground; both actions being accompanied by tremendous yawning. Then that is over too, cannot be spun out any longer, and if you have just finished an exhaustive stretching you cannot do it over again just at once. He stands still and looks gloomily at the ground. Then he begins to turn round on himself, slowly and consideringly, as though he wanted to lie down, yet was not quite certain of the best way to do it. Finally he decides not to; he moves off sluggishly to the middle of the grass-plot, and once there flings himself violently on his back and scrubs to and fro as though to cool off on the shaven turf. Quite a blissful sensation, this, it seems, for his paws jerk and he snaps in all directions in a delirium of release and satisfaction. He drains this joy down to its vapid dregs, aware that it is fleeting, that you cannot roll and tumble more than ten seconds at most, and that no sound and soul-contenting weariness will result from it, but only a flatness and returning boredom, such as always follows when one tries to drug oneself. He lies there on his side with his eyes rolled up, as though he were dead. Then he gets up and shakes himself, shakes as only his like can shake without fearing concussion of the brain; shakes until everything rattles, until his ears flop together under his chin and foam flies from his dazzling white teeth. And then? He stands perfectly still in his tracks, rigid, dead to the world, without the least idea what to do next. And then, driven to extremes, he climbs the steps once more, comes up to the glass door, lifts his paw and scratches – hesitantly, with his ears laid back, the complete beggar. He scratches only once, quite faintly; but this timidly lifted paw, this single, faint-hearted scratch, to which he has come because he simply cannot think of anything else, are too moving. I get up and open the door, though I know it can lead to no good. And he begins to dance and jump, challenging me to be a man and come abroad with him. He rumples the rugs, upsets the whole room and makes an end of all my peace and quiet. But now judge for yourself if, after I have seen Bashan wait like this, I can find it easy to go off in the tram and leave him, a pathetic little dot at the end of the poplar avenue!

In the long twilights of summer, things are not quite so bad: there is a good chance that I will take an evening walk in the open and thus even after long waiting he will come into his own and with good luck be able to start a hare. But in winter if I go off in the afternoon it is all over for the day, all hope must be buried for another four-and-twenty hours. For night will have fallen; if I go out again our hunting-grounds will lie in inaccessible darkness and I must bend my steps towards the traffic, the lighted streets, and city parks up the river – and this does not suit Bashan's simple soul. He came with me at first, but soon gave it up and stopped at home. Not only that space and freedom were lacking; he was afraid of the bright lights in the darkness, he shied at every bush, at every human form. A policeman's flapping cloak could make him swerve aside with a yelp or even lead him to attack the officer with a courage born of desperation; when the latter, frightened in his turn, would let loose a stream of abuse to our address. Unfortunate episodes mounted up when Bashan and I went out together in the dark and the damp. And speaking of policemen reminds me that there are three classes of human beings whom Bashan does especially abhor: policemen, monks, and chimney-sweeps. He cannot stand them, he assails them with a fury of barking wherever he sees them or when they chance to pass the house.

And winter is of course the time of year when freedom and sobriety are with most difficulty preserved against snares; when it is hardest to lead a regular, retired, and concentrated existence; when I may even seek the city a second time in the day. For the evening has its social claims, pursuing which I may come back at midnight, with the last tram, or losing that am driven to return on foot, my head in a whirl with ideas and wine and smoke, full of roseate views of the world and of course long past the point of normal fatigue. And then the embodiment of that other, truer, soberer life of mine, my own

hearthstone, in person, as it were, may come to meet me; not
wounded, not reproachful, but on the contrary giving me joyous
welcome and bringing me back to my own. I mean, of course,
Bashan. In pitchy darkness, the river roaring in my ears, I turn
into the poplar avenue, and after the first few steps I am enveloped in a soundless storm of prancings and swishings; on the
first occasion I did not know what was happening. 'Bashan?' I
inquire into the blackness. The prancings and swishings re-
double – is this a dancing dervish or a berserk warrior here on
my path? But not a sound; and directly I stand still, I feel those
honest, wet, and muddy paws on the lapels of my raincoat, and
a snapping and flapping in my face, which I draw back even as
I stoop down to pat the lean shoulder, equally wet with snow or
rain. Yes, the good soul has come to meet the tram. Well informed as always upon my comings and goings, he has got up
at what he judged to be the right time, to fetch me from the
station. He may have been waiting a long while, in snow or rain,
yet his joy at my final appearance knows no resentment at my
faithlessness, though I have neglected him all day and brought
his hopes to naught. I pat and praise him, and as we go home
together I tell him what a fine fellow he is and promise him
(that is to say, not so much him as myself) that tomorrow, no
matter what the weather, we two will follow the chase together.
And resolving thus, I feel my worldly preoccupations melt
away; sobriety returns; for the image I have conjured up of our
hunting-ground and the charms of its solitude is linked in my
mind with the call to higher, stranger, more obscure concerns of
mine.

There are still other traits of Bashan's character which I
should like to set down here, so that the gentle reader may get as
lively and speaking an image of him as is anyway possible.
Perhaps the best way would be for me to compare him with our
deceased Percy; for a better-defined contrast than that between
these two never existed within the same species. First and foremost we must remember that Bashan was entirely sound in
mind, whereas Percy, as I have said, and as often happens
among aristocratic canines, had always been mad, through and
through, a perfectly typical specimen of frantic over-breeding. I

have referred to this subject before, in a somewhat wider connection; here I only want, for purposes of comparison, to speak of Bashan's infinitely simpler, more ordinary mentality, expressed for instance in the way he would greet you, or in his behaviour on our walks. His manifestations were always within the bounds of a hearty and healthy common sense; and never even bordered on the hysterical, whereas Percy's on all such occasions overstepped them in a way that was at times quite shocking.

And even that does not quite cover the contrast between these two creatures; the truth is more complex and involved still. Bashan is coarser-fibred, true, like the lower classes; but like them also he is not above complaining. His noble predecessor, on the other hand, united more delicacy and a greater capacity for suffering, with an infinitely firmer and prouder spirit; despite all his foolishness he far excelled in self-discipline the powers of Bashan's peasant soul. In saying this I am not defending any aristocratic system of values. It is simply to do honour to truth and actuality that I want to bring out the mixture of softness and hardiness, delicacy and firmness in the two natures. Bashan, for instance, is quite able to spend the coldest winter night out of doors, behind the sacking curtains of his kennel. He has a weakness of the bladder which makes it impossible for him to remain seven hours shut up in a room; we have to fasten him out, even in the most inhospitable weather, and trust to his robust constitution. Sometimes after a particularly bitter and foggy winter night he comes into the house with his moustache and whiskers like delicately frosted wires; with a little cold, even, and coughing in the odd, one-syllabled way that dogs have. But in a few hours he has got all over it and takes no harm at all. Whereas we should never have dared to expose our silken-haired Percy to such rigours. Yet Bashan is afraid of the slightest pain, behaving so abjectly that one would feel disgusted if the plebeian simplicity of his behaviour did not make one laugh instead. When he goes stalking in the underbrush, I constantly hear him yelping because he has been scratched by a thorn or a branch has struck him in the face. If he hurts his foot or skins his belly a little, jumping over a fence, he sets up a cry like an antique hero in his death-agony; comes to me hobbling on three legs, howling and lamenting in an abandonment of self-pity – the more piercingly, the more sympathy he gets – and this although in fifteen minutes he will be running and jumping again as though nothing had happened.

With Percival it was otherwise; he clenched his jaws and was still. He was afraid of the dog-whip, as Bashan is too; and tasted it, alas, more often than the latter, for in his day I was younger and quick-tempered and his witlessness often assumed a vicious aspect which cried out for chastisement and drove me on to administer it. When I was quite beside myself and took down the lash from the nail where it hung, Percy might crawl under a table or a bench. But not a sound would escape him under punishment; even at a second flailing he would give vent only to a fervent moan if it stung worse than usual – whereas the base-born Bashan will howl abjectly if I so much as raise my arm. In short, no sense of honour, no strictness with himself. And anyhow, it seldom comes to corporal punishment, for I long ago ceased to make demands upon him contrary to his nature, of a kind which would lead to conflict between us.

For example, I never asked him to learn tricks; it would be of no use. He is not talented, no circus dog, no trained clown. He is a sound, vigorous young hunter, not a professor. I believe I remarked that he is a capital jumper. No obstacle too great, if the incentive be present: if he cannot jump it he will scrabble up somehow and let himself fall on the other side – at least, he conquers it one way or another. But it must be a genuine obstacle, not to be jumped through or crawled under; otherwise he would think it folly to jump. A wall, a ditch, a fence, a thickset hedge, are genuine obstacles; a crosswire bar, a stick held out, are not, and you cannot jump over them without going contrary to reason and looking silly. Which Bashan refuses to do. He refuses. Try to make him jump over some such unreal obstacle; in the end you will be reduced to taking him by the scruff of the neck, in your anger, and flinging him over, while he whimpers and yaps. Once on the other side he acts as though he had done just what you wanted and celebrates the

event in a frenzy of barking and capering. You may coax or
you may punish; you cannot break down his reasonable resistance to performing a mere trick. He is not unaccommodating, he
sets store by his master's approval, he will jump over a hedge at
my will or my command, and not only when he feels like it
himself, and enjoys very much the praise I bestow. But over a
bar or a stick he will not jump, he will crawl underneath – if he
were to die for it. A hundred times he will beg for forgiveness,
forbearance, consideration; he fears pain, fears it to the point of
being abject. But no fear and no pain can make him capable of a
performance which in itself would be child's-play for him, but
for which he obviously lacks all mental equipment. When you
confront him with it, the question is not whether he will jump
or not; that is already settled, and the command means nothing
to him but a beating. To demand of him what reason forbids
him to understand and hence to do is simply in his eyes to seek
a pretext for blows, strife, and disturbance of friendly relations
– it is merely the first step towards all these things. Thus
Bashan looks at it, so far as I can see, and I doubt whether one
may properly charge him with obstinacy. Obstinacy may be
broken down, in the last analysis it cries out to be broken down;
but Bashan's resistance to performing a trick he would seal with
his death.

Extraordinary creature! So close a friend and yet so remote;
so different from us, in certain ways, that our language has not
power to do justice to his canine logic. For instance, what is the
meaning of that frightful circumstantiality – unnerving alike to
the spectator and to the parties themselves – attendant on the
meeting of dog and dog; or on their first acquaintance or even
on their first sight of each other? My excursions with Bashan
have made me witness to hundreds of such encounters, or, I
might better say, forced me to be an embarrassed spectator at
them. And every time, for the duration of the episode, my old
familiar Bashan was a stranger to me, I found it impossible to
enter into his feelings or behaviour or understand the tribal laws
which governed them. Certainly the meeting in the open of two
dogs, strangers to each other, is one of the most painful, thrilling, and pregnant of all conceivable encounters; it is surrounded

by an atmosphere of the last uncanniness, presided over by a constraint for which I have no preciser name; they simply cannot pass each other, their mutual embarrassment is frightful to behold.

I am not speaking of the case where one of the parties is shut up behind a hedge or a fence. Even then it is not easy to interpret their feelings – but at least the situation is less acute. They sniff each other from far off, and Bashan suddenly seeks shelter in my neighbourhood, whining a little to give vent to a distress and oppression which simply no words can describe. At the same time the imprisoned stranger sets up a violent barking, ostensibly in his character as a good watch-dog, but passing over unconsciously into a whimpering much like Bashan's own, an unsatisfied, envious, distressful whine. We draw near. The strange dog is waiting for us, close to the hedge, grousing and bemoaning his impotence; jumping at the barrier and giving every sign – how seriously one cannot tell – of intending to tear Bashan to pieces if only he could get at him. Bashan might easily stick close to me and pass him by; but he goes up to the hedge. He has to, he would even if I forbade him; to remain away would be to transgress a code older and more inviolable than any prohibition of mine. He advances, then, and with a modest and inscrutable bearing performs that rite which he knows will soothe and appease the other – even if temporarily – so long as the stranger performs it too, though whining and complaining in the act. Then they both chase wildly along the hedge, each on his own side, as close as possible, neither making a sound. At the end of the hedge they both face about and dash back again. But in full career both suddenly halt and stand as though rooted to the spot; they stand still, facing the hedge, and put their noses together through it. For some space of time they stand thus, then resume their curious, futile race shoulder to shoulder on either side of the barrier. But in the end my dog avails himself of his freedom and moves off – a frightful moment for the prisoner! He cannot stand it, he finds it namelessly humiliating that the other should dream of simply going off like that. He raves and slavers and contorts himself in his rage; runs like one mad up and down his enclosure; threatens to

30

jump the hedge and have the faithless Bashan by the throat; he yells insults behind the retreating back. Bashan hears it all, it distresses him, as his manner shows. But he does not turn round, he jogs along beside me, while the cursings in our rear die down into whinings and are still.

Such the procedure when one of the parties is shut up. Embarrassments multiply when both of them are free. I do not relish describing the scene: it is one of the most painful and equivocal imaginable. Bashan has been bounding light-heartedly beside me; he comes up close, he fairly forces himself upon me, with a sniffling and whimpering that seem to come from his very depths. I still do not know what moves his utterance, but I recognize it at once and gather that there is a strange dog in the offing. I look about – yes, there he comes, and even at this distance his strained and hesitating mien betrays that he has already seen Bashan. I am scarcely less upset than they; I find the meeting most undesirable. 'Go away,' I say to Bashan. 'Why do you glue yourself to my leg? Can't you go off and do your business by yourselves?' I try to frighten him off with my cane. For if they start biting – which may easily happen, with reason or without – I shall find it most unpleasant to have them between my feet. 'Go away!' I repeat, in a lower voice. But Bashan does not go away, he sticks in his distress the closer to me, making as brief a pause as he can at a tree-trunk to perform the accustomed rite; I can see the other dog doing the same. We are now within twenty paces, the suspense is frightful. The strange dog is crawling on his belly, like a cat, his head thrust out. In this posture he awaits Bashan's approach, poised to spring at the right moment for his throat. But he does not do it, nor does Bashan seem to expect that he will. Or at least he goes up to the crouching stranger, though plainly trembling and heavy-hearted; he would do this, he is obliged to do it, even though I were to act myself and leave him to face the situation alone by striking into a side path. However painful the encounter, he has no choice, avoidance is not to be thought of. He is under a spell, he is bound to the other dog, they are bound to each other with some obscure and equivocal bond which may not be denied. We are now within two paces.

31

Then the other gets up, without a sound, as though he had never been behaving like a tiger, and stands there just as Bashan is standing, profoundly embarrassed, wretched, at a loss. They cannot pass each other. They probably want to, they turn away their heads, rolling their eyes sideways; evidently the same sense of guilt weighs on them both. They edge cautiously up to each other with a hang-dog air; they stop flank to flank and sniff under each other's tails. At this point the growling begins, and I speak to Bashan low-voiced and warn him, for now is the decisive moment, now we shall know whether it will come to biting or whether I shall be spared that rude shock. It does come to biting, I do not know how, still less why: quite suddenly they are nothing but a raging tumult and whirling coil out of which issue the frightful guttural noises that animals make when they engage. I may have to engage too, with my cane, to forestall a worse calamity; I may try to get Bashan by the neck or the collar and hold him up at arm's length in the air, the stranger dog hanging on by his teeth. Other horrors there are, too, which I may have to face – and feel them afterwards in all my limbs during the rest of our walk. But it may be, too, that after all the preliminaries the affair will pass tamely off and no harm done. At best it is hard to part the two; even if they are not clenched by the teeth, they are held by that inward bond. They may seem to have passed each other, they are no longer flank to flank, but in a straight line with their heads in opposite directions; they may not even turn their heads, but only be rolling their eyes backwards. There may even be a space between them – and yet the painful bond still holds. Neither knows if the right moment for release has come, they would both like to go, yet each seems to have conscientious scruples. Slowly, slowly, the bond loosens, snaps; Bashan bounds lightly away, with, as it were, a new lease of life.

I speak of these things only to show how under stress of circumstance the character of a near friend may reveal itself as strange and foreign. It is dark to me, it is mysterious; I observe it with head-shakings and can only dimly guess what it may mean. And in all other respects I understand Bashan so well. I feel such lively sympathy for all his manifestations! For

example, how well I know that whining yawn of his when our
walk has been disappointing, too short, or devoid of sporting
interest; when I have begun the day late and only gone out for a
quarter of an hour before dinner. At such times he walks beside
me and yawns – an open, impudent yawn to the whole extent of
his jaws, an animal, audible yawn insultingly expressive of his
utter boredom. 'A fine master I have!' it seems to say. 'Far in
the night last night I met him at the bridge and now he sits
behind his glass door and I wait for him dying of boredom.
And when he does go out he only does it to come back again
before there is time to start any game. A fine master! Not a
proper master at all – really a rotten master, if you ask me!'

Such was the meaning of his yawn, vulgarly plain beyond all
misunderstanding. And I admit that he is right, that he has a
just grievance, and I put out a hand to pat his shoulder con-
solingly or to stroke his head. But he is not, under such circumstances, grateful for caresses; he yawns again, if possible
more rudely than before, and moves away from my hand,
although by nature, in contrast to Percy and in harmony with
his own plebeian sentimentality, he sets great store by caresses.
He particularly likes having his throat scratched and has a
funny way of guiding one's hand to the right place by energetic
little jerks of his head. That he has no room just now for en-
dearments is partly due to his disappointment, but also to the
fact that when he is in motion – and that means that I also am –
he does not care for them. His mood is too manly; but it
changes directly I sit down. Then he is all for friendliness again
and responds to it with clumsy enthusiasm.

When I sit reading in a corner of the garden wall, or on the
lawn with my back to a favourite tree, I enjoy interrupting my
intellectual preoccupations to talk and play with Bashan. And
what do I say to him? Mostly his own name, the two syllables
which are of the utmost personal interest because they refer to
himself and have an electric effect upon his whole being. I rouse
and stimulate his sense of his own ego by impressing upon him
– varying my tone and emphasis – that he *is* Bashan and that
Bashan is his name. By continuing this for a while I can actually produce in him a state of ecstasy, a sort of intoxication with

33

his own identity, so that he begins to whirl round on himself and send up loud exultant barks to heaven out of the weight of dignity that lies on his chest. Or we amuse ourselves, I by tapping him on the nose, he by snapping at my hand as though it were a fly. It makes us both laugh, yes, Bashan has to laugh too; and as I laugh I marvel at the sight, to me the oddest and most touching thing in the world. It is moving to see how under my teasing his thin animal cheeks and the corners of his mouth will twitch, and over his dark animal mask will pass an expression like a human smile, or at least some ungainly, pathetic semblance of one. It gives way to a look of startled embarrassment, then transforms the face by appearing again ...

But I will go no further nor involve myself in more detail of the kind. Even so I am dismayed at the space I have been led on to give to this little description; for what I had in mind to do was merely to display, as briefly as I might, my hero in his element, on the scene where he is most at home, most himself, and where his gifts show to best advantage; I mean, of course, the chase. But first I must give account to my reader of the theatre of these delights, my landscape by the river and Bashan's hunting-ground. It is a strip of land intimately bound up with his personality, familiar, loved, and significant to me like himself; which fact, accordingly, without further literary justification or embellishment, must serve as the occasion for my description.

The Hunting-Ground

The spacious gardens of the suburb where we live contain many large old trees that rise above the villa roofs and form a striking contrast to the saplings set out at a later period. Unquestionably they are the earliest inhabitants, the pride and adornment of a settlement which is still not very old. They have been carefully protected and preserved, so far as was possible; when any one of them came into conflict with the boundaries of the parcels of land, some venerable silvery moss-grown trunk standing exactly on a border-line, the hedge makes a little curve round it, or an accommodating gap is left in a wall, and the ancient towers up half on public, half on private ground, with bare snow-covered boughs or adorned with its tiny, late-coming leaves.

They are a variety of ash, a tree that loves moisture more than most – and their presence here shows what kind of soil we have. It is not so long since human brains reclaimed it for human habitation; not more than a decade or so. Before that it was a marshy wilderness, a breeding-place for mosquitoes, where willows, dwarf poplars, and other stunted growths mirrored themselves in stagnant pools. The region is subject to floods. There is a stratum of impermeable soil a few yards under the surface; it has always been boggy, with standing water in the hollows. They drained it by lowering the level of the river – engineering is not my strong point, but anyhow it was some such device, by means of which the water which cannot sink into the earth now flows off laterally into the river by several subterranean channels, and the ground is left comparatively dry – but only comparatively, for Bashan and I, knowing it as we do, are acquainted with certain low, retired, and rushy spots, relics of the primeval condition of the region, whose damp coolness defies the summer heat and makes them a grateful place wherein to draw a few long breaths.

The whole district has its peculiarities, indeed, which distinguish it at a glance from the pine forests and moss-grown meadows which are the usual setting of a mountain stream. It has preserved its original characteristics even since it was acquired by the real-estate company; even outside the gardens the original vegetation preponderates over the newly planted. In the avenues and parks, of course, horse-chestnuts and quick-growing maple trees, beeches, and all sorts of ornamental shrubs have been set out; also rows of French poplars standing erect in their sterile masculinity. But the ash trees, as I said, are the aborigines; they are everywhere, and of all ages, century-old giants and tender young seedlings pushing their way by hundreds, like weeds, through the gravel. It is the ash, together with the silver poplar, the aspen, the birch, and the willow, that gives the scene its distinctive look. All these trees have small leaves, and all this small-leaved foliage is very striking by contrast with the huge trunks. But there are elms too, spreading their large, varnished, saw-edged leaves to the sun. And everywhere too are masses of creeper, winding round the young trees in the underbrush and inextricably mingling its leaves with theirs. Little thickets of slim alder trees stand in the hollows. There are few lime trees, no oaks or firs at all, in our domain, though there are some on the slope which bounds it to the east, where the soil changes and with it the character of the vegetation. There they stand out black against the sky, like sentinels guarding our little valley.

It is not more than five hundred yards from slope to river – I have paced it out. Perhaps the strip of river-bank widens a little, farther down, but not to any extent; so it is remarkable what landscape variety there is in this small area, even when one makes such moderate use of the playground it affords along the river as do Bashan and I, who rarely spend more than two hours there, counting our going and coming. There is such diversity that we need hardly take the same path twice or ever tire of the view or be conscious of any limitations of space; and this is due to the circumstance that our domain divides itself into three quite different regions or zones. We may confine ourselves to one of these or we may combine all three: they are the neighbourhood of the river and its banks, the neighbourhood of the opposite slope, and the wooded section in the middle.

The wooded zone, the parks, the osier brakes, and the river-side shrubbery take up most of the breadth. I search in vain for a word better than 'wood' to describe this strange tract of land. For it is no wood in the usual sense of the word: not a pillared hall of even-sized trunks, carpeted with moss and fallen leaves. The trees in our hunting-ground are of uneven growth and size, hoary giants of willows and poplars, especially along the river, though also deeper in; others ten or fifteen years old, which are probably as large as they will grow; and lastly a legion of slender trees, young ashes, birches, and alders in a nursery garden planted by nature herself. These look larger than they are; and all, as I said, are wound round with creepers which give a look of tropical luxuriance to the scene. But I suspect them of choking the growth of their hosts, for I cannot see that the trunks have grown any thicker in all the years I have known them.

The trees are of few and closely related species. The alder

belongs to the birch family, the poplar is after all not very different from a willow. And one might say that they all approach the willow type; foresters tell us that trees tend to adapt themselves to their local conditions, showing a certain conformity, as it were, to the prevailing mode. It is the distorted, fantastic, witchlike silhouette of the willow tree, dweller by still and by flowing waters, that sets the fashion here, with her branches like broom-splints and her crooked-fingered tips; and all the others visibly try to be like her. The silver poplar apes her best; but often it is hard to tell poplar from birch, so much is the latter beguiled by the spirit of the place to take on misshapen forms. Not that there are not also plenty of very shapely and well-grown single specimens of this lovable tree, and enchanting they look in the favouring glow of the late afternoon sun. In this region the birch appears as a slender silver bole with a crown of little, separate leaves atop; as a lovely, lithe, and well-grown maiden; it has the prettiest of chalk-white trunks, and its foliage droops like delicate languishing locks of hair. But there are also birches colossal in size, that no man could span with his arms, the bark of which is only white high up, but near the ground has turned black and coarse and is seamed with fissures.

The soil is not like what one expects in a wood. It is loamy, gravelly, even sandy. It seems anything but fertile, and yet, within its nature, is almost luxuriantly so; for it is overgrown with tall, rank grass, often the dry, sharp-cornered kind that grows on dunes. In winter it covers the ground like trampled hay; not seldom it cannot be distinguished from reeds, but in other places it is soft and fat and juicy, and among it grow hemlock, coltsfoot, nettles, all sorts of low-growing things, mixed with tall thistles and tender young tree shoots. Pheasants and other wildfowl hide in this vegetation, which rolls up to and over the gnarled roots of the trees. And everywhere the wild grape and the hop-vine clamber out of the thicket to twine round the trunks in garlands of flapping leaves, or in winter with bare stems like the toughest sort of wire.

Now, all this is not a wood, it is not a park, it is simply an enchanted garden, no more and no less. I will stand for the word – though of course nature here is stingy and sparse and tends to the deformed; a few botanical names exhausting the catalogue of her performance. The ground is rolling, it constantly rises and falls away, so that the view is enclosed on every hand, with a lovely effect of remoteness and privacy. Indeed, if the wood stretched for miles to right and left, as far as it reaches lengthwise, instead of only a hundred and some paces on each side from the middle, one could not feel more secluded. Only by the sense of sound is one made aware of the friendly nearness of the river; you cannot see it, but it whispers gently from the west. There are gorges choked with shrubbery – elder, privet, jasmine, and wild cherry – on close June days the scent is almost overpowering. And again there are low-lying spots, regular gravel-pits, where nothing but a few willow-shoots and a little sage can grow, at the bottom or on the sides.

And all this scene never ceases to exert a strange influence upon me, though it has been my almost daily walk for some years. The fine massed foliage of the ash puts me in mind of a giant fern; these creepers and climbers, this barrenness and this damp, this combination of lush and dry, have a fantastic effect; to convey my whole meaning, it is a little as though I were transported to another geological period, or even to the bottom of the sea – and the fantasy has this much of fact about it, that water did stand here once, for instance in the square low-lying meadow basins thick with shoots of self-sown ash, which now serve as pasture for sheep. One such lies directly behind my house.

The wilderness is crossed in all directions by paths, some of them only lines of trodden grass or gravelly trails, obviously born of use and not laid out – though it would be hard to say who trod them, for only by way of unpleasant exception do Bashan and I meet anyone here. When that happens he stands stock-still and gives a little growl which very well expresses my own feelings too. Even on the fine summer Sunday afternoons which bring crowds of people to walk in these parts – for it is always a few degrees cooler here – we remain undisturbed in our fastness. They know it not; the water is the great attraction, as a rule, the river in its course; the human stream gets as close as it can, down to the very edge if there is no flood, rolls along beside it, and then back home again. At most we may come on a pair of lovers in the shrubbery; they look at us wide-eyed and startled out of their nest, or else defiantly as though to ask what objection we have to their presence or their behaviour. All which we disclaim by beating swift retreat, Bashan with the indifference he feels for everything that does not smell like game; I with a face utterly devoid of all expression, either approving or the reverse.

But these woodland paths are not the only way we have of reaching my park. There are streets as well – or rather there are traces, which once were streets, or which once were to have been streets, or which, by God's will, may yet become streets. In other words: there are signs that the pickaxe has been at work, signs of a hopeful real-estate enterprise for some distance beyond the built-up section and the villas. There has been some far-sighted planning on the part of the company which some years ago acquired the land; but their plans went beyond their capacity for carrying them out, for the villas were only a part of what they had in mind. Building-lots were laid out; an area extending for nearly a mile down the river was prepared, and doubtless still remains prepared, to receive possible purchasers and home-loving settlers. The building society conceived things on a rather large scale. They enclosed the river between dykes, they built quays and planted gardens, and, not content with that, they had embarked on clearing the woods, dumped piles of gravel, cut roads through the wilderness, one or two lengthwise and several across the width: fine, well-planned roads, or at least the first steps towards them, made of coarse gravel, with a wide foot-path and indications of a kerb-stone. But no one walks there save Bashan and myself, he on the good stout leather of his four paws, I in hobnailed boots on account of the gravel. For the stately villas projected by the company are still non-existent, despite the good example I set when I built my own house. They have been, I say, non-existent for ten, no, fifteen years; it is no wonder that a kind of blight has settled upon the enterprise and discouragement reigns in the bosom of the building society, a disinclination to go on with their project.

However, things had got so far forward that these streets, though not built up, have all been given names, just as though they were in the centre of the town or in a suburb. I should very much like to know what sort of speculator he was who named them; he seems to have been a literary chap with a fondness for the past : there is an Opitzstrasse, a Flemmingstrasse, a Bürgerstrasse, even an Adalbert-Stifterstrasse – I walk on the last-named with especial reverence in my hobnailed boots. At all the corners stakes have been driven in the ground with street signs affixed to them, as is usual in suburbs where there are no house-corners to receive them; they are the usual little blue enamel plates with white lettering. But alas, they are rather the worse for wear. They have stood here far too long, pointing out the names of vacant sites where nobody wants to live; they are monuments to the failure, the discouragement, and the arrested development of the whole enterprise. They have not been kept up or renewed, the climate has done its worst by them. The enamel has scaled off, the lettering is rusty, there are ugly broken-edged gaps which make the names sometimes almost illegible. One of them, indeed, puzzled me a good deal when I first came here and was spying about the neighbourhood. It was a long name, and the word 'street' was perfectly clear, but most of the rest was eaten by rust; there remained only an *S* at the beginning, an *E* somewhere about the middle, and another *E* at the end. I could not reckon with so many unknown quantities. I studied the sign a long time with my hands behind my back, then continued along the footpath with Bashan. I thought I was thinking about something else, but all the time my brains were privately cudgelling themselves, and suddenly it came over me. I stopped with a start, stood still, and then hastened back, took up my former position, and tested my guess. Yes, it fitted. The name of the street where I was walking was Shakespeare Street.

The streets suit the signboards and the signboards suit the streets – it is a strange and dreamlike harmony in decay. The streets run through the wood they have broken into; but the wood does not remain passive. It does not let the streets stop as they were made, through decade after decade, until at last

people come and settle on them. It takes every step to close them
again; for what grows here does not mind gravel, it flourishes in
it. Purple thistles, blue sage, silvery shoots of willow, and green
ash seedlings spring up all over the road and even on the pavement; the streets with the poetic names are going back to the
wilderness, whether one likes it or not; in another ten years
Opitzstrasse, Flemmingstrasse, and the rest will be closed, they
will probably as good as disappear. There is at present no
ground for complaint; for from the romantic and picturesque
point of view there are no more beautiful streets in the world
than they are now. Nothing could be more delightful than
strolling through them in their unfinished, abandoned state, if
one has on stout boots and does not mind the gravel. Nothing
more agreeable to the eye than looking from the wild garden
beneath one's feet to the humid massing of fine-leafed foliage
that shuts in the view – foliage such as Claude Lorrain used to
paint, three centuries ago. Such as he used to paint, did I say?
But surely he painted *this*. He was here, he knew this scene, he
studied it. If my building-society man had not confined himself
to the literary field, one of these rusty street signs might have
borne the name of Claude.

Well, that is our middle or wooded region. But the eastern
slope has its own charms not to be despised, either by me or by
Bashan, who has his own reasons, which will appear hereafter. I
might call this region the zone of the brook; for it takes its
idyllic character as landscape from the stream that flows through
it, and the peaceful loveliness of its beds of forget-me-not makes
it a fit companion-piece to the zone on the other side with its
rushing river, whose flowing, when the west wind blows, can be
faintly heard even all the way across our hunting-ground. The
first of the made crossroads through the wood runs like a
causeway from the poplar avenue to the foot of the hillside,
between low-lying pasture-ground on one side and wooded lots
of land on the other. And from there a path descends to the left,
used by the children to coast on in winter. The brook rises in
the level ground at the bottom of this descent. We love to stroll
beside it, Bashan and I, on the right or the left bank at will,
through the varied territory of our eastern zone. On our left is

an extent of wooded meadow, and a nursery-gardening establishment; we can see the backs of the buildings, and sheep cropping the clover, presided over by a rather stupid little girl in a red frock. She keeps propping her hands on her knees and screaming at her charges at the top of her lungs in a harsh, angry, and imperious voice. But she seems to be afraid of the majestic old ram, who looks enormously fat in his thick fleece and who does as he likes regardless of her bullying ways. The child's screams rise to their height when the sheep are thrown into a panic by the appearance of Bashan; and this almost always happens quite against his will or intent, for he is profoundly indifferent to their existence, behaves as though they were not there, or even deliberately and contemptuously ignores them in an effort to forestall an attack of panic folly on their part. Their scent is strong enough to me, though not unpleasant; but it is not a scent of game, so Bashan takes no interest in harrying them. But let him make a single move, or merely appear on the scene, and the whole flock, but now grazing peacefully over the meadow and bleating in their curiously human voices, some bass, some treble, suddenly collect in a huddled mass of backs and go dashing off, while the imbecile child stoops over and screams at them until her voice cracks and her eyes pop out of her head. Bashan looks up at me as though to say: Am I to blame, did I do anything at all?

But once something quite the opposite happened, that was even more extraordinary and distressing than any panic. A sheep, a quite ordinary specimen, of medium size and the usual sheepish face, save for a narrow-lipped little mouth turned up at the corners into a smile which gave the creature an uncommonly sly and fatuous look – this sheep appeared to be smitten with Bashan's charms. It followed him; it left the flock and the pasture-ground and followed at his heels, wherever he went, smiling with extravagant stupidity. He left the path, and it followed. He ran, it galloped after. He stopped, it did the same, close behind him and smiling its inscrutable smile. Embarrassment and dismay were painted on Bashan's face, and certainly his position was highly distasteful. For good or for ill it lacked any kind of sense or reason. Nothing so consummately silly had ever happened to either of us. The sheep got farther and farther away from its base, but it seemed not to care for that; it followed the exasperated Bashan apparently resolved to part from him nevermore, but to be at his side whithersoever he went. He stuck close at my side; not so much alarmed – for the which there was no cause – as ashamed of the disgraceful situation. At last, as though he had had enough of it, he stood still, turned round, and gave a menacing growl. The sheep bleated – it was like a man's laugh, a spiteful laugh – and put poor Bashan so beside himself that he ran away with his tail between his legs, the sheep bounding absurdly behind him.

Meanwhile we had got a good way from the flock; the addlepated little girl was screaming fit to burst, and not only bending her knees but jerking them up and down as she screamed till they touched her face, and she looked from a distance like a demented dwarf. A dairymaid in an apron came running, her attention being drawn by the shrieks or in some other way. She had a pitchfork in one hand; with the other she held her breasts, that shook up and down as she ran. She tried to drive back the sheep with the pitchfork – it had started after Bashan again – but unsuccessfully. The sheep did indeed spring away from the fork in the right direction, but then swung round again to follow Bashan's trail. It seemed no power on earth would divert it. But at last I saw what had to be done and turned round. We all marched back, Bashan beside me, behind him the sheep, behind the sheep the maid with the pitchfork, the child in the red frock bouncing and stamping at us all the while. It was not enough to go back to the flock, we had to do the job thoroughly. We went into the farmyard and to the sheep-pen, where the farm girl rolled back the big door with her strong right arm. We all went inside, all of us; and then the rest of us had to slip out again and shut the door in the face of the poor deluded sheep, so that it was taken prisoner. And then, after receiving the farm girl's thanks, Bashan and I might resume our interrupted walk, to the end of which Bashan preserved a sulky and humiliated air.

So much for the sheep. Beyond the farm buildings is an extensive colony of allotments, that looks rather like a cemetery, with its arbours and little summer-houses like chapels and each tiny garden neatly enclosed. The whole colony has a fence round it, with a latticed gate, through which only the owners of the plots have admission. Sometimes I have seen a man with his sleeves rolled up digging his few yards of vegetable-plot – he looked as though he were digging his own grave. Beyond this come open meadows full of mole-hills, reaching to the edge of the middle wooded region; besides the moles, the place abounds in field-mice – I mention them on account of Bashan and his multifarious joy of the chase.

But on the other, the right side, the brook and the hillside continue, the latter, as I said, with great variety in its contours. The first part is shadowed and gloomy and set with pines. Then comes a sand-pit which reflects the warm rays of the sun; then a gravel-pit, then a cataract of bricks, as though a house had been demolished up above and the rubble simply flung down the hill, damming the brook at the bottom. But the brook rises until its waters flow over the obstacle and go on, reddened with brick-dust and dyeing the grass along its edge, to flow all the more blithely and pellucidly farther on, with the sun making diamonds spark on its surface.

I am very fond of brooks, as indeed of all water, from the ocean to the smallest reedy pool. If in the mountains in the summertime my ear but catch the sound of plashing and prattling from afar, I always go to seek out the source of the liquid sounds, a long way if I must; to make the acquaintance and to look in the face of that conversable child of the hills, where he hides. Beautiful are the torrents that come tumbling with mild thunderings down between evergreens and over stony terraces; that form rocky bathing-pools and then dissolve in white foam to fall perpendicularly to the next level. But I have pleasure in the brooks of the flatland too, whether they be so shallow as hardly to cover the slippery, silver-gleaming pebbles in their bed, or as deep as small rivers between overhanging, guardian willow trees, their current flowing swift and strong in the centre, still and gently at the edge. Who would not choose to follow the sound of running waters? Its attraction for the normal man is of a natural, sympathetic sort. For man is water's child, nine

44

tenths of our body consists of it, and at a certain stage the foetus possesses gills. For my part I freely admit that the sight of water in whatever form or shape is my most lively and immediate kind of natural enjoyment; yes, I would even say that only in contemplation of it do I achieve true self-forgetfulness and feel my own limited individuality merge into the universal. The sea, still-brooding or coming on in crashing billows, can put me in a state of such profound organic dreaminess, such remoteness from myself, that I am lost to time. Boredom is unknown, hours pass like minutes, in the unity of that companionship. But then, I can lean on the rail of a little bridge over a brook and contemplate its currents, its whirlpools, and its steady flow for as long as you like; with no sense or fear of that other flowing within and about me, that swift gliding away of time. Such love of water and understanding of it make me value the circumstance that the narrow strip of ground where I dwell is enclosed on both sides by water.

But my little brook here is the simplest of its kind, it has no particular or unusual characteristics, it is quite the average brook. Clear as glass, without any guile, it does not dream of seeming deep by being turbid. It is shallow and candid and makes no bones of betraying that there are old tins and the mouldering remains of a laced shoe in its bed. But it is deep enough to serve as a home for pretty, lively, silver-grey little fish, which dart away in zigzags at our approach. In some places it broadens into a pool, and it has willows on its margin, one of which I love to look at as I pass. It stands on the hillside, a little removed from the water; but one of the boughs has bent down and reached across and actually succeeded in plunging its silvery tip into the flowing water. Thus it stands revelling in the pleasure of this contact.

It is pleasant to walk here in the warm breeze of summer. If the weather is very warm Bashan goes into the stream to cool his belly; not more than that, for he never of his own free will wets the upper parts. He stands there with his ears laid back and a look of virtue on his face and lets the water stream round and over him. Then he comes back to me to shake himself, being convinced that this can only be accomplished in my vicinity –

although he does it so thoroughly that I receive a perfect shower-bath in the process. It is no good waving him off with my stick or with shoutings. Whatever seems to him natural and right and necessary, that he will do.

The brook flows on westward to a little hamlet that faces north between the wood and the hillside. At the beginning of this hamlet is an inn, and at this point the brook widens into another pool where women kneel to wash their clothes. Crossing the little footbridge, you strike into a road going back towards the city between wood and meadow. But on the right of the road is another through the wood, by which in a few minutes you can get back to the river.

And so here we are at the river zone, and the river itself is in front of us, green and roaring and white with foam. It is really nothing more than a mountain torrent; but its ceaseless roaring pervades the whole region round, in the distance subdued, but here a veritable tumult which – if one cannot have the ocean itself – is quite a fair substitute for its awe-inspiring swell. Numberless gulls fill the air with their cries; autumn, winter, and spring they circle screaming round the mouths of the drain-pipes which issue here, seeking their food. In summer they depart once more for the lakes higher up. Wild and half-wild duck also take refuge here in the neighbourhood of the town for the winter months. They rock on the waves, are whirled round and carried off by the current, rise into the air to escape being engulfed, and then settle again on quieter water.

And this river tract also is divided into areas of varying character. At the edge of the wood is the gravelly expanse into which the poplar avenue issues; it extends for nearly a mile downstream, as far as the ferry-house, of which I will speak presently. At this point the underbrush comes nearly down to the river-bed. And all the gravel, as I am aware, constitutes the beginnings of the first and most important of the lengthwise streets, magnificently conceived by the real-estate company as an esplanade, a carriage-road bordered by trees and flowers – where elegantly turned-out riders were to hold sweet converse with ladies leaning back in shiny landaus. Beside the ferry-house, indeed, is a sign, already rickety and rotting, from which one can gather that the site was intended for the erection of a café. Yes, there is the sign – and there it remains, but there is no trace of the little tables, the hurrying waiters and coffee-sipping guests; nobody has bought the site, and the esplanade is nothing but a desert of gravel, where sage and willow-shoots are almost as thick as in Opitz- and Flemmingstrasse.

Down close to the river is another, narrower gravel waste, as full of weeds as the bigger one. Along it are grassy mounds supporting telegraph poles. I like to use this as a path, by way of variety – also because it is cleaner, though more difficult, to walk on it than on the actual footpath, which in bad weather is often very muddy, though it is actually the proper path, extending for miles along the river, finally going off into trails along the bank. It is planted on the river side with young maple and birch trees; on the other side the original inhabitants stand in a row – willows, aspens, and silver poplars of enormous size. The river-bank is steep and high and is ingeniously shored up with withes and concrete to prevent the flooding which threatens two or three times in the year, after heavy rains or when the snows melt in the hills. At several points there are ladderlike wooden steps leading down to the river-bed – an extent of mostly dry gravel, six or eight yards wide. For this mountain torrent behaves precisely as its like do, whether large or small: it may be, according to the conditions up above, either the merest green trickle, hardly covering the stones, where long-legged birds seem to be standing on the water; or it may be a torrent alarming in its power and extent, filling the wide bed with raging fury, whirling round tree-branches and old baskets and dead cats and threatening to commit much damage. Here, too, there is protection against floods in the shape of woven hurdles put in slanting to the stream. When dry, the bed is grown up with wiry grass and wild oats, as well as that omnipresent shrub the blue sage; there is fairly good walking, on the strip of flat stones at the extreme outer edge, and it affords me a pleasant variety, for though the stone is not of the most agreeable to walk on, the close proximity of the river atones for much, and there is even sometimes sand between the gravel and the grass; true, it is mixed with clay, it has not the exquisite cleanness of sea-sand,

but after all it is sand. I am taking a walk on the beach that
stretches into the distance at the edge of the wave, and there is
the sound of the surge and the cry of the gulls, there is that
monotony that swallows time and space and shuts one up as in
a dream. The river roars eddying over the stones, and halfway
to the ferry-house the sound is augmented by a waterfall that
comes down by a diagonal canal and tumbles into the larger
stream, arching as it falls, shining glassily like a leaping fish, and
seething perpetually at its base.

Lovely to walk here when the sky is blue and the ferry-boat
flies a flag, perhaps in honour of the fine weather or because it is
a feast-day of some sort. There are other boats here too, but the
ferry-boat is fast to a wire cable attached to another, thicker
cable that is spanned across the stream and runs along it on a
little pulley. The current supplies the motive power, the steering
is done by hand. The ferryman lives with his wife and child in
the ferry-house, which is a little higher up than the upper footpath; the house has a kitchen-garden and a chicken-house and
the man undoubtedly gets it rent-free in his office as ferryman.
It is a sort of dwarf villa, rather flimsy, with funny little out-
croppings of balconies and bay-windows, and seems to have two
rooms below and two above. I like to sit on the little bench on
the upper footpath close to the tiny garden – with Bashan
squatting on my foot and the ferryman's chickens stalking
round about me, jerking their heads forward with each step.
The cock usually comes and perches on the back of the bench
with his green bersaglieri tail-feathers hanging down behind; he
sits thus beside me and measures me with a fierce side-glance of
his red eye. I watch the traffic; it is not crowded, hardly even
lively; indeed, the ferry-boat runs only at considerable intervals.
The more do I enjoy it when on one side or the other a man appears, or a woman with a basket, and wants to be put across; the
'Boat ahoy!' is an age-old, picturesque cry, with a poetry not im-
paired by the fact that the business is done somewhat differently
nowadays. Double flights of steps for those coming and going
lead down to the river-bed and to the landings, and there is an
electric push-button at the side of each. So when a man appears
on the opposite bank and stands looking across the water, he

does not put his hands round his mouth and call. He goes up to
the push-button, puts out his hand, and pushes. The bell rings
shrilly in the ferryman's villa; that is the 'Boat ahoy!' even so,
and it is poetic still. Then the man waits and looks about. And
almost at the moment when the bell rings, the ferryman comes
out of his little official dwelling, as though he had been standing
behind the door or sitting on a chair waiting for the signal. He
comes out, and the way he walks suggests that he has been
mechanically put in motion by the ringing of the bell. It is like a
shooting-booth when you shoot at the door of a little house and
if you hit it a figure comes out, a sentry or a cow-girl. The
ferryman crosses his garden at a measured pace, his arms swinging regularly at his sides; over the path and down the steps to
the river, where he pushes off the ferry-boat and holds the
steering-gear while the little pulley runs along the wire above
the stream and the boat is driven across. The man springs in,
and once safely on this side hands over his penny and runs
briskly up the steps, going off right or left. Sometimes, when the
ferryman is not well or is very busy in the house, his wife or
even his little child comes out to ferry the stranger across. They
can do it as well as he, and so could I, for it is an easy office,
requiring no special gift or training. He can reckon himself
lucky to have the job and live in the dwarf villa. Anyone, however stupid, could do what he does, and he knows this, of
course, and behaves with becoming modesty. On the way back
to his house he very politely says: 'Grüss Gott' to me as I sit
there on the bench between Bashan and the cock; you can see
that he likes to be on good terms with everybody.

There is a tarry smell, a breeze off the water, a slapping sound
against the ferry-boat. What more can one want? Sometimes
these things call up a familiar memory: the water is deep, it has
a smell of decay – that is the Lagoon, that is Venice. But sometimes there is a heavy storm, a deluge of rain; in my macintosh,
my face streaming with wet, I take the upper path, leaning
against the strong west wind, which in the poplar avenue has
torn the saplings away from their supports. Now one can see
why all the trees are bent in one direction and have somewhat
lop-sided tops. Bashan has to stop often to shake himself, the

water flies off him in every direction. The river is quite changed: swollen and dark yellow it rolls threateningly along, rushing and dashing in a furious hurry this way and that; its muddy tide takes up the whole extra bed up to the edge of the undergrowth, pounding against the cement and the willow hurdles – until one is glad of the forethought that put them there. The strange thing about it is that the water is *quiet*; it makes almost no noise at all. And there are no rapids in its course now, the stream is too high for that. You can only see where they were by the fact that its waves are higher and deeper there than elsewhere, and that their crests break backwards instead of forwards like the surf on a beach. The waterfall is insignificant now, its volume is shrunken, no longer vaulted, and the boiling water at its base is almost obliterated by the height of the flood. Bashan's reaction to all this is simple unmitigated astonishment that things can be so changed. He cannot get over it, cannot understand how it is that the dry territory where he is wont to run about has disappeared, is covered by water. He flees up into the undergrowth to get away from the lashing of the flood; looks at me and wags his tail, then back at the water, and has a funny, puzzled way of opening his jaws crookedly, shutting them again and running his tongue round the corner of his mouth. It is not a very refined gesture, in fact rather common, but very speaking, and as human as it is animal – in fact it is just what an ordinary simple-minded man might do in face of a surprising situation, very likely scratching his neck at the same time.

Having gone into some detail in describing the river zone, I believe I have covered the whole region and done all I can to bring it before my reader's eye. I like my description pretty well, but I like the reality of nature even better. It is more vivid and various; just as Bashan himself is warmer, more living and hearty than his imaginary presentment. I am attached to this landscape, I owe it something, and am grateful; therefore, I have described it. It is my park and my solitude; my thoughts and dreams are mingled and interwoven with images from it, as the tendrils of climbing plants are with the boughs of its trees. I have seen it at all times of day and all seasons of the year: in autumn, when the chemical odour of decaying vegetation fills the air, when all the thistles have shed their down, when the great beeches in my park have spread a rust-coloured carpet of leaves on the meadow and the liquid golden afternoons merge into romantic, theatrical early evenings, with the moon's sickle swimming in the sky, when a milk-brewed mist floats above the lowlands and a crimson sunset burns through the black silhouettes of the tree-branches. In autumn, but in winter too, when the gravel is covered with snow and softly levelled off so that one can walk on it in overshoes; when the river looks black as it flows between sallow frost-bound banks, and the cries of hundreds of gulls fill the air from morning to night. But my freest and most familiar intercourse with it is in the milder months, when no extra clothing is required, to dash out quickly, between two showers, for a quarter of an hour; to bend aside in passing a bough of black alder and get a glimpse of the river as it flows. We may have had guests, and I am left somewhat worn down by conversation, between my four walls, where it seems the breath of the strangers still hovers on the air. Then it is good not to linger but to go out at once and stroll in Gellertstrasse or Stifterstrasse, to draw a long breath and get the air into one's lungs. I look up into the sky, I gaze into the tender depths of the masses of green foliage, and peace returns once more and dwells within my spirit.

And Bashan is always with me. He had not been able to prevent the influx of strange persons into our dwelling though he had lifted up his voice and objected. But it did no good, so he had withdrawn. Now he rejoices to be with me again in our hunting-ground. He runs before me on the gravel path, one ear negligently cocked, with that sidewise gait dogs have, the hind legs not just exactly behind the forelegs. And suddenly I see him gripped, as it were, body and soul, his stump of tail switching furiously, erect in the air. His head goes forward and down, his body lengthens out, he makes short dashes in several directions, and then shoots off in one of them with his nose to the ground. He has struck a scent. He is off after a hare.

A Man and His Dog

The Chase

The region round is full of game, and we hunt it; that is,
Bashan does and I look on. Thus we go hunting: hares, part-
ridges, fieldmice, moles, ducks, and gulls. Neither do we shrink
from larger game, we stalk pheasant, even deer, if one of them,
in winter, happens to stray into our preserve. It is quite a
thrilling sight to see the slender long-legged creature, yellow
against the snow, running away, with its white buttocks bobbing
up and down, in flight from my little Bashan. He strains every
nerve, I look on with the greatest sympathy and suspense. Not
that anything would ever come of it, nothing ever has or will.
But the lack of concrete results does not affect Bashan's passionate eagerness or mar my own interest at all. We pursue the
chase for its own sake, not for the prey nor for any other
material advantage. Bashan is, as I have said, the active partner.
He does not expect from me anything more than my moral
support, having no experience, immediate and personal, that is,
of more direct co-operation. I say immediate and personal for
it is more than likely that his forebears, at least on the pointer
side, know what the chase should really be like. I have sometimes
asked myself whether some memory might still linger in him,
ready to be awakened by a chance sight or sound. At his level
the life of the individual is certainly less sharply distinguished
from the race than is the case with human beings, birth and
death must be a less far-reaching shock; perhaps the traditions
of the stock are preserved unimpaired, so that it would only be
an apparent contradiction to speak of inborn experiences,
unconscious memories which, when summoned up, would have
the power to confuse the creature as to what were its own individual experiences or give rise to dissatisfaction with them. I
indulged in this thought, but finally put it from me, as Bashan
obviously put from him the rather brutal episode which gave
rise to my speculations.

When we get out to follow the chase it is usually midday, half
past eleven or twelve; sometimes, on particularly warm summer
days, we go late in the afternoon, six o'clock or so – or perhaps
we go then for the second time. But on the afternoon walk

things are very different with me – not at all as they were on my careless morning stroll. My freshness and serenity have departed long since, I have been struggling and taking thought, I have overcome difficulties, have had to grit my teeth and tussle with a single detail while at the same time holding a more extended and complex context firmly in mind, concentrating my mental powers upon it down to its furthermost ramifications. And my head is tired. It is the chase with Bashan that relieves and distracts me, gives me new life, and puts me back into condition for the rest of the day, in which there is still something to be done.

Of course we do not select each day a certain kind of game to hunt – only hares, for instance, or only ducks. Actually we hunt everything that comes – I was going to say, within reach of our guns. So that we do not need to go far before starting something, actually the hunt can begin just outside the garden gate; for there are quantities of moles and field-mice in the meadow bottom behind the house. Of course these fur-bearing little creatures are not properly game at all. But their mysterious, burrowing little ways, and especially the slyness and dexterity of the field-mice, which are not blind by day like their brethren the moles, but scamper discreetly about on the ground, whisking into their holes at the approach of danger, so that one cannot even see their legs moving – all this works powerfully upon Bashan's instincts. Besides, they are the only wild creatures he ever catches. A field-mouse, a mole, makes a morsel not to be despised, in these lean days, when he often finds nothing more appetizing than porridge in the dish beside his kennel.

So then I and my walking-stick will scarcely have taken two or three steps up the poplar avenue, and Bashan will have scarcely opened the ball with his usual riotous plunges, when I see him capering off to my right – already he is in the grip of his passion, sees and hears nothing but the maddening invisible activities of the creatures all round him. He slinks through the grass, his whole body tense, wagging his tail and lifting his legs with great caution; stops, with one foreleg and one hind leg in the air, eyes the ground with his head on one side, muzzle pointed, ear muscles stiffly erected – so that his ear-laps fall

down in front, each side of his eyes. Then with both forepaws
raised he makes a sudden forward plunge, and another; looking
with a puzzled air at the place where something just now was
but is not any more. Then he begins to dig. I feel a strong desire
to follow him and see what he gets. But if I did we should
never get farther, his whole zeal for the chase would be expended here on the spot. So I go on. I need not worry about his
losing me. Even if he stops behind a long time and has not seen
which way I turned, my trail will be as clear to him as though I
were the game he seeks, and he will follow it, head between his
paws, even if I am out of sight; already I can hear his licence-
tag clinking and his stout paws thudding in my rear. He shoots
past me, turns round, and wags his tail to announce that he is
on the spot.

But in the woods, or out on the meadows by the brook, I do
stop often and watch him digging for a mouse, even though the
time allotted for my walk is nearly over. It is so fascinating to
see his passionate concentration, I feel the contagion myself and
cannot help a fervent wish that he may catch something and I
be there to see. The spot where he has chosen to dig looks, like
any other – perhaps a mossy little mound among the roots at the
foot of a birch tree. But he has heard and scented something at
that spot, perhaps even viewed it as it whisked away; he is
convinced that it is there in its burrow underground, he has only
to get at it – and he digs away for dear life, oblivious of all else,
not angry, but with the professional passion of the sportsman –
it is a magnificent sight. His little striped body, the ribs showing
and muscles playing under the smooth skin, is drawn in at the
middle, his hind quarters stand up in the air, the stump of a tail
vibrating in quick time; his head with his forepaws is down in
the slanting hole he has dug and he turns his face aside as he
plies his iron-shod paws. Faster and faster, till earth and little
stones and tufts of grass and fragments of tree-roots fly up
almost into my face. Sometimes he snorts in the silence, when he
has burrowed his nose well into the earth, trying to smell out the
motionless, clever, frightened little beast that is besieged down
there. It is a muffled snorting; he draws in the air hastily and
empties his lungs again the better to scent the fine, keen, far-

away, and buried effluvium. How does the creature feel when he hears the snorting? Ah, that is its own affair, or God's, who has made Bashan the enemy of field-mice. Even the emotion of fear is an enhancement of life; and who knows, if there were no Bashan the mouse might find time hang heavy on its hands. Besides, what would be the use of all its beady-eyed cleverness and mining skill, which more than balance what Bashan can do, so that the attacker's success is always more than problematical? In short, I do not feel much pity for the mouse, privately I am on Bashan's side and cannot always stick to my role of onlooker. I take my walking-stick and dig out some pebble or gnarled piece of root that is too firmly lodged for him to move. And he sends up a swift, warm glance of understanding to me as he works. With his mouth full of dirt, he chews away at the stubborn earth and the roots running through it, tears out whole chunks and throws them aside, snorts again into his hole and is encouraged by the freshened scent to renewed attack on it with his claws.

In nearly every case all this labour is vain. Bashan will give one last cursory look at the scene and then with soil sticking to his nose, and his legs black to the shoulder, he will give it up and trot off indifferently beside me. 'No go, Bashan,' I say when he looks up at me. 'Nothing there,' I repeat, shaking my head and shrugging my shoulders to make my meaning clear. But he needs no consolation, he is not in the least depressed by his failure. The chase is the thing, the quarry a minor matter. It was a good effort, he thinks, in so far as he casts his mind back at all to his recent strenuous performance – for already he is bent on a new one, and all three of our zones will furnish him plenty of opportunity.

But sometimes he actually catches the mouse. I have my emotions when that happens, for he gobbles it alive, without compunction, with the fur and the bones. Perhaps the poor little thing was not well enough advised by its instincts, and chose for its hole a place where the earth was too soft and loose and easy to dig. Perhaps its gallery was not long enough and it was too terrified to go on digging, but simply crouched there with its beady eyes popping out of its head for fright, while the horrible snorting came nearer and nearer. And so at last the iron-shod paw laid it bare and scooped it up – out into the light of day, a lost little mouse! It was justified of its fears; luckily these most likely reduced it to a semi-conscious state, so that it will hardly have noticed being converted into porridge.

Bashan holds it by the tail and dashes it against the ground, once, twice, thrice; there is the faintest squeak, the very last sound which the godforsaken little mouse is destined to make on this earth, and now Bashan snaps it up in his jaws, between his strong white teeth. He stands with his forelegs braced apart, his neck bent, and his head stuck out while he chews, shifting the morsel in his mouth and then beginning to munch once more. He crunches the tiny bones, a shred of fur hangs from the corner of his mouth, it disappears and all is over. Bashan begins to execute a dance of joy and triumph round me as I stand leaning on my stick as I have been standing to watch the whole procedure. 'You are a fine one!' I say, nodding in grim tribute to his prowess. 'You are a murderer, you know, a cannibal!' He only redoubles his activity – he does everything but laugh aloud. So I walk on, feeling rather chilled by what I have seen, yet inwardly amused by the crude humours of life. The event was in the natural order of things, and a mouse lacking in the instinct of self-preservation is on the way to be turned into pulp. But I feel better if I happen not to have assisted the natural order with my stick but to have preserved throughout my attitude of onlooker.

It is startling to have a pheasant burst out of the undergrowth where it was perched asleep or else hoping to be undiscovered, until Bashan's unerring nose ferreted it out. The big, rust-coloured, long-tailed bird rises with a great clapping and flapping and a frightened, angry, cackling cry. It drops its excrement into the brush and takes flight with the absurd headlessness of a chicken to the nearest tree, where it goes on shrieking murder, while Bashan claws at the trunk and barks furiously up at it. 'Get up, get up!' he is saying. 'Fly away, you silly object of my sporting instincts, that I may chase you!' And the bird cannot resist his loud voice, it rises rustling from the bough and flies on heavy wing through the tree-tops, squawking and complaining, Bashan following below, with ardour, but preserving a stately silence.

This is his joy. He wants and knows no other. For what would happen if he actually caught the pheasant? Nothing at all: I have seen him with one in his claws – he may have stolen upon it while it slept so that the awkward bird could not rise – and he stood over it embarrassed by his triumph, without an idea what to do. The pleasant lay in the grass with its neck and one wing sprawled out and shrieked without stopping – it sounded as though an old woman were being murdered in the bushes, and I hastened up to prevent, if I could, something frightful happening. But I quickly convinced myself that there was no danger. Bashan's obvious helplessness, the half curious, half disgusted look he bent on his capture, with his head on one side, quite reassured me. The old-womanish screaming at his feet got on his nerves, the whole affair made him feel more bothered than triumphant. Perhaps, for his honour as a sportsman, he plucked at the bird – I think I saw him pulling out a couple of feathers with his lips, not using his teeth, and tossing them to one side with an angry shake of the head. But then he moved away and let it go. Not out of magnanimity, but because the affair seemed not to have anything to do with the joyous hunt and so was merely stupid. Never have I seen a more non-plussed bird. It had given itself up for lost, and appeared not to be able to convince itself to the contrary: awhile it lay in the grass as though it were dead. Then it staggered along the ground a little way, fluttered up on a tree, looked like falling off it, but pulled itself together and flew away heavily, with dishevelled plumes. It did not squawk, it kept its bill shut. Without a sound it flew across the park, the river, the woods on the other side, as far away as possible and certainly it never came back.

But there are plenty of its kind in our hunting-ground and Bashan hunts them in all honour and according to the rules of the game. Eating mice is the only blood-guilt he has on his head and even that is incidental and superfluous. The tracking out, the driving up, the chasing – these are ends in themselves to the sporting spirit, and are plainly so to him, as anybody would see who watched him at his brilliant performance. How beautiful he becomes, how consummate, how ideal! Like a clumsy peasant lad, who will look perfect and statuesque as a huntsman among his native rocks. All that is best in Bashan, all that is genuine and fine, comes out and reaches its flower at these times. Hence his yearning for them, his repining when they fruitlessly slip away. He is no terrier, he is true hunter and pointer, and joy in himself as such speaks in every virile, valiant, native pose he assumes. Not many other things rejoice my eye as does the sight of him going through the brush at a swinging trot, then standing stock-still, with one paw daintily raised and turned in, sagacious, serious, alert, with all his faculties beautifully concentrated. Then suddenly he whimpers. He has trod on a thorn and cries out. Ah, yes, that too is natural, it is amusing to see that he has the courage of his simplicity. It could only passingly mar his dignity, next moment his posture is as fine as ever.

I look at him and recall a time when he lost all his nobility and distinction and reverted to the low physical and moral state in which we found him in the kitchen of that mountain inn and from which he climbed painfully enough to some sort of belief in himself and the world. I do not know what ailed him; he had bleeding from the mouth or nose or throat, I do not know which to this day. Wherever he went he left traces of blood behind: on the grass in our hunting-ground, the straw in his kennel, on the floor in the house – though we could not discover any wound. Sometimes his nose looked as though it had been dipped in red paint. When he sneezed he showered blood all over, and then trod in it and left the marks of his paws about. He was carefully examined without result, and we felt more and more disturbed. Was he tubercular? Or had he some other complaint to which his species was prone? When the mysterious affliction did not pass off after some days, we decided to take him to a veterinary clinic.

Next day at about noon I kindly but firmly adjusted his muzzle, the leather mask which Bashan detests as he does few other things, always trying to get rid of it by shaking his head or rubbing it with his paws. I put him on the plaited leather lead and led him thus harnessed up the poplar avenue, through the

English Gardens, and along a city street to the Academy, where we went under the arch and crossed the courtyard. We were received into a waiting-room where several people sat, each holding like me a dog on a lead. They were dogs of all sizes and kinds, gazing dejectedly at each other over their muzzles. There was a matron with her apoplectic pug, a liveried manservant with a tall, snow-white Russian greyhound, which from time to time gave a hoarse, aristocratic cough; a countryman with a dachshund which seemed to need orthopaedic assistance, its legs being entirely crooked and put on all wrong. And many more. The attendant let them in one by one into the consulting-room, and after a while it became the turn of Bashan and me.

The Professor was a man in advanced years, wearing a white surgeon's coat and a gold eye-glass. His hair was curly, and he seemed so mild, expert, and kindly that I would have unhesitatingly entrusted myself and all my family to him in any emergency. During my recital he smiled benevolently at his patient, who sat there looking up at him with equal trustfulness. 'He has fine eyes,' said he, passing over Bashan's moustaches in silence. He said he would make an examination at once, and poor Bashan, too astounded to offer any resistance, was with the attendant's help stretched out on the table forthwith. And then it was touching to see the physician apply his black stethoscope and auscultate my little man just as I have more than once had it done to me. He listened to his quick-breathing doggish heart, listened to all his organs, in various places. Then with his stethoscope under his arm he examined Bashan's eyes and nose and the cavity of his mouth, and gave a temporary opinion. The dog was a little nervous and anaemic, he said, but otherwise in good condition. The origin of the bleeding was unclear. It might be an epistaxis or a haematemesis. But equally well it might be tracheal or pharyngeal haemorrhage. Perhaps for the present one might characterize it as a case of haemoptysis. It would be best to keep the animal under careful observation. I might leave it with them and look in at the end of a week.

Thus instructed, I expressed my thanks and took my leave, patting Bashan on the shoulder by way of good-bye. I saw the attendant take the new patient across the courtyard to some

back buildings opposite the entrance, Bashan looking back at me
with a frightened and bewildered face. And yet he might have
felt flattered, as I could not help feeling myself, at having the
Professor call him nervous and anaemic. No one could have
foretold of him in his cradle that he would one day be called
those things or discussed with such gravity and expert knowledge.

But after that my walks abroad were as unseasoned food to
the palate; I had little relish of them. No dumb paean of joy
accompanied my going out, no glorious excitement of the chase
surrounded my footsteps. The park was a desert, time hung on
my hands. During the period of waiting I telephoned several
times for news. Answer came through a subordinate that the
patient was doing as well as possible under the circumstances –
but the circumstances – for better or worse – were never described in more detail. So when the week came round again, I
betook myself to the clinic.

Guided by numerous signs and arrows I arrived without difficulty before the entrance of the department where Bashan was
lodged, and, warned by another sign on the door, forbore to
knock and went straight in. The medium-sized room I found
myself in reminded me of a carnivora-house – a similar atmosphere prevailed. Only here the menagerie odour seemed to be
kept down by various sweetish-smelling medicinal fumes – a
disturbing and oppressive combination. Wire cages ran round
the room, most of them occupied. Loud baying greeted me from
one of these, at the open door of which a man, who seemed to
be the keeper, was busy with rake and shovel. He contented
himself with returning my greeting while going on with his
work, and left me to my own devices.

I had seen Bashan directly I entered the door, and went up to
him. He was lying behind his bars on a pile of tan-bark or some
such stuff, which contributed its own special odour to the
animal and chemical smells in the room. He lay there like a
leopard – but a very weary, sluggish, and disgusted leopard. I
was startled by the sullen indifference with which he met me.
His tail thumped the floor once or twice, weakly; only when I
spoke to him did he lift his head from his paws, and even then

he let it fall again at once and blinked gloomily to one side. There was an earthenware dish of water at the back of his pen. A framed chart, partly printed and partly written, was fastened to the bars, giving his name, species, sex, and age and showing his temperature curve. 'Bastard pointer,' it said, 'named Bashan. Male. Two years old. Admitted on such and such a day of the month and the year, for observation of occult blood.' Underneath followed the fever curve, drawn with a pen and showing small variations; also daily entries of his pulse. Yes, his temperature was taken, and his pulse felt, by a doctor; in his direction everything was being done. But I was distressed about his state of mind.

'Is that one yours?' asked the keeper, who had now come up, his tools in his hands. He had on a sort of gardening apron and was a squat red-faced man with a round beard and rather bloodshot brown eyes that were quite strikingly like a dog's in their humid gaze and faithful expression.

I answered in the affirmative, referred to my telephone conversations and the instructions I had had to come back today, and said I should like to hear how things stood. The man looked at the chart. Yes, the dog was suffering from occult blood, that was always a long business, especially when one did not know where it came from. But was not that always the case? No, they did not really know yet. But the dog was there to be observed, and he would be. And did he still bleed? Yes, now and then he did. And had he fever? I asked, trying to read the chart. No, no fever. His temperature and pulse were quite normal, about ninety beats a minute, he ought to have that much, and if he had not, then they would have to observe him even more carefully. Except for the bleeding, the dog was really doing all right. He had howled at first, of course; he had howled for twenty-four hours, but after that he was used to it. He didn't eat much, for a fact, but then he hadn't much exercise, and perhaps he wasn't a big eater. What did they give him? Soup, said the man. But as he had said, the dog didn't eat much at all. 'He seems depressed,' I remarked with an assumption of objectivity. Yes, that was true, but it didn't mean much. After all it wasn't very much fun for a dog to lie cooped

61

up like that under observation. They were all depressed, more or less. That is, the good-natured ones, some dogs got mean and treacherous. He could not say that of Bashan. He was a good dog, he would not get mean if he stayed there all his days. I agreed with the man, but I did so with pain and rebellion in my heart. How long then, I asked, did they reckon to keep him here? The man looked at the chart again. Another week, he said, would be needed for the observation, the Herr Professor had said. I'd better come and ask again in another week; that would be two weeks in all, then they would be able to say more about the possibility of getting rid of the haemorrhages.

I went away, after trying once more to rouse up Bashan by renewed calls and encouragement. In vain. He cared as little for my going as for my coming. He seemed weighed down by bitter loathing and despair. He had the air of saying: 'Since you were capable of having me put in this cage, I expect nothing more from you.' And, actually, had he not enough ground to despair of reason and justice? What had he done that this should happen to him and that I not only let it happen but took steps to bring it about? And yet my intentions had been of the best. He had bled, and though it seemed to make no difference to him, I thought it sensible that we should call in medical advice, he being a dog in good circumstances. And then we had learned that he was anaemic and nervous – as though he were the daughter of some upper-class family. And then it had to come out like this! How could I explain to him we were treating him with great distinction, in shutting him up like a jaguar, without sun, air, or exercise, and plaguing him every day with a thermometer?

On the way home I asked myself these things; and if before then I had missed Bashan, now worry about him was added to my distress: worry over his state and reproaches to my own address. Perhaps after all I had taken him to the clinic only out of vanity and arrogance. And added to that may I not have secretly wished to get rid of him for a while? Perhaps I had a craving to see what it would be like to be free of his incessant watching of me; to be able to turn calmly to right or left as I pleased, without having to realize that I had been to another

living creature the source of joy or of bitter disappointment.
Certainly while Bashan was interned I felt a certain inner
independence which had long been strange to me. No one
exasperated me by looking through the glass door with the air of
a martyr. No one put up a hesitating paw to move me to laughter and relenting and persuade me to go out sooner than I
wished. Whether I sought the park or kept my room concerned
no one at all. It was quiet, pleasant, and had the charm of
novelty. But lacking the accustomed spur I hardly went out at
all. My health suffered, gradually I approached the condition of
Bashan in his cage; and the moral reflection occurred to me that
the bonds of sympathy were probably more conducive to my own
well-being than the selfish independence for which I had longed.

The second week went by, and on the appointed day I stood
with the round-bearded keeper before Bashan's cage. Its inmate
lay on his side on the tan-bark, there were bits of it on his coat.
He had his head flung back as he lay and was staring with dull,
glazed eyes at the bare whitewashed wall. He did not stir. I
could scarcely see him breathe; but now and then his chest rose
in a long sigh that made the ribs stand out, and fell again with a
faint, heart-rending resonance from the vocal cords. His legs
seemed to have grown too long, and his paws large out of all
proportion, as a result of his extraordinary emaciation. His coat
was rough and dishevelled and had, as I said, tan-bark sticking
in it. He did not look at me, he seemed not to want to look at
anything ever any more.

The bleeding, so the keeper said, had not altogether and entirely disappeared, it came back now and again. Where it came
from was still not quite clear; in any case it was harmless. If I
liked I could leave the dog here for further observation, to be
quite certain, or I could take him home, because the bleeding
might disappear just as well there as here. I drew the plaited
lead out of my pocket – I had brought it with me – and said
that I would take him with me. The keeper thought that was a
sensible thing to do. He opened the grating and we summoned
Bashan by name, both together and in turn, but he did not
come, he kept on staring at the whitewashed wall. But he did
not struggle when I put my arm into the cage and pulled him

out by the collar. He gave a spring and landed with his four feet on the floor, where he stood with his tail between his legs and his ears laid back, the picture of wretchedness. I picked him up, tipped the keeper, and went to the front office to pay my debt; at the rate of seventy-five pfennigs a day plus the medical examination it came to twelve marks fifty. I led Bashan home, breathing the animal-chemical odours which still clung to his coat.

He was broken, in body and in spirit. Animals are more primitive and less inhibited in giving expression to their mental state – there is a sense in which one might say they are more human: descriptive phrases which to us have become mere metaphor still fit them literally, we get a fresh and diverting sense of their meaning when we see it embodied before our eyes. Bashan, as we say, 'hung his head'; that is, he did it literally and visibly, till he looked like a worn-out cab-horse, with sores on its legs, standing at the cab-rank, its skin twitching and its poor fly-infested nose weighed down towards the pavement. It was as I have said: those two weeks at the clinic had reduced him to the state he had been in at the beginning. He was the shadow of his former self – if that does not insult the proud and joyous shadow our Bashan once cast. The hospital smell he had brought with him wore off after repeated soapy baths till you got only an occasional whiff; but it was not with him as with human beings: he got no symbolic refreshment from the physical cleansing. The very first day, I took him out to our hunting-grounds, but he followed at my heel with his tongue lolling out; even the pheasants perceived that it was the close season. For days he lay as he had lain in his cage at the clinic, staring with glazed eyes, flabby without and within. He showed no healthy impatience for the chase, did not urge me to go out – indeed it was rather I who had to go and fetch him from his kennel. Even the reckless and indiscriminate way he wolfed his food recalled those early unworty days. But what a joy to see him slowly finding himself again! Little by little he began to greet me in the morning in his old naïve, impetuous way, storming upon me at my first whistle instead of limping morosely up; putting his forepaws on my chest and snapping playfully at my face. Gradually there returned to him his old out-of-doors pride and joy in his own physical prowess; once more he delighted my eyes with the bold and beautiful poses he took, the sudden bounds with his feet drawn up, after some creature stirring in the long grass ... He forgot. The ugly and to Bashan senseless episode sank into the past, unresolved indeed, unclarified by comprehension, that being of course impossible; it was covered by the lapse of time, as must happen sometimes to human beings. We went on living and what had not been expressed became by degrees forgotten ... For several weeks, at lengthening intervals, Bashan's nose showed red. Then the phenomenon disappeared, it was no more, it only had been, and so it was no matter whether it had been an epistaxis or a haematemesis.

Well, there! Contrary to my own intentions, I have told the story of the clinic. Perhaps my reader will forgive the lengthy digression and come back to the park and the pleasures of the chase, where we were before the interruption. Do you know that long-drawn wailing howl to which a dog gives vent when he summons up his utmost powers to give chase to a flying hare? In it rage and rapture mingle, desire and the ecstasy of despair. How often have I heard it from Bashan! It is passion itself, deliberate, fostered passion, drunkenly revelled in, shrilling through our woodland scene, and every time I hear it near or far a fearful thrill of pleasure shoots through my limbs. Rejoiced that Bashan will come into his own today, I hasten to his side, to see the chase if I can; when it roars past me I stand spellbound – though the futility of it is clear from the first – and look on with an agitated smile on my face.

And the hare, the common, frightened little hare? The air whistles through its ears, it lays back its head and runs for its life, it scrabbles and bounds with Bashan behind it yelling all he can; its yellow–white scut flies up in the air. And yet at the bottom of its soul, timid as that is and acquainted with fear, it must know that its peril cannot be grave, that it will get away, as its brothers and sisters have done before it, and itself too under like circumstances. Never in his life has Bashan caught one of them, nor will he ever; the thing is as good as impossible. Many dogs, they say, are the death of a hare, a single dog cannot achieve it, even one much speedier and more enduring than Bashan. The hare can 'double' and Bashan cannot – and that is all there is to it. For the double is the unfailing natural weapon of those born to seek safety in flight; they always have it by them, to use at the decisive moment; when Bashan's hopes are highest – then they are dashed to the ground, and he is betrayed.

There they come, dashing diagonally through the brush, across the path in front of me, and on towards the river: the hare silently hugging his little trick in his heart, Bashan giving tongue in high head-tones. 'Be quiet!' I think. 'You are wasting your wind and your lung-power and you ought to save them if you want to catch him up.' Thus I think because in my heart I am on Bashan's side, some of his fire has kindled me, I fervently hope he may catch the hare – even at the risk of seeing it torn to shreds before my eyes. How he runs! It is beautiful to see a creature expending the utmost of its powers. He runs better than the hare does, he has stronger muscles, the distance between them visibly diminishes before I lose sight of them. And I make haste too, leaving the path and cutting across the park towards the river-bank, reaching the gravelled street in time to see the chase come raging on – the hopeful, thrilling chase, with Bashan on the hare's very heels; he is still, he runs with his jaw set, scent just in front of his nose urges him to a final effort. – 'One more push, Bashan!' I think, and feel like shouting: 'Well run, old chap, remember the double!' But there it is; Bashan does make one more push, and the misfortune is upon us: at that moment the hare gives a quick, easy, almost malicious twitch at right angles to the course, and Bashan shoots past from his rear, howling helplessly and braking his very best so that dirt and pebbles fly into the air. Before he can stop, turn round, and get going in the other direction, yelling all the time as in great mental torment, the hare has gained so much ground that it is out of sight; for while he was braking so desperately Bashan could not watch where it went.

It is no use, I think; it is beautiful but futile; this while the chase fades away through the park. It takes a lot of dogs, five or six, a whole pack. Some of them to take it on the flank, some to cut off its way in front, some to corner it, some to catch it by the neck. And in my excited fancy I see a whole pack of blood-hounds with their tongues out rushing on the hare in their midst.

It is my passion for the chase makes me have these fancies, for what has the hare done to me that I should wish him such a horrible death? Bashan is nearer to me, of course, it is natural that I should feel with him and wish for his success. But the hare is after all a living creature too, and he did not play his trick on my huntsman out of malice, but only from the compelling desire to live yet awhile, nibble young tree-shoots, and beget his kind. It would be different, I go on in my mind, if this cane of mine – I lift it and look at it – were not a harmless stick, but a more serious weapon, effective like lightning and at a distance, with which I could come to Bashan's assistance and hold up the hare in mid career, so that it would turn a somersault and lie dead on the ground. Then we should not need another dog, and it would be Bashan's only task to rouse the game. Whereas as things stand it is Bashan who sometimes rolls over and over in his effort to brake. The hare sometimes does too, but it is nothing to it, it is used to such things, they do not make it feel miserable, whereas it is a shattering experience for Bashan, and might even quite possibly break his neck.

Often such a chase is all over in a few minutes; that is, when the hare succeeds after a short length in ducking into the bushes and hiding, or else by doubling and feinting in throwing off its pursuer, who stands still, hesitating, or makes short springs in this and that direction, while I in my bloodthirstiness shout encouragement and try to show him with my stick the direction the hare took. But often the hunt sways far and wide across the landscape and Bashan's furious baying sounds like a distant bugle-horn, now near, now remote; I go my own way, knowing that he will return. But in what a state he does return, at last! Foam drips from his lips, his ribs flutter, and his loins are lank and expended, his tongue lolls out of his jaws, which yawn so wide as to distort his features and give his drunken, swimming eyes a weird Mongolian slant. His breath goes like a trip-hammer. 'Lie down and rest, Bashan,' say I, 'or your lungs will burst!' and I wait to give him time to recover. I am alarmed for him when it is cold, when he pumps the air by gasps into his overheated insides and it gushes out again in a white stream; when he swallows whole mouthfuls of snow to quench his furious thirst. He lies there looking helplessly up at me, now and then licking up the slaver from his lips, and I cannot help teasing him a bit about the invariable futility of all his exertions. 'Where is the hare, Bashan?' I ask. 'Why don't you bring it to me?' He thumps with his tail on the ground when I speak; his sides pump in and out less feverishly, and he gives a rather embarrassed snap – for how can he know that I am mocking him because I feel guilty myself and want to conceal it? For I did not play my part in his enterprise, I was not man enough to hold the hare, as a proper master should have done. He does not know this, and so I can make fun of him and behave as though it were all his fault.

Strange things sometimes happen on these occasions. Never shall I forget the day when the hare ran into my arms. It was on the narrow clayey path above the river. Bashan was in full cry; I came from the wood into the river zone, struck across through the thistles of the gravelly waste, and jumped down the grassy slope to the path just in time to see the hare, with Bashan fifteen paces behind it, come bounding from the direction of the ferry-house towards which I was facing. It leaped right into the path and came towards me. My first impulse was that of the hunter towards his prey: to take advantage of the situation and cut off its escape, driving it back if possible into the jaws of the pursuer joyously yelping behind. I stood fixed on the spot, quite abandoned to the fury of the chase, weighing my cane in my hand as the hare came towards me. A hare's sight is poor, that I knew; hearing and smell are the senses that guide and preserve it. It might have taken me for a tree as I stood there; I hoped and foresaw it would do so and thus fall victim to a frightful error, the possible consequences of which were not very clear to me, though I meant to turn them to our advantage. Whether it did at any time make this mistake is unclear. I think it did not see me at all until the last minute, and what it did was so unexpected as to upset all my plans in a trice and cause a complete and sudden revulsion in my feelings. Was it beside itself with fright? Anyhow, it jumped straight at me, like a dog, ran up my overcoat with its forepaws and snuggled its head into me, me whom it should most fear, the master of the chase! I stood bent back with my arms raised, I looked down at the hare and it looked up at me. It was only a second, perhaps only part of a second, that this lasted. I saw the hare with such extraordinary distinctness, its long ears, one of which stood up, the other hung down; its large, bright, short-sighted, prominent eyes, its cleft lip and the long hairs of its moustache, the white on its breast and little paws; I felt or thought I felt the throbbing of its hunted heart. And it was strange to see it so clearly and have it so close to me, the little genius of the place, the inmost beating heart of our whole region, this ever-fleeing little being which I had never seen but for brief moments in our meadows and bottoms, frantically and drolly getting out of the way – and now, in its hour of need, not knowing where to turn, it came to me, it clasped as it were my knees, a human being's knees: not the knees, so it seemed to me, of Bashan's master, but the knees of a man who felt himself master of hares and this hare's master as well as Bashan's. It was, I say, only for the smallest second. Then the hare had dropped off, taken again to its uneven legs, and bounded up the slope on my left; while in its place there was Bashan, Bashan giving tongue in all the horrid head-tones of his hue-and-cry. When he got within reach he was abruptly checked by a deliberate and well-aimed blow from the stick of the hare's master, which sent him yelping down the slope with a temporarily disabled hind quarter. He had to limp painfully back again before he could take up the trail of his by this time vanished prey.

Finally, there are the waterfowl, to our pursuit of which I must devote a few lines. We can only go after them in winter and early spring, before they leave their town quarters – where they stay for their food's sake, and return to their lakes in the mountains. They furnish, of course, much less exciting sport than can be got out of the hares; still, it has its attractions for hunter and hound – or, rather, for the hunter and his master. For me the charm lies in the scenery, the intimate bond with living water; also it is amusing and diverting to watch the creatures swimming and flying and try provisionally to exchange one's personality for theirs and enter into their mode of life.

The ducks lead a quieter, more comfortable, more bourgeois life than do the gulls. They seem to have enough to eat, on the whole, and not to be tormented by the pangs of hunger – their kind of food is regularly to be had, the table, so to speak, always laid. For everything is fish that comes to their net: worms, snails, insects – even the ooze of the river-bed. So they have plenty of time to sit on the stones in the sun, doze with their bills tucked under one wing, and preen their well-oiled plumes, off which the water rolls in drops. Sometimes they take a pleasure-ride on the waves, with their pointed rumps in the air; paddling this way and that and giving little self-satisfied shrugs.

But the nature of gulls is wilder and more strident; there is a dreary monotony about what they do, they are the eternally hungry bird of prey, swooping all day long in hordes across the waterfall, croaking about the drainpipes that disgorge their brown streams into the river. Single gulls hover and pounce down upon a fish now and then, but this does not go far to satisfy their inordinate mass hunger; they have to fill in with most unappetizing-looking morsels from the drains, snatching them from the water in flight and carrying them off in their crooked beaks. They do not like the river-bank. But when the river is low, they huddle together on the rocks that stick out of the water – the scene is white with them, as the cliffs and islets of northern oceans are white with hosts of nesting eider-duck. I like to watch them rise all together with a great cawing and take to the air, when Bashan barks at them from the bank, across the intervening stream. They need not be frightened, certainly they are in no danger. He has a native aversion to water; but aside from that he would never trust himself to the current, and he is quite right, it is much stronger than he and would soon sweep him away and carry him God knows where. Perhaps into the Danube – but he would only arrive there after having suffered a river-change of a very drastic kind, as we know from seeing the bloated corpses of cats on their way to some distant bourne.

Bashan never goes farther into the water than the point where it begins to break over the stones. Even when he seems most tense with the pleasure of the chase and looks exactly as though he meant to jump in the very next minute, one knows that under all the excitement his sense of caution is alert and that the dashings and rushings are pure theatre – empty threats, not so much dictated by passion as cold-bloodedly undertaken in order to terrify the web-footed tribe.

But the gulls are too witless and poor-spirited to make light of his performance. He cannot get to them himself, but he sends his voice thundering across the water; it reaches them, and it, too, has actuality; it is an attack which they cannot long resist. They try to at first, they sit still, but a wave of uneasiness goes through the host, they turn their heads, a few lift their wings, and suddenly they all rush up into the air, like a white cloud, whence issue the bitterest, most fatalistic screams, Bashan springing hither and thither on the rocks, to scatter their flight and keep them in motion, for it is motion that he wants, they are not to sit quiet, they must fly, fly up and down the river so that he may chase them.

He scampers along the shore far and wide, for everywhere there are ducks, sitting with their bills tucked in homely comfort under their wings; and wherever he comes they fly up before him. He is like a jolly little hurricane making a clean sweep of the beach. Then they plump down on the water again, where they rock and ride in comfort and safety, or else they fly away over his head with their necks stretched out, while below on the shore he measures the strength of his leg-muscles quite creditably against those of their wings.

He is enchanted, and really grateful to them if they will only fly and give him occasion for this glorious race up and down the beach. It may be that they know what he wants and turn the fact to their own advantage. I saw a mother duck with her brood – this was in spring, all the birds had forsaken the river and only this one was left with her fledglings, not yet able to fly. She had them in a stagnant puddle left by the last flood in the low-lying bed of the shrunken river, and there Bashan found them, while I watched the event from the upper path. He jumped into the puddle and lashed about, furiously barking, driving the family of ducklings into wild disorder. He did them no harm, of course, but he frightened them beyond measure; the ducklings flapped their stumps of wings and scattered in all directions, and the duck was overtaken by an attack of the maternal heroism which will hurl itself blind with valour upon the fiercest foe to protect her brood; more, will even by a frenzied and unnatural display of intrepidity bully the attacker into surrender. She opened her beak to a horrific extent, she ruffled up her feathers, she flew repeatedly into Bashan's face, she made onslaught after onslaught, hissing all the while. The grim seriousness of her behaviour was so convincing that Bashan actually gave ground in confusion, though without definitely retiring from the field, for each time after retreating he would bark and advance anew. Then the mother duck changed her tactics: heroics having failed, she took refuge in strategy. Probably she knew Bashan already and was aware of his foibles and the childish nature of his desires. She left her children in the lurch – or she pretended to; she took to flight, she flew up above the river, 'pursued' by Bashan. At least, he thought he was pursuing her, in reality it was she who was leading him on, playing on his childish passion, leading him by the nose. She flew downstream, then upstream, she flew farther and farther away, Bashan racing equal with her along the bank; they left the pool with the ducklings far behind, and at length both dog and duck disappeared from my sight. Bashan came back to me after a while; the simpleton was quite winded and panting for dear life. But when we passed the pool again on our homeward way, it was empty of its brood.

So much for the mother duck. As for Bashan, he was quite grateful for the sport she had given him. For he hates the ducks who selfishly prefer their bourgeois comfort and refuse to play his game with him, simply gliding off into the water when he comes rushing along, and rocking there in base security before his face and eyes, heedless of his mighty barking, heedless too – unlike the nervous gulls – of all his feints and plungings. We stand there, Bashan and I, on the stones at the water's edge, and two paces away a duck floats on the wave, floats impudently up and down, her beak pressed coyly against her breast; safe and untouched and sweetly reasonable she bobs up and down out there, let Bashan rave as he will. Paddling against the current, she keeps abreast of us fairly well; yet she is being slowly carried down, closer and closer to one of those beautiful foaming eddies in the stream. In her folly she rides with her tail turned towards it – and now it is only a yard away. Bashan loudly gives tongue, standing with his forelegs braced against the stones; and in my heart I am barking with him, I am on his side and against that impudent, self-satisfied floating thing out there. I wish her ill. Pay attention to our barking, I address her mentally; do not hear the whirlpool roar – and then presently you will find yourself in an unpleasant and undignified situation and I shall be glad! But my malicious hopes are not fulfilled. For at the rapid's very edge she flutters up into the air, flies a few yards upstream, and then, oh, shameless hussy, settles down again.

I recall the feelings of baffled anger with which we looked at that duck – and I am reminded of another occasion, another and final episode in this tale of our hunting-ground. It was attended by a certain satisfaction for my companion and me, but had its painful and disturbing side as well; yes, it even gave rise to some coolness between us, and if I could have foreseen it I would have avoided the spot where it took place.

It was a long way out, beyond the ferry-house, downstream, where the wilds that border the river approach the upper road along the shore. We were going along this, I at an easy pace, Bashan in front with his easy, lop-sided lope. He had roused a hare – or, if you like, it had roused him – had stirred up four pheasants, and now was minded to give his master a little attention. A small bevy of ducks were flying above the river, in v-formation, their necks stretched out. They flew rather high and closer to the other shore, so that they were out of our reach as game, but moving in the same direction as ourselves. They paid no attention to us and we only cast casual glances at them now and then.

Then it happened that opposite to us on the other bank, which like ours was steep here, a man struck out of the bushes, and directly he appeared upon the scene he took up a position which fixed our attention, Bashan's no less than mine, upon him at once. We stopped in our tracks and faced him. He was a fine figure of a man, though rather rough-looking; with drooping moustaches, wearing puttees, a frieze hat cocked down over his forehead, wide velveteen trousers and jerkin to match, over which hung numerous leather straps, for he had a rucksack slung on his back and a gun over his shoulder. Or rather he had had it over his shoulder; for he no sooner appeared than he took it in his hand, laid his cheek along the butt, and aimed it diagonally upwards at the sky. He took a step forwards with one putteed leg, the gun-barrel rested in the hollow of his left hand, with the arm stretched out and the elbow against his side. The other elbow, with the hand on the trigger, stuck out at his side, and we could see his bold, foreshortened face quite clearly as he sighted upwards. It looked somehow very theatrical, this figure standing out above the boulders on the bank, against a background of shrubbery, river, and open sky. But we could have gazed for only a moment when the dull sound of the explosion made me start, I had waited for it with such inward tension. There was a tiny flash at the same time; it looked pale in the broad daylight; a puff of smoke followed. The man took one slumping pace forwards, like an operatic star, with his face and chest lifted towards the sky, his gun hanging from the strap in his right fist. Something was going on up there where he was looking and where we now looked too. There was a great confusion and scattering, the ducks flew in all directions wildly flapping their wings with a noise like wind in the sails, they tried to volplane down – then suddenly a body fell like a stone onto the water near the other shore.

This was only the first half of the action. But I must interrupt my narrative here to turn the vivid light of my memory upon the figure of Bashan. I can think of large words with which to describe it, phrases we use for great occasions: I could say that he was thunderstruck. But I do not like them, I do not want to use them. The large words are worn out, when the great occasion comes they do not describe it. Better use the small ones and put into them every ounce of their weight. I will simply say that when Bashan heard the explosion, saw its meaning and

consequence, he started; and it was the same start which I have
seen him give a thousand times when something surprises him,
only raised to the nth degree. It was a start which flung his
whole body backwards with a right-and-left motion, so sudden
that it jerked his head against his chest and almost bounced it
off his shoulders with the shock; a start which made his whole
body seem to be crying out: What! What! What was that?
Wait a minute, in the devil's name! *What was that?* He looked
and listened with that sort of rage in which extreme astonishment expresses itself; listened within himself and heard things
that had always been there, however novel and unheard-of the
present form they took. Yes, from this start, which flung him to
right and left and halfway round on his axis, I got the impression that he was trying to look at himself, trying to ask: What
am I? Who am I? Is this me? At the moment when the duck's
body plopped on the water he bounded forwards to the edge of
the bank, as though he were going to jump down to the river-
bed and plunge in. But he bethought himself of the current and
checked his impulse; then, rather shamefaced, devoted himself
to staring, as before.

I looked at him, somewhat disturbed. After the duck had
fallen I felt that we had had enough and suggested that we go
on our way. But he had sat down on his haunches, facing the
other shore, his ears erected as high as they would go. When I
said: 'Well, Bashan, shall we go on?' he turned his head only
the briefest second as though saying, with some annoyance:
Please don't disturb me! And kept on looking. So I resigned
myself, crossed my legs, leaned on my cane, and watched to see
what would happen.

The duck – no doubt one of those that had rocked in such
pert security on the water in front of our noses – went driving
like a wreck on the water, you could not tell which was head and
which tail. The river is quieter at this point, its rapids are not so
swift as they are farther up. But even so, the body was seized by
the current, whirled round, and swept away. If the man was not
concerned only with sport but had a practical goal in view, then
he would better act quickly. And so he did, not losing a moment
– it all went very fast. Even as the duck fell he had rushed

forward stumbling and almost falling down the slope, with his gun held out at arm's length. Again I was struck with the picturesqueness of the sight, as he came down the slope like a robber or smuggler in a melodrama, in the highly effective scenery of boulder and bush. He held somewhat leftwards, allowing for the current, for the duck was drifting away and he had to head it off. This he did successfully, stretching out the butt end of the gun and bending forward with his feet in the water. Carefully and painstakingly he piloted the duck towards the stones and drew it to shore.

The job was done, the man drew a long breath. He put down his weapon against the bank, took his knapsack from his shoulders, and stuffed the duck inside; buckled it on again, and thus satisfactorily laden and using his gun as a stick, he clambered over the boulders and up the slope.

'Well, he got his Sunday joint,' thought I, half enviously, half approvingly. 'Come, Bashan, let's go now, it's all over.' Bashan got up and turned round on himself, but then he sat down again and looked after the man, even after he had left the scene and disappeared among the bushes. It did not occur to me to ask him twice. He knew where we lived, and he might sit here goggling, after it was all over, as long as he thought well. It was quite a long walk home and I meant to be stirring. So then he came.

He kept beside me on our whole painful homeward way, and did not hunt. Nor did he run diagonally a little ahead, as he does as a rule when not in a hunting mood; he kept behind me, at a jog-trot, and put on a sour face, as I could see when I happened to turn round. I could have borne with that and should not have dreamed of being drawn; I was rather inclined to laugh and shrug my shoulders. But every thirty or forty paces he *yawned* – and that I could not stand. It was that impudent gape of his, expressing the extreme of boredom, accompanied by a throaty little whine which seems to say: Fine master I've got! No master at all! Rotten master, if you ask me! – I am always sensitive to the insulting sound, and this time it was almost enough to shake our friendship to its foundations.

76

'Go away!' said I. 'Get out with you! Go to your new friend with the blunderbuss and attach yourself to him! He does not seem to have a dog, perhaps he could use you in his business. He is only a man in velveteens, to be sure, not a gentleman, but in your eyes he may be one; perhaps he is the right master for you, and I honestly recommend you to suck up to him – now that he has put a flea in your ear to go with your others.' (Yes, I actually said that!) 'We'll not ask if he has a hunting-licence, or if you won't both get into fine trouble some day at your dirty game – that is your affair, and, as I tell you, my advice is perfectly sincere. You think so much of yourself as a hunter! Did you ever bring me a hare of all those I let you chase? Is it my fault that you do not know how to double, but must come down with your nose in the gravel at the moment when agility is required? Or a pheasant, which in these lean times would be equally welcome? And now you yawn! Get along, I tell you. Go to your master with the puttees and see if he knows how to scratch your neck and make you laugh. I'll wager he does not know how to laugh a decent laugh himself. Do you think he is likely to have you put under scientific observation when you decide to suffer from occult blood, or that when you are his dog you will be pronounced nervous and anaemic? If you do, then you'd better get along. But you may be overestimating the respect which that kind of master would have for you. There are certain distinctions – that kind of man with a gun is very keen on them: native advantages or disadvantages, to make my meaning clearer, troublesome questions of pedigree and breeding, if I must be plain. Not everybody passes these over on grounds of humanity and fine feeling; and if your wonderful master reproaches you with your moustaches the first time you and he have a difference of opinion, then you may remember me and what I am telling you now.'

With such biting words did I address Bashan as he slunk behind me on our way home. And though I did not utter but only thought them, for I did not care to look as though I were mad, yet I am convinced that he got my meaning perfectly, at least in its main lines. In short, it was a serious quarrel, and when we got home I deliberately let the gate latch behind me so that he could not slip through and had to climb over the fence. I went into the house without even looking round, and shrugged my shoulders when I heard him yelp because he scratched his belly on the rail.

But all that is long ago, more than six months. Now, like our little clinical episode, it has dropped into the past. Time and forgetfulness have buried it, and on their alluvial deposit where all life lives, we too live on. For a few days Bashan appeared to mope. But long ago he recovered all his joy in the chase, in mice and moles and pheasant, hares and waterfowl. When we return home, at once begins his period of waiting for the next time. I stand at the house door and turn towards him; upon that signal he bounds in two great leaps up the steps and braces his forepaws against the door, reaching as far up as he can that I may pat him on the shoulder. 'Tomorrow, Bashan,' say I; 'that is, if I am not obliged to pay a visit to the outer world.' Then I hasten inside, to take off my hobnailed boots, for the soup stands waiting on the table.

DISORDER AND EARLY SORROW

(1925)

THE principal dish at dinner had been croquettes made of turnip greens. So there follows a trifle, concocted out of one of those dessert powders we use nowadays, that taste like almond soap. Xaver, the youthful manservant, in his outgrown striped jacket, white woollen gloves, and yellow sandals, hands it round, and the 'big folk' take this opportunity to remind their father, tactfully, that company is coming today.

The 'big folk' are two, Ingrid and Bert. Ingrid is brown-eyed, eighteen, and perfectly delightful. She is on the eve of her exams, and will probably pass them, if only because she knows how to wind masters, and even headmasters, round her finger. She does not, however, mean to use her certificate once she gets it; having leanings towards the stage, on the ground of her ingratiating smile, her equally ingratiating voice, and a marked and irresistible talent for burlesque. Bert is blond and seventeen. He intends to get done with school somehow, anyhow, and fling himself into the arms of life. He will be a dancer, or a cabaret actor, possibly even a waiter – but not a waiter anywhere else save at the Cairo, the night-club, whither he has once already taken flight, at five in the morning, and been brought back crestfallen. Bert bears a strong resemblance to the youthful manservant Xaver Kleinsgutl, of about the same age as himself; not because he looks common – in features he is strikingly like his father, Professor Cornelius – but by reason of an approximation of types, due in its turn to far-reaching compromises in matters of dress and bearing generally. Both lads wear their heavy hair very long on top, with a cursory parting in the middle, and give their heads the same characteristic toss to throw it off the forehead. When one of them leaves the house, by the garden gate, bareheaded in all weathers, in a blouse rakishly girt

with a leather strap, and sheers off bent well over with his head
on one side; or else mounts his push-bike – Xaver makes free
with his employers', of both sexes, or even, in acutely irrespons-
ible mood, with the Professor's own – Dr Cornelius from his
bedroom window cannot, for the life of him, tell whether he is
looking at his son or his servant. Both, he thinks, look like
young moujiks. And both are impassioned cigarette-smokers,
though Bert has not the means to compete with Xaver, who
smokes as many as thirty a day, of a brand named after a popular
cinema star. The big folk call their father and mother the 'old
folk' – not behind their backs, but as a form of address and in
all affection: 'Hullo, old folks,' they will say; though Cornelius
is only forty-seven years old and his wife eight years younger.
And the Professor's parents, who lead in his household the
humble and hesitant life of the really old, are on the big folk's
lips the 'ancients'. As for the 'little folk', Ellie and Snapper,
who take their meals upstairs with blue-faced Ann – so-called
because of her prevailing facial hue – Ellie and Snapper follow
their mother's example and address their father by his first
name, Abel. Unutterably comic it sounds, in its pert, confiding
familiarity; particularly on the lips, in the sweets accents, of five-
year-old Eleanor, who is the image of Frau Cornelius's baby
pictures and whom the Professor loves above everything else in
the world.

'Darling old thing,' says Ingrid affably, laying her large but
shapely hand on his, as he presides in proper middle-class style
over the family table, with her on his left and the mother opposite: 'Parent mine, may I ever so gently jog your memory, for
you have probably forgotten: this is the afternoon we were to
have our little jollification, our turkey-trot with eats to match.
You haven't a thing to do but just bear up and not funk it;
everything will be over by nine o'clock.'

'Oh – ah!' says Cornelius, his face falling. 'Good!' he goes
on, and nods his head to show himself in harmony with the
inevitable. 'I only meant – is this really the day? Thursday, yes.
How time flies! Well, what time are they coming?'

'Half past four they'll be dropping in, I should say,' answers
Ingrid, to whom her brother leaves the major role in all dealings

with the father. Upstairs, while he is resting, he will hear scarcely anything, and from seven to eight he takes his walk. He can slip out by the terrace if he likes.

'Tut!' says Cornelius deprecatingly, as who should say: 'You exaggerate.' But Bert puts in: 'It's the one evening in the week Wanja doesn't have to play. Any other night he'd have to leave by half past six, which would be painful for all concerned.'

Wanja is Ivan Herzl, the celebrated young leading man at the Stadttheater. Bert and Ingrid are on intimate terms with him, they often visit him in his dressing-room and have tea. He is an artist of the modern school, who stands on the stage in strange and, to the Professor's mind, utterly affected dancing attitudes, and shrieks lamentably. To a professor of history, all highly repugnant; but Bert has entirely succumbed to Herzl's influence, blackens the lower rim of his eyelids – despite painful but fruitless scenes with the father – and with youthful carelessness of the ancestral anguish declares that not only will he take Herzl for his model if he becomes a dancer, but in case he turns out to be a waiter at the Cairo he means to walk precisely thus.

Cornelius slightly raises his brows and makes his son a little bow – indicative of the unassumingness and self-abnegation that befits his age. You could not call it a mocking bow or suggestive in any special sense. Bert may refer it to himself or equally to his so talented friend.

'Who else is coming?' next inquires the master of the house. They mention various people, names all more or less familiar, from the city, from the suburban colony, from Ingrid's school. They still have some telephoning to do, they say. They have to phone Max. This is Max Hergesell, an engineering student; Ingrid utters his name in the nasal drawl which according to her is the traditional intonation of all the Hergesells. She goes on to parody it in the most abandonedly funny and lifelike way, and the parents laugh until they nearly choke over the wretched trifle. For even in these times when something funny happens people have to laugh.

From time to time the telephone bell rings in the Professor's study, and the big folk run across, knowing it is their affair. Many people had to give up their telephones the last time the price rose, but so far the Corneliuses have been able to keep theirs, just as they have kept their villa, which was built before the war, by dint of the salary Cornelius draws as professor of history—a million marks, and more or less adequate to the chances and changes of post-war life. The house is comfortable, even elegant, though sadly in need of repairs that cannot be made for lack of materials, and at present disfigured by iron stoves with long pipes. Even so, it is still the proper setting of the upper middle class, though they themselves look odd enough in it, with their worn and turned clothing and altered way of life. The children, of course, know nothing else; to them it is normal and regular, they belong by birth to the 'villa proletariat'. The problem of clothing troubles them not at all. They and their like have evolved a costume to fit the time, by poverty out of taste for innovation: in summer it consists of scarcely more than a belted linen smock and sandals. The middle-class parents find things rather more difficult.

The big folk's table-napkins hang over their chair-backs, they talk with their friends over the telephone. These friends are the invited guests who have rung up to accept or decline or arrange; and the conversation is carried on in the jargon of the clan, full of slang and high spirits, of which the old folk understand hardly a word. These consult together meantime about the hospitality to be offered to the impending guests. The Professor displays a middle-class ambitiousness: he wants to serve a sweet – or something that looks like a sweet – after the Italian salad and brown-bread sandwiches. But Frau Cornelius says that would be going too far. The guests would not expect it, she is sure – and the big folk, returning once more to their trifle, agree with her.

The mother of the family is of the same general type as Ingrid, though not so tall. She is languid; the fantastic difficulties of the housekeeping have broken and worn her. She really ought to go and take a cure, but feels incapable; the floor is always swaying under her feet, and everything seems upside down. She speaks of what is uppermost in her mind: the eggs, they simply must be bought today. Six thousand marks apiece they are, and just so many are to be had on this one day of the week at one single shop fifteen minutes' journey away. Whatever else they do, the big folk must go and fetch them immediately after luncheon, with Danny, their neighbour's son, who will soon be calling for them; and Xaver Kleinsgutl will don civilian garb and attend his young master and mistress. For no single household is allowed more than five eggs a week; therefore the young people will enter the shop singly, one after another, under assumed names, and thus wring twenty eggs from the shopkeeper for the Cornelius family. This enterprise is the sporting event of the week for all participants, not excepting the moujik Kleinsgutl, and most of all for Ingrid and Bert, who delight in misleading and mystifying their fellow-men and would revel in the performance even if it did not achieve one single egg. They adore impersonating fictitious characters; they love to sit in a bus and carry on long lifelike conversations in a dialect which they otherwise never speak, the most commonplace dialogue about politics and people and the price of food, while the whole bus listens open-mouthed to this incredibly ordinary prattle, though with a dark suspicion all the while that something is wrong somewhere. The conversation waxes ever more shameless, it enters into revolting detail about these people who do not exist. Ingrid can make her voice sound ever so common and twittering and shrill as she impersonates a shop-girl with an illegitimate child, said child being a son with sadistic tendencies, who lately out in the country treated a cow with such unnatural cruelty that no Christian could have borne to see it. Bert nearly explodes at her twittering, but restrains himself and displays a grisly sympathy; he and the unhappy shop-girl entering into a long, stupid, depraved, and shuddery conversation over the particular morbid cruelty involved; until an old gentleman opposite, sitting with his ticket folded between his index finger and his seal ring, can bear it no more and makes public protest against the nature of the themes these young folk are discussing with such particularity. He uses the Greek plural: 'themata'. Whereat Ingrid pretends to be dissolving in tears, and Bert behaves as though his wrath against the old gentleman was with difficulty being held in check and would probably burst out before long. He clenches his fists, he gnashes his teeth, he shakes from head to foot; and the unhappy old gentleman, whose intentions had been of the best, hastily leaves the bus at the next stop.

Such are the diversions of the big folk. The telephone plays a prominent part in them: they ring up any and everybody – members of government, opera singers, dignitaries of the Church – in the character of shop assistants, or perhaps as Lord or Lady Doolittle. They are only with difficulty persuaded that they have the wrong number. Once they emptied their parents' card-tray and distributed its contents among the neighbours' letter-boxes, wantonly, yet not without enough impish sense of the fitness of things to make it highly upsetting, God only knowing why certain people should have called where they did.

Xaver comes in to clear away, tossing the hair out of his eyes. Now that he has taken off his gloves you can see the yellow chain-ring on his left hand. And as the Professor finishes his watery eight-thousand-mark beer and lights a cigarette, the little folk can be heard scrambling down the stairs, coming, by established custom, for their after-dinner call on Father and Mother. They storm the dining-room, after a struggle with the latch, clutched by both pairs of little hands at once; their clumsy small feet twinkle over the carpet, in red felt slippers with the socks falling down on them. With prattle and shoutings each makes for his own place: Snapper to Mother, to climb on her lap, boast of all he has eaten, and thump his fat little tum; Ellie to her Abel, so much hers because she is so very much his; because she consciously luxuriates in the deep tenderness – like all deep feeling, concealing a melancholy strain – with which he holds her small form embraced; in the love in his eyes as he kisses her little fairy hand or the sweet brow with its delicate tracery of tiny blue veins.

The little folk look like each other, with the strong undefined likeness of brother and sister. In clothing and hair-cut they are twins. Yet they are sharply distinguished after all, and quite on sex lines. It is a little Adam and a little Eve. Not only is Snapper the sturdier and more compact, he appears consciously to emphasize his four-year-old masculinity in speech, manner, and carriage, lifting his shoulders and letting the little arms hang down quite like a young American athlete, drawing down his mouth when he talks and seeking to give his voice a gruff and forthright ring. But all this masculinity is the result of effort rather than natively his. Born and brought up in these desolate, distracted times, he has been endowed by them with an unstable and hypersensitive nervous system and suffers greatly under life's disharmonies. He is prone to sudden anger and outbursts of bitter tears, stamping his feet at every trifle; for this reason he is his mother's special nursling and care. His round, round eyes are chestnut brown and already inclined to squint, so that he will need glasses in the near future. His little nose is long, the mouth small – the father's nose and mouth they are, more plainly than ever since the Professor shaved his pointed beard and goes smooth-faced. The pointed beard had become impossible – even professors must make some concessions to the changing times.

But the little daughter sits on her father's knee, his Eleonorchen, his little Eve, so much more gracious a little being, so much sweeter-faced than her brother – and he holds his cigarette away from her while she fingers his glasses with her dainty wee hands. The lenses are divided for reading and distance, and each day they tease her curiosity afresh.

At bottom he suspects that his wife's partiality may have a firmer basis than his own: that Snapper's refractory masculinity perhaps is solider stuff than his own little girl's more explicit charm and grace. But the heart will not be commanded, that he knows; and once and for all his heart belongs to the little one, as it has since the day she came, since the first time he saw her. Almost always when he holds her in his arms he remembers that first time: remembers the sunny room in the Women's Hospital, where Ellie first saw the light, twelve years after Bert was born. He remembers how he drew near, the mother smiling the while, and cautiously put aside the canopy of the diminutive bed that stood beside the large one. There lay the little miracle among the pillows: so well formed, so encompassed, as it were, with the harmony of sweet proportions, with little hands that even then, though so much tinier, were beautiful as now; with wide-open eyes blue as the sky and brighter than the sunshine – and almost in that very second he felt himself captured and held fast. This was love at first sight, love everlasting: a feeling unknown, unhoped for, unexpected – in so far as it could be a matter of conscious awareness; it took entire possession of him, and he understood, with joyous amazement, that this was for life.

But he understood more. He knows, does Dr Cornelius, that there is something not quite right about this feeling, so unaware, so undreamed of, so involuntary. He has a shrewd suspicion that it is not by accident it has so utterly mastered him and bound itself up with his existence; that he had – even subconsciously – been preparing for it, or, more precisely, been prepared for it. There is, in short, something in him which at a given moment was ready to issue in such a feeling; and this something, highly extraordinary to relate, is his essence and quality as a professor of history. Dr Cornelius, however, does not actually say this, even to himself; he merely realizes it, at odd times, and smiles a private smile. He knows that history professors do not love history because it is something that comes to pass, but only because it is something that *has* come to pass; that they hate a revolution like the present one because they feel it is lawless, incoherent, irrelevant – in a word, unhistoric; that their hearts belong to the coherent, disciplined, historic past. For the temper of timelessness, the temper of eternity – thus the scholar communes with himself when he takes his walk by the river before supper – that temper broods over the past; and it is a temper much better suited to the nervous system of a history professor than are the excesses of the present. The past is immortalized; that is to say, it is dead; and death is the root of all godliness and all abiding significance. Dr Cornelius, walking alone in the dark, has a profound insight into this truth. It is this conservative instinct of his, his sense of the eternal, that has found in his love for his little daughter a way to save itself from the wounding inflicted by the times. For father love, and a little child on its mother's breast – are not these timeless, and thus very, very holy and beautiful? Yet Cornelius, pondering there in the dark, descries something not perfectly right and good in his love. Theoretically, in the interests of science, he admits it to himself. There is something ulterior about it, in the nature of it; that something is hostility, hostility against the history of today, which is still in the making and thus not history at all, on behalf of the genuine history that has already happened – that is to say, death. Yes, passing strange though all this is, yet it is true; true in a sense, that is. His devotion to this priceless little morsel of life and new growth has something to do with death, it clings to death as against life; and that is neither right nor beautiful – in a sense. Though only the most fanatical asceticism could be capable, on no other ground than such casual scientific perception, of tearing this purest and most precious of feelings out of his heart.

He holds his darling on his lap and her slim rosy legs hang down. He raises his brows as he talks to her, tenderly, with a half-teasing note of respect, and listens enchanted to her high, sweet little voice calling him Abel. He exchanges a look with the mother, who is caressing her Snapper and reading him a gentle lecture. He must be more reasonable, he must learn self-control; today again, under the manifold exasperations of life, he has given way to rage and behaved like a howling dervish. Cornelius casts a mistrustful glance at the big folk now and then, too; he thinks it not unlikely they are not unaware of those scientific preoccupations of his evening walks. If such be the case they do not show it. They stand there leaning their arms on their chairbacks and with a benevolence not untinctured with irony look on at the parental happiness.

The children's frocks are of a heavy, brick-red stuff, embroidered in modern 'arty' style. They once belonged to Ingrid and Bert and are precisely alike, save that little knickers come out beneath Snapper's smock. And both have their hair bobbed. Snapper's is a streaky blond, inclined to turn dark. It is bristly and sticky and looks for all the world like a droll, badly fitting wig. But Ellie's is chestnut brown, glossy and fine as silk, as pleasing as her whole little personality. It covers her ears – and these ears are not a pair, one of them being the right size, the other distinctly too large. Her father will sometimes uncover this little abnormality and exclaim over it as though he had never noticed it before, which both makes Ellie giggle and covers her with shame. Her eyes are now golden brown, set far apart and with sweet gleams in them – such a clear and lovely look! The brows above are bionde; the nose still unformed, with thick nostrils and almost circular holes; the mouth large and expressive, with a beautifully arching and mobile upper lip. When she laughs, dimples come in her cheeks and she shows her teeth like loosely strung pearls. So far she has lost but one tooth, which her father gently twisted out with his handkerchief after it had grown very wobbling. During this small operation she had paled and trembled very much. Her cheeks have the softness proper to her years, but they are not chubby; indeed, they are rather concave, due to her facial structure, with its somewhat prominent jaw. On one, close to the soft fall of her hair, is a downy freckle.

Ellie is not too well pleased with her looks – a sign that already she troubles about such things. Sadly she thinks it is best to admit it once for all, her face is 'homely'; though the rest of her, 'on the other hand', is not bad at all. She loves expressions like 'on the other hand'; they sound choice and grown-up to her, and she likes to string them together, one after the other: 'very likely', 'probably', 'after all'. Snapper is self-critical too, though more in the moral sphere: he suffers from remorse for his attacks of rage and considers himself a tremendous sinner. He is quite certain that heaven is not for such as he; he is sure to go to 'the bad place' when he dies, and no persuasions will convince him to the contrary – as that God sees the heart and gladly makes allowances. Obstinately he shakes his head, with the comic, crooked little peruke, and vows there is no place for him in heaven. When he has a cold he is immediately quite choked with mucus; rattles and rumbles from top to toe if you even look at him; his temperature flies up at once and he simply puffs. Nursy is pessimistic on the score of his constitution: such fat-blooded children as he might get a stroke any minute. Once she even thought she saw the moment at hand: Snapper had been in one of his berserker rages, and in the ensuing fit of penitence stood himself in the corner with his back to the room. Suddenly Nursy noticed that his face had gone all blue, far bluer, even, than her own. She raised the alarm, crying out that the child's all too rich blood had at length brought him to his final hour; and Snapper, to his vast astonishment, found himself, so far from being rebuked for evil-doing, encompassed in tenderness and anxiety – until it turned out that his colour was not caused by apoplexy but by the distempering on the nursery wall, which had come off on his tear-wet face.

Nursy has come downstairs too, and stands by the door, sleek-haired, owl-eyed, with her hands folded over her white apron, and a severely dignified manner born of her limited intelligence. She is very proud of the care and training she gives her nurslings and declares that they are 'enveloping wonderfully'. She has had seventeen suppurated teeth lately removed from her jaws and been measured for a set of symmetrical yellow ones in dark rubber gums; these now embellish her peasant face. She is obsessed with the strange conviction that these teeth of hers are the subject of general conversation, that, as it were, the sparrows on the house-tops chatter of them. 'Everybody knows I've had a false set put in,' she will say; 'there has been a great deal of foolish talk about them.' She is much given to dark hints and veiled innuendo: speaks, for instance, of a certain Dr Bleifuss, whom every child knows and 'there are even some in the house who pretend to be him.' All one can do with talk like this is charitably to pass it over in silence. But she teaches the children nursery rhymes: gems like:

> Puff, puff, here comes the train
> Puff, puff, toot, toot,
> Away it goes again.

Or that gastronomical jingle, so suited, in its sparseness, to the times, and yet seemingly with a blitheness of its own:

> Monday we begin the week,
> Tuesday there's a bone to pick.
> Wednesday we're half way through,
> Thursday what a great to-do!
> Friday we eat what fish we're able,
> Saturday we dance round the table.
> Sunday brings us pork and greens –
> Here's a feast for kings and queens!

Also a certain four-line stanza with a romantic appeal, un-utterable and unuttered:

> Open the gate, open the gate
> And let the carriage drive in.
> Who is it in the carriage sits?
> A lordly sir with golden hair.

Or, finally that ballad about golden-haired Marianne who sat on a, sat on a, sat on a stone, and combed out her, combed out her, combed out her hair; and about bloodthirsty Rudolph, who pulled out a, pulled out a, pulled out a knife – and his ensuing direful end. Ellie enunciates all these ballads charmingly, with her mobile little lips, and sings them in her sweet little voice – much better than Snapper. She does everything better than he does, and he pays her honest admiration and homage and obeys her in all things except when visited by one of his attacks. Sometimes she teaches him, instructs him upon the birds in the picture-book and tells him their proper names: 'This is a chaffinch, Buddy, this is a bullfinch, this is a cowfinch.' He has to repeat them after her. She gives him medical instruction too, teaches him the names of diseases, such as inflammation of the lungs, inflammation of the blood, inflammation of the air. If he does not pay attention and cannot say the words after her, she stands him in the corner. Once she even boxed his ears, but was so ashamed that she stood herself in the corner for a long time. Yes, they are fast friends, two souls with but a single thought, and have all their adventures in common. They come home from a walk and relate as with one voice that they have seen two moollies and a teenty-weenty baby calf. They are on familiar terms with the kitchen, which consists of Xaver and the ladies Hinterhofer, two sisters once of the lower middle class who, in these evil days, are reduced to living '*au pair*' as the phrase goes and officiating as cook and housemaid for their board and keep. The little ones have a feeling that Xaver and the Hinterhofers are on much the same footing with their father and mother as they are themselves. At least sometimes, when they have been scolded, they go downstairs and announce that the master and mistress are cross. But playing with the servants lacks charm compared with the joys of playing upstairs. The kitchen could never rise to the height of the games their father can invent. For instance, there is 'four gentlemen taking a walk'. When they play it Abel will crook his knees until he is the same height with themselves and go walking with them, hand in hand. They never get enough of this sport; they could walk round and round the dining-room a whole day on end, five gentlemen in all, counting the diminished Abel.

Then there is the thrilling cushion game. One of the children, usually Ellie, seats herself, unbeknownst to Abel, in his seat at table. Still as a mouse she awaits his coming. He draws near with his head in the air, descanting in loud, clear tones upon the surpassing comfort of his chair; and sits down on top of Ellie. 'What's this, what's this?' says he. And bounces about, deaf to the smothered giggles exploding behind him. 'Why have they put a cushion in my chair? And what a queer, hard, awkward-shaped cushion it is!' he goes on. 'Frightfully uncomfortable to sit on!' And keeps pushing and bouncing about more and more on the astonishing cushion and clutching behind him into the rapturous giggling and squeaking, until at last he turns round, and the game ends with a magnificent climax of discovery and recognition. They might go through all this a hundred times without diminishing by an iota its power to thrill.

Today is no time for such joys. The imminent festivity disturbs the atmosphere, and besides there is work to be done, and, above all, the eggs to be got. Ellie has just time to recite 'Puff, puff', and Cornelius to discover that her ears are not mates, when they are interrupted by the arrival of Danny, come to fetch Bert and Ingrid. Xaver, meantime, has exchanged his striped livery for an ordinary coat, in which he looks rather rough-and-ready, though as brisk and attractive as ever. So then Nursy and the children ascend to the upper regions, the Professor withdraws to his study to read, as always after dinner, and his wife bends her energies upon the sandwiches and salad that must be prepared. And she has another errand as well. Before the young people arrive she has to take her shopping-basket and dash into town on her bicycle, to turn into provisions a sum of money she has in hand, which she dares not keep lest it lose all value.

Cornelius reads, leaning back in his chair, with his cigar between his middle and index fingers. First he reads Macaulay on the origin of the English public debt at the end of the seventeenth century; then an article in a French periodical on the rapid increase in the Spanish debt towards the end of the sixteenth. Both these for his lecture on the morrow. He intends to compare the astonishing prosperity which accompanied the phenomenon in England with its fatal effects a hundred years earlier in Spain, and to analyse the ethical and psychological grounds of the difference in results. For that will give him a chance to refer back from the England of William III, which is the actual subject in hand, to the time of Philip II and the Counter-Reformation, which is his own special field. He has already written a valuable work on this period; it is much cited and got him his professorship. While his cigar burns down and gets strong, he excogitates a few pensive sentences in a key of gentle melancholy, to be delivered before his class next day: about the practically hopeless struggle carried on by the belated Philip against the whole trend of history: against the new, the kingdom-disrupting power of the Germanic ideal of freedom and individual liberty. And about the persistent, futile struggle of the aristocracy, condemned by God and rejected of man, against the forces of progress and change. He savours his sentences; keeps on polishing them while he puts back the books he has been using; then goes upstairs for the usual pause in his day's work, the hour with drawn blinds and closed eyes, which he so imperatively needs. But today, he recalls, he will rest under disturbed conditions, amid the bustle of preparations for the feast. He smiles to find his heart giving a mild flutter at the thought. Disjointed phrases on the theme of black-clad Philip and his times mingle with a confused consciousness that they will soon be dancing down below. For five minutes or so he falls asleep.

As he lies and rests he can hear the sound of the garden gate and the repeated ringing at the bell. Each time a little pang goes through him, of excitement and suspense, at the thought that the young people have begun to fill the floor below. And each time he smiles at himself again – though even his smile is slightly nervous, is tinged with the pleasurable anticipations people always feel before a party. At half past four – it is already dark – he gets up and washes at the wash-stand. The basin has been out of repair for two years. It is supposed to tip, but has broken away from its socket on one side and cannot be mended because there is nobody to mend it; neither replaced because no shop can supply another. So it has to be hung up above the vent and emptied by lifting in both hands and pouring out the water. Cornelius shakes his head over this basin, as he does several times a day – whenever, in fact, he has occasion to use it. He finishes his toilet with care, standing under the ceiling light to polish his glasses till they shine. Then he goes downstairs.

On his way to the dining-room he hears the gramophone already going, and the sound of voices. He puts on a polite, society air; at his tongue's end is the phrase he means to utter: 'Pray don't let me disturb you,' as he passes directly into the dining-room for his tea. 'Pray don't let me disturb you' – it seems to him precisely the *mot juste*; towards the guests cordial and considerate, for himself a very bulwark.

The lower floor is lighted up, all the bulbs in the chandelier are burning save one that has burned out. Cornelius pauses on a lower step and surveys the entrance hall. It looks pleasant and cosy in the bright light, with its copy of Marées over the brick chimney-piece, its wainscoted walls – wainscoted in soft wood – and red-carpeted floor, where the guests stand in groups, chatting, each with his teacup and slice of bread-and-butter spread with anchovy paste. There is a festal haze, faint scents of hair and clothing and human breath come to him across the room, it is all characteristic and familiar and highly evocative. The door into the dressing-room is open, guests are still arriving.

A large group of people is rather bewildering at first sight. The Professor takes in only the general scene. He does not see Ingrid, who is standing just at the foot of the steps, in a dark silk frock with a pleated collar falling softly over the shoulders, and bare arms. She smiles up at him, nodding and showing her lovely teeth.

'Rested?' she asks, for his private ear. With a quite unwarranted start he recognizes her, and she presents some of her friends.

'May I introduce Herr Zuber?' she says. 'And this is Fräulein Plaichinger.'

Herr Zuber is insignificant. But Fräulein Plaichinger is a perfect Germania, blonde and voluptuous, arrayed in floating draperies. She has a snub nose, and answers the Professor's salutation in the high, shrill pipe so many stout women have.

'Delighted to meet you,' he says. 'How nice of you to come! A classmate of Ingrid's, I suppose?'

And Herr Zuber is a golfing partner of Ingrid's. He is in business; he works in his uncle's brewery. Cornelius makes a few jokes about the thinness of the beer and professes to believe that Herr Zuber could easily do something about the quality if he would. 'But pray don't let me disturb you,' he goes on, and turns towards the dining-room.

'There comes Max,' says Ingrid. 'Max, you sweep, what do you mean by rolling up at this time of day?' For such is the way they talk to each other, offensively to an older ear; of social forms, of hospitable warmth, there is no faintest trace. They all call each other by their first names.

A young man comes up to them out of the dressing-room and makes his bow; he has an expanse of white shirt-front and a little black string tie. He is as pretty as a picture, dark, with rosy cheeks, clean-shaven of course, but with just a sketch of side-whisker. Not a ridiculous or flashy beauty, not like a gypsy fiddler, but just charming to look at, in a winning, well-bred way, with kind dark eyes. He even wears his dinner-jacket a little awkwardly.

'Please don't scold me, Cornelia,' he says; 'it's the idiotic lectures.' And Ingrid presents him to her father as Herr Hergesell.

Well, and so this is Herr Hergesell. He knows his manners, does Herr Hergesell, and thanks the master of the house quite ingratiatingly for his invitation as they shake hands. 'I certainly seem to have missed the bus,' says he jocosely. 'Of course I have lectures today up to four o'clock; I would have; and after that I had to go home to change.' Then he talks about his pumps, with which he has just been struggling in the dressing-room.

'I brought them with me in a bag,' he goes on. 'Mustn't tramp all over the carpet in our brogues – it's not done. Well, I was ass enough not to fetch along a shoehorn, and I find I simply can't get in! What a sell! They are the tightest I've ever had, the numbers don't tell you a thing, and all the leather today is just cast iron. It's not leather at all. My poor finger' – he confidingly displays a reddened digit and once more characterizes the whole thing as a 'sell', and a putrid sell into the bargain. He really does talk just as Ingrid said he did, with a peculiar nasal drawl, not affectedly in the least, but merely because that is the way of all the Hergesells.

Dr Cornelius says it is very careless of them not to keep a shoehorn in the cloakroom and displays proper sympathy with the mangled finger. 'But now you *really* must not let me disturb you any longer,' he goes on. '*Auf wiedersehen!*' And he crosses the hall into the dining-room.

There are guests there too, drinking tea; the family table is pulled out. But the Professor goes at once to his own little upholstered corner with the electric light bulb above it – the nook where he usually drinks his tea. His wife is sitting there talking with Bert and two other young men, one of them Herzl, whom Cornelius knows and greets; the other a typical 'Wander-vogel' named Möller, a youth who obviously neither owns nor cares to own the correct evening dress of the middle classes (in fact, there is no such thing any more), nor to ape the manners of a gentleman (and, in fact, there is no such thing any more either). He has a wilderness of hair, horn spectacles, and a long neck, and wears golf stockings and a belted blouse. His regular occupation, the Professor learns, is banking, but he is by way of being an amateur folklorist and collects folksongs from all localities and in all languages. He sings them, too, and at Ingrid's command has brought his guitar; it is hanging in the dressing-room in an oilcloth case. Herzl, the actor, is small and slight, but he has a strong growth of black beard, as you can tell

by the thick coat of powder on his cheeks. His eyes are larger
than life, with a deep and melancholy glow. He has put on
rouge besides the powder – those dull carmine highlights on
the cheeks can be nothing but a cosmetic. 'Queer,' thinks the
Professor. 'You would think a man would be one thing or the
other – not melancholic and use face paint at the same time. It's
a psychological contradiction. How can a melancholy man
rouge? But here we have a perfect illustration of the abnormality of the artist soul-form. It can make possible a contradiction
like this – perhaps it even consists in the contradiction. All very
interesting – and no reason whatever for not being polite to him.
Politeness is a primitive convention – and legitimate ... Do
take some lemon, Herr Hofschauspieler!'

Court actors and court theatres – there are no such things any
more, really. But Herzl relishes the sound of the title, notwithstanding he is a revolutionary artist. This must be another
contradiction inherent in his soul-form; so, at least, the Professor assumes, and he is probably right. The flattery he is guilty
of is a sort of atonement for his previous hard thoughts about
the rouge.

'Thank you so much – it's really too good of you, sir,' says
Herzl, quite embarrassed. He is so overcome that he almost
stammers; only his perfect enunciation saves him. His whole
bearing towards his hostess and the master of the house is exaggeratedly polite. It is almost as though he had a bad conscience
in respect of his rouge; as though an inward compulsion had
driven him to put it on, but now, seeing it through the Professor's eyes, he disapproves of it himself, and thinks, by an air
of humility towards the whole of unrouged society, to mitigate
its effect.

They drink their tea and chat: about Möller's folksongs,
about Basque folksongs, and Spanish folksongs; from which
they pass to the new production of *Don Carlos* at the Stadttheater, in which Herzl plays the title-rôle. He talks about his
own rendering of the part and says he hopes his conception of
the character has unity. They go on to criticize the rest of the
cast, the setting, and the production as a whole; and Cornelius
is struck, rather painfully, to find the conversation trending

towards his own special province, back to Spain and the
Counter-Reformation. He has done nothing at all to give it this
turn, he is perfectly innocent, and hopes it does not look as
though he had sought an occasion to play the professor. He
wonders, and falls silent, feeling relieved when the little folk
come up to the table. Ellie and Snapper have on their blue
velvet Sunday frocks; they are permitted to partake in the
festivities up to bedtime. They look shy and large-eyed as they
say how-do-you-do to the strangers and, under pressure, repeat
their names and ages. Herr Möller does nothing but gaze at
them solemnly, but Herzl is simply ravished. He rolls his eyes
up to heaven and puts his hands over his mouth; he positively
blesses them. It all, no doubt, comes from his heart, but he is so
addicted to theatrical methods of making an impression and
getting an effect that both words and behaviour ring frightfully
false. And even his enthusiasm for the little folk looks too much
like part of his general craving to make up for the rouge on his
cheeks.

The tea-table has meanwhile emptied of guests, and dancing
is going on in the hall. The children run off, the Professor
prepares to retire. 'Go and enjoy yourselves,' he says to Möller
and Herzl, who have sprung from their chairs as he rises from
his. They shake hands and he withdraws into his study, his
peaceful kingdom, where he lets down the blinds, turns on the
desk lamp, and sits down to his work.

It is work which can be done, if necessary, under disturbed
conditions: nothing but a few letters and a few notes. Of
course, Cornelius's mind wanders. Vague impressions float
through it: Herr Hergesell's refractory pumps, the high pipe in
that plump body of the Plaichinger female. As he writes, or
leans back in his chair and stares into space, his thoughts go
back to Herr Möller's collection of Basque folksongs, to Herzl's
posings and humility, to 'his' Carlos and the court of Philip II.
There is something strange, he thinks, about conversations, they
are so ductile, they will flow of their own accord in the direction of one's dominating interest. Often and often he has seen
this happen. And while he is thinking, he is listening to the
sounds next door – rather subdued, he finds them. He hears

only voices, no sound of footsteps. The dancers do not glide or circle round the room; they merely walk about over the carpet, which does not hamper their movements in the least. Their way of holding each other is quite different and strange, and they move to the strains of the gramophone, to the weird music of the new world. He concentrates on the music and makes out that it is a jazz-band record, with various percussion instruments and the clack and clatter of castanets, which, however, are not even faintly suggestive of Spain, but merely jazz like the rest. No, not Spain . . . His thoughts are back at their old round.

Half an hour goes by. It occurs to him it would be no more than friendly to go and contribute a box of cigarettes to the festivities next door. Too bad to ask the young people to smoke their own – though they have probably never thought of it. He goes into the empty dining-room and takes a box from his supply in the cupboard: not the best ones, nor yet the brand he himself prefers, but a certain long, thin kind he is not averse to getting rid of – after all, they are nothing but youngsters. He takes the box into the hall, holds it up with a smile, and deposits it on the mantelshelf. After which he gives a look round and returns to his own room.

There comes a lull in dance and music. The guests stand about the room in groups or round the table at the window or are seated in a circle by the fireplace. Even the built-in stairs, with their worn velvet carpet, are crowded with young folk as in an amphitheatre: Max Hergesell is there, leaning back with one elbow on the step above and gesticulating with his free hand as he talks to the shrill, voluptuous Plaichinger. The floor of the hall is nearly empty, save just in the centre: there, directly beneath the chandelier, the two little ones in their blue velvet frocks clutch each other in an awkward embrace and twirl silently round and round, oblivious of all else. Cornelius, as he passes, strokes their hair, with a friendly word; it does not distract them from their small solemn preoccupation. But at his own door he turns to glance round and sees young Hergesell push himself off the stair by his elbow – probably because he noticed the Professor. He comes down into the arena, takes Ellie out of her brother's arms, and dances with her himself. It looks very comic, without the music, and he crouches down just as Cornelius does when he goes walking with the four gentlemen, holding the fluttered Ellie as though she were grown up and taking little 'shimmying' steps. Everybody watches with huge enjoyment, the gramophone is put on again, dancing becomes general. The Professor stands and looks, with his hand on the door-knob. He nods and laughs; when he finally shuts himself into his study the mechanical smile still lingers on his lips.

Again he turns over pages by his desk lamp, takes notes, attends to a few simple matters. After a while he notices that the guests have forsaken the entrance hall for his wife's drawing-room, into which there is a door from his own study as well. He hears their voices and the sounds of a guitar being tuned. Herr Möller, it seems, is to sing – and does so. He twangs the strings of his instrument and sings in a powerful bass a ballad in a strange tongue, possibly Swedish. The Professor does not succeed in identifying it, though he listens attentively to the end, after which there is great applause. The sound is deadened by the portière that hangs over the dividing door. The young bank-clerk begins another song. Cornelius goes softly in.

It is half-dark in the drawing-room; the only light is from the shaded standard lamp, beneath which Möller sits, on the divan, with his legs crossed, picking his strings. His audience is grouped easily about; as there are not enough seats, some stand, and more, among them many young ladies, are simply sitting on the floor with their hands clasped round their knees or even with their legs stretched out before them. Hergesell sits thus, in his dinner jacket, next to the piano, with Fräulein Plaichinger beside him. Frau Cornelius is holding both children on her lap as she sits in her easy-chair opposite the singer. Snapper, the Boeotian, begins to talk loud and clear in the middle of the song and has to be intimidated with hushings and finger-shakings. Never, never would Ellie allow herself to be guilty of such conduct. She sits there daintily erect and still on her mother's knee. The Professor tries to catch her eye and exchange a private signal with his little girl; but she does not see him. Neither does she seem to be looking at the singer. Her gaze is directed lower down.

Möller sings the 'joli tambour':

> *'Sire, mon roi, donnez-moi votre*
> *fille —*

They are all enchanted. 'How good!' Hergesell is heard to say, in the odd, nasally condescending Hergesell tone. The next one is a beggar ballad, to a tune composed by young Möller himself; it elicits a storm of applause:

> 'Gypsy lassie a-goin' to the fair,
> Huzza!
> Gypsy laddie a-goin' to be
> there —
> Huzza, diddlety umpty dido!'

Laughter and high spirits, sheer reckless hilarity, reign after this jovial ballad. 'Frightfully good!' Hergesell comments again, as before. Follows another popular song, this time a Hungarian one; Möller sings it in its own outlandish tongue, and most effectively. The Professor applauds with ostentation. It warms his heart and does him good, this outcropping of artistic, historic, and cultural elements all amongst the shimmying. He goes up to young Möller and congratulates him, talks about the songs and their sources, and Möller promises to lend him a certain anno-tated book of folksongs. Cornelius is the more cordial because all the time, as fathers do, he has been comparing the parts and achievements of this young stranger with those of his own son, and being gnawed by envy and chagrin. This young Möller, he is thinking, is a capable bank-clerk (though about Möller's capacity he knows nothing whatever) and has this special gift besides, which must have taken talent and energy to cul-tivate. 'And here is my poor Bert, who knows nothing and can do nothing and thinks of nothing except playing the clown, without even talent for that!' He tries to be just; he tells himself that, after all, Bert has innate refinement; that probably there is a good deal more to him than there is to the successful Möller; that perhaps he has even something of the poet in him, and his dancing and table-waiting are due to mere boyish folly and the distraught times. But paternal envy and pessimism win the upper hand; when Möller begins another song, Dr Cornelius goes back to his room.

He works as before, with divided attention, at this and that, while it gets on for seven o'clock. Then he remembers a letter he may just as well write, a short letter and not very important, but letter-writing is wonderful for the way it takes up the time, and it is almost half past when he has finished. At half past eight the Italian salad will be served; so now is the prescribed moment for the Professor to go out into the wintry darkness to post his letters and take his daily quantum of fresh air and exercise. They are dancing again, and he will have to pass through the hall to get his hat and coat; but they are used to him now, he need not stop and beg them not to be disturbed. He lays away his papers, takes up the letters he has written, and goes out. But he sees his wife sitting near the door of his room and pauses a little by her easy-chair.

She is watching the dancing. Now and then the big folk or some of their guests stop to speak to her; the party is at its height, and there are more onlookers than these two: blue-faced Ann is standing at the bottom of the stairs, in all the dignity of her limitations. She is waiting for the children, who simply cannot get their fill of these unwonted festivities, and watching over Snapper, lest his all too rich blood be churned to the danger-point by too much twirling round. And not only the nursery but the kitchen takes an interest: Xaver and the two ladies Hinterhofer are standing by the pantry door looking on with relish. Fräulein Walburga, the elder of the two sunken sisters (the culinary section – she objects to being called a cook), is a whimsical, good-natured sort, brown-eyed, wearing glasses with thick circular lenses; the nose-piece is wound with a bit of rag to keep it from pressing on her nose. Fräulein Cecilia is younger, though not so precisely young either. Her bearing is as self-assertive as usual, this being her way of sustaining her dignity as a former member of the middle class. For Fräulein Cecilia feels acutely her descent into the ranks of domestic service. She positively declines to wear a cap or other badge of servitude, and her hardest trial is on the Wednesday evening when she has to serve the dinner while Xaver has his afternoon out. She hands the dishes with averted face and elevated nose – a fallen queen; and so distressing is it to behold her degradation that one evening when the little folk happened to be at table and saw her they both with one accord burst into tears. Such anguish is unknown to young Xaver. He enjoys serving and does it with an ease born of practice as well as talent, for he was once a 'piccolo'. But otherwise he is a thorough-paced good-for-nothing and windbag – with quite distinct traits of character of his own, as his long-suffering employers are always ready to concede, but perfectly impossible and a bag of wind for all that. One must just take him as he is, they think, and not expect figs from thistles. He is the child and product of the disrupted times, a perfect specimen of his generation, follower of the re-volution, Bolshevist sympathizer. The Professor's name for him is the 'minute-man', because he is always to be counted on in any sudden crisis, if only it address his sense of humour or love of novelty, and will display therein amazing readiness and resource. But he utterly lacks a sense of duty and can as little be trained to the performance of the daily round and common task as some kinds of dog can be taught to jump over a stick. It goes so plainly against the grain that criticism is disarmed. One becomes resigned. On grounds that appealed to him as unusual and amusing he would be ready to turn out of his bed at any hour of the night. But he simply cannot get up before eight in the morning, he cannot do it, he will not jump over the stick. Yet all day long the evidence of this free and untrammelled existence, the sound of his mouth-organ, his joyous whistle, or his raucous but expressive voice lifted in song, rises to the hearing of the world above-stairs; and the smoke of his cigarettes fills the pantry. While the Hinterhofer ladies work he stands and looks on. Of a morning while the Professor is breakfasting, he tears the leaf off the study calendar – but does not lift a finger to dust the room. Dr Cornelius has often told him to leave the calendar alone, for he tends to tear off two leaves at a time and thus to add to the general confusion. But young Xaver appears to find joy in this activity, and will not be deprived of it.

Again, he is fond of children, a winning trait. He will throw himself into games with the little folk in the garden, make and mend their toys with great ingenuity, even read aloud from their books – and very droll it sounds in his thick-lipped pronunciation. With his whole soul he loves the cinema; after an evening spent there he inclines to melancholy and yearning and talking to himself. Vague hopes stir in him that some day he may make his fortune in that gay world and belong to it by rights – hopes based on his shock of hair and his physical agility and daring. He likes to climb the ash tree in the front garden, mounting branch by branch to the very top and frightening everybody to death who sees him. Once there he lights a cigarette and smokes it as he sways to and fro, keeping a look-out for a cinema director who might chance to come along and engage him.

If he changed his striped jacket for mufti, he might easily dance with the others and no one would notice the difference. For the big folk's friends are rather anomalous in their clothing: evening dress is worn by a few, but it is by no means the rule. There is quite a sprinkling of guests, both male and female, in the same general style as Möller the ballad-singer. The Professor is familiar with the circumstances of most of this young generation he is watching as he stands beside his wife's chair; he has heard them spoken of by name. They are students at the high school or at the School of Applied Art; they lead, at least the masculine portion, that precarious and scrambling existence which is purely the product of the time. There is a tall, pale, spindling youth, the son of a dentist, who lives by speculation. From all the Professor hears, he is a perfect Aladdin. He keeps a car, treats his friends to champagne suppers, and showers presents upon them on every occasion, costly little trifles in mother-of-pearl and gold. So today he has brought gifts to the young givers of the feast: for Bert a gold lead-pencil, and for Ingrid a pair of earrings of barbaric size, great cold circlets that fortunately do not have to go through the little ear-lobe, but are fastened over it by means of a clip. The big folk come laughing to their parents to display these trophies; and the parents shake their heads even while they admire – Aladdin bowing over and over from afar.

The young people appear to be absorbed in their dancing – if the performance they are carrying out with so much still concentration can be called dancing. They stride across the carpet, slowly, according to some unfathomable prescript, strangely embraced; in the newest attitude, tummy advanced and shoulders high, waggling the hips. They do not get tired, because nobody could. There is no such thing as heightened colour or heaving bosoms. Two girls may dance together or two young men – it is all the same. They move to the exotic strains of the gramophone, played with the loudest needles to procure the maximum of sound: shimmies, foxtrots, one-steps, double foxes, African shimmies, Java dances, and Creole polkas, the wild musky melodies follow one another, now furious, now languishing, a monotonous Negro programme in unfamiliar rhythm, to a clacking, clashing, and strumming orchestral accompaniment.

'What is that record?' Cornelius inquires of Ingrid, as she passes him by in the arms of the pale young speculator, with reference to the piece then playing, whose alternate languors and furies he finds comparatively pleasing and showing a certain resourcefulness in detail.

'*Prince of Pappenheim:* "Console thee, dearest child," ' she answers, and smiles pleasantly back at him with her white teeth.

The cigarette smoke wreathes beneath the chandelier. The air is blue with a festal haze compact of sweet and thrilling ingredients that stir the blood with memories of green-sick pains and are particularly poignant to those whose youth – like the Professor's own – has been over-sensitive ... The little folk are still on the floor. They are allowed to stop up until eight, so great is their delight in the party. The guests have got used to their presence; in their own way, they have their place in the doings of the evening. They have separated, anyhow: Snapper revolves all alone in the middle of the carpet, in his little blue velvet smock, while Ellie is running after one of the dancing couples, trying to hold the man fast by his coat. It is Max Hergesell and Fräulein Plaichinger. They dance well, it is a pleasure to watch them. One has to admit that these mad modern dances, when the right people dance them, are not so bad after all – they have something quite taking. Young Hergesell is a capital leader, dances according to rule, yet with in-

dividuality. So it looks. With what aplomb can he walk backwards – when space permits! And he knows how to be graceful
standing still in a crowd. And his partner supports him well,
being unsuspectedly lithe and buoyant, as fat people often are.
They look at each other, they are talking, paying no heed to
Ellie, though others are smiling to see the child's persistence. Dr
Cornelius tries to catch up his little sweetheart as she passes and
draw her to him. But Ellie eludes him, almost peevishly; her
dear Abel is nothing to her now. She braces her little arms
against his chest and turns her face away with a persecuted
look. Then escapes to follow her fancy once more.

The Professor feels an involuntary twinge. Uppermost in his
heart is hatred for this party, with its power to intoxicate and
estrange his darling child. His love for her – that not quite
disinterested, not quite unexceptionable love of his – is easily
wounded. He wears a mechanical smile, but his eyes have
clouded, and he stares fixedly at a point in the carpet, between
the dancers' feet.

'The children ought to go to bed,' he tells his wife. But she
pleads for another quarter of an hour; she has promised already,
and they do love it so! He smiles again and shakes his head,
stands so a moment and then goes across to the cloakroom,
which is full of coats and hats and scarves and overshoes. He
has trouble in rummaging out his own coat, and Max Hergesell
comes out of the hall, wiping his brow.

'Going out, sir?' he asks, in Hergesellian accents, dutifully
helping the older man on with his coat. 'Silly business this, with
my pumps,' he says. 'They pinch like hell. The brutes are
simply too tight for me, quite apart from the bad leather. They
press just here on the ball of my great toe' – he stands on one
foot and holds the other in his hand – 'it's simply unbearable.
There's nothing for it but to take them off; my brogues will
have to do the business ... Oh, let me help you, sir.'

'Thanks,' says Cornelius. 'Don't trouble. Get rid of your own
tormentors ... Oh, thanks very much!' For Hergesell has gone
on one knee to snap the fasteners of his snow-boots.

Once more the Professor expresses his gratitude; he is pleased
.and touched by so much sincere respect and youthful readiness

to serve. 'Go and enjoy yourself,' he counsels. 'Change your shoes and make up for what you have been suffering. Nobody can dance in shoes that pinch. Good-bye, I must be off to get a breath of fresh air.'

'I'm going to dance with Ellie now,' calls Hergesell after him. 'She'll be a first-rate dancer when she grows up, and that I'll swear to.'

'Think so?' Cornelius answers, already half out. 'Well, you are a connoisseur, I'm sure. Don't get curvature of the spine with stooping.'

He nods again and goes. 'Fine lad,' he thinks as he shuts the door. 'Student of engineering. Knows what he's bound for, got a good clear head, and so well set up and pleasant too.' And again paternal envy rises as he compares his poor Bert's status with this young man's, which he puts in the rosiest light that his son's may look the darker. Thus he sets out on his evening walk.

He goes up the avenue, crosses the bridge, and walks along the bank on the other side as far as the next bridge but one. The air is wet and cold, with a little snow now and then. He turns up his coat-collar and slips the crook of his cane over the arm behind his back. Now and then he ventilates his lungs with a long deep breath of the night air. As usual when he walks, his mind reverts to his professional preoccupations, he thinks about his lectures and the things he means to say tomorrow about Philip's struggle against the Germanic revolution, things steeped in melancholy and penetratingly just. Above all just, he thinks. For in one's dealings with the young it behoves one to display the scientific spirit, to exhibit the principles of enlightenment – not only for purposes of mental discipline, but on the human and individual side, in order not to wound them or indirectly offend their political sensibilities; particularly in these days, when there is so much tinder in the air, opinions are so frightfully split up and chaotic, and you may so easily incur attacks from one party or the other, or even give rise to scandal, by taking sides on a point of history. 'And taking sides is unhistoric anyhow,' so he muses. 'Only justice, only impartiality is historic.' And could not, properly considered, be otherwise ...

For justice can have nothing of youthful fire and blithe, fresh, loyal conviction. It is by nature melancholy. And, being so, has secret affinity with the lost cause and the forlorn hope rather than with the fresh and blithe and loyal – perhaps this affinity is its very essence and without it it would not exist at all!... 'And is there then no such thing as justice?' The Professor asks himself, and ponders the question so deeply that he absently posts his letters in the next box and turns round to go home. This thought of his is unsettling and disturbing to the scientific mind but is it not after all itself scientific, psychological, conscientious, and therefore be accepted without prejudice, no matter how upsetting? In the midst of which musings Dr Cornelius finds himself back at his own door.

On the outer threshold stands Xaver, and seems to be looking for him.

'Herr Professor,' says Xaver, tossing back his hair, 'go upstairs to Ellie straight off. She's in a bad way.'

'What's the matter?' asks Cornelius in alarm. 'Is she ill?'

'No-o, not to say ill,' answers Xaver. 'She's just in a bad way and crying fit to bust her little heart. It's along o' that chap with the shirt-front that danced with her – Herr Hergesell. She couldn't be got to go upstairs peaceably, not at no price at all, and she's b'en crying bucketfuls.'

'Nonsense,' says the Professor, who has entered and is tossing off his things in the cloakroom. He says no more; opens the glass door and without a glance at the guests turns swiftly to the stairs. Takes them two at a time, crosses the upper hall and the small room leading into the nursery. Xaver follows at his heels, but stops at the nursery door.

A bright light still burns within, showing the gay frieze that runs all round the room, the large row of shelves heaped with a confusion of toys, the rocking-horse on his swaying platform, with red-varnished nostrils and raised hoofs. On the linoleum lie other toys – building blocks, railway trains, a little trumpet. The two white cribs stand not far apart, Ellie's in the window corner, Snapper's out in the room.

Snapper is asleep. He has said his prayers in loud, ringing tones, prompted by Nurse, and gone off at once into vehement, profound, and rosy slumber – from which a cannon-ball fired at close range could not rouse him. He lies with both fists flung back on the pillows on either side of the tousled head with its funny crooked little slumber-tossed wig.

A circle of females surrounds Ellie's bed : not only blue-faced Ann is there, but the Hinterhofer ladies too, talking to each other and to her. They make way as the Professor comes up and reveal the child sitting all pale among her pillows, sobbing and weeping more bitterly than he has ever seen her sob and weep in her life. Her lovely little hands lie on the coverlet in front of her, the nightgown with its narrow lace border has slipped down from her shoulder – such a thin, birdlike little shoulder – and the sweet head Cornelius loves so well, set on the neck like a flower on its stalk, her head is on one side, with the eyes rolled up to the corner between wall and ceiling above her head. For there she seems to envisage the anguish of her heart and even to nod to it – either on purpose or because her head wobbles as her body is shaken with the violence of her sobs. Her eyes rain down tears. The bow-shaped lips are parted, like a little *mater dolorosa*'s and from them issue long, low wails that in nothing resemble the unnecessary and exasperating shrieks of a naughty child, but rise from the deep extremity of her heart and wake in the Professor's own a sympathy that is well-nigh intolerable. He has never seen his darling so before. His feelings find immediate vent in an attack on the ladies Hinterhofer.

'What about the supper?' he asks sharply. 'There must be a great deal to do. Is my wife being left to do it alone?'

For the acute sensibilities of the former middle class this is quite enough. The ladies withdraw in righteous indignation, and Xaver Kleingutl jeers at them as they pass out. Having been born to low life instead of achieving it, he never loses a chance to mock at their fallen state.

'Childie, childie,' murmurs Cornelius, and sitting down by the crib enfolds the anguished Ellie in his arms. 'What is the trouble with my darling?'

She bedews his face with her tears.

'Abel ... Abel ...' she stammers between sobs. 'Why – isn't Max – my brother? Max ought to be – my brother!'

Alas, alas! What mischance is this? Is this what the party has wrought, with its fatal atmosphere? Cornelius glances helplessly up at blue-faced Ann standing there in all the dignity of her limitations with her hands before her on her apron. She purses up her mouth and makes a long face. 'It's pretty young,' she says, 'for the female instincts to be showing up.'

'Hold your tongue,' snaps Cornelius, in his agony. He has this much to be thankful for, that Ellie does not turn from him now; she does not push him away as she did downstairs, but clings to him in her need, while she reiterates her absurd, bewildered prayer that Max might be her brother, or with a fresh burst of desire demands to be taken downstairs so that he can dance with her again. But Max, of course, is dancing with Fräulein Plaichinger, that behemoth who is his rightful partner and has every claim upon him; whereas Ellie – never, thinks the Professor, his heart torn with the violence of his pity, never has she looked so tiny and birdlike as now, when she nestles to him shaken with sobs and all unaware of what is happening in her little soul. No, she does not know. She does not comprehend that her suffering is on account of Fräulein Plaichinger, fat, overgrown, and utterly within her rights in dancing with Max Hergesell, whereas Ellie may only do it once, by way of a joke, although she is incomparably the more charming of the two. Yet it would be quite mad to reproach young Hergesell with the state of affairs or to make fantastic demands upon him. No, Ellie's suffering is without help or healing and must be covered up. Yet just as it is without understanding, so it is also without restraint – and that is what makes it so horribly painful. Xaver and blue-faced Ann do not feel this pain, it does not affect them – either because of native callousness or because they accept it as the way of nature. But the Professor's fatherly heart is quite torn by it, and by a distressful horror of this passion, so hopeless and so absurd.

Of no avail to hold forth to poor Ellie on the subject of the perfectly good little brother she already has. She only casts a distraught and scornful glance over at the other crib, where Snapper lies vehemently slumbering, and with fresh tears calls again for Max. Of no avail either the promise of a long, long walk tomorow, all five gentlemen, round and round the diningroom table; or a dramatic description of the thrilling cushion games they will play. No, she will listen to none of all this, nor to lying down and going to sleep. She will not sleep, she will sit bolt upright and suffer ... But on a sudden they stop and listen, Abel and Ellie; listen to something miraculous that is coming to pass, that is approaching by strides, two strides, to the nursery door, that now overwhelmingly appears ...

It is Xaver's work, not a doubt of that. He has not remained by the door where he stood to gloat over the ejection of the Hinterhofers. No, he has bestirred himself, taken a notion; likewise steps to carry it out. Downstairs he has gone, twitched Herr Hergesell's sleeve, and made a thick-lipped request. So here they both are. Xaver, having done his part, remains by the door; but Max Hergesell comes up to Ellie's crib; in his dinner-jacket, with his sketchy side-whisker and charming black eyes; obviously quite pleased with his role of swan knight and fairy prince, as one who should say: 'See, here am I, now all losses are restored and sorrows end.'

Cornelius is almost as much overcome as Ellie herself.

'Just look,' he says feebly, 'look who's here. This is uncommonly good of you, Herr Hergesell.'

'Not a bit of it,' says Hergesell. 'Why shouldn't I come to say good night to my fair partner?'

And he approaches the bars of the crib, behind which Ellie sits struck mute. She smiles blissfully through her tears. A funny, high little note that is half a sigh of relief comes from her lips, then she looks dumbly up at her swan knight with her golden-brown eyes – tear-swollen though they are, so much more beautiful than the fat Plaichinger's. She does not put up her arms. Her joy, like her grief is without understanding; but she does not do that. The lovely little hands lie quiet on the coverlet, and Max Hergesell stands with his arms leaning over the rail as on a balcony.

'And now,' he says smartly, 'she need not "sit the livelong night and weep upon her bed"!' He looks at the Professor to make sure he is receiving due credit for the quotation. 'Ha ha!' he laughs, 'she's beginning young. "Console thee, dearest child!" Never mind, you're all right! Just as you are you'll be wonderful! You've only got to grow up ... And you'll lie down and go to sleep like a good girl, now I've come to say good night? And not cry any more, little Lorelei?'

Ellie looks up at him, transfigured. One birdlike shoulder is bare; the Professor draws the lace-trimmed nighty over it. There comes into his mind a sentimental story he once read about a dying child who longs to see a clown he had once, with unforgettable ecstasy, beheld in a circus. And they bring the clown to the bedside marvellously arrayed, embroidered before and behind with silver butterflies; and the child dies happy. Max Hergesell is not embroidered, and Ellie, thank God, is not going to die, she has only 'been in a bad way'. But, after all, the effect is the same. Young Hergesell leans over the bars of the crib and rattles on, more for the father's ear than the child's, but Ellie does not know that – and the father's feelings towards him are a most singular mixture of thankfulness, embarrassment, and hatred.

'Good night, little Lorelei,' says Hergesell, and gives her his hand through the bars. Her pretty, soft, white little hand is swallowed up in the grasp of his big, strong, red one. 'Sleep well,' he says, 'and sweet dreams! But don't dream about me – God forbid! Not at your age – ha ha!' And then the fairy clown's visit is at an end. Cornelius accompanies him to the door. 'No, no, positively, no thanks called for, don't mention it,' he large-heartedly protests; and Xaver goes downstairs with him, to help serve the Italian salad.

But Dr Cornelius returns to Ellie, who is now lying down, with her cheek pressed into her flat little pillow.

'Well, wasn't that lovely?' he says as he smooths the covers. She nods, with one last little sob. For a quarter of an hour he sits beside her and watches while she falls asleep in her turn beside the little brother who found the right way so much earlier than she. Her silky brown hair takes the enchanting fall it always does when she sleeps; deep, deep lie the lashes over the eyes that late so abundantly poured forth their sorrow; the angelic mouth with its bowed upper lip is peacefully relaxed and a little open. Only now and then comes a belated catch in her slow breathing.

111

And her small hands, like pink and white flowers, lie so quietly, one on the coverlet, the other on the pillow by her face – Dr Cornelius, gazing, feels his heart melt with tenderness as with strong wine.

'How good,' he thinks, 'that she breathes in oblivion with every breath she draws! That in childhood each night is a deep, wide gulf between one day and the next. Tomorrow, beyond all doubt, young Hergesell will be a pale shadow, powerless to darken her little heart. Tomorrow, forgetful of all but present joy, she will walk with Abel and Snapper, all five gentlemen, round and round the table, will play the ever-thrilling cushion game.'

Heaven be praised for that!

MARIO AND THE MAGICIAN

(*1929*)

THE atmosphere of Torre di Venere remains unpleasant in the memory. From the first moment the air of the place made us uneasy, we felt irritable, on edge; then at the end came the shocking business of Cipolla, that dreadful being who seemed to incorporate, in so fateful and so humanly impressive a way, all the peculiar evilness of the situation as a whole. Looking back, we had the feeling that the horrible end of the affair had been preordained and lay in the nature of things; that the children had to be present at it was an added impropriety, due to the false colours in which the weird creature presented himself. Luckily for them, they did not know where the comedy left off and the tragedy began; and we let them remain in their happy belief that the whole thing had been a play up till the end.

Torre di Venere lies some fifteen kilometres from Porto-clemente, one of the most popular summer resorts on the Tyrrhenian Sea. Portoclemente is urban and elegant and full to overflowing for months on end. Its gay and busy main street of shops and hotels runs down to a wide sandy beach covered with tents and pennanted sandcastles and sunburnt humanity, where at all times a lively social bustle reigns, and much noise. But this same spacious and inviting fine-sanded beach, this same border of pine grove and near, presiding mountains, continues all the way along the coast. No wonder then that the same competition of a quiet kind should have sprung up farther on. Torre di Venere – the tower that gave the town its name is gone long since, one looks for it in vain – is an offshoot of the larger resort, and for some years remained an idyll for the few, a refuge for more unworldly spirits. But the usual history of such places repeated itself: peace has had to retire farther along the coast, to Marina Petriera and dear knows where else. We all

113

know how the world at once seeks peace and puts her to flight –
rushing upon her in the fond idea that they two will wed, and
where she is, there it can be at home. It will even set up its
Vanity Fair in a spot and be capable of thinking that peace is
still by its side. Thus Torre – though its atmosphere so far is
more modest and contemplative than that of Portoclemente –
has been quite taken up, by both Italians and foreigners. It is no
longer the thing to go to Portoclemente – though still so much
the thing that it is as noisy and crowded as ever. One goes next
door, so to speak: to Torre. So much more refined, even, and
cheaper to boot. And the attractiveness of these qualities persists,
though the qualities themselves long ago ceased to be evident.
Torre has got a Grand Hotel. Numerous pensions have sprung
up, some modest, some pretentious. The people who own or rent
the villas and pinetas overlooking the sea no longer have it all
their own way on the beach. In July and August it looks just like
the beach at Portoclemente: it swarms with a screaming, squab-
bling, merrymaking crowd, and the sun, blazing down like mad,
peels the skin off their necks. Garish little flat-bottomed boats
rock on the glittering blue, manned by children, whose mothers
hover afar and fill the air with anxious cries of Nino! and
Sandro! and Bice! and Maria! Pedlars step across the legs of
recumbent sunbathers, selling flowers and corals, oysters,
lemonade, and *cornetti al burro*, and crying their wares in the
breathy, full-throated southern voice.

Such was the scene that greeted our arrival in Torre: pleasant enough, but after all, we thought, we had come too soon. It
was the middle of August, the Italian season was still at its
height, scarcely the moment for strangers to learn to love the
special charms of the place. What an afternoon crowd in the
cafés on the front! For instance, in the Esquisito, where we
sometimes sat and were served by Mario, that very Mario of
whom I shall have presently to tell. It is well-nigh impossible to
find a table; and the various orchestras contend together in the
midst of one's conversation with bewildering effect. Of course, it
is in the afternoon that people come over from Portoclemente.
The excursion is a favourite one for the restless denizens of that
pleasure resort, and a Fiat motor-bus plies to and fro, coating

inch-thick with dust the oleander and laurel hedges along the highroad – a notable if repulsive sight.

Yes, decidedly one should go to Torre in September, when the great public has left. Or else in May, before the water is warm enough to tempt the Southerner to bathe. Even in the before and after seasons Torre is not empty, but life is less national and more subdued. English, French, and German prevail under the tent-awnings and in the pension dining-rooms; whereas in August – in the Grand Hotel, at least, where, in default of private addresses, we had engaged rooms – the stranger finds the field so occupied by Florentine and Roman society that he feels quite isolated and even temporarily *déclassé*.

We had, rather to our annoyance, this experience on the evening we arrived, when we went in to dinner and were shown to our table by the waiter in charge. As a table, it had nothing against it, save that we had already fixed our eyes upon those on the veranda beyond, built out over the water, where little red-shaded lamps glowed – and there were still some tables empty, though it was as full as the dining-room within. The children went into raptures at the festive sight, and without more ado we announced our intention to take our meals by preference on the veranda. Our words, it appeared, were prompted by ignorance; for we were informed, with somewhat embarrassed politeness. that the cosy nook outside was reserved for the clients of the hotel: *di nostri clienti*. Their clients? But we were their clients. We were not tourists or trippers, but boarders for a stay of some three or four weeks. However, we forbore to press for an explanation of the difference between the likes of us and that clientèle to whom it was vouchsafed to eat out there in the glow of the red lamps, and took our dinner by the prosaic common light of the dining-room chandelier – a thoroughly ordinary and monotonous hotel bill of fare, be it said. In Pensione Eleonora, a few steps landward, the table, as we were to discover, was much better.

And thither it was that we moved, three or four days later, before we had had time to settle in properly at the Grand Hotel. Not on account of the veranda and the lamps. The children, straightway on the best of terms with waiters and pages, absorbed in the joys of life on the beach, promptly forgot those colourful seductions. But now there arose, between ourselves and the veranda clientèle – or perhaps more correctly with the compliant management – one of those little unpleasantnesses which can quite spoil the pleasure of a holiday. Among the guests were some high Roman aristocracy, a Principe X and his family. These grand folk occupied rooms close to our own, and the Principessa, a great and a passionately maternal lady, was thrown into a panic by the vestiges of a whooping-cough which our little ones had lately got over, but which now and then still faintly troubled the unshatterable slumbers of our youngest-born. The nature of this illness is not clear, leaving some play for the imagination. So we took no offence at our elegant neighbour for clinging to the widely held view that whooping-cough is acoustically contagious and quite simply fearing lest her children yield to the bad example set by ours. In the fullness of her feminine self-confidence she protested to the management, which then, in the person of the proverbial frock-coated manager, hastened to represent to us, with many expressions of regret, that under the circumstances they were obliged to transfer us to the annexe. We did our best to assure him that the disease was in its very last stages, that it was actually over, and presented no danger of infection to anybody. All that we gained was permission to bring the case before the hotel physician – not one chosen by us – by whose verdict we must then abide. We agreed, convinced that thus we should at once pacify. the Princess and escape the trouble of moving. The doctor appeared, and behaved like a faithful and honest servant of science. He examined the child and gave his opinion: the disease was quite over, no danger of contagion was present. We drew a long breath and considered the incident closed – until the manager announced that despite the doctor's verdict it would still be necessary for us to give up our rooms and retire to the *dépendance*. Byzantinism like this outraged us. It is not likely that the Principessa was responsible for the wilful breach of faith. Very likely the fawning management had not even dared to tell her what the physician said. Anyhow, we made it clear to his understanding that we preferred to leave the hotel altogether and at once – and packed our trunks. We could do so with a light heart, having already set up casual friendly relations with Casa Eleonora. We had noticed its pleasant exterior and formed the acquaintance of its proprietor, Signora Angiolieri, and her husband: she slender and black-haired, Tuscan in type, probably at the beginning of the thirties, with the dead ivory complexion of the southern woman, he quiet and bald and carefully dressed. They owned a larger establishment in Florence and presided only in summer and early autumn over the branch in Torre di Venere. But earlier, before her marriage, our new landlady had been companion, fellow-traveller, wardrobe mistress, yes, friend, of Eleonora Duse and manifestly regarded that period as the crown of her career. Even at our first visit she spoke of it with animation. Numerous photographs of the great actress, with affectionate inscriptions, were displayed about the drawing-room, and other souvenirs of their life together adorned the little tables and *étagères*. This cult of a so interesting past was calculated, of course, to heighten the advantages of the signora's present business. Nevertheless our pleasure and interest were quite genuine as we were conducted through the house by its owner and listened to her sonorous and staccato Tuscan voice relating anecdotes of that immortal mistress, depicting her suffering saintliness, her genius, her profound delicacy of feeling.

Thither, then, we moved our effects, to the dismay of the staff of the Grand Hotel, who, like all Italians, were very good to children. Our new quarters were retired and pleasant, we were within easy reach of the sea through the avenue of young plane trees that ran down to the esplanade. In the clean, cool dining-room Signora Angiolieri daily served the soup with her own hands, the service was attentive and good, the table capital. We even discovered some Viennese acquaintances, and enjoyed chatting with them after luncheon, in front of the house. They, in their turn, were the means of our finding others – in short, all seemed for the best, and we were heartily glad of the change we had made. Nothing was now wanting to a holiday of the most gratifying kind.

And yet no proper gratification ensued. Perhaps the stupid occasion of our change of quarters pursued us to the new ones we had found. Personally, I admit that I do not easily forget these collisions with ordinary humanity, the naïve misuse of power, the injustice, the sycophantic corruption. I dwelt upon the incident too much, it irritated me in retrospect – quite futilely, of course, since such phenomena are only all too natural and all too much the rule. And we had not broken off relations with the Grand Hotel. The children were as friendly as ever there, the porter mended their toys, and we sometimes took tea in the garden. We even saw the Principessa. She would come out, with her firm and delicate tread, her lips emphatically corallined, to look after her children, playing under the super-vision of their English governess. She did not dream that we were anywhere near, for so soon as she appeared in the offing we sternly forbade our little one even to clear his throat.

The heat – if I may bring it in evidence – was extreme. It was African. The power of the sun, directly one left the border of the indigo-blue wave, was so frightful, so relentless, that the mere thought of the few steps between the beach and luncheon was a burden, clad though one might be only in pyjamas. Do you care for that sort of thing? Weeks on end? Yes, of course, it is proper to the south, it is classic weather, the sun of Homer, the climate wherein human culture came to flower – and all the rest of it. But after a while it is too much for me, I reach a point where I begin to find it dull. The burning void of the sky, day after day, weighs one down; the high coloration, the enormous naïveté of the unrefracted light – they do, I dare say, induce light-heartedness, a carefree mood born of immunity from downpours and other meteorological caprices. But slowly, slowly, there makes itself felt a lack: the deeper, more complex needs of the northern soul remain unsatisfied. You are left barren – even, it may be, in time, a little contemptuous. True, without that stupid business of the whooping-cough I might not have been feeling these things. I was annoyed, very likely I wanted to feel them and so half-unconsciously seized upon an idea lying ready to hand to induce, or if not to induce, at least to justify and strengthen my attitude. Up to this point, then, if you like, let us grant some ill will on our part. But the sea; and the mornings spent extended upon the fine sand in face of its eternal splendours – no, the sea could not conceivably induce such feelings. Yet it was none the less true that, despite all previous experience, we were not at home on the beach, we were not happy.

It was too soon, too soon. The beach, as I have said, was still in the hands of the middle-class native. It is a pleasing breed to look at, and among the young we saw much shapeliness and charm. Still, we were necessarily surrounded by a great deal of very average humanity – a middle-class mob, which, you will admit, is not more charming under this sun than under one's own native sky. The voices these women have! It was some-times hard to believe that we were in the land which is the western cradle of the art of song. '*Fuggièro!*' I can still hear that cry, as for twenty mornings long I heard it close behind me, breathy, full-throated, hideously stressed, with a harsh open *e*, uttered in accents of mechanical despair. '*Fuggièro! Rispondi almeno!*' Answer when I call you! The *sp* in *rispondi* was pronounced like *shp*, as Germans pronounce it; and this, on top of what I felt already, vexed my sensitive soul. The cry was addressed to a repulsive youngster whose sunburn had made disgusting raw sores on his shoulders. He outdid anything I have ever seen for ill-breeding, refractoriness, and temper and was a great coward to boot, putting the whole beach in an uproar, one day, because of his outrageous sensitiveness to the slightest pain. A sand-crab had pinched his toe in the water, and the minute injury made him set up a cry of heroic propor-tions – the shout of an antique hero in his agony – that pierced one to the marrow and called up visions of some frightful tragedy. Evidently he considered himself not only wounded, but poisoned as well; he crawled out on the sand and lay in appar-ently intolerable anguish, groaning '*Ohi!*' and '*Ohimè!*' and threshing about with arms and legs to ward off his mother's tragic appeals and the questions of the bystanders. An audience gathered round. A doctor was fetched – the same who had pronounced objective judgement on our whooping-cough – and here again acquitted himself like a man of science. Good-naturedly he reassured the boy, telling him that he was not hurt at all, he should simply go into the water again to relieve the smart. Instead of which, Fuggièro was borne off the beach, followed by a concourse of people. But he did not fail to appear next morning, nor did he leave off spoiling our children's sand-castles. Of course, always by accident. In short, a perfect terror.

And this twelve-year-old lad was prominent among the influences that, imperceptibly at first, combined to spoil our holiday and render it unwholesome. Somehow or other, there was a stiffness, a lack of innocent enjoyment. These people stood on their dignity – just why, and in what spirit, it was not easy at first to tell. They displayed much self-respectingness; towards each other and towards the foreigner their bearing was that of a person newly conscious of a sense of honour. And wherefore? Gradually we realized the political implications and understood that we were in the presence of a national ideal. The beach, in fact, was alive with patriotic children – a phenomenon as unnatural as it was depressing. Children are a human species and a society apart, a nation of their own, so to speak. On the basis of their common form of life, they find each other out with the greatest ease, no matter how different their small vocabularies. Ours soon played with natives and foreigners alike. Yet they were plainly both puzzled and disappointed at times. There were wounded sensibilities, displays of assertiveness – or rather hardly assertiveness, for it was too self-conscious and too didactic to deserve the name. There were quarrels over flags, disputes about authority and precedence. Grown-ups joined in, not so much to pacify as to render judgement and enunciate principles. Phrases were dropped about the greatness and dignity of Italy, solemn phrases that spoilt the fun. We saw our two little ones retreat, puzzled and hurt, and were put to it to explain the situation. These people, we told them, were just passing through a certain stage, something rather like an illness, perhaps; not very pleasant, but probably unavoidable.

We had only our own carelessness to thank that we came to blows in the end with this 'stage' – which, after all, we had seen and sized up long before now. Yes, it came to another 'cross-purposes', so evidently the earlier ones had not been sheer accident. In a word, we became an offence to the public morals.

Our small daughter – eight years old, but in physical development a good year younger and thin as a chicken – had had a
good long bathe and gone playing in the warm sun in her wet
costume. We told her that she might take off her bathing-suit,
which was stiff with sand, rinse it in the sea, and put it on
again, after which she must take care to keep it cleaner. Off goes
the costume and she runs down naked to the sea, rinses her little
jersey, and comes back. Ought we to have foreseen the outburst
of anger and resentment which her conduct, and thus our conduct, called forth? Without delivering a homily on the subject,
I may say that in the last decade our attitude towards the nude
body and our feelings regarding it have undergone, all over the
world, a fundamental change. There are things we 'never think
about' any more, and among them is the freedom we had permitted to this by no means provocative little childish body. But
in these parts it was taken as a challenge. The patriotic children
hooted. Fuggièro whistled on his fingers. The sudden buzz of
conversation among the grown people in our neighbourhood
boded no good. A gentleman in city togs, with a not very
apropos bowler hat on the back of his head, was assuring his
outraged womenfolk that he proposed to take punitive
measures; he stepped up to us, and a philippic descended on
our unworthy heads, in which all the emotionalism of the sense-
loving south spoke in the service of morality and discipline. The
offence against decency of which we had been guilty was, he
said, the more to be condemned because it was also a gross
ingratitude and an insulting breach of his country's hospitality.
We had criminally injured not only the letter and spirit of the
public bathing regulations, but also the honour of Italy; he, the
gentleman in the city togs, knew how to defend that honour and
proposed to see to it that our offence against the national dignity should not go unpunished.

We did our best, bowing respectfully, to give ear to this
eloquence. To contradict the man, overheated as he was, would
probably be to fall from one error into another. On the tips of
our tongues we had various answers: as, that the word 'hospitality', in its strictest sense, was not quite the right one, taking
all the circumstances into consideration. We were not literally

121

the guests of Italy, but of Signora Angiolieri, who had assumed
the role of dispenser of hospitality some years ago on laying down
that of familiar friend to Eleonora Duse. We longed to say that
surely this beautiful country had not sunk so low as to be
reduced to a state of hypersensitive prudishness. But we confined ourselves to assuring the gentleman that any lack of respect, any provocation on our parts, had been the farthest from
our thoughts. And as a mitigating circumstance we pointed out
the tender age and physical slightness of the little culprit. In
vain. Our protests were waved away, he did not believe in them;
our defence would not hold water. We must be made an
example of. The authorities were notified, by telephone, I believe, and their representative appeared on the beach. He said
the case was *'molto grave'*. We had to go with him to the
Municipio up in the Piazza, where a higher official confirmed
the previous verdict of *'molto grave'*, launched into a stream of
the usual didactic phrases – the selfsame tune and words as the
man in the bowler hat – and levied a fine and ransom of fifty
lire. We felt that the adventure must willy-nilly be worth to us
this much of a contribution to the economy of the Italian
government; paid, and left. Ought we not at this point to have
left Torre as well?

If we only had! We should thus have escaped that fatal
Cipolla. But circumstances combined to prevent us from making up our minds to a change. A certain poet says that it is
indolence that makes us endure uncomfortable situations. The
aperçu may serve as an explanation for our inaction. Anyhow,
one dislikes voiding the field immediately upon such an event.
Especially if sympathy from other quarters encourages one to
defy it. And in the Villa Eleonora they pronounced as with one
voice upon the injustice of our punishment. Some Italian after-
dinner acquaintances found that the episode put their country
in a very bad light, and proposed taking the man in the bowler
hat to task, as one fellow-citizen to another. But the next day he
and his party had vanished from the beach. Not on our account,
of course. Though it might be that the consciousness of his
impending departure had added energy to his rebuke; in any
case his going was a relief. And, furthermore, we stayed because

our stay had by now become remarkable in our own eyes, which is worth something in itself, quite apart from the comfort or discomfort involved. Shall we strike sail, avoid a certain experience so soon as it seems not expressly calculated to increase our enjoyment or our self-esteem? Shall we go away whenever life looks like turning in the slightest uncanny, or not quite normal, or even rather painful and mortifying? No, surely not. Rather stay and look matters in the face, brave them out; perhaps precisely in so doing lies a lesson for us to learn. We stayed on and reaped as the awful reward of our constancy the unholy and staggering experience with Cipolla.

I have not mentioned that the after season had begun, almost on the very day we were disciplined by the city authorities. The worshipful gentleman in the bowler hat, our denouncer, was not the only person to leave the resort. There was a regular exodus, on every hand you saw luggage-carts on their way to the station. The beach denationalized itself. Life in Torre, in the cafés and the pinetas, become more homelike and more European. Very likely we might even have eaten at a table on the glass veranda, but we refrained, being content at Signora Angiolieri's – as content, that is, as our evil star would let us be. But at the same time with this turn for the better came a change in the weather: almost to an hour it showed itself in harmony with the holiday calendar of the general public. The sky was overcast; not that it grew any cooler, but the unclouded heat of the entire eighteen days since our arrival, and probably long before that, gave place to a stifling sirocco air, while from time to time a little ineffectual rain sprinkled the velvety surface of the beach. Add to which, that two thirds of our intended stay at Torre had passed. The colourless, lazy sea, with sluggish jellyfish floating in its shallows, was at least a change. And it would have been silly to feel retrospective longings after a sun that had caused us so many sighs when it burned down in all its arrogant power.

At this juncture, then, it was that Cipolla announced himself. Cavaliere Cipolla he was called on the posters that appeared one day stuck up everywhere, even in the dining-room of Pensione Eleonora. A travelling virtuoso, an entertainer, *'forzatore, illusionista, prestidigitatore*', he called himself, who proposed to wait upon the highly respectable population of Torre di Venere with a display of extraordinary phenomena of a mysterious and staggering kind. A conjuror! The bare announcement was enough to turn our children's heads. They had never seen anything of the sort, and now our present holiday was to afford them this new excitement. From that moment on they besieged us with prayers to take tickets for the performance. We had doubts, from the first, on the score of the lateness of the hour, nine o'clock; but gave way, in the idea that we might see a little of what Cipolla had to offer, probably no great matter, and then go home. Besides, of course, the children could sleep late next day. We bought four tickets of Signora Angiolieri herself, she having taken a number of the stalls on commission to sell them to her guests. She could not vouch for the man's performance, and we had no great expectations. But we were conscious of a need for diversion, and the children's violent curiosity proved catching.

The Cavaliere's performance was to take place in a hall where during the season there had been a cinema with a weekly programme. We had never been there. You reached it by following the main street under the wall of the *'palazzo'*, a ruin with a 'For sale' sign, that suggested a castle and had obviously been built in lordlier days. In the same street were the chemist, the hairdresser, and all the better shops; it led, so to speak, from the feudal past the bourgeois into the proletarian, for it ended off between two rows of poor fishing-huts, where old women sat mending nets before the doors. And here, among the proletariat, was the hall, not much more, actually, than a wooden shed, though a large one, with a turreted entrance, plastered on either side with layers of gay placards. Some while after dinner, then, on the appointed evening, we wended our way thither in the dark, the children dressed in their best and blissful with the sense of so much irregularity. It was sultry, as it had been for days; there was heat lightning now and then, and a little rain; we proceeded under umbrellas. It took us a quarter of an hour.

Our tickets were collected at the entrance, our places we had to find ourselves. They were in the third row left, and as we sat down we saw that, late though the hour was for the performance, it was to be interpreted with even more laxity. Only very slowly did an audience – who seemed to be relied upon to come late – begin to fill the stalls. These comprised the whole auditorium; there were no boxes. This tardiness gave us some concern. The children's cheeks were already flushed as much with fatigue as with excitement. But even when we entered, the standing-room at the back and in the side aisles was already well occupied. There stood the manhood of Torre di Venere, all and sundry, fisherfolk, rough-and-ready youths with bare forearms crossed over their striped jerseys. We were well pleased with the presence of this native assemblage, which always adds colour and animation to occasions like the present; and the children were frankly delighted. For they had friends among these people – acquaintances picked up on afternoon strolls to the farther ends of the beach. We would be turning homeward, at the hour when the sun dropped into the sea, spent with the huge effort it had made and gilding with reddish gold the oncoming surf; and we would come upon bare-legged fisherfolk standing in rows, bracing and hauling with long-drawn cries as they drew in the nets and harvested in dripping baskets their catch, often so scanty, of *frutta di mare*. The children looked on, helped to pull, brought out their little stock of Italian words, made friends. So now they exchanged nods with the 'standing-room' clientèle; there was Guiscardo, there Antonio, they knew them by name and waved and called across in half-whispers, getting answering nods and smiles that displayed rows of healthy white teeth. Look, there is even Mario, Mario from the Esquisito, who brings us the chocolate. He wants to see the conjuror, too, and he must have come early, for he is almost in front; but he does not see us, he is not paying attention; that is a way he has, even though he is a waiter. So we wave instead to the man who lets out the little boats on the beach; he is there too, standing at the back.

It had got to a quarter past nine, it got to almost half past. It was natural that we should be nervous. When would the children get to bed? It had been a mistake to bring them, for now it would be very hard to suggest breaking off their enjoyment

125

before it had got well under way. The stalls had filled in time; all
Torre, apparently, was there: the guests of the Grand Hotel, the
guests of Villa Eleonora, familiar faces from the beach. We heard
English and German and the sort of French that Rumanians
speak with Italians. Madame Angiolieri herself sat two rows
behind us, with her quiet, bald-headed spouse, who kept stroking his moustache with the two middle fingers of his right hand.
Everybody had come late, but nobody too late. Cipolla made us
wait for him.

He made us wait. That is probably the way to put it. He
heightened the suspense by his delay in appearing. And we
could see the point of this, too – only not when it was carried to
extremes. Towards half past nine the audience began to clap –
an amiable way of expressing justifiable impatience, evincing as it
does an eagerness to applaud. For the little ones, this was a joy
in itself – all children love to clap. From the popular sphere
came loud cries of *'Pronti!' 'Cominciamo!'* And lo, it seemed
now as easy to begin as before it had been hard. A gong
sounded, greeted by the standing rows with a many-voiced
'Ah-h!' and the curtains parted. They revealed a platform furnished more like a schoolroom than like the theatre of a
conjuring performance – largely because of the blackboard in
the left foreground. There were a common yellow hatstand, a
few ordinary straw-bottomed chairs, and farther back a little
round table holding a water carafe and glass, also a tray with a
liqueur glass and a flask of pale yellow liquid. We had still a few
seconds of time to let these things sink in. Then, with no
darkening of the house, Cavaliere Cipolla made his entry.

He came forward with a rapid step that expressed his eagerness to appear before his public and gave rise to the illusion that
he had already come a long way to put himself at their service –
whereas, of course, he had only been standing in the wings. His
costume supported the fiction. A man of an age hard to determine, but by no means young; with a sharp, ravaged face,
piercing eyes, compressed lips, small black waxed moustache,
and a so-called imperial in the curve between mouth and chin.
He was dressed for the street with a sort of complicated evening
elegance, in a wide black pelerine with velvet collar and satin

lining; which, in the hampered state of his arms, he held together in front with his white-gloved hands. He had a white scarf round his neck; a top hat with a curving brim sat far back on his head. Perhaps more than anywhere else the eighteenth century is still alive in Italy, and with it the charlatan and mountebank type so characteristic of the period. Only there, at any rate, does one still encounter really well-preserved specimens. Cipolla had in his whole appearance much of the historic type; his very clothes helped to conjure up the traditional figure with its blatantly, fantastically foppish air. His pretentious costume sat upon him, or rather hung upon him, most curiously, being in one place drawn too tight, in another a mass of awkward folds. There was something not quite in order about his figure, both front and back – that was plain later on. But I must emphasize the fact that there was not a trace of personal jocularity or clownishness in his pose, manner, or behaviour. On the contrary, there was complete seriousness, an absence of any humorous appeal; occasionally even a cross-grained pride, along with that curious, self-satisfied air so characteristic of the deformed. None of all this, however, prevented his appearance from being greeted with laughter from more than one quarter of the hall.

All the eagerness had left his manner. The swift entry had been merely an expression of energy, not of zeal. Standing at the footlights he negligently drew off his gloves, to display long yellow hands, one of them adorned with a seal ring with a lapis-lazuli in a high setting. As he stood there, his small hard eyes, with flabby pouches beneath them, roved appraisingly about the hall, not quickly, rather in a considered examination, pausing here and there upon a face with his lips clipped together, not speaking a word. Then with a display of skill as surprising as it was casual, he rolled his gloves into a ball and tossed them across a considerable distance into the glass on the table. Next from an inner pocket he drew forth a packet of cigarettes; you could see by the wrapper that they were the cheapest sort the government sells. With his fingertips he pulled out a cigarette and lighted it, without looking, from a quick-firing benzine lighter. He drew the smoke deep into his lungs and let it out again, tapping his foot, with both lips drawn in an arrogant grimace and the grey smoke streaming out between broken and saw-edged teeth.

With a keenness equal to his own his audience eyed him. The youths at the rear scowled as they peered at this cocksure creature to search out his secret weaknesses. He betrayed none. In fetching out and putting back the cigarettes his clothes got in his way. He had to turn back his pelerine, and in so doing revealed a riding-whip with a silver claw-handle that hung by a leather thong from his left forearm and looked decidedly out of place. You could see that he had on not evening clothes but a frock-coat, and under this, as he lifted it to get at his pocket, could be seen a striped sash worn about the body. Somebody behind me whispered that this sash went with his title of Cavaliere. I give the information for what it may be worth – personally, I never heard that the title carried such insignia with it. Perhaps the sash was sheer pose, like the way he stood there, without a word, casually and arrogantly puffing smoke into his audience's face.

People laughed, as I said. The merriment had become almost general when somebody in the 'standing seats', in a loud, dry voice, remarked: *'Buona sera.'*

Cipolla cocked his head. 'Who was that?' asked he, as though he had been dared. 'Who was that just spoke? Well? First so bold and now so modest? *Paura*, eh?' He spoke with a rather high, asthmatic voice, which yet had a metallic quality. He waited.

'That was me,' a youth at the rear broke into the stillness, seeing himself thus challenged. He was not far from us, a handsome fellow in a woollen shirt, with his coat hanging over one shoulder. He wore his curly, wiry hair in a high, dishevelled mop, the style affected by the youth of the awakened Fatherland; it gave him an African appearance that rather spoiled his looks. *'Bè!* That was me. It was your business to say it first, but I was trying to be friendly.'

More laughter. The chap had a tongue in his head. *'Ha sciolto la scilinguàgnolo,'* I heard near me. After all, the retort was deserved.

128

'Ah, bravo!' answered Cipolla. 'I like you, *giovanotto*. Trust me, I've had my eye on you for some time. People like you are just in my line. I can use them. And you are the pick of the lot, that's plain to see. You do what you like. Or is it possible you have ever not done what you liked – or even, maybe, what you didn't like? What somebody else liked, in short? Hark ye, my friend, that might be a pleasant change for you, to divide up the willing and the doing and stop tackling both jobs at once. Division of labour, *sistema americano, sa'!* For instance, suppose you were to show your tongue to this select and honourable audience here – your whole tongue, right down to the roots?'

'No, I won't,' said the youth, hostilely. 'Sticking out your tongue shows a bad bringing-up.'

'Nothing of the sort,' retorted Cipolla. 'You would only be *doing* it. With all due respect to your bringing-up, I suggest that before I count ten, you will perform a right turn and stick out your tongue at the company here farther than you knew yourself that you could stick it out.'

He gazed at the youth, and his piercing eyes seemed to sink deeper into their sockets. *'Uno!'* said he. He had let his riding-whip slide down his arm and made it whistle once through the air. The boy faced about and put out his tongue, so long, so extendedly, that you could see it was the very uttermost in tongue which he had to offer. Then turned back, stony-faced, to his former position.

'That was me,' mocked Cipolla, with a jerk of his head towards the youth. *'Bè!* That was me.' Leaving the audience to enjoy its sensations, he turned towards the little round table, lifted the bottle, poured out a small glass of what was obviously cognac, and tipped it up with a practised hand.

The children laughed with all their hearts. They had understood practically nothing of what had been said, but it pleased them hugely that something so funny should happen, straight-away, between that queer man up there and somebody out of the audience. They had no preconception of what an 'evening' would be like and were quite ready to find this a priceless beginning. As for us, we exchanged a glance and I remember that involuntarily I made with my lips the sound that Cipolla's whip had made when it cut the air. For the rest, it was plain that people did not know what to make of a preposterous beginning like this to a sleight-of-hand performance. They could not see why the *giovanotto*, who after all in a way had been their spokesman, should suddenly have turned on them to vent his incivility. They felt that he had behaved like a silly ass and withdrew their countenances from him in favour of the artist, who now came back from his refreshment table and addressed them as follows:

'Ladies and gentlemen,' said he, in his wheezing, metallic voice, 'you saw just now that I was rather sensitive on the score of the rebuke this hopeful young linguist saw fit to give me' – '*questo linguista di belle speranze*' was what he said, and we all laughed at the pun. 'I am a man who sets some store by himself, you may take it from me. And I see no point in being wished a good evening unless it is done courteously and in all seriousness. For anything else there is no occasion. When a man wishes me a good evening he wishes himself one, for the audience will have one only if I do. So this lady-killer of Torre di Venere' (another thrust) 'did well to testify that I have one tonight and that I can dispense with any wishes of his in the matter. I can boast of having good evenings almost without exception. One not so good does come my way now and again, but very seldom. My calling is hard and my health not of the best. I have a little physical defect which prevented me from doing my bit in the war for the greater glory of the Fatherland. It is perforce with my mental and spiritual parts that I conquer life – which after all only means conquering oneself. And I flatter myself that my achievements have aroused interest and respect among the educated public. The leading newspapers have lauded me, the *Corriere della Sera* did me the courtesy of calling me a phenomenon, and in Rome the brother of the *Duce* honoured me by his presence at one of my evenings. I should not have thought that in a relatively less important place' (laughter here, at the expense of poor little Torre) 'I should have to give up the small personal habits which brilliant and elevated audiences had been ready to overlook. Nor did I think I had to stand being heckled by a person who seems to have been rather spoilt by the favours of the fair sex.' All this of course at the expense of the youth whom Cipolla never tired of presenting in the guise of *donnaiuolo* and rustic Don Juan. His persistent thin-skinnedness and animosity were in striking contrast to the self-confidence and the wordly success he boasted of. One might have assumed that the *giovanotto* was merely the chosen butt of Cipolla's customary professional sallies, had not the very pointed witticisms betrayed a genuine antagonism. No one looking at the physical parts of the two men need have been at a loss for the explanation, even if the deformed man had not constantly played on the other's supposed success with the fair sex. 'Well,' Cipolla went on, 'before beginning our entertainment this evening, perhaps you will permit me to make myself comfortable.'

And he went towards the hatstand to take off his things.

'*Parla benissimo,*' asserted somebody in our neighbourhood. So far, the man had done nothing; but what he had said was accepted as an achievement, by means of that he had made an impression. Among southern peoples speech is a constituent part of the pleasure of living, it enjoys far livelier social esteem than in the north. That national cement, the mother tongue, is paid symbolic honours down here, and there is something blithely symbolical in the pleasure people take in their respect for its form and phonetics. They enjoy speaking, they enjoy listening; and they listen with discrimination. For the way a man speaks serves as a measure of his personal rank; carelessness and clumsiness are greeted with scorn, elegance and mastery are rewarded with social éclat. Wherefore the small man too, where it is a question of getting his effect, chooses his phrase nicely and turns it with care. On this count, then, at least, Cipolla had won his audience; though he by no means belonged to the class of men which the Italian, in a singular mixture of moral and aesthetic judgements, labels '*simpatico*'.

After removing his hat, scarf, and mantle he came to the front of the stage, settling his coat, pulling down his cuffs with their large cuff-buttons, adjusting his absurd sash. He had very ugly hair; the top of his head, that is, was almost bald, while a narrow, black-varnished frizz of curls ran from front to back as

though stuck on; the side hair, likewise blackened, was brushed forward to the corners of the eyes – it was, in short, the hairdressing of an old-fashioned circus-director, fantastic, but entirely suited to his outmoded personal type and worn with so much assurance as to take the edge off the public's sense of humour. The little physical defect of which he had warned us was now all too visible, though the nature of it was even now not very clear: the chest was too high, as is usual in such cases; but the corresponding malformation of the back did not sit between the shoulders, it took the form of a sort of hips or buttocks hump, which did not indeed hinder his movements but gave him a grotesque and dipping stride at every step he took. However, by mentioning his deformity beforehand he had broken the shock of it, and a delicate propriety of feeling appeared to reign throughout the hall.

'At your service,' said Cipolla. 'With your kind permission, we will begin the evening with some arithmetical tests.'

Arithmetic? That did not sound much like sleight-of-hand. We began to have our suspicions that the man was sailing under a false flag, only we did not yet know which was the right one. I felt sorry on the children's account; but for the moment they were content simply to be there.

The numerical test which Cipolla now introduced was as simple as it was baffling. He began by fastening a piece of paper to the upper right-hand corner of the blackboard; then lifting it up, he wrote something underneath. He talked all the while, relieving the dryness of his offering by a constant flow of words, and showed himself a practised speaker, never at a loss for conversational turns of phrase. It was in keeping with the nature of his performance, and at the same time vastly entertained the children, that he went on to eliminate the gap between stage and audience, which had already been bridged over by the curious skirmish with the fisher lad: he had representatives from the audience mount the stage, and himself descended the wooden steps to seek personal contact with his public. And again, with individuals, he fell into his former taunting tone. I do not know how far that was a deliberate feature of his system; he preserved a serious, even a peevish air, but his audience, at least the more popular section, seemed convinced that that was all part of the game. So then, after he had written something and covered the writing by the paper, he desired that two persons should come up on the platform and help to perform the calculations. They would not be difficult, even for people not clever at figures. As usual, nobody volunteered, and Cipolla took care not to molest the more select portion of his audience. He kept to the populace. Turning to two sturdy young louts standing behind us, he beckoned them to the front, encouraging and scolding by turns. They should not stand there gaping, he said, unwilling to oblige the company. Actually, he got them in motion; with clumsy tread they came down the middle aisle, climbed the steps, and stood in front of the blackboard, grinning sheepishly at their comrades' shouts and applause. Cipolla joked with them for a few minutes, praised their heroic firmness of limb and the size of their hands, so well calculated to do this service for the public. Then he handed one of them the chalk and told him to write down the numbers as they were called out. But now the creature declared that he could not write! 'Non so scrivere,' said he in his gruff voice, and his companion added that neither did he.

God knows whether they told the truth or whether they wanted to make game of Cipolla. Anyhow, the latter was far from sharing the general merriment which their confession aroused. He was insulted and disgusted. He sat there on a straw-bottomed chair in the centre of the stage with his legs crossed, smoking a fresh cigarette out of his cheap packet; obviously it tasted the better for the cognac he had indulged in while the yokels were stumping up the steps. Again he inhaled the smoke and let it stream out between curling lips. Swinging his leg, with his gaze sternly averted from the two shamelessly chuckling creatures and from the audience as well, he stared into space as one who withdraws himself and his dignity from the contemplation of an utterly despicable phenomenon.

'Scandalous,' said he, in a sort of icy snarl. 'Go back to your places! In Italy everybody can write – in all her greatness there is no room for ignorance and unenlightenment. To accuse her of them, in the hearing of this international company, is a cheap joke, in which you yourselves cut a very poor figure and humiliate the government and the whole country as well. If it is true that Torre di Venere is indeed the last refuge of such ignorance, then I must blush to have visited the place – being, as I already was, aware of its inferiority to Rome in more than one respect –'

Here Cipolla was interrupted by the youth with the Nubian coiffure and his jacket across his shoulder. His fighting spirit, as we now saw, had only abdicated temporarily, and he now flung himself into the breach in defence of his native heath. 'That will do,' said he loudly. 'That's enough jokes about Torre. We all come from the place and we won't stand strangers making fun of it. These two chaps are our friends. Maybe they are no scholars, but even so they may be straighter than some folks in the room who are so free with their boasts about Rome, though they did not build it either.'

That was capital. The young man had certainly cut his eye-teeth. And this sort of spectacle was good fun, even though it still further delayed the regular performance. It is always fascinating to listen to an altercation. Some people it simply amuses, they take a sort of kill-joy pleasure in not being principals. Others feel upset and uneasy, and my sympathies are with these latter, although on the present occasion I was under the impression that all this was part of the show – the analphabetic yokels no less than the *giovanotto* with the jacket. The children listened well pleased. They understood not at all, but the sound of the voices made them hold their breath. So this was a 'magic evening' – at least it was the kind they have in Italy. They expressly found it 'lovely'.

Cipolla had stood up and with two of his scooping strides was at the footlights.

'Well, well, see who's here!' said he with grim cordiality. 'An old acquaintance! A young man with his heart at the end of his tongue' (he used the word *linguaccia*, which means a coated tongue, and gave rise to much hilarity). 'That will do, my friends,' he turned to the yokels. 'I do not need you now, I have business with this deserving young man here, *con questo torregiano de Venere,* this tower of Venus, who no doubt expects the gratitude of the fair as a reward for his prowess –'

'*Ah, non scherziamo!* We're talking earnest,' cried out the youth. His eyes flashed, and he actually made as though to pull off his jacket and proceed to direct methods of settlement.

Cipolla did not take him too seriously. We had exchanged apprehensive glances; but he was dealing with a fellow-countryman and had his native soil beneath his feet. He kept quite cool and showed complete mastery of the situation. He looked at his audience, smiled, and made a sideways motion of the head towards the young cockerel as though calling the public to witness how the man's bumptiousness only served to betray the simplicity of his mind. And then, for the second time, something strange happened, which set Cipolla's calm superiority in an uncanny light, and in some mysterious and irritating way turned all the explosiveness latent in the air into matter for laughter.

Cipolla drew still nearer to the fellow, looking him in the eye with a peculiar gaze. He even came halfway down the steps that led into the auditorium on our left, so that he stood directly in front of the troublemaker, on slightly higher ground. The riding-whip hung from his arm.

'My son, you do not feel much like joking,' he said. 'It is only too natural, for anyone can see that you are not feeling too well. Even your tongue, which leaves something to be desired on the score of cleanliness, indicates acute disorder of the gastric system. An evening entertainment is no place for people in your state; you yourself, I can tell, were of several minds whether you would not do better to put on a flannel bandage and go to bed. It was not good judgement to drink so much of that very sour white wine this afternoon. Now you have such a colic you would like to double up with the pain. Go ahead, don't be embarrassed. There is a distinct relief that comes from bending over, in cases of intestinal cramp.'

He spoke thus, word for word, with quiet impressiveness and a kind of stern sympathy, and his eyes, plunged the while deep in the young man's, seemed to grow very tired and at the same time burning above their enlarged tear-ducts – they were the strangest eyes, you could tell that not manly pride alone was preventing the young adversary from withdrawing his gaze. And presently, indeed, all trace of its former arrogance was gone from the bronzed young face. He looked open-mouthed at the Cavaliere and the open mouth was drawn in a rueful smile.

'Double over,' repeated Cipolla. 'What else can you do? With a colic like that you *must* bend. Surely you will not struggle against the performance of a perfectly natural action just because somebody suggests it to you?'

Slowly the youth lifted his forearms, folded and squeezed them across his body; it turned a little sideways, then bent, lower and lower, the feet shifted, the knees turned inward, until he had become a picture of writhing pain, until he all but grovelled upon the ground. Cipolla let him stand for some seconds thus, then made a short cut through the air with his whip and went with his scooping stride back to the little table, where he poured himself out a cognac.

'*Il boit beaucoup,*' asserted a lady behind us. Was that the only thing that struck her? We could not tell how far the audience grasped the situation. The fellow was standing upright again, with a sheepish grin – he looked as though he scarcely knew how it had all happened. The scene had been followed with tense interest and applauded at the end; there were shouts of '*Bravo, Cipolla!*' and '*Bravo, giovanotto!*' Apparently the issue of the duel was not looked upon as a personal defeat for the young man. Rather the audience encouraged him as one does an actor who succeeds in an unsympathetic role. Certainly his way of screwing himself up with cramp had been highly picturesque, its appeal was directly calculated to impress the gallery – in short, a fine dramatic performance. But I am not sure how far the audience were moved by that natural tactfulness in which the south excels, or how far it penetrated into the nature of what was going on.

The Cavaliere, refreshed, had lighted another cigarette. The numerical tests might now proceed. A young man was easily found in the back row who was willing to write down on the blackboard the numbers as they were dictated to him. Him too we knew; the whole entertainment had taken on an intimate character through our acquaintance with so many of the actors. This was the man who worked at the greengrocer's in the main street; he had served us several times, with neatness and dispatch. He wielded the chalk with clerkly confidence, while Cipolla descended to our level and walked with his deformed gait through the audience, collecting numbers as they were given, in two, three, and four places, and calling them out to the grocer's assistant, who wrote them down in a column. In all this, everything on both sides was calculated to amuse, with its jokes and its oratorical asides. The artist could not fail to hit on foreigners, who were not ready with their figures, and with them he was elaborately patient and chivalrous, to the great amusement of the natives, whom he reduced to confusion in their turn, by making them translate numbers that were given in English or French. Some people gave dates concerned with great events in Italian history. Cipolla took them up at once and made patriotic comments. Somebody shouted 'Number one!' The Cavaliere, incensed at this as at every attempt to make game of him, retorted over his shoulder that he could not take less than two-place figures. Whereupon another joker cried out 'Number two!' and was greeted with the applause and laughter which every reference to natural functions is sure to win among southerners.

When fifteen numbers stood in a long straggling row on the board, Cipolla called for a general adding-match. Ready reckoners might add in their heads, but pencil and paper were not forbidden. Cipolla, while the work went on, sat on his chair near the blackboard, smoked and grimaced, with the complacent, pompous air cripples so often have. The five-place addition was soon done. Somebody announced the answer, somebody else confirmed it, a third had arrived at a slightly different result, but the fourth agreed with the first and second. Cipolla got up, tapped some ash from his coat, and lifted the paper at the upper right-hand corner of the board to display the writing. The correct answer, a sum close on a million, stood there; he had written it down beforehand.

Astonishment, and loud applause. The children were overwhelmed. How had he done that, they wanted to know. We told them it was a trick, not easily explainable offhand. In short, the

137

man was a conjuror. This was what a sleight-of-hand evening was like, so now they knew. First the fisherman had cramp, and then the right answer was written down beforehand – it was all simply glorious, and we saw with dismay that despite the hot eyes and the hand of the clock at almost half past ten, it would be very hard to get them away. There would be tears. And yet it was plain that this magician did not 'magick' – at least not in the accepted sense, of manual dexterity – and that the entertainment was not at all suitable for children. Again, I do not know, either, what the audience really thought. Obviously there was grave doubt whether its answers had been given of 'free choice'; here and there an individual might have answered of his own motion, but on the whole Cipolla certainly selected his people and thus kept the whole procedure in his own hands and directed it towards the given result. Even so, one had to admire the quickness of his calculations, however much one felt disinclined to admire anything else about the performance. Then his patriotism, his irritable sense of dignity – the Cavaliere's own countrymen might feel in their element with all that and continue in a laughing mood; but the combination certainly gave us outsiders food for thought.

Cipolla himself saw to it – though without giving them a name – that the nature of his powers should be clear beyond a doubt to even the least-instructed person. He alluded to them, of course, in his talk – and he talked without stopping – but only in vague, boastful, self-advertising phrases. He went on awhile with experiments on the same lines as the first, merely making them more complicated by introducing operations in multiplying, subtracting, and dividing; then he simplified them to the last degree in order to bring out the method. He simply had numbers 'guessed' which were previously written under the paper; and the guess was nearly always right. One guesser admitted that he had had in mind to give a certain number, when Cipolla's whip went whistling through the air, and a quite different one slipped out, which proved to be the 'right' one. Cipolla's shoulders shook. He pretended admiration for the powers of the people he questioned. But in all his compliments there was something fleering and derogatory; the victims could scarcely have relished them much, although they smiled, and although they might easily have set down some part of the applause to their own credit. Moreover, I had not the impression that the artist was popular with his public. A certain ill will and reluctance were in the air, but courtesy kept such feelings in check, as did Cipolla's competency and his stern self-confidence. Even the riding-whip, I think, did much to keep rebellion from becoming overt.

From tricks with numbers he passed to tricks with cards. There were two packs, which he drew out of his pockets, and so much I still remember, that the basis of the tricks he played with them was as follows: from the first pack he drew three cards and thrust them without looking at them inside his coat. Another person then drew three out of the second pack, and these turned out to be the same as the first three – not invariably all the three, for it did happen that only two were the same. But in the majority of cases Cipolla triumphed, showing his three cards with a little bow in acknowledgment of the applause with which his audience conceded his possession of strange powers – strange whether for good or evil. A young man in the front row, to our right, an Italian, with proud, finely chiselled features, rose up and said that he intended to assert his own will in his choice and consciously to resist any influence, of whatever sort. Under these circumstances, what did Cipolla think would be the result? 'You will,' answered the Cavaliere, 'make my task somewhat more difficult thereby. As for the result, your resistance will not alter it in the least. Freedom exists, and also the will exists; but freedom of the will does not exist, for a will that aims at its own freedom aims at the unknown. You are free to draw or not to draw. But if you draw, you will draw the right cards – the more certainly, the more wilfully obstinate your behaviour.'

One must admit that he could not have chosen his words better, to trouble the waters and confuse the mind. The refractory youth hesitated before drawing. Then he pulled out a card and at once demanded to see if it was among the chosen three. 'But why?' queried Cipolla. 'Why do things by halves?' Then, as the other defiantly insisted, '*E servito*,' said the juggler, with a gesture of exaggerated servility; and held out the three cards fanwise, without looking at them himself. The left-hand card was the one drawn.

Amid general applause, the apostle of freedom sat down. How far Cipolla employed small tricks and manual dexterity to help out his natural talents, the deuce only knew. But even without them the result would have been the same: the curiosity of the entire audience was unbounded and universal, everybody both enjoyed the amazing character of the entertainment and unanimously conceded the professional skill of the performer. '*Lavora bene*,' we heard, here and there in our neighbourhood; it signified the triumph of objective judgement over antipathy and repressed resentment.

After his last, incomplete, yet so much the more telling success, Cipolla had at once fortified himself with another cognac. Truly he did 'drink a lot', and the fact made a bad impression. But obviously he needed the liquor and the cigarettes for the replenishment of his energy, upon which, as he himself said, heavy demands were made in all directions. Certainly in the intervals he looked very ill, exhausted and hollow-eyed. Then the little glassful would redress the balance, and the flow of lively, self-confident chatter run on, while the smoke he inhaled gushed out grey from his lungs. I clearly recall that he passed from the card-tricks to parlour games – the kind based on certain powers which in human nature are higher or else lower than human reason: on intuition and 'magnetic' transmission; in short, upon a low type of manifestation. What I do not remember is the precise order things came in. And I will not bore you with a description of these experiments; everybody knows them, everybody has at one time or another taken part in this finding of hidden articles, this blind carrying out of a series of acts, directed by a force that proceeds from organism to organism by unexplored paths. Everybody has had his little glimpse into the equivocal, impure, inexplicable nature of the occult, has been conscious of both curiosity and contempt, has shaken his head over the human tendency of those who deal in it to help themselves out with humbuggery, though, after all, the humbuggery is no disproof whatever of the genuineness of the other elements in the dubious amalgam. I can only say here that each single circumstance gains in weight and the whole greatly in impressiveness when it is a man like Cipolla who is the chief actor and guiding spirit in the sinister business. He sat smoking at the rear of the stage, his back to the audience while they conferred. The object passed from hand to hand which it was his task to find, with which he was to perform some action agreed upon beforehand. Then he would start to move zigzag through the hall, with his head thrown back and one hand outstretched, the other clasped in that of a guide who was in the secret but enjoined to keep himself perfectly passive, with his thoughts directed upon the agreed goal. Cipolla moved with the bearing typical in these experiments: now groping upon a false start, now with a quick forward thrust, now pausing as though to listen and by sudden inspiration correcting his course. The roles seemed reversed, as the artist himself pointed out, in his ceaseless flow of discourse. The suffering, receptive, performing part was now his, the will he had before imposed on others was shut out, he acted in obedience to a voiceless common will which was in the air. But he made it perfectly clear that it all came to the same thing. The capacity for self-surrender, he said, for becoming a tool, for the most unconditional and utter self-abnegation, was but the reverse side of that other power to will and to command. Commanding and obeying formed together one single principle, one indissoluble unity; he who knew how to obey knew also how to command, and conversely; the one idea was comprehended in the other, as people and leader were comprehended in one another. But that which was *done,* the highly exacting and exhausting performance, was in every case his, the leader's and mover's, in whom the will became obedience, the obedience will, whose person was the cradle and womb of both, and who thus suffered enormous hardship. Repeatedly he emphasized the fact that his lot was a hard one – presumably to account for his need of stimulant and his frequent recourse to the little glass.

Thus he groped his way forward, like a blind seer, led and sustained by the mysterious common will. He drew a pin set with a stone out of its hiding-place in an Englishwoman's shoe, carried it, halting and pressing on by turns, to another lady –

Signora Angiolieri – and handed it to her on bended knee, with the words it had been agreed he was to utter. 'I present you with this in token of my respect,' was the sentence. Their sense was obvious but the words themselves not easy to hit upon, for the reason that they had been agreed on in French; the language complication seemed to us a little malicious, implying as it did a conflict between the audience's natural interest in the success of the miracle, and their desire to witness the humiliation of this presumptuous man. It was a strange sight: Cipolla on his knees before the signora, wrestling, amid efforts at speech, after knowledge of the preordained words. 'I must say something,' he said, 'and I feel clearly what it is I must say. But I also feel that if it passed my lips it would be wrong. Be careful not to help me unintentionally!' he cried out, though very likely that was precisely what he was hoping for. '*Pensez très fort*,' he cried all at once, in bad French, and then burst out with the required words – in Italian, indeed, but with the final substantive pronounced in the sister tongue, in which he was probably far from fluent: he said *vénération* instead of *venerazione*, with an impossible nasal. And this partial success, after the complete success before it, the finding of the pin, the presentation of it on his knees to the right person – was almost more impressive than if he had got the sentence exactly right, and evoked bursts of admiring applause.

Cipolla got up from his knees and wiped the perspiration from his brow. You understand that this experiment with the pin was a single case, which I describe because it sticks in my memory. But he changed his method several times and improvised a number of variations suggested by his contact with his audience; a good deal of time thus went by. He seemed to get particular inspiration from the person of our landlady; she drew him on to the most extraordinary displays of clairvoyance. 'It does not escape me, madame,' he said to her, 'that there is something unusual about you, some special and honourable distinction. He who has eyes to see descries about your lovely brow an aureola – if I mistake not, it once was stronger than now – a slowly paling radiance ... hush, not a word! Don't help me. Beside you sits your husband – yes?' He turned to-

wards the silent Signor Angiolieri. 'You are the husband of this
lady, and your happiness is complete. But in the midst of this
happiness memories rise ... the past, signora, so it seems to me,
plays an important part in your present. You knew a king ...
has not a king crossed your path in bygone days?'

'No,' breathed the dispenser of our midday soup, her golden-
brown eyes gleaming in the noble pallor of her face.

'No? No, not a king; I meant that generally, I did not mean
literally a king. Not a king, not a prince, and a prince after all, a
king of a loftier realm; it was a great artist, at whose side you
once – you would contradict me, and yet I am not wholly
wrong. Well, then! It was a woman, a great, a world-renowned
woman artist, whose friendship you enjoyed in your tender
years, whose sacred memory overshadows and transfigures your
whole existence. Her name? Need I utter it, whose fame has
long been bound up with the Fatherland's, immortal as its own?
Eleonora Duse,' he finished, softly and with much solemnity.

The little woman bowed her head, overcome. The applause
was like a patriotic demonstration. Nearly everyone there knew
about Signora Angiolieri's wonderful past; they were all able to
confirm the Cavaliere's intuition – not least the present guests of
Casa Eleonora. But we wondered how much of the truth he had
learned as the result of professional inquiries made on his
arrival. Yet I see no reason at all to cast doubt, on rational
grounds, upon powers which, before our very eyes, became fatal
to their possessor.

At this point there was an intermission. Our lord and master
withdrew. Now I confess that almost ever since the beginning of
my tale I have looked forward with dread to this moment in it.
The thoughts of men are mostly not hard to read; in this case
they are very easy. You are sure to ask why we did not choose
this moment to go away – and I must continue to owe you an
answer. I do not know why. I cannot defend myself. By this
time it was certainly eleven, probably later. The children were
asleep. The last series of tests had been too long, nature had had
her way. They were sleeping in our laps, the little one on mine,
the boy on his mother's. That was, in a way, a consolation; but
at the same time it was also ground for compassion and a clear

leading to take them home to bed. And I give you my word that we wanted to obey this touching admonition, we seriously wanted to. We roused the poor things and told them it was now high time to go. But they were no sooner conscious than they began to resist and implore – you know how horrified children are at the thought of leaving before the end of a thing. No cajoling has any effect, you have to use force. It was so lovely, they wailed. How did we know what was coming next? Surely we could not leave until after the intermission; they liked a little nap now and again – only not go home, only not go to bed, while the beautiful evening was still going on!

We yielded, but only for the moment, of course – so far as we knew – only for a little while, just a few minutes longer. I cannot excuse our staying, scarcely can I even understand it. Did we think, having once said A, we had to say B – having once brought the children hither we had to let them stay? No, it is not good enough. Were we ourselves so highly entertained? Yes, and no. Our feelings for Cavaliere Cipolla were of a very mixed kind, but so were the feelings of the whole audience, if I mistake not, and nobody left. Were we under the sway of a fascination which emanated from this man who took so strange a way to earn his bread; a fascination which he gave out independently of the programme and even between the tricks and which paralysed our resolve? Again, sheer curiosity may account for something. One was curious to know how such an evening turned out; Cipolla in his remarks having all along hinted that he had tricks in his bag stranger than any he had yet produced.

But all that is not it – or at least it is not all of it. More correct it would be to answer the first question with another. Why had we not left Torre di Venere itself before now? To me the two questions are one and the same, and in order to get out of the impasse I might simply say that I had answered it already. For, as things had been in Torre in general: queer, uncomfortable, troublesome, tense, oppressive, so precisely they were here in this hall tonight. Yes, more than precisely. For it seemed to be the fountain-head of all the uncanniness and all the strained feelings which had oppressed the atmosphere of our holiday. This man whose return to the stage we were awaiting was the personification of all that; and, as we had not gone away in general, so to speak, it would have been inconsistent to do it in the particular case. You may call this an explanation, you may call it inertia, as you see fit. Any argument more to the purpose I simply do not know how to adduce.

Well, there was an interval of ten minutes, which grew into nearly twenty. The children remained awake. They were enchanted by our compliance, and filled the break to their own satisfaction by renewing relations with the popular sphere, with Antonio, Guiscardo, and the canoe man. They put their hands to their mouths and called messages across, appealing to us for the Italian words. 'Hope you have a good catch tomorrow, a whole netful!' They called to Mario, Esquisito Mario: *'Mario, una cioccolata e biscotti!'* And this time he heeded and answered with a smile: *'Subito, signorini!'* Later we had reason to recall this kindly, if rather absent and pensive smile.

Thus the interval passed, the gong sounded. The audience, which had scattered in conversation, took their places again, the children sat up straight in their chairs with their hands in their laps. The curtain had not been dropped. Cipolla came forward again, with his dipping stride, and began to introduce the second half of the programme with a lecture.

Let me state once for all that this self-confident cripple was the most powerful hypnotist I have ever seen in my life. It was pretty plain now that he threw dust in the public eye and advertised himself as a prestidigitator on account of police regulations which would have prevented him from making his living by the exercise of his powers. Perhaps this eyewash is the usual thing in Italy; it may be permitted or even connived at by the authorities. Certainly the man had from the beginning made little concealment of the actual nature of his operations; and this second half of the programme was quite frankly and exclusively devoted to one sort of experiment. While he still practised some rhetorical circumlocutions, the tests themselves were one long series of attacks upon the will-power, the loss or compulsion of volition. Comic, exciting, amazing by turns, by midnight they were still in full swing; we ran the gamut of all the phenomena this natural–unnatural field has to show, from the unimpressive at one end of the scale to the monstrous at the other. The audience laughed and applauded as they followed the grotesque details; shook their heads, clapped their knees, fell very frankly under the spell of this stern, self-assured personality. At the same time I saw signs that they were not quite complacent, not quite unconscious of the peculiar ignominy which lay, for the individual and for the general, in Cipolla's triumphs.

Two main features were constant in all the experiments: the liquor glass and the claw-handled riding-whip. The first was always invoked to add fuel to his demoniac fires; without it, apparently, they might have burned out. On this score we might even have felt pity for the man; but the whistle of his scourge, the insulting symbol of his domination, before which we all cowered, drowned out every sensation save a dazed and outbraved submission to his power. Did he then lay claim to our sympathy to boot? I was struck by a remark he made – it suggested no less. At the climax of his experiments, by stroking and breathing upon a certain young man who had offered himself as a subject and already proved himself a particularly susceptible one, he had not only put him into the condition known as deep trance and extended his insensible body by neck and feet across the backs of two chairs, but had actually sat down on the rigid form as on a bench, without making it yield. The sight of this unholy figure in a frock-coat squatted on the stiff body was horrible and incredible; the audience, convinced that the victim of this scientific diversion must be suffering, expressed its sympathy: *'Ah, poveretto!'* Poor soul, poor soul! *'Poor soul!'* Cipolla mocked them, with some bitterness. 'Ladies and gentlemen, you are barking up the wrong tree. *Sono io il poveretto*. I am the person who is suffering. I am the one to be pitied.' We pocketed the information. Very good. Maybe the experiment was at his expense, maybe it was he who had suffered the cramp when the *giovanotto* over there had made the faces. But appearances were all against it; and one does not feel like saying *poveretto* to a man who is suffering to bring about the humiliation of others.

I have got ahead of my story and lost sight of the sequence of events. To this day my mind is full of the Cavaliere's feats of endurance; only I do not recall them in their order – which does not matter. So much I do know: that the longer and more circumstantial tests, which got the most applause, impressed me less than some of the small ones which passed quickly over. I remember the young man whose body Cipolla converted into a board, only because of the accompanying remarks which I have quoted. An elderly lady in a cane-seated chair was lulled by Cipolla into the delusion that she was on a voyage to India and gave a voluble account of her adventures by land and sea. But I found this phenomenon less impressive than one which followed immediately after the intermission. A tall, well-built, soldierly man was unable to lift his arm, after the hunchback had told him that he could not and given a cut through the air with his whip. I can still see the face of that stately, mustachioed colonel smiling and clenching his teeth as he struggled to regain his lost freedom of action. A staggering performance! He seemed to be exerting his will, and in vain; the trouble, however, was probably simply that he could not will. There was involved here that recoil of the will upon itself which paralyses choice – as our tyrant had previously explained to the Roman gentleman.

Still less can I forget the touching scene, at once comic and horrible, with Signora Angiolieri. The Cavaliere, probably in his first bold survey of the room, had spied out her ethereal lack of resistance to his power. For actually he bewitched her, literally drew her out of her seat, out of her row, and away with him whither he willed. And in order to enhance his effect, he bade Signor Angiolieri call upon his wife by her name, to throw, as it were, all the weight of his existence and his rights in her into the scale, to rouse by the voice of her husband everything in his spouse's soul which could shield her virtue against the evil assaults of magic. And how vain it all was! Cipolla was standing at some distance from the couple, when he made a single cut with his whip through the air. It caused our landlady to shudder violently and turn her face towards him. 'Sofronia!' cried Signor Angiolieri – we had not known that Signora Angiolieri's name was Sofronia. And he did well to call,

everybody saw that there was no time to lose. His wife kept
her face turned in the direction of the diabolical Cavaliere, who
with his ten long yellow fingers was making passes at his victim,
moving backwards as he did so, step by step. Then Signora
Angiolieri, her pale face gleaming, rose up from her seat, turned
right round, and began to glide after him. Fatal and forbidding
sight! Her face as though moonstruck, stiff-armed, her lovely
hands lifted a little at the wrists, the feet as it were together, she
seemed to float slowly out of her row and after the tempter.
'Call her, sir, keep on calling,' prompted the redoubtable man.
And Signor Angiolieri, in a weak voice, called: 'Sofronia!' Ah,
again and again he called; as his wife went farther off he even
curved one hand round his lips and beckoned with the other as
he called. But the poor voice of love and duty echoed unheard,
in vain, behind the lost one's back; the signora swayed along,
moonstruck, deaf, enslaved; she glided into the middle aisle and
down it towards the fingering hunchback, towards the door. We
were convinced, we were driven to the conviction, that she
would have followed her master, had he so willed it, to the ends
of the earth.

'*Accidente!*' cried out Signor Angiolieri, in genuine affright,
springing up as the exit was reached. But at the same moment
the Cavaliere put aside, as it were, the triumphal crown and
broke off. 'Enough, signora, I thank you,' he said, and offered
his arm to lead her back to her husband. 'Signor,' he greeted the
latter, 'here is your wife. Unharmed, with my compliments, I
give her into your hands. Cherish with all the strength of your
manhood a treasure which is so wholly yours, and let your zeal
be quickened by knowing that there are powers stronger than
reason or virtue, and not always so magnanimously ready to re-
linquish their prey!'

Poor Signor Angiolieri, so quiet, so bald! He did not look as
though he would know how to defend his happiness, even
against powers much less demoniac than these which were now
adding mockery to frightfulness. Solemnly and pompously the
Cavaliere retired to the stage, amid applause to which his
eloquence gave double strength. It was this particular episode, I
feel sure, that set the seal upon his ascendancy. For now he

made them dance, yes, literally; and the dancing lent a disso-
lute, abandoned, topsy-turvy air to the scene, a drunken abdication of the critical spirit which had so long resisted the spell of
this man. Yes, he had had to fight to get the upper hand – for
instance against the animosity of the young Roman gentleman,
whose rebellious spirit threatened to serve others as a rallying-
point. But it was precisely upon the importance of example that
the Cavaliere was so strong. He had the wit to make his attack at
the weakest point and to choose as his first victim that feeble,
ecstatic youth whom he had previously made into a board. The
master had but to look at him, when this young man would
fling himself back as though struck by lightning, place his hands
rigidly at his sides, and fall into a state of military somnambul-
ism, in which it was plain to any eye that he was open to the
most absurd suggestion that might be made to him. He seemed
quite content in his abject state, quite pleased to be relieved of
the burden of voluntary choice. Again and again he offered
himself as a subject and gloried in the model facility he had in
losing consciousness. So now he mounted the platform, and a
single cut of the whip was enough to make him dance to the
Cavaliere's orders, in a kind of complacent ecstasy, eyes closed,
head nodding, lank limbs flying in all directions.

It looked unmistakably like enjoyment, and other recruits
were not long in coming forward: two other young men, one
humbly and one well dressed, were soon jigging alongside the
first. But now the gentleman from Rome bobbed up again,
asking defiantly if the Cavaliere would engage to make him
dance too, even against his will.

'Even against your will,' answered Cipolla, in unforgettable
accents. That frightful *'anche se non vuole'* still rings in my
ears. The struggle began. After Cipolla had taken another little
glass and lighted a fresh cigarette he stationed the Roman at a
point in the middle aisle and himself took up a position some
distance behind him, making his whip whistle through the air as
he gave the order: *'Balla!'* His opponent did not stir. *'Balla!'*
repeated the Cavaliere incisively, and snapped his whip. You
saw the young man move his neck round in his collar; at the
same time one hand lifted slightly at the wrist, one ankle turned

outward. But that was all, for the time at least; merely a tendency to twitch, now sternly repressed, now seeming about to get the upper hand. It escaped nobody that here a heroic obstinacy, a fixed resolve to resist, must needs be conquered; we were beholding a gallant effort to strike out and save the honour of the human race. He twitched but danced not; and the struggle was so prolonged that the Cavaliere had to divide his attention between it and the stage, turning now and then to make his riding-whip whistle in the direction of the dancers, as it were to keep them in leash. At the same time he advised the audience that no fatigue was involved in such activities, however long they went on, since it was not the automatons up there who danced, but himself. Then once more his eye would bore itself into the back of the Roman's neck and lay siege to the strength of purpose which defied him.

One saw it waver, that strength of purpose, beneath the repeated summons and whip-crackings. Saw with an objective interest which yet was not quite free from traces of sympathetic emotion – from pity, even from a cruel kind of pleasure. If I understand what was going on, it was the negative character of the young man's fighting position which was his undoing. It is likely that *not* willing is not a practicable state of mind; *not* to want to do something may be in the long run a mental content impossible to subsist on. Between not willing a certain thing and not willing at all – in other words, yielding to another person's will – there may lie too small a space for the idea of freedom to squeeze into. Again, there were the Cavaliere's persuasive words, woven in among the whip-crackings and commands, as he mingled effects that were his own secret with others of a bewilderingly psychological kind. *'Balla!'* said he. 'Who wants to torture himself like that? Is forcing yourself your idea of freedom? *Una ballatina!* Why, your arms and legs are aching for it. What a relief to give way to them – there, you are dancing already! That is no struggle any more, it is a pleasure!' And so it was. The jerking and twitching of the refractory youth's limbs had at last got the upper hand; he lifted his arms, then his knees, his joints quite suddenly relaxed, he flung his legs and danced, and amid bursts of applause the Cavaliere led him to join the row of puppets on the stage. Up there we could see his face as he 'enjoyed' himself; it was clothed in a broad grin and the eyes were half-shut. In a way, it was consoling to see that he was having a better time than he had had in the hour of his pride.

His 'fall' was, I may say, an epoch. The ice was completely broken, Cipolla's triumph had reached its height. The Circe's wand, that whistling leather whip with the claw handle, held absolute sway. At one time – it must have been well after midnight – not only were there eight or ten persons dancing on the little stage, but in the hall below a varied animation reigned, and a long-toothed Anglo-Saxoness in a pince-nez left her seat of her own motion to perform a tarantella in the centre aisle. Cipolla was lounging in a cane-seated chair at the left of the stage, gulping down the smoke of a cigarette and breathing it impudently out through his bad teeth. He tapped his foot and shrugged his shoulders, looking down upon the abandoned scene in the hall; now and then he snapped his whip backwards at a laggard upon the stage. The children were awake at the moment. With shame I speak of them. For it was not good to be here, least of all for them; that we had not taken them away can only be explained by saying that we had caught the general devil-may-careness of the hour. By that time it was all one. Anyhow, thank goodness, they lacked understanding for the disreputable side of the entertainment, and in their innocence were perpetually charmed by the unheard-of indulgence which permitted them to be present at such a thing as a magician's 'evening'. Whole quarter-hours at a time they drowsed on our laps, waking refreshed and rosy-cheeked, with sleep-drunken eyes, to laugh to bursting at the leaps and jumps the magician made those people up there make. They had not thought it would be so jolly; they joined with their clumsy little hands in every round of applause. And jumped for joy upon their chairs, as was their wont, when Cipolla beckoned to their friend Mario from the Esquisito, beckoned to him just like a picture in a book, holding his hand in front of his nose and bending and straightening the forefinger by turns.

Mario obeyed. I can see him now going up the stairs to Cipolla, who continued to beckon him, in that droll, picturebook sort of way. He hesitated for a moment at first; that, too, I recall quite clearly. During the whole evening he had lounged against a wooden pillar at the side entrance, with his arms folded, or else with his hands thrust into his jacket pockets. He was on our left, near the youth with the militant hair, and had followed the performance attentively, so far as we had seen, if with no particular animation and God knows how much comprehension. He could not much relish being summoned thus, at the end of the evening. But it was only too easy to see why he obeyed. After all, obedience was his calling in life; and then, how should a simple lad like him find it within his human capacity to refuse compliance to a man so throned and crowned as Cipolla at that hour? Willy-nilly he left his column and with a word of thanks to those making way for him he mounted the steps with a doubtful smile on his full lips.

Picture a thickset youth of twenty years, with clipped hair, a low forehead, and heavy-lidded eyes of an indefinite grey, shot with green and yellow. These things I knew from having spoken with him, as we often had. There was a saddle of freckles on the flat nose, the whole upper half of the face retreated behind the lower, and that again was dominated by thick lips that parted to show the salivated teeth. These thick lips and the veiled look of the eyes lent the whole face a primitive melancholy – it was that which had drawn us to him from the first. In it was not the faintest trace of brutality – indeed, his hands would have given the lie to such an idea, being unusually slender and delicate for a southerner. They were hands by which one liked being served.

We knew him humanly without knowing him personally, if I may make that distinction. We saw him nearly every day, and felt a certain kindness for his dreamy ways, which might at times be actual inattentiveness, suddenly transformed into a redeeming zeal to serve. His mien was serious, only the children could bring a smile to his face. It was not sulky, but uningratiating, without intentional effort to please – or rather, it seemed to give up being pleasant in the conviction that it could not succeed. We should have remembered Mario in any case, as one of those homely recollections of travel which often stick in the mind better than more important ones. But of his circumstances we knew no more than that his father was a petty clerk in the Municipio and his mother took in washing.

His white waiter's-coat became him better than the faded striped suit he wore, with a gay coloured scarf instead of a collar, the ends tucked into his jacket. He neared Cipolla, who however did not leave off that motion of his finger before his nose, so that Mario had to come still closer, right up to the chair-seat and the master's legs. Whereupon the latter spread out his elbows and seized the lad, turning him so that we had a view of his face. Then gazed him briskly up and down, with a careless, commanding eye.

'Well, *ragazzo mio*, how comes it we make acquaintance so late in the day? But believe me, I made yours long ago. Yes, yes, I've had you in my eye this long while and known what good stuff you were made of. How could I go and forget you again? Well, I've had a good deal to think about ... Now tell me, what is your name? The first name, that's all I want.'

'My name is Mario,' the young man answered, in a low voice.

'Ah, Mario. Very good. Yes, yes, there is such a name, quite a common name, a classic name too, one of those which preserve the heroic traditions of the Fatherland. *Bravo! Salve!*' And he flung up his arm slantingly above his crooked shoulder, palm outward, in the Roman salute. He may have been slightly tipsy by now, and no wonder; but he spoke as before, clearly, fluently, and with emphasis. Though about this time there had crept into his voice a gross, autocratic note, and a kind of arrogance was in his sprawl.

'Well, now, Mario *mio*,' he went on, 'it's a good thing you came this evening, and that's a pretty scarf you've got on; it is becoming to your style of beauty. It must stand you in good stead with the girls, the pretty pretty girls of Torre –'

From the row of youths, close by the place where Mario had been standing, sounded a laugh. It came from the youth with the militant hair. He stood there, his jacket over his shoulder, and laughed outright, rudely and scornfully.

Mario gave a start. I think it was a shrug, but he may have started and then hastened to cover the movement by shrugging his shoulders, as much as to say that the neckerchief and the fair sex were matters of equal indifference to him.

The Cavaliere gave a downward glance.

'We needn't trouble about him,' he said. 'He is jealous, because your scarf is so popular with the girls, maybe partly because you and I are so friendly up here. Perhaps he'd like me to put him in mind of his colic – I could do it free of charge. Tell me, Mario. You've come here this evening for a bit of fun – and in the daytime you work in an ironmonger's shop?'

'In a café,' corrected the youth.

'Oh, in a café. That's where Cipolla nearly came a cropper! What you are is a cup-bearer, a Ganymede – I like that, it is another classical allusion – *Salvietta!*' Again the Cavaliere saluted, to the huge gratification of his audience.

Mario smiled too. 'But before that,' he interpolated, in the interest of accuracy, 'I worked for a while in a shop in Portoclemente.' He seemed visited by a natural desire to assist the prophecy by dredging out its essential features.

'There, didn't I say so? In an ironmonger's shop?'

'They kept combs and brushes,' Mario got round it.

'Didn't I say that you were not always a Ganymede? Not always at the sign of the serviette? Even when Cipolla makes a mistake, it is a kind that makes you believe in him. Now tell me: Do you believe in me?'

An indefinite gesture.

'A halfway answer,' commented the Cavaliere. 'Probably it is not easy to win your confidence. Even for me, I can see, it is not so easy. I see in your features a reserve, a sadness, *un tratto di malinconia* ... tell me' (he seized Mario's hand persuasively) 'Have you troubles?'

'*Nossignore*,' answered Mario, promptly and decidedly.

'You *have* troubles,' insisted the Cavaliere, bearing down the denial by the weight of his authority. 'Can't I see? Trying to pull the wool over Cipolla's eyes, are you? Of course, about the girls – it is a girl, isn't it? You have love troubles?'

Mario gave a vigorous head-shake. And again the *giovanotto*'s brutal laugh rang out. The Cavaliere gave heed. His eyes were roving about somewhere in the air; but he cocked an ear to the sound, then swung his whip backwards, as he had once or twice before in his conversation with Mario, that none of his puppets might flag in their zeal. The gesture had nearly cost him his new prey: Mario gave a sudden start in the direction of the steps. But Cipolla had him in his clutch.

'Not so fast,' said he. 'That would be fine, wouldn't it? So you want to skip, do you, Ganymede, right in the middle of the fun, or rather, when it is just beginning? Stay with me, I'll show you something nice. I'll convince you. You have no reason to worry, I promise you. This girl – you know her and others know her too – what's her name? Wait! I read the name in your eyes, it is on the tip of my tongue and yours too –'

'Silvestra!' shouted the *giovanotto* from below.

The Cavaliere's face did not change.

'Aren't there the forward people?' he asked, not looking down, more as in undisturbed converse with Mario. 'Aren't there the young fighting-cocks that crow in season and out? Takes the word out of your mouth, the conceited fool, and seems to think he has some special right to it. Let him be. But Silvestra, your Silvestra – ah, what a girl that is! What a prize! Brings your heart into your mouth to see her walk or laugh or breathe, she is so lovely. And her round arms when she washes, and tosses her head back to get the hair out of her eyes! An angel from paradise!'

Mario stared at him, his head thrust forward. He seemed to have forgotten the audience, forgotten where he was. The red rings round his eyes had got larger, they looked as though they were painted on. His thick lips parted.

'And she makes you suffer, this angel,' went on Cipolla, 'or, rather, you make yourself suffer for her – there is a difference, my lad, a most important difference, let me tell you. There are misunderstandings in love, maybe nowhere else in the world are there so many. I know what you are thinking: what does this Cipolla, with his little physical defect, know about love? Wrong, all wrong, he knows a lot. He has a wide and powerful understanding of its workings, and it pays to listen to his advice. But let's leave Cipolla out, cut him out altogether and think only of Silvestra, your peerless Silvestra! What! Is she to

155

give any young gamecock the preference, so that he can laugh while you cry? To prefer him to a chap like you, so full of feeling and so sympathetic? Not very likely, is it? It is impossible – we know better, Cipolla and she. If I were to put myself in her place and choose between the two of you, a tarry lout like that – a codfish, a sea-urchin – and a Mario, a knight of the serviette, who moves among gentlefolk and hands round refreshments with an air – my word, but my heart would speak in no uncertain tones – it knows to whom I gave it long ago. It is time that he should see and understand, my chosen one! It is time that you see me and recognize me, Mario, my beloved! Tell me, who am I?'

It was grisly, the way the betrayer made himself irresistible, wreathed and coquetted with his crooked shoulder, languished with the puffy eyes, and showed his splintered teeth in a sickly smile. And alas, at his beguiling words, what was come of our Mario? It is hard for me to tell, hard as it was for me to see; for here was nothing less than an utter abandonment of the inmost soul, a public exposure of timid and deluded passion and rapture. He put his hands across his mouth, his shoulders rose and fell with his pantings. He could not, it was plain, trust his eyes and ears for joy, and the one thing he forgot was precisely that he could not trust them. 'Silvestra!' he breathed, from the very depths of his vanquished heart.

'Kiss me!' said the hunchback. 'Trust me, I love thee. Kiss me here.' And with the tip of his index finger, hand, arm, and little finger outspread, he pointed to his cheek, near the mouth. And Mario bent and kissed him.

It had grown very still in the room. That was a monstrous moment, grotesque and thrilling, the moment of Mario's bliss. In that evil span of time, crowded with a sense of the illusiveness of all joy, one sound became audible, and that not quite at once, but on the instant of the melancholy and ribald meeting between Mario's lips and the repulsive flesh which thrust itself forward for his caress. It was the sound of a laugh, from the *giovanotto* on our left. It broke into the dramatic suspense of the moment, coarse, mocking, and yet – or I must have been grossly mistaken – with an undertone of compassion for the poor

bewildered, victimized creature. It had a faint ring of that
'*Poveretto*' which Cipolla had declared was wasted on the
wrong person, when he claimed the pity for his own.

The laugh still rang in the air when the recipient of the caress
gave his whip a little swish, low down, close to his chair-leg,
and Mario started up and flung himself back. He stood in that
posture staring, his hands one over the other on those desecrated
lips. Then he beat his temples with his clenched fists, over and
over; turned and staggered down the steps, while the audience
applauded, and Cipolla sat there with his hands in his lap, his
shoulders shaking. Once below, and even while in full retreat,
Mario hurled himself round with legs flung wide apart; one
arm flew up, and two flat shattering detonations crashed
through applause and laughter.

There was instant silence. Even the dancers came to a full
stop and stared about, struck dumb. Cipolla bounded from his
seat. He stood with his arms spread out, slanting as though to
ward everybody off, as though next moment he would cry out:
'Stop! Keep back! Silence! What was that?' Then, in that
instant, he sank back in his seat, his head rolling on his chest; in
the next he had fallen sideways to the floor, where he lay
motionless, a huddled heap of clothing, with limbs awry.

The commotion was indescribable. Ladies hid their faces,
shuddering, on the breasts of their escorts. There were shouts
for a doctor, for the police. People flung themselves on Mario in
a mob, to disarm him, to take away the weapon that hung from
his fingers – that small, dull-metal, scarcely pistol-shaped tool
with hardly any barrel – in how strange and unexpected a direction had fate levelled it!

And now – now finally, at last – we took the children and led
them towards the exit, past the pair of *carabinieri* just entering.
Was that the end, they wanted to know, that they might go in
peace? Yes, we assured them, that was the end. An end of
horror, a fatal end. And yet a liberation – for I could not, and I
cannot, but find it so!

THE TRANSPOSED HEADS
(*1940*)

THE story of Sita of the beautiful hips, daughter of the cattle-breeder Sumantra of the warrior caste, and of her two husbands (if one may put it like that) is so sanguinary, so amazing to the senses, that it makes the greatest demands on the hearer's strength of mind and his power to resist the gruesome guiles of Maya. It would be well for the listener to take pattern from the fortitude of the teller, for it requires, if anything, more courage to tell such a tale than to hear it. But here it is, from first to last, just as it fell out:

At the time when memory mounted in the mind of man, as the vessel of sacrifice slowly fills up from the bottom with drink or with blood; when the womb of stern patriarchal piety opened to the seed of the primeval past, nostalgia for the Mother re-invested with new shudderings the ancient images and swelled the number of pilgrims thronging in the spring to the shrines of the great World-Nurse; at such a time it was that two youths, little different in age and caste, but very unlike in body, were vowed to friendship. The younger was named Nanda, the some-what elder Shridaman. The first was eighteen years old, the second already one-and-twenty; both, each on his proper day, had been girt with the sacred cord and received into the com-pany of the twice-born. Their homes were in the temple village called Welfare of Cows, which had been settled in time past on a sign from the gods in its place in the land of Kosala. It was surrounded by a cactus hedge and a wooden wall; its gates, facing the four points of the compass, had been blessed by a wandering wise man and familiar of the goddess Speech – who uttered no unrighteous word, and had been given to eat in the village – with the blessing that its door-posts and lintels should drop fatness and honey.

The friendship between the two youths was based on the diversity in their I- and my-feelings, those of the one yearning towards those of the other. Incorporation, that is, makes for isolation, isolation for difference, difference makes for comparisons, comparisons give rise to uneasiness, uneasiness to wonderment, wonderment tends to admiration; and finally admiration turns to a yearning for mutual exchange and unity. *Etad vai tad*. This is that. And the doctrine applies especially in youth, when the clay of life is still soft and the I- and my-feelings not yet hardened into the conflicts of the single personality.

Young Shridaman was a merchant, and the son of a merchant; Nanda, on the other hand, both a smith and cowherd, for his father Garga not only kept cattle on the meadow and in the byre, but also plied the hammer and fanned the fire with a feather fan. As for Shridaman's sire, Bhavabhuti by name, he traced his line on the male side from a Brahman stock versed in the Vedas, which Garga and his son were far from doing. Still, they were no Sudras, and although somewhat goat-nosed, were quite distinctly members of human society. Anyhow, for Shridaman, and even for Bhavabhuti, the Brahman way of life was only a memory, for Bhavabhuti's father had deliberately abandoned it at the stage of householder, which follows that of student, and never gone on to be either forest hermit or ascetic to the end of his days. He had scorned to live only on gifts from pious respecters of his knowledge of the Vedas, perhaps he had not been content with these; for he had opened up a good business in mull, silk and calico, camphor and sandalwood. And his son in his turn, though begotten for the service of the gods, had become a vanija or merchant in the village of Welfare of Cows, and Bhavabhuti's son Shridaman followed in his father's footsteps, after having previously devoted some years to grammar and the elements of astronomy and ontology, under the supervision of a guru or spiritual preceptor.

Not so Nanda, son of Garga. His Karma was otherwise; and never, either by tradition or by inheritance, had he had to do with things of the mind. No, he was just as he was, a son of the people, simple and blithe, a Krishna-manifestation, dark of skin and hair; he even had the 'lucky-calf' lock on his breast. His work as a smith had made powerful his arms; that as a shepherd had been further an advantage, for he had a well-set-up body, which he loved to rub with mustard oil and drape with gold ornaments and chains of wild flowers. There was harmony between it and the pleasant beardless face, despite the rather thick lips and the suggestion of a goat-nose; even these were attractive in their way, and his black eyes almost always wore a laugh.

Shridaman very much liked all this, comparing it with himself, who was several shades lighter in both head and limbs, with a face too quite otherwise shaped. The ridge of his nose was thin as a blade; eyes he had, soft of pupil and lid, and on his cheeks a soft fan-shaped beard. Soft too were his limbs, not moulded by exercise as cow-herd and smith, even rather Brahman-like, as well as clerkly, with a rather soft, narrow breast and some fat on the little belly, but otherwise flawless, with fine knee-joints and feet. It was a body proper to serve as adjunct and appendage to a noble and knowledgeable headpiece, that was of course head and front of the whole, whereas with the whole Nanda the body was, so to speak, the main thing, and the head merely a pleasing appendage. All in all the two were like Siva in his double manifestation, lying sometimes as dead, a bearded ascetic, at the feet of the goddess, but sometimes erect, a figure in the bloom of youth, stretching his young limbs as he turns towards her.

But after all they were not one like Siva, who is life and death, world and eternity in the Mother, but manifested as two entities here below; thus they were to each other like images. The my-feeling of each was tired of itself, and though each was aware that after all everything consists of what it has not got, yet on account of their very differences they intrigued each other. The fine-lipped, soft-bearded Shridaman found pleasure in the rude primeval Krishna-nature of the thick-lipped Nanda; while he, partly flattered, but partly and even more, because he felt impressed by Shridaman's light complexion, his noble headpiece and correct diction – all that, of course, being from the beginning of things inseparable from wisdom and philosophy, and one with these – on his side knew nothing more lovely than intercourse with Shridaman; thus it was they became fast friends. Certainly in the inclination of each for the other some slight humour inhered; Nanda privately made fun of Shridaman's plumpness and blondness, his thin nose and punctilious speech. Shridaman, on the other hand, smiled at Nanda's goat-nose and rustic simplicity. This sort of private criticism is a common feature of the uneasiness born of comparison; it is a tribute to the I- and my-feeling, and does no least violence to the Maya longing born of the same.

2

Well, then, it came about that in the lovely springtime, when the air was full of the song of birds, Nanda and Shridaman took a walking-tour together through the country, each on his own occasions. Nanda had from his father Garga the task of buying a certain quantity of black ore from a community of humble folk, clad only in reed aprons, who were skilful smelters and with whom Nanda knew how to talk. These folk dwelt in mud huts some days' journey from the friends' village, and nearer the town of Kurukshetra, which, in its turn, was some-what north of the thickly populated Indraprastha, on the river Jumna. Here Shridaman's errand lay, with a business friend of the family, himself a Brahman who had not got farther than the stage of householder. With this man Shridaman was to barter to the best advantage some fine-coloured cloths woven by the village women at home, for some rice-mallets and a particularly practical kind of tinder, of which there was need at Welfare of Cows.

They had travelled a day and a half, on peopled highways and through empty woods and wastes, each bearing his fardel on his back: Nanda a box of betel-nuts, cowrie-shells, and alta-red on bast paper to redden the soles of the feet, for with these he thought to pay the humble folk for their ore; Shridaman his cloths sewed up in a doeskin. Nanda out of sheer friend-liness carried the other's burden too, from time to time. They came now to a bathing-place, sacred to Kali, the All-Embrac-ing, Mother of the worlds and of all beings, who is the dream-drunkenness of Vishnu. It lay on the stream Goldfly, which rushes, like a colt let loose, out of the mountain's womb, to moderate its flow and unite at a holy place with the river Jumna; that in its turn issuing, at a place yet more holy, into the eternal Ganges. But the Ganges flows by its many mouths into the sea. Many bathing-places of high repute, which cleanse all defilement, where one drawing up the water of life and plunging into its bosom may receive new birth – many such stand on the banks and mouths of the Ganges, and at the junction of other rivers with the terrestrial Milky Way, as at the point where Goldfly, little daughter of the snows, joins with the Jumna. Everywhere in this region, in short, such shrines and sites of purification abound, convenient to all for sacrifice and communion. They are provided with consecrated steps, so that the pious need not plump awkwardly and irreligiously through reed and lotus into the water, but may step down in dignity to drink and to lave themselves.

Now, this bathing-place the friends had hit on was not one of the larger ones, full of offerings, renowned for its miracles, and thronged by noble and simple, though at different hours. No, it was a quiet, retired little spot, not a meeting of rivers, just somewhere on the river-bank, which at that point climbed above the bed of the Goldfly. On the top of the bank stood the little temple, built simply of wood and already somewhat rickety though carved in pleasing designs. It was the temple of the Mistress of all desires and joys, with a bulbous tower above the cella. The steps leading to the spring were wooden too and rather broken, yet good enough for a dignified descent.

The youths expressed their pleasure at having hit on this spot, which gave them opportunity for worship, refreshment, and rest in the shade. It was already very hot at midday; the heavy summer threatened untimely, and at the sides of the little temple the growth of mangoes, teak and kadamba trees, magnolias, tamarisks, and tala palms made shelter where it would be good to rest and breakfast. The friends first performed their religious duties, as well as circumstances permitted. There was no priest from whom to purchase oil or clarified butter to anoint the stone linga images on the little terrace before the temple.

They found a ladle, scooped up water from the river, and did their pious service, murmuring the appropriate words. Then they descended, cupping their hands, into the green river-bed; drank, poured the ritual water, dipped, and gave thanks. Out of pure enjoyment they stopped in the water a little longer than the spiritually requisite time; then, feeling in all their limbs the blessing of purification, returned to the resting-place they had selected under the trees.

Here like brothers they shared their bite, though one had no different from the other, and each might have eaten his own. When Nanda broke a barley cake, he handed half of it to Shridaman saying: 'There, old fellow.' Shridaman, dividing a piece of fruit, gave half to Nanda with the same words. Shridaman sat to eat, sideways to his food, knees and feet together, in the grass that was here still green and unsinged. Nanda squatted rustically with his knees up and feet in front of him, as one cannot long sit without being born to it. They took up these attitudes unconsciously and without thought; if they had paid heed to the manner of their sitting, Shridaman, out of sheer inclination to the primitive, would have sat with his knees up and Nanda put himself sideways in the contrary desire. He wore a little cap on his sleek black hair, still wet from the bath, a loincloth of white cotton cloth, rings on his upper arms, and round his neck a necklace of stone-pearls held together with gold bands. Through it one could see the 'lucky-calf' lock on his breast. Shridaman had a white cloth wound around his head and wore his white cotton short-sleeved smock falling over his full draped apron, that hung like trousers. In the neck-opening of the smock there showed an amulet-pouch on a thin chain. Both wore the sign of their faith painted in mineral-white on their foreheads.

When they had eaten they put aside the remnants and talked. It was so delightful here that princes and kings could not have fared better. Between the tall stems of calamus and bamboo, whose foliage and clusters of blossoms made a light rustling, they could see the pool and the lower steps going down to it. Clinging water-plants made charming garlands from bough to bough. The chirping and trilling of unseen birds mingled with the humming of insects that darted to and fro returning ever and anon to the flowering grasses. The cool freshness and warm breath of all these plants perfumed the air; there was the headiness of the jasmine, the peculiar scent of the tala-fruit; sandalwood and mustard oil – Nanda had anointed himself with this last after the ritual of the bath.

'Here we seem to be beyond the six waves of hunger and thirst, age and death, suffering and blindness,' said Shridaman. 'It is extraordinarily peaceful. It is as though we were moved from the restless whirl of life and placed in its motionless centre where we can draw a long breath. Hark! How cosy and hushed it is here! I use the word 'hushed' because we say hush when we want to listen; and listening can only properly be done where there is a hush. It lets us listen to everything in it which is not entirely still, so that the stillness speaks as in a dream and we hear it to, as though we were dreaming.'

'It is verily true as thy word sayeth,' responded Nanda. 'In the noise of the marketplace one does not listen; that is only done where there is a hush that even so holds this and that to listen to. Quite soundless, filled with silence, is only Nirvana, and so you could never call it hushed, nor yet cosy.'

'No,' answered Shridaman, and could not help laughing. 'It has probably not occurred to anyone to call Nirvana hushed, and certainly not cosy; yet you do it, in a sort of way, if only by negation, when you say that one cannot do it; and so you find out the funniest of all the negations – for only so can Nirvana be spoken of, of course – that could ever be uttered about it. You do say such shrewd things sometimes, if I may use the word 'shrewd' about something which is at once absurd and perfectly correct. I like it very much, sometimes it makes my diaphragm contract suddenly, almost like a sob. Thus we see how close together are laughing and weeping; so that it is an illusion to make any distinction between pleasure and pain, and like the one and hate the other, when, after all, both can be called good and both bad. But there is a combination of laughter and tears which one can most readily assent to and call good among all things that move us in life. We have a word for it, we call it touching; it has to do with sympathy on the cheerful side, and is just what makes the contraction of my diaphragm so much like a sob. And it is that that hurts me about your shrewdness.'

'But why does it hurt you?' Nanda asked.

'Because after all you are actually a child of Samsara and thus completely taken up with life,' answered Shridaman; 'you do not belong among the souls who feel the need to emerge above the frightful ocean of laughing and weeping as lotus flowers rise above the surface of the stream and open their cups to the sky. You are perfectly at home in the depths, where such a complex profusion and variety of shapes and forms exist. You are well off, and that is why one feels good at the sight of you. Then you suddenly get the idea in your head to meddle with Nirvana and talk about its negative condition and how it cannot be called hushed nor cosy, and all that is funny enough to make one weep, or, to use the word made on purpose, it is touching, because it makes me grieve for that well-being of yours that is so good to see.'

'But listen to me,' countered Nanda. 'I don't understand. You might be sorry I am so taken up with Samsara and cannot go in for being a lotus. That is all right. But to be hurt because I try to take an interest in Nirvana, as well as I can – that might not be so good. You have hurt me too, let me tell you.'

'And how so?' Shridaman asked.

'Because you have read the Vedas and learned about the nature of being,' replied Nanda, 'but even so you are more easily blinded by Samsara than people who have not. That is what really tickles me; it gives me, as you say, a feeling of sympathy on the cheerful side. It is more or less hushed in this spot where we are; so you let yourself go on about being beyond the six waves of hunger and thirst, and think you are in life's resting centre. And yet all the hush, and all the things you can listen to in it, are just a sign that there is a lot going on and your notions about peace and quiet are just notions. The birds coo because they are making love; all these bees and bugs and cockchafers are darting about in search of food; the grass is alive with sounds of life-and-death struggles we cannot hear. The very vines so tenderly embracing the trees would like to strangle them to take their sap and air to batten on. And there you have the true knowledge of life.'

'I know it well,' Shridaman said. 'I do not blind myself to it, or at least only for the moment and because I want to. For there is not only the truth and knowledge of the understanding, but also the insight of the human heart, which sees as in an allegory and knows how to read the handwriting of all phenomena, not only in its first and simple sense but also in its second and higher one, using it as a means whereby to look through at the pure and spiritual. How will you arrive at a perception of peace, and feel the joy of a cessation from conflict, unless you have a Maya-image to give you a hold on it – though in itself a Maya-image is by no means peace and joy! It is granted and vouchsafed to man to make actuality serve him to see the truth by; language has coined the word "poetry" to express this boon.'

'Ah, so that is what you think,' laughed Nanda. 'According to that, and if one listens to you, poetry would also be the stupidity that comes after the cleverness, and, suppose a man is stupid, it is in order to ask whether he is still being stupid or being stupid again. I must say, you clever ones do not make it easy for the likes of us. We think the point is to become clever; but before one reaches it, one finds out the real point is to become stupid again. You ought not to show us the new and higher stages, for fear we lose courage to climb the first ones.'

'From me,' said Shridaman, 'you have not heard that one must be clever. Come, let us stretch out in the soft grass after our meal and look through the branches of the trees into the sky. It is such a wonderful thing to look from a station which does not actually oblige us to look up, because the eyes are already directed upwards, and to see the sky in the way that Mother Earth sees it.'

'Siya, be it so,' Nanda agreed.

'Siyat!' Shridaman corrected him, in the pure tongue. Nanda laughed at himself and them both.

'Siyat, Siyat!' he repeated. 'Hair-splitter, leave me my lingo! When I speak Sanskrit it sounds like the snuffling of a young heifer with a rope through her nose.'

166

At this bucolic simile Shridaman too laughed heartily; and they stretched themselves out as he had said and looked straight up through the swaying boughs and flowering bushes into the blue of Vishnu's heaven, waving broken-off branches to protect themselves from the red-and-white flies, called Children of Indra, that came to settle on their skins. Nanda had lain down, not because he cared in particular to look at the sky as Mother Earth did, merely out of good nature. He soon sat up again and assumed his Dravidian attitude, with a flower in his mouth.

'The Child of Indra is a confounded nuisance,' he said, speaking of the darting host of flies as one and the same individual. 'Probably he is attracted by my good mustard oil. Or it might be he has orders from his protector the elephant-rider, lord of the thunderbolt, the great god, to torment us as punishment – you know already why.'

'That should not affect you,' responded Shridaman; 'for you voted under the tree that Indra's thanksgiving feast last autumn should be celebrated in the old or shall we rather say in the newer way, according to the ritual and the Brahmanic observance; you can wash your hands of the rest, even if we did afterwards in council decide otherwise and give Indra notice that we were turning to a newer or rather an older thanksgiving service, one which seems more natural to the religious feeling of us village folk than the patter of the Brahman service for Indra the Thunderer, who burst the strongholds of the aborigines.'

'Certainly, as thy word sayeth, so is it,' replied Nanda. 'For my part, I still have an uncanny feeling, for even when I gave my voice under the tree for Indra, I was afraid he might not bother himself about such small matters and would just make all of us generally responsible for being done out of his feast at Welfare of Cows. Then it occurs to the people and comes into their heads, I don't know from where, that the Indra thanksgiving service is no longer the right thing, at least not for us shepherds and farmers and we must think about pious simplification. What, said they, have we to do with the great Indra? The Brahmans, with their knowledge of the Vedas, may pay their homage with endless repetitions. As for us, we will sacrifice to the cows and mountains and forest meadows because they are our true and proper deities. And it seems to us that is what we had done before Indra came, who preceded the Coming One, and burst the strongholds of the primitive inhabitants; and even though we no longer rightly know what is to be done, yet it will come to us, and our hearts shall teach us. We will pay homage to our Bright Peak and its pastures, in our own countryside, with pious rites which are in so far new that we shall have to look for them in our hearts, remember and fetch them out again. To Bright Peak will we sacrifice the perfect of the herd, to him bring offerings of sour milk, flowers, fruit, and uncooked rice. Afterwards the herd of cows, wearing garlands of autumn flowers, shall rove over the mountain turning to him their right flanks, and the steers shall bellow to him with the thunder-voice of clouds heavy with rain. And that shall be our mountain worship, new and old. But in order that the Brahmans may have naught against it, we will feast them to the number of many hundreds; and from all the herds we will collect milk so that they can eat their fill of curds and rice-milk, and so may they be content. Thus spake some of those under the tree, and some agreed with them, but others did not. I voted from the first against the mountain rites, for I had great fear and reverence for Indra, who broke the strongholds of the blacks; and I do not hold with reviving things that nobody any longer rightly knows. But you spoke and uttered pure and right words – I mean right in respect to the language – in favour of the new form of the feast and for the renewal of the mountain rites over Indra's head, and so I was silent. For I thought: when those who have gone to school and learned something about the nature of being, speak against Indra and in favour of simplification, then we others can have nothing to say, we can only hope that the great Comer and Breaker of strongholds will have some judgement and be satisfied with the feeding of multitudes of Brahmans, so that he does not afflict us with drought or overwhelm us with rains. Perhaps, I thought, he is tired of his feast himself and thinks it would be more fun to have the mountain sacrifice and the procession of cows instead. We simple ones had great reverence for him; but perhaps he has not so much for himself these days. In the end I very much liked the revived rite and enjoyed helping to drive the garlanded cows about the mountain. Yet I will say, when you corrected my Prakrit and wanted me to say Siyat, it struck me again how strange it is that you are using your correct and cultured speech in the interest of simplification.'

'You have no ground to reproach me,' Shridaman answered, 'for you yourself have been using the popular tongue to uphold the Brahman rites. You probably took pleasure in it. But let me tell you: there is far more pleasure in using correct and cultured words to support the claims of simplicity.'

3

They were silent for a while. Shridaman still lay as he was and gazed up into the sky. Nanda held his muscular arms clasped round his knees and looked between the trees down the slope towards the bathing-place of Mother Kali.

'Sh-h! Thunder and lightning! Bolts and blazes!' he whispered all of a sudden, and laid his finger to his thick lips. 'Shridaman, brother, sit up and look very quietly. Going down to bathe, I mean. Open your eyes, it's worth the trouble! She cannot see us, but we can see her.'

A young girl stood at the lonely shrine, about to perform the ritual of the bath. She had laid her sari and bodice on the steps and stood there quite nude, save only for some beads round her neck, her swaying earrings, and a white ribbon round her thick hair. The loveliness of her body was dazzling. Made of Maya it seemed, and of the most enchanting tint, neither too dark nor too pale, and more like a bronze with golden lights. Gloriously formed she was, after the thoughts of Brahma, with the sweetest childish shoulders, and hips deliciously curved, making a spacious pelvic cavity, with maidenly firm, budlike breasts and splendidly spreading buttocks that narrowed above to the smallest, most tender back. How supply it curved, as she raised her slender arms and clasped her hands at the back of her neck, so that the delicate armpits showed darkly! In all this the most striking thing, the most adequately representative of Brahma's thoughts – yet without prejudice to the dazzling sweetness of

169

the breasts, which must infallibly win over any soul to the life of sense – was the conjunction of the magnificent rear with the slimness and pliant suppleness of a back of elfin delicacy. By way of emphasis was the other contrast, between the splendid swing of the hips – this of itself worthy of a whole paean of praise – and the dainty attenuation round the waist. Just such a shape must have had the heavenly maid Pramlocha, sent by Indra to the ascetic Kandu to wean him from his austerity lest he attain to divine power.

'Let us withdraw,' Shridaman said, as he sat up, his eyes resting on the maiden's form. 'It is not right that she sees us not, yet we see her.'

'Why not?' answered Nanda in a whisper. 'We were here first, to enjoy the peace and the hush; and whatever else may come along, we cannot help it. We will not stir; it would be cruel if we made off, crackling the bushes, and she learned she had been seen while she saw not. I look with pleasure – you do not? Your eyes are red, as when you recite texts from the Rig-Veda.'

'Be quiet!' Shridaman admonished him in turn. 'And be serious. This is a serious, a sacred sight; that we look on at it is only excusable if we do it with serious and pious minds.'

'Yes, of course,' answered Nanda. 'Certainly such a thing is no joke; but say what you like, it is a pleasure. You wanted to look into the sky from the flat earth. Now you see one can sometimes see into heaven only by standing up and looking straight ahead.'

They were silent awhile, moved not at all, and looked. The gold-bronze maid did as they had done a little before, laid her cupped palms together and prayed, before descending to her purification.

They saw her a little from one side, so it did not escape them that not only her body but her face as well, between the hanging earrings, was of the rarest sweetness: little nose, lips, brows, and especially the long slanting eyes like lotus petals. She turned her head slightly, startling the friends lest she might be aware of them; and they could see that this charming figure suffered no least detraction from an ugly face; rather that harmony ruled throughout and the loveliness of the features fully bore out the loveliness of the form.

'But I know her!' Nanda suddenly murmured, with a snap of his fingers. 'This very minute do I recognize her; only up to now did she escape me. That is Sita, daughter of Sumantra from the village of the Bisons near here. She came hither from her home to do her ablutions, of course. Why should I not know her? I swung her up to the sun.'

'You swung her?' asked Shridaman, low-voiced but urgently. And Nanda replied:

'Why not? With all the strength of my arms, before all the people. In her clothes I should have known her at once. But who would recognize a naked person straight off? That's Sita of Bisonbull. I was there last spring to visit my aunt, and it was at the feast of aid to the sun; but she —'

'Later, I pray you,' Shridaman interrupted in an anxious whisper. 'The great good fortune that we may see her so close has also the misfortune that she might hear us. Not another word or we shall alarm her.'

'Then she might run away and you would see her no more, and you have not seen your fill,' Nanda said teasingly. But the other motioned him peremptorily, and once more they sat silent, watching Sita perform her ritual. She prayed first, then, with her face turned heavenwards, stepped cautiously into the pool, took up water and drank, and dipped in as far as the crown of her head, on which she laid her hand. Afterwards for a while she dipped and played and slipped in and out; after a time she stepped back on dry land, cool and dripping and most beautiful to see. Even therewith was not quite an end to the favour vouchsafed to the friends; for after the purificatory bath the maid sat down on the steps that the sun might dry her. And her native charm, released by the conviction that she was quite alone, made her fall into first one, then another most pleasing posture. Only after some little time, and then only slowly, did she don her clothes and disappear up the temple stair.

'Well, that's all there is of that,' said Nanda. 'Now we can at least speak and move about. In the long run it gets tiresome to act as though you were not there.'

'I do not see how you can use such a word,' retorted Shridaman. 'Could there be a more blissful state than to lose oneself in such a sight and be present only in its presence? I should have liked to hold my breath the whole time; not out of fear of losing sight of her face, but for fear of undeceiving her belief that she was alone; for that I trembled and felt myself sacredly responsible. She is called Sita, you say? I am glad to know, it consoles me for my offence, that I may pay her honour by name to myself. And you know her from swinging her?'

'As I tell you,' Nanda assured him. 'She was chosen as sunmaiden last spring when I was in her village, and I swung her in aid of the sun so high in the heavens that one could hardly hear her screams. Or else they were lost in the screaming of the crowd.'

'You were lucky,' said Shridaman. 'You are always lucky. It must have been on account of your stout arms they chose you to swing her. I can just see how she rose and flew up into the blue. My imaginary picture of her flight blends with the one we saw just now, where she stood like a statue, bowed in prayer.'

'Anyhow,' said Nanda, 'she has ground for prayer and penance; not on account of her behaviour, for she is a very good girl, but on account of her looks. Certainly she cannot help them, yet after all, strictly speaking, she is responsible for them. A figure like that is taking. But why taking? Just because it takes us captive, makes us prisoners to the world of delights and desires. It tangles the beholder deeper in the snares of Samsara, so he simply loses consciousness just the way one loses one's breath. That is the effect she has even if it is not her intention. But her lengthening her eyes in the shape of a lotus leaf makes it look like intention. You may say the fine figure was given her, she did not deliberately take it, so she has nothing to repent on that score. But the truth is, there are cases where no real difference exists between 'given' and 'taken': she knows that herself, probably she prays for pardon just because she is so 'taking'. This figure of hers, she has taken it – not as one just accepts something that is given, she really put it on, of herself. No amount of ritual bathing can alter that: she comes out with the very same taking behind she took in.'

'You should not speak so coarsely,' Shridaman chided him with feeling, 'of such a tender and sacred being. True, you have ventured into the field of metaphysics, but I must tell you you express yourself very rustically there; and the use you make of what knowledge you have makes it clear you were not worthy of the vision. For everything depended on the spirit in which we looked on.'

Nanda received the reproach in all modesty.

'Teach me, then, Dau-ji (elder brother),' he begged, 'in what spirit you looked on and how I should have done.'

'Lo,' said Shridaman, 'all beings have two sorts of existence: one for themselves and one for the eyes of others. They are, and also they are to be seen, soul and image; and ever is it sinful to let oneself be influenced by the image only and not to heed the soul. It is necessary to overcome the disgust inspired in us at sight of the scurvy beggar. We must not stop at the effect it has on our eyes and senses. For what affects us is impression, not reality; we must go behind it to reach the knowledge to which every phenomenon can lay claim, for it is more than appearance, and one must find the being, the soul, behind it. But not only shall we not stop at the disgust aroused in us by the sight of misery. Just as little must we dwell on the desire which the image of the beautiful inspires; this, too, being more than image, although the temptation of the senses to take it only as such is perhaps even greater than in the case of the repulsive beggar. The beautiful, that is, seems to make no claim on our conscience, no demand that we enter into its soul, whereas the image of the beggar, by its very misery, does. Yet we are equally guilty if we simply feast on the sight of beauty without inquiring into its being. And our debt to it is even greater, so it seems to me, if we see it while it does not see us. Let me tell you, Nanda, it was a real boon to me that you could name the name of her whom we watched, Sita, daughter of Sumantra; for it gave me to know something of that which is more than the image, since the name is a part of the essence and of the soul. Happier still I was to hear from you that she is a good maiden; for that was a means still more easily to go behind her image and understand her soul. And then her lengthening her eyes in

173

the shape of a lotus leaf, and painting the lashes a little – that, you might say, is all only custom and has nothing to do with morality; she does it in all innocence, her morals being dependent upon convention. But, after all, beauty too has a duty towards its image; perhaps in fulfilling it she only seeks to increase the desire to ask after her soul. I like to imagine that she has a good father in Sumantra, and a careful mother, and has been brought up in piety; I can fancy her life and occupations as daughter of the house, how she grinds the corn on the stone, makes the porridge on the hearth, or spins the wool to a fine thread. Having been guilty of beholding her image, my heart cries out to have it become a person.'

'That I can understand,' responded Nanda. 'But you must remember that this wish cannot be so lively with me, since she already was more of a person to me, because I swung her up to the sun.'

'Only too much,' replied Shridaman, whose voice had betrayed a certain quiver throughout. 'Obviously only too much; for this familiarity which you were vouchsafed – whether with justice or not, I will not say, for you owed it to your strong arms and your whole sturdy body, not to your head and the thoughts of your head – this familiarity seems to have made her entirely a material being in your eyes and dulled your gaze for the higher meaning of such a manifestation. Otherwise you would not have spoken with such unpardonable coarseness of the fine shape it has taken on. Do you not know, then, that in every female shape – child, maid, mother, or grey-haired woman – *she*, the All-Mother, hides herself, the all-nourisher, Sakti, the great goddess; of whose womb all things come, into whose womb all things go; whom we honour and praise in every manifestation that bears her sign? In her most worshipful shape she has revealed herself to us here on the bank of the little stream Goldfly; shall we not then be most deeply moved by her revealing herself thus – to the extent that in fact, now that I notice it, my voice somewhat trembles – though that may in part be due to displeasure at your manner of speaking?'

'And your cheeks and forehead are red as fire,' said Nanda, 'and your voice, though it trembles, has a fuller ring than common. I can assure you that I too in my way was quite affected.'

'Then I do not understand,' answered Shridaman, 'how you can talk so inadequately and reproach her for her fine figure that so confuses people that the breath of consciousness goes out of them! That is to look at things with culpable one-sidedness and to show yourself entirely empty of the true and real essence of her who revealed herself to us in so sweet an image. For she is All and not only one; life and death, madness and wisdom, enchantress and liberatress, knowest thou not that? Knowest only that she befools and bewitches the host of created beings and not also that she leads them out beyond the darkness of confusion to knowledge of the truth? Then you know very little and have not grasped a great and difficult mystery: that the very drunkenness she puts upon us is the same as the exaltation which bears us on to truth and freedom. For so it is, that what enchains us frees us, and that exaltation it is that binds together beauty of sense and beauty of spirit.'

Nanda's black eyes glittered with tears, for he was easily moved and could scarcely listen to metaphysical language without weeping; especially at this moment, when Shridaman's otherwise rather thin voice had suddenly taken on a deep note that went to his heart. He drew a breath rather like a sob through his goat-nose as he said:

'How you speak today, Dau-ji, so solemnly! I think I have never heard you speak so strangely; it touches me very near. I could wish you would not go on, I feel it so much. And yet I beg you to, do please go on about the spirit and the chains and the All-Embracing one!'

'So you see,' Shridaman went on in his exalted strain, 'the meaning of it all, and how it is not only madness but wisdom that she confers. If what I say moves you, it is because she is mistress of the fluent word, mingled with the wisdom of Brahma. In her twofold shape we recognize her greatness; for she is the wrathful one, black and terrifying, drinking the blood of creatures out of steaming vessels; but at the same time is she the white and gracious one, source of all being, cherishing all forms of life at her nourishing breast. Vishnu's great Maya is

175

she, she holds him embraced, he dreams in her; but we dream in him. Many waters flow into the eternal Ganges, but the Ganges flows into the sea. So we flow into Vishnu's world-dreaming godhead; but that into the sea of the Mother. Lo, we came to a place where our life-dream flowed into the sacred bathing-place, and there appeared to us the All-Mother, the All-Consumer, in whose womb we bathed, in her sweetest shape, to amaze and to exalt us – very likely as a reward, because we honoured her procreative emblem and poured water to it. Linga and Yoni – there is no greater sign and no greater hour in life than when the man is summoned with his Sakti to circle round the bridal fire, their hands are united with the flowery bond and he speaks the words: "I have received her!" When he takes her from the hand of her parents and speaks the royal word: "He am I, this is you; heaven I, earth you; I the music of the song, you the words; so shall we make the journey together." When they celebrate the meeting – no longer human beings more, not he and she, one male one female, but the great pair, he Siva, she Durga, the high and awful goddess; when their words wander and are no more *their* words, but a stammering out of the drunken deeps and they die away to the highest life in the supernal joy of their embrace. Such is the holy hour which laves us in wisdom and grants us release from the delusions of the ego in the womb of the Mother. For as sense and spirit flow together in rapture, so do life and death in love!'

Nanda was utterly ravished by these metaphysical words.

'No,' said he, shaking his head, while the tears sprang from his eyes, 'but the goddess of eloquence is gracious to you, endowing you with the wisdom of Brahma till I can hardly bear to listen, yet would have you go on for ever. If I could sing and say even a fifth part of all that comes out of your headpiece I would love and honour myself in all my members. That is why you are so necessary to me, my elder brother; what I have not you have, and you are my friend, so that it is almost as though I had it myself. For as your fellow I have a part in you, and so I am a little bit Shridaman; but without you I were only Nanda, and that is not enough. I tell you freely, I could not bear to survive a parting from you; I would erect the funeral pyre and burn myself. So much for that. Take this before we go!'

And he rummaged in his bundle with his dark beringed hands and drew out a roll of betel, such as is pleasant to chew after the meal to give sweet odour to the mouth. This he handed to Shridaman, with his face averted and wet with tears, as a present-giving and a sign and seal to their friendship and their compact.

4

So they went on, and their respective errands took them for a time upon different ways. When they had reached the river Jumna with its crowding sails and saw on the horizon the outline of the city Kurukshetra, Shridaman took to the high-road full of ox-carts and entered the narrow city streets to seek the house of the man from whom he was to buy the rice-mallets and tinder. Nanda struck off on a narrow lane leading to the mud huts of the humble folk who were to give him crude iron for his father's smithy. They blessed each other and took their leave, agreeing to meet again on this same spot at a certain hour on the third day, their business being done, and then to return home as they had come.

But when the sun had risen three times, Nanda, riding a grey ass which he had got from the humble folk to transport his iron, had to wait some time at the place of parting and meeting, for Shridaman was late. At length he came along the highway with his pack; his steps were slow and dragging, his cheeks hollow in the soft fan-shaped beard, and his eyes full of gloom. He showed no joy at sight of his friend, and when Nanda hastened to take his burden and put it on the ass, Shridaman's manner did not change; he walked by Nanda's side, as drooped and depressed as before, his words were hardly more than Yea, yea, even when they ought to have been Nay, nay. He did say no, too, but precisely when he should have said yes, namely at the hour for rest and refreshment, when he declared he would not and could not eat. In answer to a question, he also said that he could not sleep.

177

All this looked like illness. Indeed, when on the second evening they were walking along by the light of the stars, and the anxious Nanda got him to speak a few words, he not only said that he was ill, but also added in a strangled voice that the illness was incurable, a sickness unto death. It was of such a nature, he said, that he not only must but would die, the must and the will being entirely interwoven and indistinguishable, so that they formed a single compelling desire, each issuing inevitably from the other. 'If you are serious in your friendship,' he said to Nanda, always in that strangled and wildly agitated voice, 'then do me love's last service and build me the funeral hut that I may go into it and burn in the fire. For the incurable disease burns me within with such torments that the consuming ardour of the fire will feel by contrast like soothing oil and a healing bath in the holy stream.'

Oh, ye great gods, what will become of you? thought Nanda when his ears heard this. But we must say that despite his goatnose and his physical habit, which stood midway between the lowly folk who had sold him his iron and Shridaman, the grandchild of Brahmans, Nanda was equal to the difficult situation and did not lose his head in face of his companion's morbid state, however high-class. He made use of the advantage which the sound person has over the ailing, and, suppressing his inclination to shudder, loyally put himself at his friend's service and spoke with reason and tact.

'You may be sure,' said he, 'if it is true, as you say, and as I cannot doubt, that your ailment is incurable, I will not hesitate to carry out your directions and erect the pyre for you. And I will make it large enough that after I have kindled it there will be room for me beside you; for I do not think to survive the parting an hour, but will enter with you into the flames. Just for that reason, and because the thing concerns me too so nearly, you must tell me what is the matter and call your illness by name, if only so that I may gain the conviction of its incurableness and prepare to turn us both into ashes. You must admit that what I say is right and just, and if even I with my limited understanding see that, how much more must you, the wiser, agree! If I put myself in your place and try to use your head as though it sat on my shoulders, I cannot but think that my – I mean your – conviction of the incurableness of your disease needs confirmation and proof by others before we begin to carry out such far-reaching intentions. And therefore speak!'

For a long time the lank-cheeked Shridaman would not come out with it; he declared that the mortal hopelessness of his sufferings needed no evidence and no explanation. But at last after much urging he complied, with the following confession, putting as he spoke one hand over his eyes, that he need not look at his friend.

'Since,' said he, 'we watched that maiden, nude but virtuous, whom you once swung up to the sun, Sita, daughter of Suman-tra, at the bathing-place of Devi, suffering to do with her nakedness as well as her virtue, and having its origin in both, has been planted like a seed in my soul and there flourished until it has penetrated all my limbs down to their smallest fibre; consumed my mental powers, robbed me of sleep and appetite, and now slowly but surely leads me on to destruction.' He went on to say that his anguish was mortal because the cure – namely, the fulfilment of the wishes founded on the beauty and virtue of the maiden – was unthinkable, unimaginable, and of an extrava-gance, in short, far beyond mortal pretensions. If a man were afflicted by desire for a happiness of which no mortal but only a god might dream, and if he could not live without this happi-ness, then it was clear the man must die. 'If,' he concluded, 'I may not possess her, Sita of the partridge-eyes, the glorious colour, the divine hips, then of itself my spirit will dissolve and pass away. So build me the pyre, for only in the fire is salvation from the conflict of the human and the divine. It pains me that you would enter it with me, on account of your youth and your blithe young nature and lucky-calf lock; yet there is some justice in it too. For the thought that you swung her up to the sun adds to the fire in my breast, and I should hate to leave upon earth anyone to whom this had been granted.'

Nanda had no sooner heard Shridaman out than to his friend's utter amazement he burst out laughing, and continued to laugh as he danced up and down and embraced his friend by turns.

'Lovesick!' he cried. 'Lovesick, lovesick! That is all there is to it. That is the mortal illness. What fun, what a joke!' And he began to sing:

'The clever man, the clever man,
How wisely did he reason!
But now, alack, his wits are gone,
His wisdom's out of season.

The glances of a maiden's eye
Have turned his head to jelly;
A monkey tumbled from a tree
Could not look half so silly!'

Then he went on roaring, clapping his hands on his knees, and crying out:

'Shridaman, brother, how I rejoice to know it is nothing worse, and you are only thinking of the funeral pyre because your heart is on fire like a straw thatch! The little witch stood there too long in your sight; Kama, the god with the flowery arrow, has pierced you through. What we thought was the humming of bees was the whirr of his bolt; and Rati, sister of the springtime and desire, she has done this to you. And it is all quite normal and jolly, happens every day, and is no more than proper to a man. To you it looks as though only a god could hope for such bliss; but that only shows the warmth of your desires, and proves that they do indeed come from a god, that is to say Kama, but not that they are fitting to him instead of to you. Take it not unfriendly, but only as cooling counsel to your overheated sense, when I say that you are mistaken if you think only gods have a right to the goal of your desires. This is exaggerated; indeed, nothing is more human and natural than that you are driven to sow in this furrow.' (He put it like this because the word Sita means a furrow.) 'But to you,' he went on, 'the proverb applies: "The owl is blind by day, by night the crow. But whom love blinds nor light nor darkness know." I repeat this edifying saying that you may see yourself in it and bethink you that Sita of Bisonbull is no goddess, although she might so seem to you as she stood naked at the bathing-place of Durga, but a quite ordinary though extremely pretty little thing; she lives like other people, grinds the corn, cooks the porridge, and spins the wool and has parents who are like other folk, even though Sumantra, her father, can boast of a little warrior blood in his veins – too far away to amount to much! In short, they are people one can talk to; and why have you a friend like your Nanda if he should not get on his legs and arrange this whole quite regular and ordinary business for you, so you can be happy? Well? Hey? What, stupid! Instead of laying the bonfire and squatting in it beside you, I will help you build your bridal house where you can live in bliss with your bride of the beautiful hips!'

Shridaman, after a pause, answered and said: 'Your words – not to mention your song – contained much that was offensive. For offensive it is to call my anguished desires quite ordinary and everyday when they are past my power to endure and are nigh to split my heart in twain. A yearning stronger than we are, too strong to sustain – we are right in calling it unfitting for man, only fit for a god to know. But I am sure you mean well by me, you want to console me, so I forgive you the vulgar and ignorant way you express yourself about my mortal illness. Indeed, not only do I forgive you; for your last words seem to hold out a possibility which has already stimulated my heart, but now resigned to death, to new and violent throbbing. It is the picture you hold up that has done this, though as yet I am incapable of belief in it. I have moments of divining that unscathed mortals, in another frame of mind than mine, may be able to judge more clearly and objectively. But I immediately mistrust any other view than my own and believe only in the way which points me to death. Consider how probable it is that the divine Sita was contracted in marriage as a child and is soon to be united with a bridegroom who grew up with her! The mere thought is such a burning torment that I can only flee from it into the coolness of the funeral pyre.'

But Nanda swore by their friendship that his fear was utterly baseless; Sita was not bound by any child-marriage. Her father Sumantra had objected to such an arrangement, on the ground that it would expose her to the ignominy of widowhood in case the boy husband died untimely. In fact, she could not have been chosen as the swinging maiden if she had been betrothed. No, Sita was free, she was to be wooed; and with Shridaman's good caste, his family connections, and his conversance with the Vedas, it only needed that he formally commission his friend to take the thing in hand and set in motion the negotiations between the families, to make a happy issue to the affair as good as certain.

Shridaman's cheek had twitched with pain at mention of the swinging episode. But on the whole he showed himself grateful for his friend's readiness to serve him. Slowly he let himself be turned by Nanda's sound reasoning away from his yearning for death towards a belief that the fulfilment of his desire, to enfold Sita as a bride in his arms, did not lie outside the realms of the possible and human. Even so, he stuck to it that if the wooing went wrong, Nanda would have to erect the funeral pyre with his stout arms. The son of Garga soothed him by promising this; but found it more pertinent to discuss in detail all the steps leading up to the happy consummation. Shridaman was to retire entirely and await the issue; Nanda for his part had first to open the affair to Bhavabhuti, Shridaman's father, and persuade him to undertake negotiations with the maiden's parents. Then Nanda, representing the wooer, would betake himself as suitor of the bride to Bisonbull and in his character of friend carry out the further approach between the couple.

No sooner said than done. Bhavabhuti, the *vanija* of Brahman stock, was rejoiced at the communication which his son's friend made to him. Sumantra, the cow-breeder, of warrior blood, was not displeased by the proposals, accompanied by considerable presents. Nanda in homely but convincing phrases sang the praises of his friend in the house of the wooing. Not less auspicious was the return visit of Sita's parents to Welfare of Cows, to convince themselves of the suitor's good faith. In such exchanges as these the days passed, and the maiden Sita learned from afar to see in Shridaman, the merchant's son, her destined lord and master. The marriage contract was drawn up and the signing of it celebrated with a feast and the exchange of appropriate gifts. The day of the wedding, selected by advice of those learned in the heavenly signs, drew on; and Nanda, who knew that it would do so – quite aside from the fact that Shridaman's union with Sita depended upon him, which prevented Shridaman from believing it would ever come – ran about inviting kin and friends to the nuptials. The nuptial bonfire was laid on a base of cakes of dried dung in the inner court of Sita's parents' house. Nanda's strong arms did yeoman service here too, while the priest of Brahma stood by and recited texts.

So came on the day when Sita the fine-limbed, her body anointed with sandalwood, camphor, and coconut oils, adorned with jewellery, in wedding bodice and robe, her head enveloped in a cloudy veil, for the first time set eyes on her appointed husband. He, as we are aware, had seen her before. For the first time she called him by his name. The hour had indeed been waited for, but here it was at last and took on presentness, when he spoke the words: 'I have received her'; when with offerings of rice and butter he took her from her parents' hands, called himself heaven and her earth, himself the melody, her the words; and to the singing and hand-clapping of the women went with her thrice round the glowing fire. Then in solemn procession, with a team of white oxen he led her home to his village and to his mother's heart.

Here there were more good-luck ceremonies to be performed, here too they went round about the fire; he fed her with sugar-cane, let the ring fall in her lap. At the festal meal they sat again with kin and friends. But when they had eaten and drunk and been sprinkled with rose-water and water from the Ganges, they were accompanied by all the guests to the bridal chamber or 'room of the happy pair', where the flower-garlanded bed had been set up. There, among kisses, jesting, and tears, everyone took leave of them. Nanda, who had been at their side throughout, was last upon the threshold.

5

Here we warn the listener, perhaps misled by the so far pleasing course of the tale, not to fall prey to a misconception of its real character. For a little space there was silence, it turned its face away; when it turns back it is no more the same, but changed to a frightful mask, a face of horror, distracting, Medusa-like, turning the beholder to stone, or maddening him to wild acts of abnegation – for so Shridaman, Nanda, and Sita saw it, on the journey which they ... But everything in its turn.

Six months had passed since Shridaman's mother had taken the lovely Sita to her maternal bosom and Sita had granted to her narrow-nosed husband the full enjoyment of wedded bliss. The heavy summer had passed, and now the rainy season, covering the sky with floods of cloud, the earth with freshets of flowers, would soon be over too. Heaven's tent was spotless, the autumn lotus was in bloom, when the newly wedded pair discussed with their friend Nanda, after winning the consent of Shridaman's parents, a visit to Sita's family. Her parents had not seen her since she embraced her husband, and they wished to convince themselves that her wedded bliss became her. Although Sita had begun of late to look forward to the joys of motherhood, they ventured on the journey, which was not long and in the cool of the year not very trying.

They travelled in a cart with a top and side curtains, drawn by a zebu and a dromedary; friend Nanda being the driver. He sat in front of the wedded pair, his little cap on one ear and his legs dangling down. He seemed to be paying too much attention to his driving to turn round often to speak to his passengers. Sometimes he called out to his beasts; from time to time burst into song, very loud and clear – but after the first notes his voice would die down to a humming, ending in a vague chirrup to his team. If the burst of song was rather startling, like a relief to an overcharged breast, its dying away was no less so.

Behind him the wedded pair sat silent. They had Nanda immediately before them, their gaze if directed straight ahead would rest on the back of his neck; as the young wife's sometimes did, rising slowly from contemplation of her lap and after a short pause swiftly returning there. Shridaman avoided the sight entirely, keeping his face averted towards the canvas curtains. Gladly he would have changed places with Nanda and become the driver, in order not to have, like his wife beside him, a view of the brown back with the spinal column and the flexible shoulder-blades. But it was no matter, he thought; for any other arrangement would have been no better. And so in silence they took their way, but the breath of all three came quickly as though they had been running; their eyes were blood-shot, and that is always a bad sign. A person gifted with second sight would certainly have seen a shadow, like a black pinion, covering them as they drove.

And they drove, by preference, in the shadow of darkness; in other words, before the dawn; thus avoiding the burden of the midday sun – a sensible course, for which, however, they had other grounds than good sense. The confusion of their own souls was favoured by the darkness, and unconsciously they projected their inward bewilderment into outward space – with the result that they lost their way. Nanda did not guide his zebu and dromedary into the turning off the highroad that led to Sita's home. With no moon, and only the stars to guide him, he took the wrong turn, and the road they found themselves on was soon no road at all, but only a thinning among the trees, and even that only apparent, for they thickened again and became a forest wherein the thinning soon disappeared through which they might have made their way back.

It was impossible to get forward with their cart among the tree-trunks and on the soft floor of the forest. They confessed to each other that they had gone astray; but not that they had brought about a situation corresponding to confusion of their own minds. Shridaman and Sita, sitting behind Nanda as he drove, had not even been asleep; open-eyed, they allowed him to take them into the wrong road. There was nothing for it but to make a fire where they were, and await the sunrise with more security against beasts of prey. When day at length dawned, they cast about in all directions; unharnessed their team and let them go single file; then with great difficulty pushed and shoved the cart wherever the teak and sandalwood trees would let them through, and reached the edge of the jungle, where they found a stone gully. This might be possible for the cart; and Nanda declared that it would certainly lead in the direction of Sita's home.

Following the steep gully, with many jolts, they came on a temple hewn out of the rock, and recognized it as a shrine of

Devi-Durga the terrible and unapproachable, Kali the dark Mother. Obeying an impulse of his heart, Shridaman expressed a wish to get out and pay honour to the goddess. 'I will only look at her, say a prayer, and come back in a few minutes,' he said to his companions. 'Just wait here!' And he left the wagon and clambered up the rude steps leading to the temple.

It was a shrine no more important than the little mother-house by the secluded bathing-place on the river Goldfly; but its columns and ornamentation had been carved with infinite piety and care. The entrance seemed to crouch beneath the wild mountain itself, supported by columns flanked by snarling leopards. There were painted pictures to right and left, also at the sides of the inner entrance, carven out of the rock; visions of life in the flesh, all jumbled together out of skin and bones, marrow and sinews, sperm and sweat and tears and ropy rheum, filth and urine and gall; thick with passions, anger, lust, envy, and despair; lovers' partings and bonds unloved; with hunger, thirst, old age, sorrow, and death; all this for ever fed by the sweet, hot streaming blood-stream, suffering and enjoying in a thousand shapes, teeming, devouring, turning into one another. And in that all-encompassing labyrinthine flux of the animal, human, and divine, there would be an elephant's trunk that ended in a man's hand, or a boar's head seemed to take the place of a woman's. Shridaman heeded not the pictures, he thought not to see them; yet his red-veined eyeballs skimmed them in passing, and they stirred in his soul feelings of slight giddiness and of tender pity, to prepare it for the beholding of the Mother.

Twilight reigned in the rocky cell, lighted only from above by light falling through the mountain into the audience hall, which he crossed to go into the lower vestibule adjoining it. There a door on a still lower level, to which steps led down, admitted him into the heart of the house, the womb of the great Mother.

At the foot of the steps he trembled and staggered back, his hands spread out against the two linga stones on either side. Kali's image was fearsome. Did it only seem so to his bloodshot eyes, or had he never anywhere beheld the raging one in such triumphantly horrible guise? Framed in an arch composed of skulls and hacked-off hands and feet, the idol stood out from the living rocky wall in colours that snatched up all the light to hurl it glaringly back. She was adorned with a dazzling crown; clothed and girt with bones and severed limbs, and her eighteen arms were a whirling wheel. Swords and fiery beacons the Mother brandished. Blood steamed hot in the skull she held with one hand to her lips, and blood was at her feet in a spreading pool. The frightful one stood in a bark on the flooding sea of life, it swam in a sea of blood. The very smell of blood saluted Shridaman's thin nostrils, it smelt old and sweetish in the stagnant air of this mountain cave, this subterranean charnelhouse, where coagulating blood choked and made sticky the runnels in the pavement grooved to carry off the quick-flowing life-stream of the beheaded sacrifices. Four or five heads of animals, bison, swine, and goats, their eyes open and glazed, were piled in a pyramid on the altar before the image of the Unescapable, and the sword that had served to behead them, sharp-edged and shining, though spotted with dried blood, lay on the flags at one side.

Shridaman stared at the wild glaring visage, his horror mounting by the moment to fever heat. This was She, the Deathbringer-Lifegiver, Compeller of Sacrifice – her whirling arms made his own senses go round in drunken circles. He pressed his clenched fists against his mightily throbbing breast; uncanny shudderings, cold and hot, surged over his frame in successive floods. In the back of his head, in the very pit of his stomach, in the woeful excitation of his organs of sex, he felt one single urge, driving on to the extremity of a deed against his own life in the service of the eternal womb. With lips already bloodless he prayed:

'Beginningless, that wast before all created! Mother without man, whose garment none lifteth! All-embracing horror and desire, sucking back into thyself the worlds and images thou givest forth! With offerings of living creatures the people honour thee, for to thee is due the life-blood of all! How shall I not find grace to my healing, if I bring thee myself as offering? Well I know I shall not thereby escape life, even though that were desirable. But let me enter again into thee through the door of

the womb that I may be free of this self; let me no more be
Shridaman, to whom all desire is but bewilderment, since it is
not he who gives it!'

Spoke these sinister words, seized up the sword from the
floor, and severed his own head from his neck.

Quickly said; and not otherwise than quickly done. Yet the
teller has here but one wish: that the hearer may not accept the
fact with thoughtless indifference, as something quite common
and natural, simply because it has been often told and stands in
the records, that people practise cutting off their own heads.
The single case is never common; the most common of all the
things we think and talk about are birth and death; yet attend at
a birth or a deathbed and ask yourself, ask the groaning or the
parting soul, whether it is common or not. Self-beheading, however often it may be reported, is an act well-nigh impossible; to
carry it through takes enormous determination, a fearful sum-
moning up of purpose and energy. That Shridaman, the little
Brahman with the mild pensive eyes and thin clerkly arms, did
in fact perpetrate it, must not be taken as in the common run,
but as something scarcely credible at all.

Enough, in all conscience, that he performed the gruesome
sacrifice in the twinkling of an eye; here lay his noble head, with
the soft beard on the cheeks, and there his body, that less important appendage, its two hands still grasping the sacrificial
sword by the hilt. From the trunk the blood gushed out and ran
into the channels in the floor. There was only a slight incline; so
once in the channels it crept but slowly towards the pit under
the altar – very like the little river Goldfly, that comes rushing,
like a colt let loose, out of Himawant's gate but flows more and
more quietly as it nears its mouth.

6

Returning now from the bowels of this rocky cell back to the
pair waiting outside, we need not be surprised that they spent
the first part of the time in silence, but after that began to
question aloud. After all Shridaman had only wanted to make a
brief devotion; where was he lingering so long? The lovely Sita,

sitting behind Nanda in the cart, had gazed by turns at his neck and into her lap and kept as still as he, whose goat-nose and thick lips remained turned towards his team. But at length both began to wriggle in their seats, and after a while friend Nanda resolutely turned round to the young wife and asked:

'Have you any idea why he keeps us waiting and what he is doing there so long?'

'I cannot imagine, Nanda,' responded she, in the sweet lilting and trilling voice he had been afraid to hear. She had quite superfluously added his name, and he had been afraid of that too – it was unnecessary, and he himself had not said: 'Where is Shridaman', but simply: 'Where is he?'

'I have been wondering a long time,' she went on, 'and if you had not turned round to me and asked me, I should very soon have asked you.'

He shook his head, partly out of surprise at his friend's delay, but partly to ward off the unnecessary words she always used. 'Turned round' would have been enough, the 'to me', although quite correct, was unnecessary and even dangerous, spoken as it was, while they waited for Shridaman, and in that sweetly lilting, slightly affected voice.

He said nothing, afraid lest he too might speak in an unnatural voice and address her by her name, for he felt drawn to follow the example she had set. It was she who after a short pause made the suggestion:

'I will tell you what, Nanda, you must go after him and see where he is, give him a shake with those strong arms of yours, if he has forgotten himself in prayer – we cannot wait any longer, and it is very strange of him to leave us sitting here, and waste the time while the sun is getting higher. We are late anyhow by reason of losing the way, and my parents must be beginning to worry about me, for they love me beyond aught in the world. Do, pray, go fetch him, Nanda! Even though he does not want to come and protests a little, yet make him come. You are stronger than he.'

'Good, I will go fetch him,' Nanda replied. 'Of course in all friendliness. I need only remind him of the time. It was my fault we lost the way. I had already thought of going, and only feared you might not like to wait here alone. But it is only for a few seconds.'

With that he lowered himself from the driver's seat and went up into the shrine.

And we, who know what a sight awaited him there! We must accompany him through the audience hall where he walked all unconscious; and through the vestibule where still he was unaware; then finally down into the mother-cell. Now, indeed, he faltered, he staggered, a dull cry of horror on his lips, struggling to hold fast to the linga stones, just as Shridaman had done. But his horror was not, like Shridaman's, for the image, but for the awful sight on the floor. There lay his friend, the waxen face with loosened neckcloth severed from the trunk, his blood flowing by many ways towards the pit.

Poor Nanda quivered like an elephant's ear. He held his cheeks with his dark beringed hands and from between his thick lips came chokingly over and over the name of his friend. He bent and made helpless motions towards the two parts of him on the ground, not knowing which part to embrace or to address. To the head he turned at last, that having always been so decidedly the main part; knelt down to the pallid shape and spoke, his goat-nosed face awry with bitter weeping. He laid one hand on the body and turned to it now and again as he talked.

'Shridaman,' he sobbed, 'dear friend, what hast thou done, and how couldst thou bring thyself to do this with thy hands and arms, a deed so hard to do! It was not anything for thee! No one urged thee to this, yet hast thou accomplished it. Always have I admired thy spirit, now must I in tears admire thy body too, because thou hast been able to do this hardest of all deeds! But what must have gone on in thy soul, to bring thee to it! How in thy breast must generosity and despair have gone hand in hand, in sacrificial dance, ere thou couldst slay thyself! Oh woe, oh woe! Severed the fine head from the fine body! Still remains the soft plumpness where it was, but reft of sense and meaning, unallied with that noble head of thine. Say, am I guilty? Am I indeed guilty of thy death by my very being, if also not by my deed? Lo, since my head still thinks, I try to think as thou wouldst, and perhaps in thy wisdom thou wouldst have called the guilt of being more essential than that of action. But what more can a man do than avoid doing? I have kept silent as much as possible in order not to speak with a cooing voice. I have said no unnecessary word, nor added her name when I addressed her. I am my own witness, there is indeed no other, that I took no advantage when she carped at you. But what good is all that, when I am guilty by my very existence in the flesh? I should have gone into the desert and as an anchorite performed strict observance! I ought to have done it, without any word from you, I confess it humbly. But in my defence I can say that had you spoken I would have done so! Why did you never speak, dear head, before you lay there sundered and still sat on your shoulders? Always have our heads spoken together, yours wise and mine simple; yet in the most serious and dangerous concern of all, then you were silent! Now it is too late; you have not spoken, you have acted greatly and cruelly and shown me how I too must act. Surely you did not believe I would fail you, that my strong arms would falter at a deed your slender ones have carried out! Often had I told you I did not think to survive a parting from you; when in your lovesickness you ordered me to build the funeral hut, I declared to you that if I did it at all I would do it for two and squat inside it with you. What now must happen I long have known, even though only now does it stand out clear from the confusion of my thoughts when I came in and saw you lying – by "you" I mean body there and head here beside it – then was Nanda's resolve made on the instant. I would have burned with you, so will I also bleed with you, for nothing else remains to me. Shall I go out to her to tell her what you have done and in the cries of horror she will utter hear her secret joy? Shall I go about with tarnished name and have people say, as they certainly will: "The villain Nanda has wronged his friend, has murdered him out of lust for his wife?" No, not that! Not ever that. I will follow you, and may the eternal womb drink my blood with yours!'

Thus saying, he turned from the head to the body, loosed the hilt of the sword from the already stiffening fingers, and with his stout arms carried out most thoroughly the sentence he himself had pronounced; so that his body, to mention it first, fell across Shridaman's, and his simple head bounced alongside that of his friend, where it lay with its eyes rolled up. But his blood too burst quick and furiously forth and then trickled slowly through the runnels to the mouth of the pit.

7

Meanwhile, Sita, the furrow, sat outside, alone in her tented cart, and the time was longer to her because she had no nape of a neck to look at any more. What – while she yielded to quite commonplace feelings of annoyance – was happening to that neck, of course she never dreamed. Possibly, in her inmost soul – far beneath her ill-humour, which was lively, but belonged to the sphere of small possible mischances, and merely made her scuffle with her feet – the suspicion stirred of something frightful, some explanation of the delay which would make impatience and annoyance irrelevant because it belonged to an order of possibilities beyond the scope of kicking and scuffling. We must reckon with a secret receptivity of the young wife for imaginings of this order, because she had been living under certain conditions, and having certain experiences, which, to put it mildly, were themselves rather extravagant in their nature. But nothing of that sort entered into the things she was saying to herself.

'It is just unspeakable, it is almost intolerable,' she thought. 'Men are all alike, one must not set one above another, for there is no dependence on any. One of them leaves you sitting with the other, so that he deserves I don't know what for it; and when you send the other, then you sit here alone. And that with the sun getting high, because we had already lost so much time. I shall soon fly out of my skin with rage. There is not a single excuse, in the whole range of reasonable, sensible possibilities, for one disappearing and then the other too. The utmost I can think is that they have fallen foul of each other, because Shridaman is so set on praying that he will not stir from the spot, and Nanda is trying to force him, but out of respect for my husband's weak frame will not use his full strength; for if he wanted to, he could carry him like a child in his arms; they feel like iron when one happens to touch them. It would be humiliating for Shridaman, yet the annoyance almost makes me wish Nanda would do just that. I must say, you both deserve I should take the reins and drive on alone to my parents, and you would find me gone when you finally came out. If it were not so embarrassing to arrive alone like that, without husband or friend, because both of them went and left me, I would just do it at once. Otherwise all I can do – and it is certainly high time – is to go after them and see what in the world they are up to. No wonder I feel somewhat alarmed, being with child as I am, at their strange behaviour, for fear of what is behind it. But the worst thing I can think of, after all, is that for some reason unknown, they have quarrelled, and the quarrel is keeping them from coming back. I will just step in and straighten them both out.'

With that the lovely Sita got down from the cart, her hips billowing beneath her enveloping garment, and betook herself to the shrine – and fifteen seconds later she was confronted by that most hideous of sights.

She flung up her arms, her eyes started from their sockets; bereft of her senses she sank full length on the ground. But that helped her not at all, the situation would keep, it had been keeping all the time Sita waited; and it would keep on keeping. When the unhappy Sita came to herself it was still there. She tried to faint again, but thanks to her sound constitution she could not. So she cowered on the stone pavement, her fingers in her hair, and stared at the severed heads, the bodies lying across each other, and all the crawling blood.

'Ye gods, saints, and hermits!' she whispered blue-lipped, 'I am lost! Both men, both at once. All is over! My lord and husband, who went about the fire with me, my Shridaman with the estimable head and the body, which after all was warm, for he taught me lust, as far as I know it, in nights of holy wedlock – severed the honoured head from the body, lost and gone. Lost and gone – and the other, Nanda, who swung me and wooed me for Shridaman – severed and bleeding body from head – there he lies, the lucky-calf lock still on his breast – once so merry, but headless, what now? I could touch him, I could feel the strength and beauty of his arms and thighs, if I would. But I care not, blood and death have set a barrier between him and wanton desire as honour and friendship did before. They have cut off each other's heads! For a reason I no longer conceal from myself, their anger blazed up, like a fire on which one has thrown butter; their strife was such that it came to this mutual deed – I see all clearly. But only one sword is here – and Nanda holds it! How could they fight with only one? Shridaman, forgotten all wisdom and mildness, seized the sword and hewed off Nanda's head, who then – but no! It was Nanda, for reasons at which I shudder, beheaded Shridaman, who then – oh no, oh no! Think on it no more, it avails nothing, there is nothing but blood and darkness in the darkness of this horrible place, and only one thing is clear, they behaved like savages and not for a moment thought of me. Or rather, of course they thought of me, their horrible masculine deed was on my account. Poor thing, I shudder at the thought. But only with reference to themselves did they think of me, not about me and what would become of me – that in their madness they never thought of, as little as they do now, lying there still and headless, leaving to me what I shall do next! Do? There is nothing to be done, since now I am undone. Shall I go through life a widow, shunned as a woman who cared so ill for her husband that he perished? That is a widow's common lot; but how much worse stain will attach to me when I return alone to the house of my father and my father-in-law? Only one sword – they cannot have killed each other with it in turn, one sword is not enough for two. But there is a third person left, and that is I. They will say I am an abandoned woman and murdered my husband and his foster-brother, my brother-in-law – the chain of evidence is complete. It is false, but it is conclusive and they will brand me, though innocent. Not innocent, no, there might be some sense in lying, it would be worth the trouble to lie, if everything were not at an end, but as it is there is no sense. Innocent I am not, have not been for long; and as for being abandoned there is something in it – much, much indeed, though not quite as people will think. Is there such a thing as mistaken justice? I must prevent that, I

must do justice on myself. I must follow them – nothing else in
the world is left me. The sword I cannot wield with my little
hands, they are too small, and they tremble too much to destroy
the body to which they belong, these alluring curves – that are
yet naught but weakness. A pity for its loveliness – yet it must
become as stiff and lifeless as these, and nevermore awake desire
or suffer lust. So must it be, though the number of the sacrifice
mount to four. What would it have from life, the orphaned
child? Crippled by misfortune, pale and blind because I went
pale with affliction when it was conceived, and shut my eyes
not to see him who begot it. What I do now is what they have
left me to do. Lo, then, let them see I know how to help
myself!'

She pulled herself up, staggered to and fro, tottered up the
step, and ran, with her gaze bent on destruction, back through
the temple into the open air. A fig tree stood in front of the
shrine hung with climbing vines. She seized one of these, made
a noose, put it round her neck, and was just in the act of
strangling herself.

8

At that moment a voice was manifest to her out of the air: no
other, of course, than the voice of Devi-Durga the Unapproachable, Kali the dark, the voice of the World-Mother herself. It
was a deep, harsh voice, with a maternal firmness about it.

'Will you just let that be for a minute, you silly ape!' it said.
'Is it not enough to have let the blood of my sons, so that it
flows in the runnels, but you will also mutilate my tree, and
make your body – which is not a half-bad image of me – carrion
for crows, together with the dear sweet warm little seed of life
growing inside it? Perhaps you have not noticed, you goose,
that you have missed your times and are in expectation from my
son? If you cannot add two and two in women's matters, then
hang yourself, do! But not here in my bailiwick, to make it look
as though dear life should all at once perish and go out of the
world, just on account of your silliness. My ears are full as it is
of these quack philosophers who say that human existence is a

disease, communicating itself through lust from one generation to the next – and now you, you ninny, start playing games like this with me! Take your neck out of the noose, or you'll get your ears boxed!'

'Holy goddess,' answered Sita, 'certainly, I obey. I hear the thunder of thy voice and interrupt of course at once my desperate enterprise as thou commandest. But I must defend myself against the idea that I did not realize my condition and not know that you had made me pause and had blessed me. I only thought it would surely be pale and blind and a child of misfortune.'

'Be so good as to let me take care of that! In the first place that is a silly female superstition, and in the second, in my activities there is room for pale and blind cripples too. But justify yourself, confess why the blood of my sons has flowed to me in the pit, both of them in their way very decent youths. Not that their blood would not have been grateful to me; only I should rather have let it flow awhile yet in their veins. Speak then, but tell the truth! You realize that I know everything anyhow.'

'They killed each other, holy goddess, and left me forlorn. They quarrelled on my account and with one and the same sword hewed off their –'

'Nonsense! Really, only a female can talk such sheer rubbish. They sacrificed themselves to me one after the other in manly piety, let me tell you. But why did they do it?'

The lovely Sita began to weep. She answered, sobbing:

'Ah, holy goddess, I know and confess my guilt, but how can I help it? It was such a misfortune, however inevitable; such a fatality, if you permit me to say so' (here she sobbed several times); 'such a calamity, an evil and poisonous mischance, that I became a wife, being the pert and tongue-tied and ignorant girl that I was, tending in peace my father's hearth until I knew my husband and was initiated into thy matters. For the blithe child that I was, it was like eating poison berries, changing her for ever through and through, so that sin, with its irresistible sweetness, has power over her awakened senses. Not that I can wish myself back in that pert and unthinking ignorance – I cannot; it is possible to no one. I only know that in that early time I did not know man, I did not see him, he did not trouble me, and my soul was free of him and all burning curiosity about his mysteries; I tossed him jesting words and went my saucy way. Had ever I blushed at the sight of a youth's breast or felt my eyes burn when I looked at his arms and legs? No, that was all like nothing at all to me, it did not touch ever so little my coolness and poise, for I was like a closed book. A youth came, with a flat nose and black eyes, built like an image, Nanda was his name, from Welfare of Cows; he swung me up to the sun in the feast of the sun, but I felt no glow at all. I got warm – from the caressing air but from nothing else; and for thanks I gave him a tweak of the nose. Then he came back as wooer for his friend Shridaman, and our parents agreed on the marriage. Perhaps by then it was a little different; perhaps the unhappiness began in those days when he wooed me for another man who was to embrace me as his wife and who was not there. Only Nanda was there.

'He was always there; before the wedding and during the wedding feast, when we marched round the fire – and afterwards too. In the daytime, I mean, he was there, for of course he was not at night, when I slept with his friend Shridaman, my husband, and we met as the godlike pair as we had for the first time on the bed of flowers our wedding night; when he unlocked me with his manly strength and put an end to my inexperience and the pert, chaste maidenliness of my early years. That he could do, why not, he was thy son, and he knew how to impart a loftiness to our physical union, and there was nothing at all against my loving, honouring, and fearing him – ah, most high goddess, I am not so made that I should not have loved my lord and husband, and even more feared and honoured him: that head so fine and wise, the beard soft as the soft mild eyes and lids, and the body that went with them. But with all my respect, I had to ask myself whether he was really the right one to make me a wife and instruct my maidenly coldness in the sweet and awful mysteries of sense. – It always seemed to me it did not become him: it was not worthy of him, it did not go with his head, and always when his flesh rose to encounter me in those wedded nights it seemed to me like a shame, and a degradation of his refinement, a shame and debasement – and for me too when I had been aroused.

'Eternal goddess, so it was. Chide me, punish me, I thy creature confess to thee in this frightful hour without reserve just how it all was; mindful that in any case all things are open to thy wisdom. Desire did not become my noble husband Shridaman, it became neither his head nor his body, which after all, you will agree, is the important factor. His body lying there, so piteously severed from his head, did not know how to shape the rites of love so that my whole heart would hang upon them. He did indeed awake me to desire but could not still it. Have mercy, goddess! The lust of thy awakened creature was greater than its satisfaction, its craving greater than its joy.

'And by day I saw our friend Nanda with the goat-nose; and in the evening before we went to bed. I saw him and I observed him, as wedlock had now taught me to observe and judge men; and the question slipped into my head and into my dreams: what would Nanda make of the act of love and what would the godlike embrace be like with him – who is very far from talking as well as Shridaman – instead of with my husband? No different, miserable wretch, I told myself, vicious and dishonouring towards thy rightful husband! It is always the same; how could such as Nanda, who is simplicity itself in all his words and members while thy lord and husband is really a person of consequence, how could Nanda know how to make any more of it? But that was no help: the question of Nanda the idea that his lust would become both his head and his limb and be without shame, and he might be the man to lift my joy to the level of my desire – it stuck in my flesh and soul like a hook in a fish's mouth, and could not be pulled out because the hook was barbed.

'How could I tear it out, when he was always with us, and Shridaman and he could not live without each other because they were so different? I had to see him by day, and dream about him by night, instead of Shridaman. I would look at his breast with the lucky-calf lock, his narrow hips, and very small hindquarters, mine being so large, and Shridaman forming in this respect a mean between me and Nanda, and my self-control forsook me. When his arm touched mine the hairs on my skin rose up for very bliss. When I thought of his glorious pair of legs, with the black hair on them, saw him walk and move them and thought of their clasping me round in amorous play, a giddiness seized me and my breasts dripped with tenderness. More and more lovely he became to me day by day. I could not understand how I saw him, on the day of my swinging, and smelt the mustard oil on his skin, and remained asleep and untouched. For now he was like the prince Gandharva Citra-ratha in his unearthly charm, like the love-god in his sweetest guise, full of beauty and youth, ravishing to the sense, adorned with heavenly ornament, with necklaces of flowers, sweet odours, and all loveliness – Vishnu, come down to the earth in Krishna's form.

'Thus it was, when Shridaman came near me in the night, I paled for very sorrow that it was he and not the other, and closed my eyes so I might think Nanda embraced me. It came about that I forbore not, in my ardour, to murmur the name of him whom I would have wished to rouse it in me; and so Shridaman became aware that I was breaking my marriage vows in his gentle arms. And then, alas, I sometimes talk in my sleep, and I must have hurt him cruelly by uttering within his hear-ing the betraying substance of my dreams. I gather this from his melancholy and his withdrawal from me – for from that time he has never touched me again. Nor did Nanda touch me; not because he was not tempted, tempted he certainly was, I would vouch for it that he was sorely tempted! But in his invincible loyalty to his friend he resisted the temptation, and I too – believe me, eternal Mother, for I at least do believe it – even if his temptation had mastered him, out of honour for my lord and husband I would have shown him the door. But the issue was that I had no husband at all; and the three of us were in a state of painful renunciation.

'Under such circumstances, Mother of the world, we under-took the journey to my parents and wandering from our right ways we came on thy house. Shridaman said he would stop only a little and in passing pay you his devotions. But in thy slaughter-cell overcome by his plight, he did this frightful deed, robbing his limbs of their revered head, or rather his revered head of its limbs, and abandoned me to this wretched widowed state. In an agony of abnegation he did it, and with good intentions towards me, the criminal. For, gracious goddess, pardon me the truth: not to thee did he bring himself a sacrifice but to me and to his friend, that we might spend our days in full enjoyment of the joys of the flesh. Then Nanda went to seek him, and would not abide by the sacrifice but hacked his own head from his Krishna limbs, so that they are now useless. But useless, yes, and much worse than useless my life is now become; I too am as good as headless, without husband or friend. The guilt for my unhappiness I must, I suppose, ascribe to my acts in an earlier existence. But after all this, canst thou wonder that I was resolved to make an end of my present one?'

'You are an unqualified goose and nothing else,' said the goddess in her voice of thunder. 'It is ridiculous, what your insatiable curiosity has made out of this Nanda, who is entirely ordinary in all his works and ways. With such arms, and on such legs, I have sons running about by the million, and you go and make a Gandharva out of him! It is pathetic, after all,' added the divine voice, more mildly. 'I, the Mother, find fleshly lust pathetic on the whole, and am of opinion that people are inclined to make too much of it. Anyhow, order there must be!' And the voice got suddenly harsh and blustering again. 'I, indeed, am Disorder; but precisely therefore I insist on order, and I must definitely protest that the institution of marriage be kept inviolate. Everything would get into a muddle if I gave rein to my good nature. But as for you, to say I am dissatisfied is to put it mildly. You make this kettle of fish for me here and on the top of it you say all sorts of impertinent things to me. You give me to understand that my sons did not offer themselves as sacrifices, that their blood might flow to my altar – you say the first sacrificed himself to you, and then the second to the first. What kind of manners are those? How could a man hew off his head – not simply cut his throat but cut off his head according to the proper rites (and an educated man to boot, like your Shridaman, who doesn't show up so well in the business of

love) – unless he got the necessary strength and wildness out of
the intoxication that came to him from me? So I forbid your
tone, quite aside from whether there is any truth in your words
or not! For there may be truth in them, in so far that a deed
has been committed with mixed motives, and is so far unclear.
It was not exclusively to seek my mercy that my son Shridaman
offered himself up; actually it was for affliction about you,
whether he himself was clear in the matter or no. And little
Nanda's sacrifice was just the inevitable consequence. I feel little
inclined to receive their blood and accept the offering. Well
then: if I now make good the double sacrifice and put all back
as it was, may I be permitted to hope that you will behave with
more decency in the future?'

'Ah, holy goddess and dear Mother!' cried Sita through her
tears. 'If you could do that, if you could cancel these frightful
deeds and give me back husband and friend so that all were as
before – how would I bless you! I would even control my
dreams and the words of them so that the noble Shridaman
need suffer no more. Indescribably thankful would I be to you,
if you brought that about and put everything back as it was!
For though it was sad enough before, and when I stood there in
your Innermost before the horrible scene, I realized clear and
plain that it could not have turned out otherwise, yet it would
be wonderful if you had the power and could succeed in reversing the past so that next time it might have a better issue.'

'What do you mean by "if I had the power" and "if I could
succeed"?' retorted the divine voice. 'I hope you do not doubt
that to my power it were the merest trifle! More than once in
the world it has come to pass that I showed it. But I am sorry
for you, I must say, although you do not deserve it, you and the
pale, blind little seedling in your womb. The two young men in
there, I pity them too. So open your ears and hear what I tell
you! Drop that natural noose of yours and get back with you
into my shrine, before my image and the mess you have made.
No fainting or whimpering, mind! You take the two heads by
the hair and fit them to the poor trunks again. Then you bless
the cuts with the sharp edge of the sword of sacrifice, and both
times call upon my name – you may say Durga or Kali or

simply Devi, it doesn't matter – and the two youths will be
restored to life. Do you understand me? Do not approach the
heads too quickly to the bodies, although you will feel strong
attraction between head and trunk; the spilt blood must have
time to run back and be sucked in again. That happens with
magic quickness, but after all it takes a moment of time. I hope
you have listened to me? Then run! But do the business properly, do not put the heads on the wrong way round in your
haste so that they have to go about with their faces backwards
and make people laugh at them! Get along! If you wait till
tomorrow it will be too late.'

9

The lovely Sita said nothing more at all, not even 'thank you';
she jumped up and ran, fast as her swathed robe would let her,
back into the mother-house. She ran through the audience
chamber and through the entrance hall and into the holy shrine,
and there before the frightful countenance of the goddess she set
to the prescribed task with flushed and feverish energy. The
attraction between heads and trunks was not so strong as one
might have expected from Devi's words. It was perceptible; but
yet there was time for the blood to flow back up the channels, as
it did with magical swiftness and a lively lapping sound. The
blessing of the sword infallibly performed its office – that and
the divine name which Sita, her voice breaking with joy, cried
out three times in each case. Each with his head in its place,
without mark or scar the youths rose before her. They looked at
her and down at themselves – or rather, in so doing they looked
at each other; for to look at themselves they had to look over at
each other, such being the nature of their restoration.

Sita, what hast thou done? Or what has happened? Or what
in thy flurry hast thou made to happen? In a word (to put the
question so that it takes proper cognizance of the fluid bound-
ary between doing and happening), what has come to pass with
you? The excitement in which you acted is understandable; but
could you not have opened your eyes a little better while you
did it? No, you did not put back the heads the wrong way

round – this did not happen at all. But – to tell it straight out and call the amazing truth by its name – the mischance, the mistake, the mess, or whatever all three of you might feel like calling it, that confronted you was this: you have fitted on to each one and sealed fast with the sword the other's head. Nanda's to Shridaman – if we may call his trunk without the chief feature of it Shridaman at all – and Shridaman's to Nanda, if the headless Nanda was in fact still Nanda. In short, they arose before you, not husband and friend in that order, but reversed. You behold Nanda – if he is Nanda, who wears Nanda's simple head atop – in the smock and draped trousers enveloping Shridaman's plump, slender-limbed body. You behold Shridaman – if the form may be so named that is equipped with his mild and gentle headpiece – standing before you on Nanda's well-shaped legs, the lucky-calf lock framed in stone-pearls on 'his' broad bronze chest!

What a state of things – all in consequence of too much haste! They lived who had been sacrifices. But they lived transformed; the body of the husband dwelt with the head of his friend, the body of the friend with the husband's head. No wonder that the rocky cave echoed and re-echoed as the three prolonged their amazed outcry! The one with the Nanda-head felt all down the limbs and the body which once had been appended, a mere detail, to the noble head of Shridaman; while that Shridaman (if we take the head as the decisive factor) stood full of embarrassment, seeking to recognize as his own the body which – when Nanda's simple head sat on its shoulders – had been the essential feature. As for the moving cause of this new order of things, she went from one to the other by turns, with cries of joy, with loud wailing and remorse; embraced first one and then the other, and at last threw herself at their feet to confess between sobs and laughter all that had happened and the late lamentable oversight.

'Forgive me, if you can!' she cried. 'Forgive me, dear Shridaman' – and she turned expressly to his head, deliberately overlooking the Nanda-body it sat on – 'forgive me too, Nanda' – again she spoke to the head in question as the essential thing, regarding it, despite its insignificance, as important and the

Shridaman-body thereto attached as the indifferent appendage. 'Oh, you ought to be able to forgive me! Think of the frightful deed to which, as you then were, you persuaded yourselves and the despair into which you flung me. Realize that I was about to strangle myself and after that had speech with the Unapproachable and heard her voice of thunder, which almost robbed me of my senses! Then you can realize that I was hardly in a frame to carry out her commands. Things swam before my eyes, I saw only unclearly whose head and limbs I had in my hands and had to trust to luck that the right would find the right. Half the chances were for it, and half against – and it has just turned out this way, and you have come out like this. How could I know whether the power of attraction between head and limbs was in the right proportion, when it was clear and strong as it was, though of course in different combination it might have been even more so? And the Unapproachable must bear some of the blame too; for she only warned me not to put your heads on wrong side before, and that I was careful about; that it could come out as it has, the high goddess never thought of that! Tell me, are you in despair over the manner of your resurrection and will you curse me for ever? If so, I will go and carry out the deed in which I was interrupted by her that was before all beginnings. Or are you inclined to forgive me, can you find it possible that under these circumstances brought about by blind chance, a new and better life could begin between us three – a better one, I mean, than would have been possible if the former situation were just restored as it was and by all human calculations must have had just the same sad issue again? Tell me, strong-limbed Shridaman! Slender Nanda, let me hear!'

The transformed youths bent over, lifted her up, the one with the other's arms, and all three stood embraced, weeping and laughing together. Two things became at once very clear: first, that Sita had been quite right in addressing the resurrected friends according to their heads; for it was definitely by these that their I- and my-feelings were conditioned. He who on narrow, light-complexioned shoulders bore the simple head of Garga's son knew himself to be Nanda. And equally the other, with the head of the grandson of Brahmans on top of a broad, bronze-coloured frame, knew and comported himself as Shridaman. But secondly, it was manifest that neither of them was angry at Sita for her mistake, but both actually found pleasure in their new guise.

'If Nanda,' said Shridaman, 'is not ashamed of the body that has fallen to his lot, and does not miss too much the breast-lock of Krishna, which would be painful to me, for myself I can only say that I count myself the happiest of men. I have always wished I could have a bodily form like this; when I feel the muscles of my arms, look at my shoulders and down at my magnificent legs, I am seized with unrestrained delight, and say to myself that from now on I shall hold my head high, in quite a new way; first in the consciousness of my new strength and beauty, and second because my spiritual leanings will now be in harmony with my physical build, and it will no longer be wrong or unfitting for me to speak in favour of simplification and cast my vote under the tree for the procession of cows round the mountain Bright Peak instead of for the Brahmanical rites, for it has become quite right and proper and what was strange is so no more. Of course, my dear friends, there is a certain sadness in this, that the strange is now become my own and no longer an object of desire and admiration, except that I admire myself and that I no longer serve something else in choosing the mountain feast instead of the Indra-feast, but rather that which I myself am. Yes – this kind of sadness, due to my now being that towards which I once yearned, I feel it, I admit. But it retreats into the background at the thought of you, sweet Sita, for you come before all thought of myself, and the advantage you will reap from my new circumstances – of which I am even now so proud and glad that for my part I can only bless this whole miracle and say: Siya, be it so!'

'You might at least be correct and say Siyat,' said Nanda, whose eyes at his friend's last words had sought the ground, 'instead of letting your peasant limbs rule your mouth. You are welcome to them, so far as I am concerned, I have had them much too long. But neither am I angry with you, Sita. I, too, say Siyat to this miracle, for I have always wanted a slender body like this, and now, when I speak for Indra's cult of words

and against simplification, it will become me better than it did
before – or at least if not my face it will become my body, which
has become a minor matter to you, Shridaman, but to me it is
the main point. I am not at all surprised that our heads and
bodies, when you put them together, Sita, displayed such strong
attraction; it was the power of the friendship which bound
Shridaman and me, and of which I can only hope it may suffer
no breach through what has happened. But one thing I may
say: my poor head cannot help thinking for the body that has
fallen to its lot, and seeing where its rights lie; and therefore I
am astonished and dismayed at certain of Shridaman's words
and the way they took Sita's future for granted. I see nothing
here that can be taken for granted. There is only a very great
question, and my head answers it otherwise than yours seems
to.'

'How so?' cried Sita and Shridaman as with one voice.

'How so?' repeated the slender-limbed friend. 'How can you
even ask? To me my body is the main point, and in this I
conform to the idea of marriage, for with the body are children
begot and not with the head. I should like to see him who would
deny that I am the father of the fruit Sita bears in her womb.'

'Pull your wits together, Nanda!' cried Shridaman, with an
involuntary shift of his powerful limbs, 'and think what you are
saying. Are you Nanda, or who are you?'

'I am Nanda,' the other replied. 'But as truly as I call this
wedded body mine and use the word "I" of it, just so truly is
Sita of the lovely curves my wife and her fruit of my begetting.'

'Indeed!' retorted Shridaman, with a quiver in his voice. 'Is
it really? I should not have dared to assert it, when your present
body was still mine and slept at Sita's side. For it was not that
body she really embraced, as I learned to my sorrow when she
muttered in her sleep. Instead it was the one I now call my own.
It is not in good taste, my friend, for you to touch on these
painful matters and force me to speak of them. How can you
insist on your head like this, or rather on your body, and
behave as though you had become I, and I you? Surely it is
clear that if that kind of exchange had taken place and you had
become Shridaman, Sita's husband, and I Nanda, then there

would be no change at all, and everything would be as it had been. The happy miracle is that only an exchange of heads and limbs has come about at Sita's hands, whereat our heads rejoice, being the decisive factor. Above all, our rejoicing is due to the happiness in store for Sita of the lovely hips. But now here you are, obstinately presuming on your present body, which is that of a married man, and assigning to me the role of friend! You display a culpable egotism, for you are thinking only of yourself and not at all of how she will profit by the change.'

'She would profit, as you call it,' retorted Nanda, not without bitterness, 'from advantages you are now proud to call your own. You are just as egotistic as I am. And you misunderstand me besides. I do not refer to this married body I now have, but to my very own proper head, which you yourself declare to be decisive, making me Nanda even when connected with my new and finer body. You are wrong to say I am not at least as mindful of Sita as you are. When she looked at me, of late – speaking in her sweetly trilling and lilting voice, which I feared to hear lest I should answer in the same tone – she looked into my face and into my eyes, seeking to read therein with her own, calling me Nanda and dear Nanda. At the time it seemed unnecessary, but I see it had great spiritual significance. It showed that she did not mean my body, which in and of itself does not deserve the name; you yourself have proved that, for now that you have it you still call yourself Shridaman. I did not reply to her, except for the most necessary things, and scarcely those, so as not to fall into the same trilling and thrilling key. I did not call her by name, I kept my eyes down so she could not read in them – all out of friendship for you and reverence for your wedded state. But now I have not only the head and the eyes she gazed into, so deep and questioningly, saying "Nanda", and "oh, dear Nanda", but the husband-body as well – and the situation is fundamentally changed in mine and Sita's favour. Hers above all! For if we are to put her happiness and satisfaction before everything else, then certainly there can be no purer and more perfect solution than the one I describe.'

'No,' said Shridaman, 'I would not have expected this from you. I was afraid lest you might be ashamed of my body; but now my former body might blush for your head, in such contradictions do you involve yourself, arbitrarily taking now the head and now the body as the important thing in marriage! You have always been a modest youth; but now all at once you scale the heights of presumption, and declare your situation the purest and perfectest in the world to guarantee Sita's happiness, when it is obvious that it is I who have the best, that is to say at once the happiest and most reassuring possible. But there is no sense or purpose in talking further. Here stands Sita. She must say to whom she belongs and be the judge of us and her own happiness.'

Sita looked bewildered from one to the other. Then she buried her face in her hands and wept.

'I cannot,' she sobbed. 'Do not force me to decide, I am only a poor female, it is too hard for me. At first, it seemed quite easy, and however ashamed I was of my mistake, yet I was happy about it, especially when I saw you were both happy too. But your words have bewildered my brain and cleft my heart in twain, so that one half opposes the other half as you do each other. In your words, dear Shridaman, there is much truth, and you have not ever put it beyond doubt that I can only go home with a husband who wears your features. Nanda's opinion too I sympathize with, when I remember how pathetic and insignificant his body looked without its head, I must agree with him that I probably meant his head more than his body when I said "dear Nanda" to him. But you used the word "reassuring", dear Shridaman; and it is difficult indeed to say whether the head or the body of my husband would reassure me more. Do not torture me! I am quite incapable of solving the riddle, I have no power to judge which of you is my husband.'

'If matters stand so,' said Nanda, after a helpless silence, 'and Sita cannot decide and judge between us, then judgement must come from a third or rather from a fourth party. When Sita just now said that she can only go home with a man who wears Shridaman's features, then I thought in my own mind that she and I would not go home but live somewhere in retirement, in case she should find a reassuring life with me as her husband. The thought of retirement and solitude has long been attractive

to me, for when Sita's voice made me doubt the loyalty of my
friendship, I would think that perhaps I might become a hermit. And I made acquaintance with such a man, practised in
self-mortification, Kamadamana by name, that he might give
me instruction in that kind of life. I visited him in the Dankaka
forest where he lives, and where there are very many other holy
men all about. His family name is just Guha; but he took the
name of Kamadamana, by which he desires, as anchorite, to be
called – so far as anybody has a chance to call him anything.
For many years he has lived in the Dankaka forest with strict
vows concerning bathing and speaking. I should say he cannot
be far from his transfiguration. Let us go to this wise man, who
knows and has vanquished life. Let us tell him our story and
put him as judge over Sita's happiness. Let him decide, if you
are agreed, which of us two is her husband, and may his words
prevail.'

'Yes, yes,' cried Sita with relief, 'Nanda is right, let us get up
and go to the holy man.'

'I see,' said Shridaman, 'that what we have here is an objective problem not to be solved from within but only by outward
wisdom; I agree to the suggestion and am ready to submit to the
judgement of the wise man.'

Being now so far agreed, they left the mother-house together
and returned to their conveyance standing down in the gully.
Here the question arose which of the friends should drive, that
being a matter of the body and the head both. Nanda, of course,
knew the way to the Dankaka forest, which was two days' journey away. He had it all in his head; while Shridaman was now
better adapted to hold the reins, just as Nanda had been before.
He gave up the office to Shridaman and sat down behind him
with Sita; but prompted his friend on the way he should take.

10

On the third day they reached the Dankaka forest, which was
green with the rains and thickly populated with holy men,
though large enough to afford each one sufficient seclusion and
his own little holding of desolation void of human kind. It was

not easy for the pilgrims to question their way through from solitude to solitude and find Kamadamana, the vanquisher of desires. All the hermits were one in wishing to know nothing of each other and each protested his conviction that he was alone in the wood, surrounded by unpeopled space. Holy men of various degrees were here: some of them had passed the stage of householder, and now, sometimes accompanied by their wives, were devoting the remainder of their lives to a mild form of contemplativeness. Others were yogi of the thick and thin kind, so to speak: they had as good as completely bridled the steeds of sense, by mortification and abstention fought their flesh to the knife, and managed to carry through the most awful vows. They fasted to the point of death; slept naked in the rain on the ground, and in the cold season wore their clothing wet. In the summer heat they lay between four firebrands to consume their earthly flesh – in part it dripped from them, in part it was consumed in the parching heat. To this they added further discipline by rolling days at a time on the ground, or stood continuously on the tips of their toes, or kept in constant motion by standing up and sitting down in quick succession. If by such practices they injured their health and the approach of their apotheosis was indicated, then they set forth on their final pilgrimage north and east, taking neither herbs nor roots to their nourishment but only water and air, until their bodies gave way and their souls were united with Brahma.

The seekers after decision encountered these various kinds as they wandered through the holdings of successive solitaries, having first left their conveyance at the edge of the woods with a hermit family they found leading a relatively light-minded life there, in touch, to some extent, with the outer world. The path to the particular unpeopled void where Kamadamana dwelt, was, as we said, hard to find. True, Nanda had once already found the way thither through the trackless waste. But he had done so in another body, and this hampered his intuition and sense of locality. The denizens of the caves and hollow trees were either ignorant or pretended to be so. It was only with the help of the wives of some former householders who behind the backs of their lords good-heartedly pointed out the way, and after another whole day and night spent in the wilderness, that they arrived in the preserve of their particular saint, and saw his whitewashed head with its sausage of braided hair, and his arms like dried branches reared up heavenwards, rising out of a swampy pool where he had been standing, God knows how long, up to his neck in water, his spirit gathered to a fine point. They refrained from calling to him out of reverence for so much burning zeal, and waited patiently for him to intermit his discipline. However he did not do so for a long time; either because he had not seen them or else just because he had. They had to wait for as much as an hour, keeping a modest distance from the pool, before he came out, quite naked, his beard and his body hair dripping with mud. His body was as good as fleshless, consisting merely of skin and bones; so there was, in a manner of speaking, nothing at all to his nakedness. As he approached the waiting group he swept the ground before his feet with a broom which he had taken from the bank. This, they knew, was in order not to crush any living creature that might be there. But he was not nearly so gentle to his unbidden guests: for as he came on he threatened them with uplifted broom, heedless that something irretrievable might happen to the creeping and crawling things where he trod, and that theirs would be the blame.

'Away,' he shouted, 'ye idlers and gapers! What seek ye in my unpeopled void?'

'O Kamadamana, vanquisher of desire,' answered Nanda with due modesty, 'forgive us that in our need we have so boldly approached you! The fame of your self-conquest has tempted us hither, driven by the urges of this fleshly life. Deign then, O most lion-hearted among wise men, to give us advice and useful counsel. Pray be so good as to remember me! Once already have I confided in you, to partake of your wisdom on the subject of the solitary life.'

'It is possible that I may recognize you,' said the recluse, looking at Nanda out of the deep caverns of his eyes, from under their threatening thatch of brow. 'At least I might recognize your face; but your form seems in the meantime to have gone through a certain refining process which I suppose I may ascribe to your former visit.'

'It did me a great deal of good,' Nanda answered evasively. 'But the change you perceive has a different cause and belongs to a story full of strangeness and stress, which is precisely the story of us three who petition you. It has set us face to face with a question we cannot solve by ourselves; we must obtain your advice and judgement. We have hope that your self-conquest may be so great that you can bring yourself to hearken to us.'

'It shall be,' answered Kamadamana. 'No one shall say that it would not. Of course it was my first impulse to chase you out of my preserve; but that too was an impulse which I reject and a temptation I am minded to resist. For if it is self-denial to avoid men, it is still greater self-denial to put up with them. Trust me, your nearness and the fumes of life you give out lie heavy on my chest and bring an unpleasant flush to my cheeks, as you could see were it not for their seemly coating of ashes. But I am ready to bear with you and your vapours, particularly since I have observed from the first that among the three of you is a woman grown, whom the senses find glorious; slender as a vine, with soft thighs and full breasts, oh yea, oh fie! Her navel is beauteous, her face lovely with partridge-eyes, and her breasts, I repeat, are full and upstanding. Goodday, O woman! When men look upon you, do not the hairs of their bodies rise up for lust? And the troubles of the three of you, are they not due to your snares and allurements? Hail! I should most likely have sent these young men to the devil, but since you are with them, my dear, pray stay, stop as long as you like! I rejoice to invite you to my hollow tree, when I will regale you with the jujube berries I have gathered there in leaves, not to eat but to renounce, and with them in my sight gnaw roots instead, since this earthly frame must from time to time be fed. And I will listen to your tale, though the fumes of life it exhales will come nigh to choke me. Word for word will I listen to it, for no one shall ever tax Kamadamana with lack of courage. True, it is hard to distinguish between courage and curiosity. It might be that I listen to you because I have got hungry here in my retreat, and lustful to have the fumes of real life in my nostrils. But the idea must be rejected, and no less the further suggestion that curiosity here too acts to prompt the rejection and nip it in the bud, so that actually it is the curiosity that ought to be nipped. But if so, then what about my courage? It is the same as it is with the jujube berries. The thought probably tempts me that I keep them beside me not so much to renounce them as to enjoy the sight of them. To which I make bold to reply that the pleasure of looking at them constitutes the temptation to eat them. Thus I should make life too easy for myself if I did not keep them beside me. And so the suspicion is done away with, that I have thought of this answer just for the sake of being able to share the alluring sight – since, even if I do not eat the berries myself but give them to you to eat, I can enjoy seeing you put them down. And that, in view of the illusory character of the divers manifestations on this earth, and of any distinction between the I and the you, is almost the same as though I ate them myself. In short, asceticism is a bottomless pit; unfathomable because the temptations of the spirit are mingled therein with the temptations of the flesh, until the whole thing is like the snake that grows two heads as soon as you cut off one. But it is all quite right, and after all the main thing is to have courage. So come with me, you life-reeking mortals of both sexes, come with me to my hollow tree and tell me of all life's manifold uncleanliness; tell me as much as you like, and I will listen, for my correction and to get rid of the idea that I am doing it for my own entertainment – the more one gets rid of, the better!'

With these words the holy man led the way for some distance through the jungle, always carefully sweeping before him with his broom. And they arrived at his own place, a huge, very old kadamba tree, still green though it was only a gaping hollow inside. Kamadamana had chosen this mossy, earthy home not for protection against the weather, for he constantly exposed his frame to the storm, wore wet clothing in cold weather, and sat between firebrands in the time of greatest heat. No, it was only that he might know where he belonged, and have a place to store his supply of roots, tubers, and fruits to eat, and firewood, flowers, and grasses for offerings.

Here he bade his guests sit down, which they hastened to do, in all modesty, well knowing that they were here only for his

asceticism, so to speak, to sharpen its teeth on. He gave them the
jujube berries as he had promised and they were no little refreshed. He himself meanwhile assumed an ascetic attitude,
which is called the Kajotsarga position: with motionless limbs,
arms directed stiffly downwards, and rigid knee-joints. He
contrived to keep separate, somehow or other, not only his
fingers but his toes as well; and thus remained, his spirit summoned to its height, in all his nakedness, which signified so very
little because of the lack of flesh. To Shridaman, because of his
headpiece, the office of narrator had fallen; so he stood in all the
magnificence of his present form beside the other, and spoke of
the events which had brought them hither and the vexed question which could only be solved by a fourth party, as some saint
or king.

He told it truthfully, as we have told it, in part in the same
words. To make clear the disputed point, it would have been
enough to tell only the final stage. But he reported it from the
beginning just as it happened in order to give the holy man
something to think about in his solitude. He began with an
account of Nanda's life and his own, the friendship between
them, and the way they broke their journey at the river Goldfly.
He described his lovesickness, his wooing and marriage, weaving
in such earlier information as Nanda's acquaintance with Sita,
at the feast of the swinging. Other points, such as the bitter
experience of his married life, he touched on with delicacy or
only by inference, not to spare himself, since his were now the
strong arms that had swung Sita up to the sun, and his the
living body of which she had dreamed in his former arms. No,
it was out of regard for Sita herself, for whom none of this could
be very pleasant and who throughout the narrative kept her
little head shrouded in her embroidered scarf.

The powerful Shridaman, thanks to his headpiece, proved a
good and skilful narrator. Even Sita and Nanda, who knew the
whole thing, of course, heard their own story, horrible as it was,
with pleasure from his lips, and Kamadamana, although he
maintained his Kajotsarga position unchanged, presumably
found it arresting too. Shridaman recounted his own and
Nanda's grisly deed, the relenting of the goddess to Sita, and

Sita's pardonable error at the work of restoration. At last he got
to the end, and put the question.

'Thus and thus was it,' said he. 'The husband's head was
bestowed on the body of his friend, the friend's on the body of
the husband. Be so gracious, then, as to pronounce in your
wisdom upon our bewildered state, holy Kamadamana! As thou
decreest, so will we be bound and act according, for we ourselves cannot decide. To whom now belongs this all-round fine-
limbed woman, and who is truly her husband?'

'Yes, tell us, tell us, O vanquisher of desire!' cried Nanda
loudly and with confidence. Sita only hastily pulled her veil
from her head to direct her lotus-eyes expectantly upon Kamadamana.

The latter drew his fingers and toes together and sighed
deeply. Then he took his broom, swept himself a spot on the
ground free from vulnerable insects, and sat down with his
guests.

'Faugh!' said he. 'You three are certainly the right people for
me! I was prepared of course for a tale full of life's headiest
fumes. But this of yours, you could fairly cut it with a knife. It
is easier for me to hold out between my four firebrands in the
hottest summer heat than to breathe in the steam you are giving
out. If I had not rouged my face with ashes you could see the
flush on my decently lank cheeks or rather on the ascetic bones
of them. Ah children, children! Like to the ox that with his
eyes bound up turns the oil-mill round and round, so you are
turned upon the wheel of life, anguished with appetite,
pricked and twitched in your flesh by the six miller's men of the
passions. Could you not leave off? Must you still go on, with
your ogling, licking, slavering, your knees giving way with desire when the object of your delusion heaves in sight? Yes, yes, I
know, I know it all: the body of love, with bitter lust bedewed –
limb-play 'neath satin skin, unguent-imbrued – the noble vault
the shoulder makes – the sniffing nose, loose mouth that seeks –
sweet breasts adorned with tender stars – the armpits' hollow
with sweat-drenched hairs – oh, pasturage for hands to rove,
fair hips, fine loins, back supple, belly breathing love – the
bliss-embrace of arms, the bloomy thighs, cool twin delight of

hillocks that behind them lies – till all agog with lust at pitch they work at coupling play in hot and reeking dark, each urging other on more bliss to capture, they flute each other to a heaven of rapture – and this and that and here and there – I know it all, of all I am aware!'

'But so are we – we know all that ourselves and of ourselves, great Kamadamana,' said Nanda with suppressed impatience in his voice. 'Will you not be so good as to come to the point and instruct us, who is Sita's husband, that we may finally know and act according?'

'The judgement,' replied the holy man, 'is as good as given. It is clear that I am surprised you are not far enough along in knowledge of the right things that you need a judge in so clear and self-evident a matter. The little tidbit there, of course, is the wife of him who has his friend's head on his shoulders. For in the marriage one reaches the right hand to the bride; but the hand belongs to the body; and the body is the friend's.'

With an exultant cry Nanda leaped to his finely shaped feet. Sita and Shridaman sat still with bowed heads.

'But that is only the premise,' Kamadamana went on in a louder voice. 'The conclusion follows to surmount and outsound it, and crown it with truth. Please wait a moment.'

With that he stood up and went inside his hollow, fetched a rude garment, a sort of apron made out of thin bark, and clothed his nakedness with it. Then he spoke:

> 'Husband is, who wears the husband's head.
> Here lies no doubt at all, must it be said,
> As woman is the highest bliss and bourne of songs,
> So among limbs to head the highest rank belongs.'

It was Sita's and Shridaman's turn to lift their heads and look joyfully at each other. Nanda, who had but now been so glad, remarked in a crestfallen voice:

'But you said something quite different before!'

'What I said last,' replied Kamadamana, 'is decisive.'

So now they had their verdict. Nanda, in his refined state, could least of all murmur against it, since he himself had proposed to take the holy man for their judge. Nor could he object to the irreproachable gallantry on which Kamadamana had based his decree.

They all bowed low before Kamadamana and departed hence. Together they went, not speaking, for some distance through the Dankaka forest, green with the rains. Then Nanda stopped in his tracks and took leave of them.

'All the best to you,' said he. 'I will now go my ways. I will find me an unpeopled void and become a hermit, as I previously intended. Anyway, in my present incorporation I feel myself a little too good for the world.'

Neither of them could blame him for his decision. They agreed with him, though it made them feel slightly depressed; and bade him farewell with the friendliness one shows towards a man who has drawn the shorter straw. Shridaman clapped him encouragingly on the shoulder that once was his own, and advised him, with a concern such as one seldom feels for anybody else, not to plague his body with extravagant discipline, and not to eat too many tubers, for he knew that a monotonous diet did not suit him.

'Let that be my affair,' said Nanda ungraciously. And when Sita tried to utter words of consolation he only shook his goat-nosed head, in bitter melancholy.

'Don't take it too much to heart,' said she. 'Don't forget that you nearly triumphed, and that you might be now about to share with me the legal joys of wedlock. Be sure I shall always feel the sweetest tenderness from head to foot for all that once was yours, and with hand and lips show gratitude for my joy, in ways so choice that only the eternal Mother can teach them to me!'

'Of all that I shall have nothing,' he replied obstinately. She even whispered to him: 'Sometimes I will dream of thy head too;' but his mien did not change, he only said sadly and stubbornly: 'Of that I shall have nothing.'

So they parted, the one and the two. But Sita turned back when Nanda was already a little distant, and flung her arms about him.

'Farewell,' said she. 'After all, you were my first husband, you first awakened me and taught me love so far as I know it; and whatever that dried-up holy man may think and sing about wives and heads, the fruit beneath my heart comes from you after all!'

With that she ran back to Shridaman the strong.

11

Once back at Welfare of Cows, Sita and Shridaman spent their days and nights in full enjoyment of the pleasures of sense; nor did any shadow trouble at first the cloudless heaven of their bliss. The little words 'at first', a faint premonitory troubling of their unclouded sky, are an addition by one narrating the story from outside; whereas they who lived in it, whose story it is, knew of no 'at first', but were only aware of their joy, which both sides considered no common thing.

It was, indeed, a happiness such as belongs to paradise and seldom to this earth. The common earthly joys, the gratifications falling to the lot of mortals in all the conditions of the moral order and social pressure under which we live, are circumscribed indeed. Makeshifts, renunciations, and resignation are the common lot. Our desires are boundless, their fulfilment sharply restricted; 'If I only could' is met on all sides by the stern 'It won't do'. Life soberly bids us put up with what we can get. A few things are granted, but more denied; that they will one day be granted is and remains a dream. A paradisial dream, of course; for in paradise, surely, that which is forbidden and that which is granted, so diverse here below, must there become one. The lovely forbidden must be crowned with legality, while the legal attains to all the charms of the forbidden. For in what other guise can paradise appear to the hankering man?

Well, it was just this unearthly kind of happiness that a capricious fate had dealt out to the wedded lovers on their return to Welfare of Cows. They drank it down in thirsty gulps – at first. For Sita, the awakened lover and friend had been two different people; but now, oh joy, they were one, and – by inevitable destiny – the best of each. What had been most individual in each had joined to form a new individuality surpassing all desire. Nightly on her lawful couch she nestled in the strong arms of Shridaman's friend and experienced his raptures as once on her husband's tender bosom she had closed her eyes and dreamed of them. Yet it was the headpiece of the descendant of Brahmans that she kissed in gratitude – the most highly favoured woman in all the world, for she possessed a husband who, so to speak, consisted of nothing but principal features.

And Shridaman, the transformed husband – how proud and glad was he not in his turn! We need not be concerned lest the change in him made an unpleasant impression on Bhavabhuti his father or on his mother (whose name does not occur in the story because she plays so modest a role) or on any other member of the Brahman merchant's family or the other inhabitants of the temple village. The idea that there was anything wrong or unnatural about Shridaman's physical improvement (as though the natural things were the only right ones!) might easily have arisen, if the metamorphosed Nanda had been there too. But he was far away, leading the hermit life, to which he had previously sometimes shown a leaning. The change in him, which might have been striking when reviewed together with his friend's, was known to nobody; there was only Shridaman, whose bronzed and beauteous limbs might be credited (so far as they were noticed at all) to the beneficial effect of married life on his masculine development. Sita's lord and husband, of course, did not go about in Nanda's loincloth, arm-bands, and stone-pearl necklace. Conformably to his headpiece, he wore as before the draped trousers and cotton smock which had always been his garb. And in all this we must see undeniable proof of the contention that the head is the all-important factor in establishing the human being's identity. Try to imagine your son or your brother or some acquaintance entering the room with his perfectly well-known head on his shoulders; whatever might be out of order with the rest of his appearance, would you entertain the smallest doubt that this was actually the brother, son, or acquaintance in question?

The description of Sita's bliss has been given precedence over Shridaman's in this narrative just as he himself, directly after his transformation, placed it, as we saw, before his own. But his happiness was in fact equal to hers and wore the same paradisial face. Indeed, I cannot sufficiently adjure the listener to put himself in Shridaman's place. Here was a lover who had shrunk in profound dejection from the beloved object, being driven to realize that she longed for the embraces of another. And now he was in the incomparable position of offering her everything she had so mortally craved. One feels tempted to rank his good fortune above that of the charming Sita. That love for Sumantra's golden child that had seized upon Shridaman when he saw her at her ritual bath – love so deep and ardent that he had thought he must die of it, to the great amusement of Nanda's vulgar mind; that violent, anguished attack of tenderness, kindled by a lovely image on which he at once hastened to confer a human dignity; that rapture, in short, born, of course, of spirit and sense combined, and of his whole personality – had been above all and in essentials a matter of his Brahman head, gifted by the goddess of speech with fervour of thought and power of imagination. That head's mild appendage, Shridaman's body, was not equal partner to it, and must in the marriage relation have betrayed the fact. Can we now realize the joy, the satisfaction of such a being, when to such a gifted, ardent, subtle head was added a good, gay, ordinary body, a body simple and strong, accurately corresponding to the spiritual passions conceived in the head? It is idle to imagine the blisses of paradise – in other words, life in the pleasure-grove called 'Joy' – otherwise than in the image of this perfection.

Even the depressing 'at first' does not come into the above description; and indeed is not pertinent there since it is not in the consciousness of those concerned, but belongs solely to the controlling sphere of the narrator's mind and thus casts only an objective, impersonal shadow. But now, indeed, it must be told that very soon, very early, it began to glide into the personal sphere; yes, probably from the beginning it played its earthly role to limit and condition in a way surely unknown in paradise. We must admit that Sita of the lovely hips had made a mistake when she carried out in the way she did the goddess's gracious command: a mistake not only in so far as she carried it out in blind haste, but also in so far as she carried it out not quite and altogether in blind haste. This sentence has been well considered and must be well understood.

Nowhere does the magic of Maya the preserver, life's fundamental law of illusion, deception, imagination, which holds all creatures in thrall – nowhere does it more show its deluding power than in love, in that tender craving of one single creature for another, which is so precisely the pattern and prime content of all the attachment, all the involvement and entanglement, all the delusions on which life feeds and by which it is lured to perpetuate itself. Not for nothing is lust called the love-god's most cunning mate; not in vain is that goddess called 'gifted with Maya'; for she it is which makes any phenomenon charming and worthy of desire, or rather makes it seem so; the sense-element is already apparent in the word itself, linking it with ideas of brilliance and beauty. Lust it was, the goddess and deceiver, made Sita's form so dazzling fair, so worship-ripe, to the youths at Durga's bathing-place, especially to the suggestible Shridaman. But note how glad and grateful the friends had been when the bather turned her head and they saw her face, that it too was lovely, the little nose and lips, and brows and eyes; so that the sweet form had not been deprived of value and meaning by ugly features. We need only to recall that to realize how much obsessed a man is, not only with the desired one but with desire itself; how he is not seeking sanity but intoxication and yearning, and fears nothing more than to be undeceived, that is to say relieved of his delusion.

And now see how this concern, that the little face the friends were spying on might be pretty too, proves dependence of the body, by its Maya-meaning and value, upon the head to which it belongs! Rightly had Kamadamana, vanquisher of desire, declared the head to be the highest of the limbs and on that statement based his judgement. Indeed, the head decides the value of the body for love, and the impression it makes. It is not enough to say that if it wore another head it would not be the same. Let one single feature, one expressive line be changed, and the whole is altered. Herein lay the error which Sita in error committed. She counted herself happy to have made it, because it seemed to her paradisial – and perhaps in the beginning had appeared so – to possess the friend's body in the sign of the husband's head. But she had not foreseen – nor in her happiness could at first admit it – that the Nanda-body, when combined with the narrow-nosed Shridaman-head, the thoughtful, mild eyes and cheeks covered with soft fan-shaped beard, was no longer Nanda's lively body but another altogether.

Another it was, at once and from the first minute after his Maya. But not only of this do I speak. For in time – the time that Sita and Shridaman spent 'at first' in perfect relish of their sensual joys, in the incomparable delights of love – the body of the friend, so hotly coveted and won at last (if one may still so designate the body of Nanda in the sign of Shridaman's head, when in actual fact the far-away husband-body had become the friend-body); in time, then, and indeed in no long time, the Nanda-body, crowned with the honoured husband-head, became itself, and aside from any Maya, quite a different one. Under the influence of the head and the laws of the head, it gradually become like a husband-body.

That is the common lot, the regular effect of married life. Sita's melancholy experience differed on this point not greatly from that of another woman who presently no longer recognizes in her easy-going spouse the slender lusty youth who wooed her. Yet here the common lot had a special bearing and cause.

The Shridaman-head had shown its influence when Sita's wedded lord continued to dress his new body as he had the old and not as Nanda did. Again, he did not follow Nanda's practice of anointing his skin with mustard oil. His head could not tolerate this odour on his own person; he stopped using the oil and that was rather disappointing to Sita. Another slight disappointment was the fact that when Shridaman sat on the ground his posture – as need hardly be said – was conditioned not by his body but by his head. He had contempt for the rustic position beloved of Nanda, and sat sidewise as he always had. But all these were trifles and belonged to early days.

Shridaman, the Brahman's grandson, continued, even with Nanda's body, to be what he had been and to live as he had lived. He was no smith nor herd, but a vanija and son of a vanija, who helped his father carry on a respectable trade; as the

father declined in strength the son took over the business. No
heavy hammer did he wield, nor pastured the kine on the mountain Bright Peak; but bought and sold mull and camphor, silk
and calico, likewise rice-mallets and firelighters to supply the
needs of the folk at Welfare of Cows. Between times he read in
the Vedas. It was no miracle then, however miraculous the tale
may otherwise sound, that Nanda's arms soon began to lose
their strength and grow thinner; his chest to narrow and relax
and some slight fat to gather on his little belly – in short that he
fell more and more into the husband pattern. Even the lucky-
calf lock failed him; not altogether, it merely grew thinner, so
that it was scarcely recognizable as Krishna's sign – Sita his wife
observed with pain. It is undeniable that a certain refinement, in
part Brahman, in part clerkly, an ennoblement, if you like, was
– aside from any Maya – bound up with the change, and extended even to his complexion, which turned some shades
lighter; his hands and feet grew smaller and finer, more delicate
the bones and knee-joints. And in short the joyous friend-body,
in its former life the chief of the whole, turned into a tame
appendage to a head, into whose noble impulses it soon neither
could nor would enter with any paradisial completeness, and
even bore them company with a certain reluctance.

Such was Sita's and Shridaman's wedded experience, once
the truly incomparable joys of the honeymoon were past. Things
did not get so far that the Nanda-body changed back completely
into the Shridaman-body – when indeed everything would have
been as before. Our narrative will not exaggerate, rather it
emphasizes the factors limiting the bodily change, and its restriction to unmistakable signs, in order to gain understanding
for the fact that the effect was reciprocal between head and
limbs; since the Shridaman-head, conditioning his I- and my-
feeling, underwent adaptation in its turn. This might be explained on natural grounds by secretions common to head and
body; but on philosophical ones by loftier considerations.

There is an intellectual beauty and one that speaks to the
senses. Some people will have it that the beautiful belongs solely
to the field of sense; they separate the intellectual entirely from
it, so that our world presents a picture of cleavage between the

two. This is the basis of the Vedic teaching; 'Bliss experienced in all the universe is of two kinds only: the joys received through the body and those through the redeeming peace of the spirit.' Yet it follows directly from the doctrine that the spirit does not stand in the same relation to the beautiful that the ugly does and is not inevitably one and the same. The things of the spirit and mind are not synonymous with the ugly, nor need they be; for they take on beauty through knowledge of the beautiful and love of it, and express that love as spiritual beauty. So their love is by no means an irrelevant and hopeless thing; for by the law of attraction of opposites the beautiful yearns in its turn towards the spiritual, admires it, and welcomes its wooing. This world is not so made that spirit is fated to love only spirit, and beauty only beauty. Indeed the very contrast between the two points out, with a clarity at once intellectual and beautiful, that the world's goal is union between spirit and beauty, a bliss no longer divided but whole and consummate. This tale of ours is but an illustration of the failures and false starts attending the effort to reach the goal.

Shridaman, son of Bhavabhuti, had by mistake been given a beautiful, sturdy body to accompany his noble head, where love of the beautiful reigned. And his mind straightway found something sad in the fact that the strange had now become his and was no longer an object of admiration – in other words, that he was not himself that after which he had yearned. This 'sadness' unfortunately persisted throughout the changes which his head suffered in combination with the new body; for these changes were such as go on in a head that through possession of the beautiful more or less loses the love of it and therewith its own spiritual beauty.

The question remains open whether this process would not have taken place anyhow, without the bodily change, simply because Shridaman now possessed the lovely Sita. We have already said that the case in general was like the common run of cases, though exaggerated by special circumstances. To the objective listener, it is merely an interesting fact, but to the lovely Sita it must have been a distressing and sobering sight, that her husband's fine thin lips got fuller and thicker in his soft beard until they finally curled over in a roll of flesh; that his nose, once thin as a knife blade, took on fleshiness too, and showed an undeniable inclination to droop and decline into the goat-like. His eyes in time wore an expression of rather heavy joviality. The final product was a Shridaman with a finer Nanda-body and a coarser Shridaman-head; there was no longer anything right about him at all. And here the narrator would particularly invoke the sympathy of his hearers for Sita's feelings as she watched the changes and drew inevitable conclusions about corresponding changes which might have taken place in the distant friend.

She thought about her husband's body, which she had embraced in not precisely blissful but sanctified and provocative bridal nights, and which she no longer possessed – or which, if you like, as it was now the friend-body, she still did not possess – and she doubted not where the lucky-calf lock was to be found. Moreover she definitely suspected that a refining process must have taken place in the loyal friend-head which now sat atop the husband-body, in the same way that the friend-body was now crowned by the husband-head. It was this speculation, even more than the other, that moved her. Soon she had no more rest by day or night, not even in her husband's moderated arms. The lonely and doubtless beautified husband-body hovered before her, wearing a pathetically refined Nanda-head, and suffering spiritually from the separation. Longing and pity for him so far away were born and grew in her, so that she closed her eyes in Shridaman's wedded embraces and in lust waxed pale for very woe.

12

When her time was come, Sita bore to Shridaman the fruit of her womb, a little boy, to whom they gave the name of Samadhi, which means 'collection'. They waved a cow's tail above the new-born to ward off evil, and put cow-dung on his head to the same end – as was right and proper. The joy of the parents (if that is the right word) was very great, for the boy was neither pale nor blind. True, he was very light-skinned; but that might come from his mother's Kshatriya or warrior blood. He turned out later to be very near-sighted. Thus do prophecies and folklore get themselves fulfilled, somewhat darkly and imperfectly. You may say they have 'come true', or that they have not, as you like.

After a while Samadhi got the nickname of Andhaka (little blind one) on account of his near-sightedness, and the name gradually ousted the first one. But the weakness lent his gazelle-like eyes a soft appealing gloss and made them even lovelier than Sita's which they resembled. Altogether, he took far more after her than after either of his two fathers. She was obviously the clearest and most unequivocal element in his composition, and it was natural that his form should shape itself to hers. He was pretty as a picture; and once he had got past the stage of soiled and crippling swaddlings he proved to be a model of symmetry and strength. Shridaman loved him as his own flesh and blood; and his soul began to register certain feelings of abdication, a desire to hand over the business of living to his son.

But the years in which Samadhi-Andhaka developed into loveliness at his mother's breast and in his hammock cradle were just the ones during which the changes slowly took place in Shridaman's head and limbs, turning his whole person so decisively into the husband-form that Sita could endure it no longer. She felt an overmastering sympathy with the far-off friend in whom she envisaged the begetter of her little son. The longing to see him again, to see what he in his turn might have become by operation of the law of assimilation; to show him his delightful offspring, that he too might have his joy in him, that longing filled her soul to overflowing, yet she dared not communicate it to her husband-head. So when Samadhi was four years old, and was called Andhaka more often than by his name; when he could run, but more often fell down, it happened that Shridaman went away on business, and Sita made up her mind, whatever the cost, to seek out Nanda the hermit to console him.

One morning in spring, by starlight and before the dawn, she put on her pilgrim shoes, took staff to hand and with the other clasped that of her little son, dressed in his shirt of cotton from Kalikat. With a sack of provisions on her back she stole away unseen, and by great good luck was soon off with him out of house and village.

Her courage in face of the hardships and perils of her pilgrimage is evidence of the great urgency of her desire. Her warrior blood, watered down though it might be, may have come to her aid; certainly her beauty did so, as well as that of her son; for everybody rejoiced to help the lovely pilgrim and her shining-eyed companion on their way with word and deed. She told people that she was journeying in search of her husband, father of her child, who had felt irresistible craving to contemplate the nature of things and so had become a forest hermit. She wished, she said, to conduct her son hither, that his father might bless and instruct him; and this too made folk's hearts soft, reverent, and gracious to her. In the villages and resting-places she got milk for her little one, almost always she procured a night's lodging for herself and him in hay-barns and on the earthen banks of furnaces. Often the jute and rice farmers took her long distances in their carts, and when there was no such conveyance, she paced onwards with her staff undaunted, in the dust of the highroads. She held Andhaka's hand and he took two steps to one of hers and with his shining eyes saw only a little space of the road before him. But she saw far ahead into the distance to be travelled, the goal of her pity and yearning fixed before her eyes.

Thus in her wanderings she reached the Dankaka forest, having guessed that her friend had sought himself out a solitude in that place. But she learned from the holy men she asked that he was not there. Many could or would say nothing more; but some good-hearted hermit-wives who had fed and petted little Samadhi told her kindly where Nanda was. For the world of the hermit is very like other worlds: when you belong to it you know your way about there, and all the gossip and jealousy and rivalry and backbiting that go on. One hermit of course knows where another hermit lives and what he is doing. So these good women could betray to Sita that Nanda the hermit had set up his rest near the river Gomati (the Cow River), seven days' journey distant by south and west. It was, they said, a spot to gladden the heart, with all kinds of trees, flowers, and clinging vines, full of bird-song and herds of animals; the river-bank had roots, tubers, and fruits in plenty. All in all Nanda had chosen his retreat in almost too pleasant a spot, and the more austere among the saints did not take his asceticism very seriously, particularly as he observed no vows save bathing and silence, and ate the fruits of the forest as they came to hand, with wild rice in the rainy season and even now and then a roast bird. In short, he was merely contemplative after the fashion of any disappointed and dejected man. As for the way thither, it was without special difficulties or hardships, except for the robbers' pass, the gorge of tigers, and the vale of serpents, where certainly one needed to have a care and to take one's courage in both hands.

Thus instructed, Sita took leave of the friendly women of the Dankaka and with fresh hopes continued her journey as before. She surmounted the difficulties each day as they came, and haply Kama the god of love, in bond with Shri-Lakshme, mistress of good fortune, guided her steps aright. Unassailed she put behind her the robbers' pass; the gorge of tigers she went round, by instruction from some friendly shepherds, and in the vale of serpents, which lay directly on her route, she carried little Samadhi-Andhaka the whole way in her arms.

But when she came to the Cow River she set him down and led him by the hand, with the other planting her staff. It was a morning shimmering with dew. Awhile she paced onwards along the flowery banks; then as she had been instructed turned landwards across the plain to a strip of woods behind which the sun was just rising. The blossoms of the red ashoka and the kinshuka tree made the woodland glow like fire. Her eyes were dazed by the bright sun; but when she shaded them with her hand she distinguished a hut at the edge of the clearing, thatched with straw and bark, and behind it a youth in bast garments girdled with grasses, working at the structure with an axe. As she drew yet nearer she saw that his arms were strong like those that had swung her up to the sun; but his nose came down towards the only moderately thick lips in a way that could not be called goat-like but only refined.

'Nanda!' she cried, her heart on fire with joy. He seemed to her like Krishna, who is overflowing with the juices of great tenderness. 'Nanda, look, it is Sita coming to you.'

He let fall his axe and ran towards her and on his breast he had the lucky-calf lock. With a hundred welcomes and by a hundred pet names he spoke to her, for he had yearned sorely for her in her entirety, with body and soul. 'Art thou come at last,' he cried, 'thou mild moon, thou partridge-eyed, thou altogether lovely-limbed, fair-hued thou, Sita, my wife, with the glorious hips! How many nights have I dreamed that you came so to the outcast and solitary across the wastes, and now it is really you, and you have conquered the robbers' pass, the tigers' gorge, and the serpents' vale, that I wilfully put between us out of anger at the judgement of fate! Ah, what a splendid woman! And who is this you bring with you?'

'It is the fruit,' she said, 'that you gave me in the first holy wedded night, when you were not yet Nanda.'

'That will not have been much,' said he. 'What is he called?'

'He is named Samadhi,' she replied, 'but more and more he is called Andhaka.'

'Why so?' he asked.

'Do not think he is blind,' she responded. 'He is no more blind than he is pale, despite his fair complexion. But he is truly very short-sighted, so that he can only see three paces before him.'

'That has its good side,' Nanda said. They set the boy a little distance from the hut, in the fresh green grass, and gave him flowers and nuts to play with. Thus he was busy; and what they played – fanned about with the fragrance of the mango flowers spring sends to heighten desire, and to the music of the kokils' trilling in the sunlit tree-tops – that lay outside the range of his vision.

The story goes on to tell that the wedded bliss of these lovers lasted but a day and a night. The sun had not risen for the second time above the fiery blossoms of the wood beside Nanda's hut when Shridaman came on the scene. He had known as soon as he got back to his empty house whither it was his wife had gone. His family at Welfare of Cows had tremblingly announced the disappearance of Sita, and had surely expected that his anger would blaze up like a fire into which butter is cast. But that did not happen; he had only nodded slowly like a man who had known it all before. Nor had he set out after his wife in wrath and lust for revenge; he went indeed without rest but also without haste, direct to Nanda's retreat, having long known the precise spot and kept the knowledge from Sita in order not to hasten fate.

Mildly, with drooping head, he came riding on a yak; dismounted under the morning star before the hut, and did not even disturb the embraces of the pair within, but sat and waited for day to break them off. For his jealousy was of no ordinary kind such as is commonly suffered with furious sighs by dissevered lovers. It was lightened by the knowledge that this was his former body with which Sita was now renewing her marriage vows – an act that might as well be called faithfulness as the reverse. Shridaman's knowledge of the nature of things taught him that it was in principle unimportant with whom Sita slept, with him or with his friend, since even though one of them had nothing from it, she always did it with both of them.

Hence his lack of haste on the journey and his patience and composure as he sat in front of the hut and awaited the dawning of day. But we shall see that notwithstanding he was not minded to let matters take their course. The story says that at the first ray of dawn, while little Andhaka still slept, Sita and Nanda came out of the hut with towels round their necks, to bathe in the near-by stream; thus they perceived the friend and husband, who sat with his back to them and did not turn round as they appeared. They came before him, greeted him with humility, and in the end wholly united their wills to his, recognizing as inevitable what he had excogitated on the way about their problem and its solution.

'Shridaman, my lord and honoured husband-head,' said Sita as she bowed low before him, 'greetings and hail – and believe not that your coming is unwelcome and awful to us. For where two of us are, the third will always be lacking; forgive me then, that I could not hold out longer with you but overcome by pity sought out the lonely friend-head.'

'And the husband-body,' answered Shridaman. 'I forgive you. I forgive you too, Nanda, as on your side you may forgive me for acting on the judgement of the holy man and taking Sita for myself, only considering my own I- and my-feeling and not troubling about yours. You would have done just the same if the holy man's judgement had been in your favour. For in the madness and divisions of this life it is the lot of human beings to stand in one another's light, and in vain do the better-constituted long for an existence in which the laughter of one would not be the weeping of another. All too much have I insisted on my head, which rejoiced in your body. For with these somewhat diminished arms you swung Sita up to the sun and in our new distribution I flattered myself I had everything to offer for which she yearned. But love has to do with the whole. So I had to suffer that our Sita abode by your head and went out of my house. If I could now believe she would find her lasting joy and satisfaction in you, my friend, I would go away and make my own retreat in the house of my fathers. But I do not believe it. Possessing the husband-head on the friend-body, she yearned for the friend-head on the husband-body. And just as certainly would she feel pity and sympathy for the husband-head on the friend-body, nor would she find any peace and satisfaction, the distant husband would ever be the friend whom she loves, to him would she bring our son Andhaka, because she sees the father in him. But with both of us she cannot live, since polyandry is not permitted among superior beings. Am I right, Sita, in what I say?'

'As thy word sayeth, so, alas, is it, my lord and friend,' answered she. 'My regret, however, which I sum up in the word "alas", refers only to part of your words, and has no reference to the abomination of polyandry, for I cannot regret that it does not come into consideration for a woman like me. Rather I am proud. From my father Sumantra's side some warrior blood still flows in my veins, and against anything so base as polyandry everything in me rises up. In all the weakness and bewilderment of the flesh one has yet one's pride and honour as a superior being.'

'I had not expected otherwise,' answered Shridaman. 'You may be sure that I have from the beginning taken into consideration this attitude, as distinct from your female feebleness. Since you cannot live with both of us, I am certain that this youth here, Nanda, my friend, with whom I exchanged heads, or bodies as you like, Nanda will agree with me that neither of us can live, and nothing remains but to put off the division we have exchanged and unite our essences once more with the All. For where the single essence has fallen into such conflict as in our case, it were best it melt in the flame of life as an offering of butter in the sacrificial fire.'

'Most rightly, Shridaman, my brother,' said Nanda, 'do you count on my agreement with your words. It is unconditional. I should not know what we could still have to seek in the flesh, since both of us have gratified our desires and slept at Sita's side. My body could rejoice in her in the consciousness of your head and yours in the consciousness of mine, as she rejoiced in me in the sign of your head and in you in the sign of mine. But our honour may count as saved, for I have only betrayed your head with your body, and that is quitted, in a way, by the fact that Sita the lovely-hipped betrayed my head with your body. Brahma has preserved us from the worst; that I who once shared the betel-roll with you in sign of loyalty should have betrayed you with her as Nanda in head and body both! But even so we cannot honourably go on like this, since we are too enlightened for polyandry and promiscuity; certainly Sita is, and so are you, even when you have my body; and I myself too, now that I have yours. Therefore I unreservedly agree with everything you say about mingling our essence. Here are these arms, they have been strengthened in the wilderness, I offer them to build the funeral pyre. You know I have already offered before. You know too that I was always resolved not to outlive you, and I followed you without hesitation into death when you sacrificed yourself to the goddess. I only betrayed you when my husband-body gave me a certain right and Sita brought me the little Samadhi, whose bodily father I must consider myself, though I willingly and respectfully concede your parenthood according to the head.'

'Where is Andhaka?' asked Shridaman.

'He is lying in the hut,' answered Sita, 'collecting in sleep strength and beauty for his older days. It is time we spoke of him; for his future ought to be more important to us than the question of how we shall come with honour out of all these perplexities. But his case and ours are closely related, and we shall be acting for his honour in acting for ours. Were I to stay behind with him, as I might, I suppose, when you withdraw into the All, then he would pass through life as a wretched orphan child forsaken of honour and joy. Only if I follow the example of those noble Satis who united themselves to the bodies of their dead husbands, and mounted with them into the fire, and monuments, a stone tablet, and obelisks were erected to their memory on the place of their burning – only if I leave him will his life be honourable and the favour of men fall upon him. Therefore I, the daughter of Sumantra, demand that Nanda build the funeral pyre for three. As I have shared the couch of life with you both, so shall also death's fiery bed unite us three. For after all, on the other we were always three.'

'Never,' said Shridaman, 'would I expect anything else from you; for from the first I have known your high spirit and your pride, and that they dwell in you along with the weakness of the flesh. In the name of our son I thank you for your resolve. But we must consider well how to rescue our honour and human pride out of the desolation into which the flesh has brought us. We must take great care for the form that rescue takes; and in this particular my thoughts and plans as I have developed them on the way hither differ somewhat from yours. The high-hearted widow turns herself to ashes beside her dead husband. But you are not a widow as long as one of us is alive; and it is a question whether you would become a widow by sitting living

233

with us in the fire and dying as we died. To make you a widow Nanda and I must kill ourselves, I mean we must each kill the other; in our case either is right and both come to the same thing. We must fight like bucks for the doe; I have provided two swords, they hang on the girth of my yak. But it may not be that one shall win and survive and carry off the fine-hipped Sita for himself. That would do no good, for ever would the dead man be the friend after whom she would consume herself with longing, till she faded away in the arms of her husband. No, we must both fall, each struck to the heart by the other's sword – for only the sword is the "other's", not the heart. That will be better than if each of us turned the sword against his own present division; for it seems to me our heads have no right to decree death to the body attached to each, any more than our bodies would have the right to wedded bliss wearing heads that do not belong to them. Indeed the battle will be sore; for the head and body of each of us must take care not to fight for itself and the possession of Sita, but to remember the double duty of giving and receiving the mortal blow. Still, each of us brought himself to cut off his own head – and this mutual suicide cannot be harder than that.'

'Bring on the swords,' cried Nanda. 'I am ready for the fray, and find it is a just solution to our rivalry. It is just, because in the process of adaptation of our bodies to our heads, our arms have come to be of almost equal strength – yours stronger on my body, mine weaker on yours. Gladly will I offer my heart to your weapon. But yours I will pierce through that Sita may not pale for love of me in your arms, but doubly widowed join us in the flames.'

Sita professed herself satisfied with these arrangements, she said they appealed to her warrior blood. Wherefore she would not withdraw from the combat but look on unflinching. So then this mortal meeting took place forthwith in front of the hut where Andhaka lay asleep, and on the flowery mead between the Cow River and the red-blossoming woodland; and both young men sank down into the flowers, each pierced through the other's heart. Their funeral, because of the religious ceremonial of suttee combined with it, became a great festival. Thousands gathered on the place of burning to watch the little Samadhi, called Andhaka. As next of kin male he brought his near-sighted gaze to bear and laid the torch to the pyre built of mango and sweet-smelling knots of sandalwood, the interstices filled with dry straw soaked in melted butter that it might catch quickly. Within the pyre Sita of Bisonbull had found her place between her husband and her friend. The pile blazed heaven-wards to a most unusual height; and if the lovely Sita shrieked awhile – because fire when one is not already dead is frightfully painful – her voice was drowned out by the yelling of conches and rolling of drums so that it was just as though she had not shrieked. But the story says, and we would believe it, that the heat was cool to her in the joy of being united with her twain beloved.

An obelisk was set up on the spot in memory of her sacrifice, and what was not entirely burnt of the bones of the three was collected, drenched with milk and honey, and buried in an earthen pot which was thrown into the holy Ganges.

But the little fruit of her womb, Samadhi, who was soon called nothing but Andhaka, he prospered upon earth. He en-joyed fame and favour as the son of a monument-widow, and to that was added a love called forth by his increasing beauty. Even at twelve years old he was like an incarnation of a Gand-harva for charm and supple strength; and on his breast the lucky-calf lock began to show. His poor eyesight, far from being a handicap, kept him from living too much in the body's con-cerns and directed his head towards the things of the mind. A wise and learned Brahman took charge of the seven-year-old lad; and taught him right and cultured speech, grammar, astronomy, and the art of thought. At the youthful age of twenty he was already reader to the King of Benares. On a splendid palace terrace he sat, in fine garments, under a white silk umbrella, and read aloud to that prince in a pleasing voice, from the sacred and profane writings, holding his book close in front of his shining eyes.

THE TABLES OF THE LAW
(*1944*)

HIS birth was disorderly. Therefore he passionately loved order, the immutable, the bidden, and the forbidden.

Early he killed in frenzy; therefore he knew better than the inexperienced that, though killing is delectable, *having* killed is detestable; he knew you should not kill.

He was sensual, therefore he longed for the spiritual, the pure, and the holy – in a word, the *invisible* – for this alone seemed to him spiritual, holy, and pure.

Among the Midianites, a nimble tribe of shepherds and merchants strewn across the desert, to whom he had to flee from Egypt, the land of his birth, because he had killed, he made the acquaintance of a god whom one could not see but who saw you. This god was a mountain-dweller who at the same time sat invisible on a transportable chest in a tent and there dispensed oracles by the drawing of lots. To the children of Midian this numen, called Jahwe, was one god among many; they did not bother very much about serving him. What service they undertook they did it to be on the safe side, just in case. For it had occurred to them that among the gods there could possibly be a bodiless one whom one did not see, and they sacrificed to him so as not to miss anything, not to offend anybody, to forestall any unpleasantness from any quarter.

But Moses, because of his desire for the pure and the holy, was deeply impressed by the invisibility of Jahwe; he believed that no visible god could compete in holiness with an invisible one, and he marvelled that the children of Midian attached so little importance to a characteristic which seemed to him full of immeasurable implications. While he minded the sheep belonging to the brother of his Midianite wife, he plunged himself into long, deep, and violent cogitations. He was moved by inspirations and visions which in one case even left his inner consciousness and returned to his soul as a flaming vision from without, as a precisely-worded pronouncement, and as an unshrinkable command. Thus he reached the conviction that Jahwe was none other than El'eljon, the Only-Highest, Elro'i, the God who sees me, He who had always been known as El Schaddai, 'the God of the Mountain', El otam, the God of the World and the Eternities – in short, the God of Abraham, Isaac, and Jacob, the God of the Father. And that meant the God of the poor, dumb, in their worship completely confused, uprooted, and enslaved tribes at home in Egypt, whose blood, from his father's side, flowed in the veins of Moses.

Full of this discovery, his soul heavy with command but trembling also with the wish to fulfil the mission, Moses ended his stay of many years with the children of Midian. He placed his wife Zipporah (a sufficiently noble woman because she was a daughter of Reuel, the priest-king of Midian, and the sister of his herd-owning son, Jethro) on a mule. He took along also his two sons, Gershom and Eliezer, and returned, travelling westward in seven day-journeys through many deserts, to the land of Egypt. That is to the lower land, the fallow country where the Nile branches out into the district called Kos, and variously known as Goschem, Gosem, and Goshen. It was here that the tribes of his fathers lived and drudged.

Here he immediately began to communicate his great experience to his kinsfolk; he talked to them whenever he went and stood, in their huts, their grazing grounds, and their workplaces. When he spoke he had a certain way of letting his arms hang limp at his sides, while his fists shook and trembled. He informed them that the God of their Fathers was found again, that He had made himself known to him, Moscheh ben 'Amram, on the mountain Hor in the desert Sin from a bush which burned but never burned out. This God was called Jahwe, which name is to be understood as 'I am that I am, from eternity to eternity', but also as flowing air and as mighty sound. This God was inclined towards their tribe and was ready under certain conditions to enter into a covenant with them, choosing them above all other peoples. The conditions were that they would devote themselves in full exclusiveness to him, and that they would form a sworn brotherhood to serve him alone in worship of the invisible, a worship without images.

Moses stormed at them and the fists on his broad wrists trembled. Yet he was not completely honest with them, and kept under cover much, indeed the essential thought, he had in mind. Fearing he might scare them off, he said nothing of the implications of invisibility, that is, its spirituality, its purity, its holiness. He preferred not to point out that as sworn servants of the invisible they would have to be a separated people, a people of the spirit, of purity and of holiness. Afraid to frighten them he kept silent. They were so miserable, so oppressed, and in their worship so confused, this kin of his father. He mistrusted them though he loved them. Yes, when he announced to them that Jahwe the Invisible was inclined towards them, he really ascribed to the God and interpreted for the God what possibly was true of the God but what certainly was true of him: for he himself was inclined to his father's kin, as the sculptor is inclined towards the shapeless lump from which he hopes to carve a high and fine figure, the work of his hands. Hence his trembling desire, hence too the great heaviness of soul which filled him directly after his departure from Midian.

He also kept back the second half of the secret; for it was a double secret. It included not only the message to his tribe of the rediscovery of their father's God and the God's inclination towards them; it included also his own belief that he was destined to guide them out of Egypt's house of bondage, out into the open, and through many deserts into the land of promise, the land of their fathers. That destiny was part of the mission, inseparably linked with it. God – and liberation for the return home; the Invisible – and release from foreign yoke: to him these were one and the same thought, but to the people he as yet said nothing of this second part of the mission, because he knew that one would inevitably follow from the other; also because he hoped that he himself could negotiate the release with Pharaoh, King of Egypt, with whom he had not-too-remote connection.

Was it, however, that his speech displeased the people – for he spoke badly and haltingly and often could not find the right word – or did they divine, while he shook his trembling fists, the implications of invisibility as well as those of the covenant? Did they perceive that they were being lured towards strenuous and. dangerous matters? Whatever the reason they remained mistrustful, stiff-necked, and fearful of his storming. They ogled their Egyptian whip-masters and mumbled between their teeth:

'Why do you spout words? And what kind of words are these you spout? Likely somebody set you up as chief or as judge over us? Well, we want to know who.'

That was nothing new to him. He had heard it from them once before he had fled to Midian.

2

His father was not his father, nor was his mother his mother. So disorderly was his birth.

One day the second daughter of the Pharaoh, Ramessu, was amusing herself – under the watchful eye of the armed guard and in company of her serving maidens – in the royal garden on the Nile. There she spied a Hebrew labourer who was carrying water. She became enamoured of him. He had sad eyes, he had a young beard encircling his chin, and he had strong arms, as one could clearly see when he drew the water. He worked by the sweat of his brow and had his troubles, but to Pharaoh's daughter he was the image of beauty and desire. She commanded that he should be admitted to her pavilion. There she plunged her precious little hands through his sweat-drenched hair, she kissed the muscles of his arms and charmed his manhood to wakefulness, so that he took possession of her; he, the foreign slave, took possession of the child of a king. When she had had enough, she let him go. But he did not go far; after thirty paces he was slain and quickly buried, so that nothing remained of the pleasure of the Sun-Daughter.

'The poor man,' said she when she heard about it. 'You are always such busybodies. He would have kept quiet. He loved me.' After that she became pregnant, and after nine months she gave birth in all secrecy to a boy. Her serving woman placed the boy in a box fashioned of tarred reeds, and they hid the box in the bulrushes on the edge of the water. There in due time they found it and exclaimed, 'O magic! A foundling, a boy from the bulrushes, an abandoned child! It is like the old tales, exactly as it happened with Sargon, whom Akki the Water Carrier found in the rushes and reared in the goodness of his heart. Such things happen all the time. What shall we do now with our find? It would be wisest if we gave it to a nursing mother, a woman of simple station who has milk to spare, so that the boy may grow up as her son and the son of her lawful husband.' And they handed the child to a Hebrew woman who carried it down into the region of Goshen and there gave it to Jochebed, the wife of Amram, who belonged to the tribe of the Tolerated Ones, to the descendants of Levi. She was nursing her son Aaron and had milk to spare. Therefore, and also because once in a while and quite secretly substantial gifts arrived at her hut from sources higher up, did she rear the unclassified child in the goodness of her heart. Before the world Amram and Jochebed became his parents and Aaron became his brother. Amram possessed cattle and fields, Jochebed was the daughter of a stonemason. She did not know how she should name the questionable child. Therefore she gave him a half-Egyptian name, that is to say, the half of an Egyptian name. For the sons of the land were often called Ptach-Moses, Amen-Moses, or Ra-Moses. They were named as sons with the names of the gods. Amram and Jochebed preferred to omit the name of the god, and called the child simply Moses. Thus he was called plain 'Son'. The only question was, whose son?

3

He grew up as one of the Tolerated Ones, and expressed himself in their dialect. The ancestors of this tribe had come into the land long ago at the time of the Drought. They whom Pharaoh's historians described as the 'hungry Bedouins from Edom' had come with the due permission of the frontier officials. They had received pasture privileges in the district of Goshen in the lower land. Anybody who believes that they received these privileges for nothing does not know their hosts, the children of Egypt. Not only did they have to pay taxes out of their cattle, and that so heavily that it hurt, but also all who had strength were forced to do manual services at the several building operations which in a country like Egypt are always under way. Especially since Ramessu, the second of his name, had become Pharaoh in Thebes, excessive building was going on, for building was his pleasure and his royal delight. He built prodigal temples all over the land. And down in the Delta region he not only renewed and greatly improved the long-neglected canal which connected the eastern arm of the Nile with the Bitter Lakes and thus the great ocean with the corner of the Red Sea, but he also constructed two arsenal cities on the banks of the canal, called Pithom and Rameses. It was for this work that the children of the Tolerated Ones were drafted. They baked bricks and carried them and drudged in the sweat of their bodies under Egypt's cudgel.

This cudgel was hardly more than a symbol of the authority vested in Pharaoh's overseers. The workers were not unnecessarily beaten with it. They also had good food with their drudgery: much fish from the Nile, bread, beer, and beef, quite as plentiful as they needed. Nevertheless, they did not take to or care for this work, for they were nomads, full of the tradition of a free, roaming life. Labour by the hour, labour which made them sweat, was foreign and insulting to their nature. The tribes, however, were far too tenuously connected and insufficiently conscious of themselves to be able to signal their dissatisfaction to each other, or to become of one firm mind about it. Because several of their generations had lived in a transitional land, pitching their tents between the home of their fathers and the real Egypt, they were now unanchored souls, wavering in spirit and without a secure doctrine. They had forgotten much; they had half assimilated some new thoughts; and because they lacked real orientation, they did not trust their own feelings. They did not trust even the bitterness that they felt towards their bondage, because fish and beer and beef made them uncertain.

Moses, also, as the supposed son of Amram, was destined to

form bricks for Pharaoh as soon as he had outgrown his boyhood. But this did not come to pass; the youth was taken away from his parents and was brought to Upper Egypt into a school, a very elegant academy where the sons of the Syrian town kings and the scions of the native nobility were educated. There was he taken, because his real mother, Pharaoh's child, who had delivered him into the bulrushes, was, though somewhat lascivious, not devoid of sentiment. She had remembered him for the sake of his buried father, the water carrier with the beard and the sad eyes. She didn't want Moses to remain with the savages, but wished him to be educated as an Egyptian and to achieve a court position. His half descent from the gods was thus to be half recognized in silence. Clothed in white linen and with a wig on his head, Moses acquired the knowledge of stars and of countries, the art of writing and of law. Yet he was not happy among the snobs of the elegant academy, but lonely was he among them, filled with aversion towards all of Egypt's refined culture. The blood of the buried one who had been sacrificed to this culture was stronger in him than was his Egyptian portion. In his soul he sided with the poor uncertain ones at home in Goshen, who did not even have the courage of their bitterness. He sided with them against the lecherous arrogance of his mother's kin.

'What was your name again?' his comrades at the school asked him.

'I am called Moses,' he answered.

'Ach-Moses or Ptach-Moses?' they asked.

'No, simply Moses,' he responded.

'That's inadequate and paltry,' said the snobs. And he became enraged, so that he almost wanted to kill and bury them. For he understood that with these questions they simply wished to pry into his uncertain history, which in nebulous outlines was known to everybody. He himself could hardly have known that he was the discreet result of Egyptian pleasure, if it had not been common though somewhat inexact knowledge. Pharaoh himself was as well aware of the trifling escapade of his child as was Moses of the fact that Ramessu, the master builder, was his illegitimate grandfather, and that his paternity was the result of iniquitous, lecherous, and murderous pleasure. Yes, Moses knew this, and he also knew that Pharaoh knew it. And when he thought about it he inclined his head menacingly, inclined it in the direction of Pharaoh's throne.

4

When he had lived two years among the whelps of the school in Thebes, he could stand it no longer, fled by night over the wall, and wandered home to Goshen to his father's tribe. With severe countenance he roamed among them, and one day he saw at the canal near the new buildings in Rameses how an Egyptian overseer beat with his cudgel one of the workers, who probably had been lazy or obdurate. Moses paled. With flaming eyes he challenged the Egyptian, who in short response smashed his nose so that Moses all his life had a nose with a broken flattened bridge. Moses seized the cudgel from the overseer, swung it mightily, and demolished the man's skull so that he lay dead on the spot. Not even once did Moses glance about to find out if anybody had observed him. Fortunately it was a lonely place and not a soul was near. Alone he buried the murdered man; for he whom Moses had defended had instantly taken to his heels. After it was over, he felt that killing and burying were what he had always desired in his soul.

His flaming deed remained hidden at least from the Egyptians, who never did find out what had become of their man. A year and a day passed over the deed. Moses continued to roam among his people and to probe into their frays with a peculiar air of authority. So it happened that once he saw two slaves quarrelling with each other. They were at the point of violence. 'Wherefore do you quarrel and seek to strike each other?' he said to them. 'Are you not miserable enough and neglected? Would it not be better for kin to side with kin, instead of baring your teeth to each other? This one is in the wrong: I saw it. Let him give in and be content; nor let the other triumph.'

But as usually happens, suddenly both of them were united against him, and they said, 'What business is it of yours?' Especially he who was in the wrong was extremely snappy and shouted quite loudly, 'Well, this caps everything! Who are you that you stick your ugly nose into things that don't concern you? Ahah! You are Moscheh, son of Amram, but that means very little. Nobody really knows who you are, not even you yourself. Curious are we to learn who has appointed you master and judge over us. Perhaps you want to choke me too, as you choked the Egyptian and buried him?'

'Be quiet,' whispered Moses, alarmed. And he thought, 'How did this get out?' But that very day he understood that it would be no longer possible for him to remain in the country, and he fled across the frontier where the frontier had a loophole, near the muddy shallows of the Bitter Lakes. Through many deserts of the land of Sinai he wandered, and came to Midian, to the Midianites, and to their priest-king, Reuel.

5

When he returned to Egypt, fraught with his discovery and his mission, he was a man at the height of his powers, sturdy, with a sunk-in nose and prominent cheek-bones, with a divided beard, eyes set far apart, and wrists that were unusually broad. He had a habit when he meditated of covering his mouth and beard with his right hand, and it was then that those broad wrists were especially noticeable. He went from hut to hut and from workplace to workplace, he shook his fists at the sides of his body and discoursed on the Invisible One, the God of the Fathers, who was ready for the covenant. Actually Moses did not speak well. His nature was halting and pent-up, and when he became excited he was apt to stammer. Nor was he master of any one language, but floundered in three. The Aramaic–Syro–Chaldee, which was the language of his father's kin and which he had learned from his parents, had been glossed over by the Egyptian which he had had to learn at school. And to this was added the Midianitic-Arabic which he had spoken so long in the desert. All of these he jumbled together.

Very helpful to him was his brother Aaron, a tall man with a black beard and with black curls at the nape of his neck. Aaron was gentle and held his large and curved eyelids piously lowered. Moses had initiated Aaron into all his beliefs and had won him over completely to the cause of the Invisible and all its implications. Because he knew how to speak from under his beard fluently and unctuously, he accompanied Moses on his preaching tours and did the talking for him. Admittedly, he spoke in a somewhat oily fashion, and not nearly transportingly enough to suit Moses, so that Moses, accompanying the speech with his shaking fists, sought to put more fire into his brother's words, and sometimes would blurt helter-skelter into the oration with his own Aramaic–Egyptian–Arabic.

Aaron's wife was named Elisheba, daughter of Amminadab. She too partook of the oath and the propaganda, and so did a younger sister of Moses and Aaron called Miriam, an inspired woman who knew how to sing and play the timbrel. Moses was especially fond of yet another disciple, a youth who devoted himself body and soul to his plans, and who never left his side. His real name was Hosea, son of Nun (that means 'fish'), of the kin of Ephraim. Moses, however, had given him the Jahwe name, Jehoschua – Joshua for short. Joshua was erect and sinewy and curly-headed, had a prominent Adam's-apple, and a clearly defined wrinkle between his brows. He carried his new name with pride, though he had his own view of the whole affair, views which were not so much religious as military. For him Jahwe, God of the Fathers, was first of all God of the fighting forces. The idea connected with the God, that is, the idea of flight from the house of bondage, was to him identical with the idea of the conquest of a new grazing ground which would belong solely to the Hebraic tribes. This was logical enough, for they had to live somewhere and nobody was going to hand them any land, promise or not, as a gift.

Joshua, young as he was, carried all the salient facts in his clear-eyed, curly head, and discussed them unceasingly with Moses, his older friend and master. Without having the means of carrying out an exact census, Joshua was able to calculate that the strength of the tribes tenting in Goshen or living in the slave cities, Pithom and Rameses, and including also the slaves who were far flung over the country, was about twelve or thirteen thousand people. This meant that there were possibly three thousand men capable of bearing arms. Later on these figures were immeasurably exaggerated, but Joshua knew them fairly correctly, and was little satisfied with them. Three thousand men – that was no terror-inspiring fighting force, even if you count on the fact that once on the way several kindred tribes roaming the desert would join them for the sake of winning new land. With such a force one could not dream of any major expeditions: with such a force it was impractical to hew one's way into the promised land. Joshua well understood that. His plan, therefore, was to seek first of all a spot in the open, a marking time and resting place, where the tribes could settle and devote themselves to the business of natural multiplication under more or less favourable circumstances. This natural growth amounted to – as Joshua knew his people – two and a half per cent per year. The youth was constantly on the lookout for such a hedged-in hatching place where they could grow further fighting forces. In his frequent consultations with Moses it appeared that Joshua saw with surprising clarity where one place in the world lay in relation to another place. He carried in his head a kind of map of all the interesting districts; he knew their dimensions measured in daytime marches, their watering places, and especially the fighting strength of their inhabitants.

Moses knew what a treasure he possessed in Joshua, knew also that he would have need of him, and loved his ardour, though he was little concerned with the immediate objectives of that ardour. Covering mouth and beard with his right hand, he listened to the strategic theories of the youth, thinking all the while of something else. For him also Jahwe meant an exodus, but not an exodus for a war of land seizure; an exodus rather for seclusion. Out in the open Moses would have his father's kin to himself, those swaying souls confused in their beliefs, the procreating men, the nursing women, the awakening youths, the dirty-nosed children. There in the open he would be able to imbue them with the holy, invisible God, the pure and spiritual God; there he could give them this God as the centre which would unite and form them, form them to his image, form them into a people different from all other peoples; a people belonging to God, denoted by the holy and the spiritual, and dis-

tinguished from all others through awe, restraint, and fear of
God. That is to say that his people would hold in awe a restrain-
ing, pure, spiritual code, a code which, since the Invisible One
was in truth the God of the entire world, would in the future
bind and unite all peoples, but would at first be given to them
alone and be their stern privilege among the heathen.

Thus was Moses' inclination towards his father's blood; it
was the sculptor's inclination, and he identified it with the
God's choice and the God's desire for the covenant. Because
Moses believed that the education towards God must precede all
other enterprises, such enterprises as the young Joshua carried
in his head, and because he knew that such education would
take time – free time out in the open – he did not mind that
there was so far many a hitch to Joshua's plans, that these plans
were thwarted by an insufficient number of fighters. Joshua
needed time so that his people could multiply in a natural way;
he also needed time so that he himself could become older, old
enough to set himself up as commander in chief. Moses needed
time for the work of education, which for the God's sake he
desired. So they both agreed, if for different reasons.

6

In the meantime he, God's delegate, and his immediate fol-
lowers, the eloquent Aaron, Elisheba, Miriam, Joshua, and a
certain Caleb, who was Joshua's bosom friend, of the same age,
and also a strong, simple, courageous youth – in the meantime,
they were not idle, not a single day. They were busy spreading
Jahwe's message and his flattering offer of alliance among their
people. They continued to stoke the people's bitterness against
slavery under the Egyptian cudgel, and they planted ever deeper
the thought that the yoke must be thrown off through migra-
tion. Each of them did it in his own way: Moses himself
through halting words and shaking fists; Aaron in unctuously
flowing speech, Elisheba with persuasive chatter; Joshua and
Caleb in the form of military command, in short and terse
slogans; and Miriam, who was soon known as 'the Prophetess',
in elevated tone to the accompaniment of the timbrel. Their

preaching did not fall on barren ground. The thought of allying themselves with Moses' agreeable god to become the chosen people of the Invisible One and under his and his proclaimer's banner to depart for the open – this thought took root among the tribes and began to be their uniting centre. This especially because Moses promised, or at least put it forth as a hopeful possibility, that he would be able to obtain the permission for their departure from Egypt through negotiations in the highest place, so that this departure would not have to take the form of a daring uprising, but of an amicable agreement. The tribes knew, if inexactly, Moses' half-Egyptian birth in the bulrushes. They knew, too, of his elegant education and of his ambiguous connections with the court. What used to be a cause of distrust and aversion, namely the fact that he was half foreign, and stood with one foot in Egypt, now became a source of confidence and lent him authority. Surely, if anybody, he was the man to stand before Pharaoh and plead their cause. And so they commissioned him to attempt to obtain their release from Ramessu, the master builder and master. They commissioned both him and his foster brother, Aaron. Moses planned to take Aaron along first because he himself could not speak fluently while Aaron could; but also because Aaron had at his disposal certain tricks with which he hoped to make an impression at court in Jahwe's honour. He could take a hooded snake and by pressing its neck make it rigid as a rod. Yet as soon as he cast this rod to the ground, it would curl up and 'it became a serpent'. Neither Moses nor Aaron took into account the fact that these miracles were quite well known to Pharaoh's magicians, and that they therefore could hardly serve as frightening proof of Jahwe's power.

Altogether, they did not have much luck – it may as well be mentioned beforehand – craftily as they had planned their campaign in counsel with the youths Joshua and Caleb. In this council it had been decided to ask the king for permission only that the Hebrew people might assemble and voyage three days across the frontier into the desert so that they could there hold a feast of offering to the god who had called them. Then they would return to work. They did not expect, of course, that

Pharaoh would swallow such a subterfuge and really believe that they would return. It was simply a mild and polite form in which to submit their petition for emancipation. Yet the king did not thank them for it.

However, it must be counted to the credit of the brothers that at least they succeeded in getting into the Great House and before Pharaoh's throne. And that not once but again and again for tenaciously prolonged conferences. In this Moses had not promised too much to his people, for he counted on the fact that Ramessu was his secret and illegitimate grandfather, and that they both knew that each knew it. Moses had a trump card in his hand which, if it was not sufficient to achieve from the king permission for the exodus, was at least potent enough to grant him audience again and again with the mighty one. For he feared Moses. To be sure, a king's fear is dangerous, and Moses was playing a dangerous game. He was courageous – how very courageous and what impression he was able to make through this courage on his people, we shall soon see. It would have been easy for Ramessu to have had Moses quietly strangled and buried, so that at last really nothing would remain of his child's escapade. But the princess cherished a sentimental memory of that hour, and very obviously did not want harm to befall her bulrush boy. He stood under her protection, ungrateful as he had been for her solicitude and for all her plans of education and advancement.

Thus Moses and Aaron were able to stand before Pharaoh, even if he refused categorically the festival-vacation out into the open to which their god had supposedly summoned them. It availed nothing that Aaron spoke with unctuous logic, while Moses shook his fists passionately. It availed nothing that Aaron changed his rod into a snake, for Pharaoh's magicians without further ado did the same thing, proving thereby that the Invisible One in whose name both of them were talking could claim no superior powers, and that Pharaoh need not listen to the voice of such a lord.

'But pestilence or the sword shall visit our people if we do not voyage three days and prepare a feast for our God,' said the brothers.

The king responded, 'That is not my affair. You are numerous enough, more than twelve thousand strong, and you will be able to stand some diminution, whether it be by pestilence or sword or hard work. What you, Moses and Aaron, really want is to permit slothfulness to your people, and to allow them to idle in their lawful labours. But that I cannot suffer nor permit. I have several unprecedented temples in work; furthermore I want to build a third arsenal city in addition to Pithom and Rameses. For that I need the arms of your people. I am obliged to you for your fluent recital, and you, Moses, I dismiss more or less with particular favour. But not a word more of desert festivals.'

The audience was terminated, and not only did it result in nothing good but it afterwards had decidedly bad consequences. For Pharaoh, his zeal for building affronted, and annoyed because he could not very well strangle Moses to death – for otherwise his daughter would have made a scene – issued the order that the people of Goshen were to be more pressed with labour than before, and that the cudgel was not to be spared should they be dilatory; on the contrary, they should be made to slave until they fell exhausted, so that all idle thoughts of a desert festival would be driven out of them. Thus it happened. The drudgery became harder from one day to the next for the very reason that Moses and Aaron had talked to Pharaoh. For example, the straw which they needed for the glazing of bricks was no longer furnished to them. They themselves had to go into the fields to gather the stubbles, nor was the number of bricks to be delivered diminished. That number had to be reached or the cudgel danced upon their poor backs. In vain did the Hebrew foremen protest to the authorities because of the exorbitant demands. The answer was, 'You are lazy, lazy are you. Therefore you cry and say, "We want to migrate and make offerings." The order remains: Gather the straw yourselves – and make the same number of bricks.'

For Moses and Aaron this was no small embarrassment. The foremen said to them, 'There you have it. And this is all the good the pact with your god has done us. Nothing have you accomplished except that you have made our savour worse before Pharaoh and his servants, and that you have given the sword into their hands for them to slaughter us.'

It was difficult to answer, and Moses had heavy hours alone with the god of the thorn bush. He confronted the god with the fact that from the very beginning he was against this mission, and from the beginning he had implored that whomsoever the god wanted to send, he should not in any case send him, for he could not speak properly. But the god answered him that Aaron was eloquent. True enough, Aaron had done the speaking, but in much too oily a fashion, and it appeared how absurd it was to undertake such a cause if one had a heavy tongue and was forced to have others plead as deputy. But the god consoled Moses and meted punishment to him from his own soul. He answered Moses from his own soul that he should be ashamed of his half-heartedness. His excuses were pure affectation, for at bottom he himself had longed for the mission, because he himself was as much inclined towards his people and the forming of them as the god. Yes, it was impossible to distinguish his own inclination from the inclination of the god; it was one and the same. This inclination had driven him to the work, and he should be ashamed to be despondent at the first misadventure.

Moses let himself be persuaded, the more so as in counsel with Joshua, Caleb, Aaron, and the inspired women they reached the conclusion that the greater oppression, though it did cause bad blood, was, rightly understood, not such a bad beginning. For the bad blood would form itself not only against Moses but also and especially against the Egyptians. It would make the people all the more receptive to the call of the saving God and to the idea of the exodus. Thus did it happen. Among the workers the discontent caused by straw and bricks was fomented, and the accusation that Moses had made their savour worse before Pharaoh and had only harmed them took second place to the wish that Amram's son should once again exploit his connections and once again go for them to Pharaoh.

This he did, but not with Aaron. Alone he went, not caring how haltingly he spoke. He shook his fists before the throne and demanded in stammering and plunging words permission for the exodus for the sake of the festival in the desert. Not once did he do so but a dozen times, for Pharaoh simply could not deny him admission to his throne, so excellent were his connections. It came to a combat between Moses and the king, a tenacious and protracted combat, the result of which was not that the king agreed to the petition and permitted the departure, but rather that one day he drove and chased the people of Goshen from his land, very glad to get rid of them. There has been much talk about this combat and the various threatening measures which were employed against the stubbornly resisting king. This talk is not entirely without basis, though it has been subjected to much ornamentation. Tradition speaks of ten plagues, one after the other, with which Jahwe smote Egypt, in order to wear down Pharaoh, while at the same time he purposely hardened Pharaoh's heart against Moses' demands, for the sake of proving his might with ever-new plagues. Blood, frogs, vermin, wild beasts, boils, pestilence, hail, locusts, darkness, and death of the first-born, these were the names of the ten plagues. And any or all of them could have happened. The question is only whether any of them, excepting the last, which has an opaque and never fully elucidated explanation, did contribute materially to the final result. Under certain circumstances the Nile takes on a blood-red colouring. Temporarily its waters become undrinkable and the fish die. That is as likely to happen as that the frogs of the marshes multiply unnaturally or that the propagation of the constantly present lice grows to the proportion of a general affliction. There were plenty of lions left in Egypt prowling along the edge of the desert and lurking in the dried-up stream beds of the jungle. And if the number of their rapacious attacks on man and beast suddenly increased, one could very well designate that as a plague. How usual are sores and blains in the land of Egypt, and how easily uncleanliness causes cankers which fester among the people like a pestilence! The heavens there are usually blue, and therefore the rare and heavy thunderstorm makes all the deeper an impression, when the descending fire of the clouds mixes with the sharp gravel of the hail, which flails the harvest and rends the trees asunder – all this without any definite purpose. The locust is an all-too-familiar guest; against their mass advance man has invented many a repellent and barricade. Yet again and again these yield to greed, so that whole regions remain gaping in bare baldness. And he who has experienced the dismal darkling mood which a shadowed sun produces on the earth can well understand that a people spoiled by the luxury of light would give to such an eclipse the name of a plague.

With this all the reported evils are accounted for. For the tenth evil, the death of the first-born, does not properly belong among them. It represents a dubious by-product of the exodus itself, one into which it is uncomfortable to probe. Some of the others, or even all of them, if spread over a sufficient period of time could have occurred. One need consider them as merely more or less decorative circumlocutions of the only actual pressure which Moses could use against Ramessu, namely and quite simply the fact that Pharaoh was his illegitimate grandfather and that Moses had the means to bruit this scandal abroad. The king was more than once at the point of yielding to this pressure; at least he made considerable concessions. He consented that the men depart for the feast of offering if their wives, children, and cattle remained behind. Moses did not accept this; with young and old, with sons and daughters, with sheep and cows, would they have to depart, to do justice to the feast of the Lord. So Pharaoh conceded wives and brood and excepted only the cattle, which were to remain as forfeit. But Moses asked where they were expected to find offerings to be burned and slaughtered if they lacked their cattle. Not one single hoof, he demanded, might remain behind, whereby, of course, it became apparent that it was not a question of a holiday but of a departure.

This resulted in a last stormy scene between His Egyptian Majesty and Jahwe's delegate. During all the negotiations

Moses had shown great patience, though there was fist-shaking rage in his soul. It got to the point that Pharaoh staked all and literally showed him the door. 'Out,' he screamed, 'and beware lest you come again into my sight. If you do, so shall you die.'

Then Moses, who had just been fiercely agitated, became completely calm, and answered only, 'You have spoken. I shall go and never again come into your sight.' What he contemplated when he thus took leave in terrible calm was not according to his desire. But Joshua and Caleb, the youths, they liked it well.

8

This is a dark chapter, one to be voiced only in half-whispered and muffled words. A day came, or more precisely a night, a wicked vesper, when Jahwe or his destroying angel went about and smote the children of Egypt with the tenth and last plague. That is, he smote a part of them, the Egyptian element among the inhabitants of Goshen and those of the towns of Pithom and Rameses. Those huts and houses whose posts were painted with the sign of blood he omitted, passed by, and spared.

What did he do? He caused death to come, the death of the Egyptian first-born, and in doing so he may well have met halfway many a secret wish and helped many a second-born to the right which would otherwise have been denied him. One has to note the difference between Jahwe and his destroying angel. It was not Jahwe himself who went about, but his destroying angel, or more properly, a whole band of such, carefully chosen. And if one wishes to search among the many for one single apparition, there is much to point to a certain straight, youthful figure with a curly head, a prominent Adam's-apple, and a determined, wrinkled brow. He becomes the traditional type of the destroying angel, who at all times is glad when unprofitable negotiations are ended and deeds begin.

During Moses' tenacious audiences with Pharaoh, the preparations for decisive deeds had not been neglected. Moses' part in them was limited: he merely sent his wife and sons secretly to Midian to his brother-in-law, Jethro. Expecting serious trouble, he did not wish to be burdened with their care. Joshua, however, whose relationship to Moses was recognizably similar to the relationship of the destroying angel to Jahwe, had acted according to his nature; though he did not possess the means or as yet the prestige to get three thousand arm-bearing comrades ready for war under his command, he at least had selected a group, had armed them, exercised them, and reared them in discipline. For a beginning, a good deal could be accomplished with them.

What then occurred is shrouded in darkness – the very darkness of that certain vesper night which was supposed to be a holiday night for the slave tribes. The Egyptians assumed that these tribes wanted to have some compensation for the festival in the desert which had been denied to them, and thus had planned to hold a celebration enhanced by feasting and illumination. For they had even borrowed gold and silver vessels from their Egyptian neighbours. Instead of this there occurred that appearance of the destroying angel, that death of the first-born, in all those dwellings unmarked with blood by the bundle of hyssop. It was a visitation which caused so great a confusion, and so sudden a revolution of legal claims and property rights, that in the next hour the way out of the land not only stood open to the people of Moses, but they were actually forced on the way. Their departure could not be quick enough for the people of Egypt. Indeed, it seems as if the second-born were less zealous to avenge the death of those to whose place they succeeded than to hasten the disappearance of those who had caused their advancement.

The word of history has it that the tenth plague at last broke Pharaoh's pride so that he dismissed Moses's people from bondage. Soon enough, however, he sent after the departed ones a pursuing armed division which miraculously came to grief.

Be that as it may, it is certain that the exodus took the form of expulsion. The haste with which it happened is indicated by the fact that nobody had time to leaven his bread for the journey. The people were provided only with unleavened emergency cakes. Later Moses formed of this occurrence a memorial feast for all time. But in other respects everybody, great and small, was quite prepared for the departure. While the destroying angel went about, they sat with girded loins near their fully packed carts, their shoes already on their feet, their staffs in their hands. The gold and silver vessels which they had borrowed from the children of the land they took with them.

My friends, at the departure from Egypt there was killing and there was theft. It was Moses's determined will that this should happen for the last time. How can people free themselves from uncleanliness without offering to that uncleanliness a last tribute, without soiling themselves thoroughly for the last time? Now Moses had the unformed mass, his father's kin, out in the open. He, with his sculptor's desire, believed that out in the open, out in freedom, the work of cleansing could begin.

9

The migrants, though their number was much smaller than the legend narrates, were yet numerous enough to be difficult to manage, to guide, and to provision. They were a heavy enough burden for him who had the responsibility for their fate and for their survival out in the open. The tribes chose the route which chose itself, for with good reason they wanted to avoid the Egyptian frontier fortifications, which began north of the Bitter Lakes. The way they took led through the Salt Lake district, a district into which projects the larger, more westerly of the two arms of the Red Sea. These arms frame the Sinai peninsula. Moses knew this district because on his flight to Midian and on his return from there he had passed and repassed it. Its characteristics were better known to him than to young Joshua, who knew it only as a map he had learned by heart. Moses had seen these strange reedy shallows, which sometimes formed an open connection between the Bitter Lakes and the sea, and which at other times and under certain peculiar conditions would be traversed as dry land. If there was a strong east wind and if the sea was at low tide, the shallows permitted free passage. The fugitives found them in this condition, thanks to Jahwe's favourable disposition.

Joshua and Caleb were the ones who spread the news among the multitude that Moses, calling to God, had held his rod over the waters, had caused the waters to divide and make way for the people. Very probably Moses actually did this, and thus assisted the east wind with solemn gesture and Jahwe's name. In any case, the faith of the people in their leader could at this moment well do with confirmation, because right here it was subjected to the first heavy trial. For it was here that Pharaoh's mighty battalion, the mounted men in those grim, scythe-studded chariots all too familiar to the people, caught up with the fugitives and were within a hair's breadth of putting a bloody end to the whole pilgrimage to God.

The news of their coming, announced by Joshua's rear guard, caused extreme terror and wild despair among the people. Regret at having followed 'that man Moses' immediately flared up, and the mass murmuring arose which was to occur, to his grief and bitterness, at every succeeding difficulty. The women whined, the men cursed and shook their fists at the sides of their bodies as Moses himself was wont to do when he was excited.

'Were there no graves in Egypt,' thus was the speech, 'which we could have entered peacefully at our appointed hour if we had stayed at home?' Suddenly Egypt was 'home', that very Egypt which used to be the foreign land of slavery. 'For it had been better for us to serve the Egyptians than that we should die in the wilderness.'

This Moses had to hear from a thousand throats. The cries even galled his joy in the deliverance, which when it came was overwhelming. He was 'the man Moses who had led us out of Egypt' – which phrase was a paean of praise as long as everything went well. When things went badly the phrase immediately changed colour and became a menacingly murmured reproach, a reproach never far removed from the thought of stoning.

Well, then, after a short fright everything went miraculously and shamefully well. Through God's miracle Moses stood before his people in all his greatness and was 'the man who has led us out of Egypt', once again with a different connotation. The people pushed through the dry shallows, after them the might of the Egyptian chariots. Suddenly the wind dies down, the flood returns, and man and horse perish gurgling in the engulfing waters.

The triumph was unprecedented. Miriam the prophetess, Aaron's sister, played the timbrel and led the round dance of the women. She sang: 'Praise the Lord – a wondrous deed – steed and man – he has flung them into the ocean.' She had written this herself. One has to imagine it to the accompaniment of the timbrel.

The people were deeply moved. The words 'mighty, holy, terrifying, praiseworthy, and miracle-dispensing' fell incessantly from their lips, and it was not clear whether these words were meant for the divinity or for Moses, delegate of the god. For they now believed that it was Moses's rod which had drawn the drowning flood over the might of Egypt. This substitution was ever present. At those times when the people were not murmuring against him, he always had his troubles trying to prevent them from looking on him as God instead of as God's proclaimer.

10

At the bottom this was not so ridiculous. For what Moses began to exact of those wretched people went far beyond the humanly customary, and could hardly have sprung from the brain of a mortal. They stood agape at hearing it. He immediately forbade Miriam's dance of triumph and all further jubilation over the destruction of the Egyptians. He proclaimed: Jahwe's heavenly hosts were at the point of joining in the song of victory, but the holy one had rebuked them. 'How so! My creatures sink into the sea, and you want to sing?' This short and surprising pronouncement Moses spread among the people. And he added, 'Thou shalt not rejoice over the fall of thine enemy, nor shall thy heart be glad over his misfortune.' This was the first time he addressed the entire mob, some twelve thousand people with three thousand capable of bearing arms, with 'Thou'. It was a form of speech which embraced them in their entirety and at the same time designated each individual, man and woman, the aged and the child, pointing a finger against each one's breast.

'Thou shalt not utter a cry of joy over the fall of thine enemy.' That was to the highest degree unnatural! But obviously this unnaturalness had some relation to the invisibility of Moses's god, who desired also to be their god. The more thinking ones among the dark-skinned mob began dimly to perceive what it meant to have allied themselves with an invisible god, and what uncomfortable and exigent matters they could expect.

The people were now in the land of Sinai, in the desert of Shur, an unlovely region which once left behind would only lead to yet another lamentable district, the desert of Paran. Why these deserts had different names is inexplicable. Barrenly they joined one another, and were both quite the same, that is, stony, waterless, and fruitless – accursed plains, dotted with dead hills, stretching for three days or four or five. It was lucky for Moses that he had fortified his reputation by impressing them with the supernatural occurrences at the shallows. For soon enough was he again 'that man Moses who has led us out of Egypt', which meant 'into misfortune'. Loud murmurings rose to his ears. After three days the water which they had taken along gave out. Thousands thirsted, the inexorable sun above their heads, and under their feet bare disconsolateness, whether it was the desert Shur or by this time the desert Paran.

'What shall we drink?' they called loudly, without consideration for the leader, who suffered because he was responsible. Gladly would he have wished that he alone had nothing to drink, that he alone would never drink again, if only he did not have to hear continually, 'Why did you carry us forth out of Egypt?' To suffer alone is little torment compared to the trial of having to be responsible for such a multitude. Moses was a much tried man, and remained so all his life, tried more than all the other people on earth.

Very soon there was nothing more to eat, for how long could the flat cakes which they hak taken with them last? 'What shall we eat?' Now this cry arose, tearful and abusing, and Moses had heavy hours alone with God. He complained how unfair it was that God had placed all the burden of all the people on one servant alone, on Moses.

'Did I conceive all these people and give them birth,' he asked, 'so that you have the right to say to me, "Carry them in your arms"? Where can I find the nourishment to give to all? They cry before me and speak, "Give us meat that we may eat!" Alone I cannot bear the weight of so many people; it is too heavy for me. And if you demand this of me, it would be better that you strangle me to death so that I need not see their misfortune and mine.'

Jahwe did not entirely leave him in the lurch. On the fifth day they espied on a high plateau a spring surrounded by trees, which incidentally was marked as the 'spring Marah' on the map which Joshua carried in his head. Unfortunately, the water tasted vile, because of certain unsalutary additions. This caused bitter disappointment and far-rumbling murmurs. However, Moses, made inventive by necessity, inserted a kind of filter apparatus which held back the foul additions, if not entirely, at least largely. Thus he performed the miracle of the spring, which changed the plaints into paeans and did much to cement his reputation. The phrase, 'He who has led us out of Egypt,' immediately took on again a rosy glow.

A miracle occurred also with the nourishment, a miracle which at first caused exultant astonishment. It appeared that great stretches of the desert Paran were covered with a lichen which was edible. This 'manna-lichen' was a sugary tomentum, round and small, looked like coriander seed and like bdellium, and was highly perishable. If one did not eat it at once, it began to smell evil. But otherwise it made quite tolerable emergency food, mashed and powdered and prepared like an ash cake. Some thought that it tasted almost like rolls with honey; others it reminded of oil cakes.

This was the first favourable judgement, which did not last. Soon, after a few days, the people became wearied of this manna and tired of staying their hunger with it. Because it was their only nourishment, they sickened of it; it made them nauseated and they complained, 'We remember the fish which we got in Egypt for nothing, the squash, the cucumbers, the leeks, the onions, and the garlic. But now our souls are weary, for our eyes see nothing but manna.' This, in addition of course to the question, 'Why did you carry us forth out of Egypt?' Moses had to hear in pain. What he asked God was, 'What shall I do with the people? They no longer want their manna. You will see, soon they shall stone me.'

11

However, from such a fate he was tolerably well protected by Jehoschua, his youth, and by the able guards whom he already had called on in Goshen and who surrounded the liberator as soon as the menacing murmurs rose among the crowd. For the time being this armed guard was small and consisted only of young men, with Caleb as lieutenant. Joshua was waiting for the right occasion to set himself up as commander in chief and leader of the battle, and to bind into a regular military force under his command *all* those capable of bearing arms, all the three thousand. He knew that such an occasion was coming.

Moses owed much to the youth whom he had baptized in the name of God. Without him he would have been lost many a time. He himself was a spiritual man and his virility, though it was strong and sturdy, though it had wrists as broad as a stonemason's, was a spiritual virility, a virility turned inward, nourished and fired by God, unconscious of outer happenings, concerned only with the holy. With a kind of foolhardiness, which stood in peculiar contrast to his reflective musings when he covered mouth and beard with his hand, all his thoughts and endeavours dealt only with his desire to have his father's kin alone for himself in seclusion, so that he might educate them, and sculpt into God's image the amorphous mass which he loved. He was little or not at all concerned with the dangers of freedom, the difficulties of the desert, and with the question how one could safely steer such a crowd out of the desert. He did not even know precisely to what spot he must guide the people. In short, he had hardly prepared himself for practical leadership. Therefore he could be doubly glad to have Joshua at his side, who in turn admired the spiritual virility in his master and placed his own direct, realistic, and useful virility unconditionally at his disposal.

It was thanks to him that they made planned progress through the wilderness and did not stray or perish. He determined the direction of the marches according to the stars, calculated the distances of the marches, and arranged it so that they arrived at watering places at bearable if sometimes even just bearable intervals. He it was who had found out that the round lichen was edible. In short, he looked after the reputation of the leader and master. He saw to it that when the phrase, 'He who has led us out of Egypt', became a murmur, it would soon again take on a laudatory meaning. He kept the goal clearly in his head, and there he steered with the help of the stars and in accord with Moses, on the shortest route. Both of them were agreed that a first provisional goal was needed. Even if this was a temporary shelter, it would be an abode where one could live and where one could gain time. Much time had to be gained, partly (in Joshua's view) that the people might multiply and furnish him as he grew older a stronger number of warriors; partly (in Moses's view) that he might lead the mass towards God and hew them into a shape that would be holy, decent, and clean. For this his soul and his wrists longed.

The goal was the oasis Kadesh. Just as the desert Shur touches the desert Paran, so does the desert Sin adjoin Paran in the south. But not on all sides and not closely. Somewhere in between lay the oasis of Kadesh. This oasis was like a precious meadow, a green refreshment amid waterless waste, with three strong springs and quite a number of smaller springs, a day's march long and half a day's march broad, covered with fresh pasture and arable ground, and enticing landscape rich in animals and in fruits and large enough to quarter and nourish a multitude like theirs.

Joshua knew of this attractive spot: it was scrupulously marked out on the map which he carried in his head. Moses too had heard something about it. But it was really Joshua who had contrived to select Kadesh as their destination. His opportunity – it lay there. It goes without saying that such a pearl as Kadesh was not without its owner. The oasis was in firm possession.

Well, perhaps not too firm, Joshua hoped. To acquire it, one had to fight those who possessed it, and that was Amalek.

A part of the tribe of Amalek held Kadesh occupied and would most certainly defend it. Joshua made it clear to Moses that this meant war, that a battle between Jahwe and Amalek was inevitable, even if it resulted in eternal enmity from generation to generation. The oasis they would have to have; it was their predestined place for growth and consecration.

Moses had his reservations. In his view one of the implications of the invisible god was that one should not covet the house of one's neighbour. He said as much to the youth, but Joshua responded: Kadesh is not, strictly speaking, Amalek's house. He knew his way about not only in space but in historic pasts, and he knew that long ago – though he could not precisely say just when – Kadesh had been inhabited by Hebrew people, and that they had been dispossessed by the people of Amalek. Kadesh was property through robbery – and one may rob a robber.

Moses doubted that, but he had his own reasons for believing that Kadesh truly was the property of Jahwe and should belong to those who were allied to him. The place bore the name of Kadesh, which means 'sanctuary', not only because of its natural charm but also because it was in a certain sense a sanctuary of the Midianitic Jahwe, whom Moses had recognized as the God of the Fathers. Not far from it, towards the east and towards Edom, lay the mountain Horeb, which Moses had visited from Midian and on whose slope the god had appeared to him in the burning bush. Horeb the mountain was the dwelling-place of Jahwe – at least it was one of them. His original dwelling was Mount Sinai in that range which lay towards midday. Thus between Sinai and Horeb there was a close connection – that is, that they both were Jahwe's dwelling-places. You could perhaps name one after the other, you could call Horeb Sinai. And you could call Kadesh what it was actually called because, speaking somewhat loosely, it lay at the foot of the sanctified mountain.

Therefore Moses consented to Joshua's scheme and permitted him to make his preparations for the combat with Amalek.

The battle took place – that is an historic fact. It was a bloody, fluctuating battle. But Israel emerged the victor. Moses had given this name Israel, which means 'God makes war', to his people before the battle, to strengthen them. He had explained that it was a very old name which had slipped into oblivion. Jacob, the original father, had first won it, and had thus called his kin. Now indeed it benefited Moses's people. The tribe which previously had only loosely held to each other, now that they were all called Israel, fought united under this armoured name. They fought grouped in battle ranks and led by Joshua, the war-worthy youth, and Caleb, his lieutenant.

The people of Amalek had no illusions as to the meaning of the approach of the wanderers. At all times such approaches have only one meaning. Without waiting for the attack on the oasis, they burst in bulging bands into the desert, greater in number than Israel, and better armed. Amid swirling dust, amid tumult and martial cries, the battle began. It was an uneven battle, uneven also because Joshua's people were troubled by thirst and had eaten nothing but manna for many days. On the other hand, they had Joshua, the clear-seeing youth, who led their movements, and they had Moses, the man of God.

At the beginning of the engagement Moses, together with Aaron, his half-brother, and Miriam, the prophetess, retired to a hill from which he could view the field of combat. Virile though he was, his duty was not to do battle. His was a priest's duty, and everyone agreed without hesitancy that that could be his only duty. With raised arms he called to the god, and voiced enflaming words, as 'Arise, Jahwe, appear to the myriads, to the thousands of Israelites, so that your enemies shall scatter and those who hate you flee before your sight.'

They did not flee nor did they scatter. Or if they did, they did so only in a few places and temporarily. For though Israel was made fierce by thirst and by satiety with manna, Amalek disposed of more 'myriads'. And, after a brief discouragement, they again and again pressed forward, at times dangerously close to the commanding hill. It clearly appeared that Israel conquered as long as Moses held up his arms in prayer to heaven. But if he let his arms sink, then Amalek was victorious. Because he could not continuously hold up his arms with his own strength, Aaron and Miriam supported him under the armpits, and even held his arms so that they might remain raised. What that means one can measure by the fact that the battle lasted from morn to evening, and in all this time Moses had to retain his painful position. Judge from that how difficult is the duty assigned to spiritual virility, up there on the hill of prayer – in truth more difficult than the duty of those who hack away below in the turmoil.

Nor was he able to perform this duty all day long. Intermittently, and for a moment only, his helpers had to let down the arms of the master. And immediately this caused much blood and affliction among Jahwe's warriors. Then the arms were again hoisted, and those below took fresh courage. What also helped to veer the battle in their favour was the strategic gift of Joshua. He was a most ingenious apprentice of war, a youth with ideas and vision. He invented manoeuvres which were utterly novel and quite unprecedented, at least in the desert. He was also a commander stoical enough to be able to view with calmness the temporary loss of territory. He assembled his prize warriors, the carefully chosen destroying angels, on the right flank of the enemy, pushed against this flank determinedly, deflected it, and harried it sufficiently to be victorious in that one spot. It mattered not that the main force of Amalek had the advantage against the ranks of the Hebrews, and storming ahead gained considerable territory from them. Because of the breakthrough at the flank, Joshua penetrated to the rear of Amalek's force so that now they had to turn around towards him, without being able to cease fighting against the main might of Israel. And they who a moment ago had almost been vanquished now took new courage. With this the Amalekites lost their head and despaired. 'Treason,' they cried, 'all is lost. Do not hope any longer to be victorious! Jahwe is above us, a god of unbounded malice.' And with this password of despair, the warriors of Amalek let their swords sink and were overcome.

Only a few succeeded in fleeing north towards their people,

where they found refuge with the main tribe. Israel occupied the oasis Kadesh, which proved to be traversed by a broad, rushing stream, rich with nut bushes and fruit trees and filled with bees, song birds, quails, and rabbits. The children of Amalek who had been left behind in the village tents augmented the number of their own progeny; the wives of Amalek became Israel's wives and servants.

13

Moses, though his arms hurt him long afterwards, was a happy man. That he remained a much tried man, tried more than all the people on earth, we shall soon see. For the time being he could well be pleased with the state of affairs. The exodus had been successful, Pharaoh's avenging might had drowned in the sea of reeds, the desert voyage was mercifully completed, and the battle for Kadesh had been won with Jahwe's help. Now he stood in all his greatness before his father's kin, in the esteem which springs from success, as 'the man Moses who has led us out of Egypt'. He needed this esteem to be able to begin his work, the work of cleansing and shaping in the sign of the Invisible One, the work of hewing, chiselling, and forming of the flesh and blood, the work for which he longed. He was happy to have this flesh and blood at last all to himself out in the open, in the oasis which bore the name 'sanctuary'. Here was his workplace.

He showed his people a certain mountain which lay towards the east of Kadesh behind the desert. This was Horeb, which one could also call Sinai. Two thirds of it as overgrown with bushes, but at the summit it was bare, and there was the seat of Jahwe. This was plausible, for it was a peculiar mountain, distinguished among its neighbours by a cloud which never vanished and which lay like a roof on its peak. During the day this cloud looked grey, but at night it glowed. There, he told the people, on the bushy slope beneath the rocky top, Jahwe had talked to him from the burning thorn bush, and had charged him to lead them out of Egypt. They listened to the tale with fear and trembling. They could not as yet feel reverence or devotion. All of them, even the bearded men, shook at their knees like cowards when he pointed to the mountain with the lasting cloud, and when he taught them that this was the dwelling of the god who was inclined towards them and was to be their sole god. Moses, shaking his fists, scolded them because of their uncouth behaviour, and endeavoured to make them feel more courageous towards Jahwe, and more intimate with him, by erecting right in their midst, in Kadesh itself, a shrine in his honour.

For Jahwe had a mobile presence. This was another attribute of his invisibility. He dwelt on Sinai, he dwelt on Horeb. And hardly had the people begun to make themselves at home in the camp of the Amalekites when Moses gave him a dwelling even there. It was a tent right next to one's own tent. He called it the meeting or assembly tent, and also the tabernacle. There he housed holy objects which would serve as aids in the service of the Invisible. Most of these objects traced back to the cult of the Midianitic Jahwe as he remembered it. First, a kind of chest carried on poles, on which, according to Moses's explanation (and he was the man to know such things), the invisible divinity was enthroned. This chest they could take along into the field and carry before them in battle, should Amalek approach and endeavour to seek revenge. Next to this chest he kept a brass rod with a serpent's head, also called the 'Brass Serpent'. This rod commemorated Aaron's well-meant trick before Pharaoh, but with the additional import that it be also the rod which Moses had held over the sea of reeds to part the waters. He also kept in the tent a satchel called an ephod, from which the oracle lots were drawn. These were the yes and no, the right and wrong, the good and bad, the 'Urim and Thummim' judgements which were Jahwe's direct decisions in those difficult disputes which man alone could not solve.

For the most part Moses himself did the judging in Jahwe's stead, in all kinds of controversies and contentions which arose among the people. As a matter of fact, the first thing he did in Kadesh was to erect a tribunal where, on designated days, he passed judgement and settled differences. There, where the strongest spring bubbled, the spring which was already called

Me-Meribah, meaning 'water of the law', there he pronounced his verdicts and let the holy judgement flow even as the water flowed from the earth. If one considers that there were twelve thousand five hundred souls who looked up to him alone for justice, then one can well imagine how sorely tried was he.

For more and more of them sought their rights and pressed towards his seat near the spring, as the idea of right was something utterly new to these forsaken and lost souls. Up to now they had hardly known that there was such a thing. Now they learned first that right was directly connected with the invisibility and holiness of God and stood under his protection, and second that the conception of right also included the conception of wrong. The mob could not understand this for a long time. They thought that there, where right was dispensed, everybody had to be in the right. At first they could not and did not want to believe that a person might obtain his right through the very fact that he was judged in the wrong and had to slink away with a long face. Such a man regretted that he had not decided the matter with his adversary as he used to decide in former times, that is, with stone in fist, even if the affair might then have had a different outcome. With difficulty did this man learn from Moses that such an action was offensive to the invisibility of God, and that no one should slink away with a long face if right had declared him wrong. For right was equally beautiful and equally dignified in its holy invisibility whether it said yea or nay to a man.

Thus Moses not only had to pass judgement but to teach judgement. And greatly was he tried. He had studied law in the academy in Thebes, and knew the Egyptian law scrolls and the Code of Hammurabi, king of the Euphrates. This knowledge helped him to a decision in many a case. For example: if an ox had gored a man or a woman to death, then the ox had to be stoned and his meat could not be eaten. But the owner of the ox was innocent unless he knew that that ox previously was wont to push with his horns and had not kept him in. Then his life was forfeit, except that he could ransom it with thirty shekels of silver. Or if somebody dug a pit and did not cover it properly, so that an ox or an ass fell into it, then the owner of that pit should make restitution in money to the other man for his loss, but the carcass should belong to the first man. Or whatever else occurred in matters of violence, mistreatment of slaves, theft and burglary, destruction of crops, arson, or abuse of confidence – in all these and a hundred other cases Moses passed judgement, leaning on the Code of Hammurabi, and decided what was right and what wrong. But there were too many cases for one judge, and his seat near the spring was overrun. If the master probed the various cases only halfway-conscientiously, he was never finished and had to postpone much. Ever-new problems arose, and he was tried above all people.

14

Therefore, it was a stroke of great good fortune that his brother-in-law, Jethro, came from Midian to visit him in Kadesh and give him good counsel, counsel in such as the overconscientious Moses could never have found for himself. Soon after the arrival in the oasis, Moses had sent to Midian to his brother-in-law for the return of his wife Zipporah and his two sons, who had been entrusted to the safety of Jethro's tent during the Egyptian tribulations. Accommodatingly, Jethro came in person to deliver wife and sons, to embrace Moses, to look around, and to hear from him how everything had gone off.

Jethro was a corpulent sheik with a pleasant mien, with even and deft gestures, a man of the world, a paladin of a civilized, mundane, and experienced people. Received with much splendour, he put up at Moses' hut. There, not without astonishment, he learned how one of his own gods – peculiarly enough, the imageless one – had one so extraordinarily well for Moses and his people, and had, as he already knew, delivered them from Egypt's power.

'Well, who would have thought it?' he said. 'Obviously this god is greater than we suspected, and what you tell me now makes me fear that we have cultivated him too negligently. I shall see to it that we shall accord him more honour in future.'

The next day public sacrifices were ordered. Moses arranged these seldom, as he had little use for a custom common to all the people of the world. Sacrifice was not essential, said he, to the Invisible One. 'Not offerings do I want,' spoke Jahwe, 'but that ye shall listen to my voice, and that is the voice of my servant, Moses. Then shall I be your God and ye my people.' Nevertheless, this once they did arrange slaughter and burnt offerings in Jahwe's honour as well as to celebrate Jethro's arrival. And again the next day, early in the morning, Moses took his brother-in-law along to the Spring of the Law so that he could attend a court session and observe how Moses sat and judged the people. And the people stood round him from morn to evening, and there was no end to it, no question of being finished.

'Now, let me ask you one thing, my honoured brother-in-law,' said the guest when, after the session, he walked home with Moses. 'Why do you plague yourself like that? There you sit all alone and all the people stand around you from morn until evening. Why do you do it?'

'I have to,' answered Moses 'The people come to me that I may judge one and all and show them the right of God and his laws.'

'But, my good friend, how can you be so inefficient?' said Jethro. 'Is that the way to govern, and is it right that the ruler should have to work himself to the bone because he does everything himself? It is a shame that you drive yourself so that you can hardly hold your head up. What is more, you lose your voice with all that judging. Nor are the people any less tired. That is no way to begin. As time passes you will not be able to transact all business yourself. Nor is this necessary – listen to my voice. If you act as the delegate of your people before God, and personally bring before him only the most important cases, those cases which concern everybody, that is all you can possibly be expected to do. As for the other cases – well, look around you,' said he with easy gestures, 'look around among the mob and search for respectable men, men of some standing, and place them as judges above the people. Let one of these men rule a group of a thousand, another a hundred, still another fifty and even ten, and let them all rule according to the law and tenets which you have set up. Only if it is a great matter should you be called. The lesser questions they can settle themselves; you do

270

not even need to know about it. That is how we do it, and so shall it be easier for you. I would not today have been able to get away to visit you, if I took it into my head that I had to know about everything that is going on and if I burdened myself as you do.'

'But the judges will accept gifts,' answered Moses with a heavy heart, 'and will declare the godless ones in the right. For gifts blind those who see and turn awry the cause of the just.'

'I know that,' answered Jethro, 'I know it quite well. But one has to close one's eyes to that, just a little. Wherever order reigns, wherever law is spoken, wherever judgements are made, they become a little involved through gifts. Does that matter so much? Look, those who accept presents, they are ordinary folk. But the people themselves are ordinary folk; therefore they understand the ordinary and the ordinary is comfortable to the community. Moreover, if a man has been wronged because the judge of the ten has accepted gifts from his godless adversary, then let that man pursue an ordinary process of law. Let him appeal to the judge who rules over the fifty, then to the one who rules over the hundred; and finally, to the one who rules over the thousand: that one gets the most gifts and has therefore the clearest vision. Our man will find his rights with this last judge, that is, if in the meantime the fellow has not wearied of the whole affair.'

Thus did Jethro discourse with even gestures, gestures which made life easier if one but saw them. Thus did he show that he was indeed the priest-king of a civilized desert people. With a heavy heart did Moses listen and nod. His was the pliable soul of the lonely spiritual man, the man who nods his head thoughtfully at the cleverness of the world and understands that the world may well be in the right. He followed the counsel of his deft brother-in-law – it was absolutely necessary. He appointed lay judges who, according to his tenets, let judgement flow next to the great spring and next to the smaller one. They judged the everyday cases (such as if an ass fell into the pit); only the capital cases came to Moses, the priest of God. And the greatest matters were decided by the holy oracles.

Moses no longer had his hands tied with everyday affairs; his hands were free for the larger work, the work of sculpting for which Joshua, the strategic youth, had won the work-place: Kadesh the oasis. Undoubtedly, the doctrine of right and wrong was one important example of the implications inherent in the invisible God. Yet it was only one example. Much work remained to be done. Mighty and long labour lay ahead, labour which would have to be achieved through anger and patience before the uncouth hordes could be formed into a people who would be more than the usual community to whom the ordinary was comfortable, but would be an extraordinary, a separated people and a unique monument erected to the Invisible One and dedicated to him.

15

The people soon learned what it meant to have fallen into the hands of an angrily patient workman who held himself accountable to an invisible god. They began to realize that that unnatural suggestion to omit the shout of triumph over the drowning of the enemy was but a beginning, though a portentous beginning, which already lay well within the domain of holiness and purity. It was a beginning which presupposed a certain understanding; the people would have to acquire that understanding before they could view Moses's command as anything less than unnatural.

What the mob was really like, to what degree it was the rawest of raw material and flesh and blood, lacking the most elementary conception of purity and holiness, how Moses had to begin at the beginning and teach them beginnings, that is to be deduced from the simple precepts with which he started to work and chisel and blast. Not to their comfort, certainly, for the stone does not take sides with the master but against him; to the stone the first stroke struck to form it appears as a most unnatural action.

Moses, with his wide-set eyes and his flattened nose, was always in their midst, here, there, in this and that encampment. Shaking his broad-wristed fists, he jogged, censured, chided, and churned their existence; he reproved, chastised, and cleansed, using as his touchstone the invisibility of the God Jahwe who had led them out of Egypt in order to choose them as his people and make them into a holy people, even as holy as himself. For the time being they were nothing more than rabble, a fact which they proved by emptying their bodies simply wherever they lay. That was a disgrace and a pestilence. Ye must have a place outside the camp where ye shall go when ye need to. Do ye understand me? And take along a litle scoop and dig a pit before ye sit down, and after ye have sat then shall ye cover it. For the Lord your God walks in your camp, therefore your camp must be holy. And that means clean, so that the Lord need not hold his nose and turn away from you. For holiness begins with cleanliness, which is purity in the rough, the rough beginning of all purity. Dost thou comprehend this, Ahiman, and thou, wife Naemi? The next time I want to see everybody with that scoop, or ye shall have to reckon with the destroying angel.

Thou must be clean and wash thyself often with live water for the sake of thy health. For without water there is no cleanliness or holiness, and disease is unclean. But if thou thinkest that vulgarity is healthier than clean custom, then thou art an imbecile and thou shalt be visited by jaundice, fig warts, and the boils of Egypt. If ye do not practise cleanliness, then evil black blains shall grow up in you and the seeds of pestilence shall travel from blood to blood. Learn to distinguish cleanliness from uncleanliness, or else ye shall fail before the Invisible One and ye are nothing but rabble. Therefore if a man or a woman have a cankerous sore or an evil fistula, if he suffer with rash or ulcers, then he or she shall be declared unclean and not permitted in the encampment, but shall be put outside, separated in uncleanliness even as the Lord has separated you that ye may become clean. And whatever such a one has touched, on whatever he has lain, the saddle on which he has sat, that shall be burned. But if he has become clean again in separation, then he shall count seven days to make sure that he be truly clean, then he shall bathe thoroughly in water and then may he return.

Distinguish, I say unto you, and be holy before God. For how else can ye be holy as I want you to be? Ye eat everything together without choice or daintiness, and to me who have to watch you that is an abomination. There are certain things that ye may eat and others that ye may not, for ye shall have your pride and you disgust. Those animals which have cloven hooves and chew their cud, those ye may eat. But those which chew their cud and divide not the hoof, like the camel, those shall be unclean to you and ye shall not eat them. Notice well: the good camel is not unclean as a living creature of God; it is merely unfit as food, as little fit as the pig, which, though it has cloven hooves, does not chew its cud. Therefore distinguish! What creatures in the water have fins and scales, those ye may eat, but those which slither in the element without fins or scales, the entire breed of salamanders, they, though they also are from God, ye shall shun as nourishment. Among the birds disdain ye the eagle, the hawk, the osprey, the vulture, and their ilk. Furthermore, all ravens, the ostrich, the night owl, the cuckoo, the screech owl, the swan, the horned owl, the bat, the bittern, the stork, the heron, and the jay, as well as the swallow. Who would eat the weasel, the mouse, the toad, or the hedgehog? Who shall be so cross as to eat the lizard, the mole, and the blindworm – in fact, anything which creeps on the earth and crawls on its belly? But ye do it, and turn your souls into loathsomeness. The one whom I shall see eating a blindworm I shall deal with so that he will never do it again. For though one does not die from eating it, though it is not harmful, yet it is reprehensible, and much shall be reprehensible to you. Therefore ye also shall eat no carcass, for that is even harmful.

Thus did he give them precepts of nourishment and circumscribe them in matters of food, though not alone in those. He did likewise in matters of lust and love, for there too were they disorderly in rabble fashion. Ye shall not commit adultery, he told them, for marriage is a holy barrier. But do ye really know what that means: ye shall not commit adultery? It means a hundred curbs out of regard for the holiness of God. It does not mean only that thou shalt not covet the wife of your neighbour: that is the least. For though ye are living in the flesh, ye are allied in oath to Invisibility. And marriage is the essence of all purity of flesh before God's visage. Therefore thou shalt not take unto thyself a wife and her mother, to name only one example; that is not seemly. And thou shalt never and under no conditions lie with thy sister so that thou shalt see her shame and she yours. For that is incest. Not even with thine aunt shalt thou lie. That is not worthy of her nor of thyself: thou shalt keep clear from it. If a woman have a sickness, then thou shalt shun her and not approach the fountain of her blood. And if something shameful should happen to a man in his sleep, then shall he be unclean until the next evening, and he shall bathe carefully in water.

I hear that thou causest thy daughter to be a whore and that thou takest whore money from her? Do this no longer, for if thou perseverest, then shall I let thee be stoned. What art thou thinking of, to sleep with a boy as well as with a woman? That is iniquity and rabble depravity. Both of you shall be put to death. But if somebody consort with an animal, be it man or woman, they shall be completely exterminated, and they and the animal choked to death.

Imagine their bewilderment over all these curbs! At first they felt life would hardly be worth living if they should observe them all. Moses struck at them with the sculptor's chisel so that the chips flew. Deadly serious was he about meting out the chastisements which he had placed on the worse transgressions. And behind his ordinances stood the young Joshua and his destroying angels.

'I am the Lord thy God,' said he, risking the danger that they might in truth take him for God, 'who have led thee out of Egypt and separated thee from all the peoples. Therefore shall ye separate the clean from the unclean, and not follow in whoredom the other tribes but be holy to me. For I, thy Lord, am holy, and have separated you so that ye shall become mine. Of all the unclean actions the one most unclean is to care for any other god. For I am a jealous god. The most unclean action is to make yourself an image, be it the likeness of a man or a woman, of an ox or a hawk, a fish or a worm. In doing that ye shall become faithless to me, even if the image shall be in my likeness, and thou mightest as well sleep with thy sister or with an animal. Such an action is not far removed and soon follows quite by itself. Take care! I am among you and I see everything.

Whosoever shall whore after the animal-and-death gods of Egypt, him shall I drown. I shall drive him into the desert and banish him like an outcast. And the same shall I do with him who sacrifices to the Moloch, whom I know ye still carry in your memory. If ye consume your force in its honour, I shall deem it evil, and heavily shall I deal with you. Nor shalt thou let thy son nor thy daughter walk through the fire according to the stupid old custom, not shalt thou pay attention to the flight of the birds and their cry, nor whisper with fortune-tellers, destiny predictors, or augurs, nor shall ye question the dead nor practise magic in my name. If one among you is a scoundrel and takes my name in false testimony, he shall not profit by such tale-bearing, for I shall devour him. It is even magic and abomination to print marks on one's body, to shave one's eyebrows and make cuttings on one's face as a sign of sorrow for the dead – I shall not suffer it.'

How great was their bewilderment! They were not even allowed to cut their faces in mourning, not even allowed to tattoo themselves a little bit. They realized now what it meant by the invisibility of God. It meant great privation, this business of being in league with Jahwe. But because behind Moses's prohibition stood the destroying angels, and because nobody wanted to be driven into the desert, that which he prohibited soon appeared to them to be worthy of fear. At first it was fearworthy only in relation to the punishment, but by and by the action itself took on the stamp of evil, and if they committed it they became ill at ease without even thinking of the punishment.

Bridle your hearts, he said to them, and do not cast your eyes on somebody else's possessions. If ye desire them, it soon follows that ye take them, be it through stealthy purloining, which is cowardice, or by killing the other, which is brutality. Jahwe and I do not want you either cowardly or brutal, but ye shall be in the middle between these two; that means decent. Have ye understood that much? To steal is slinking wretchedness, but to murder, be it from rage or from greed, or from greedy rage or from raging greed, that is flaming wrong, and against him who shall commit such a wrong shall I set my countenance so that he will not know where to hide himself. For he has shed blood and blood is holy awe and a deep secret, offering for my altar and atonement. Ye shall not eat blood nor any meat in the blood, for blood is mine. And he who is smeared with the blood of human beings, his heart shall sicken in cold terror and I shall drive him that he run away from himself unto the ends of the world. Say ye Amen to that.

And they said Amen, still hoping that with the ban on murder killing alone was meant. For few of them had the desire to kill, and those who did had it only occasionally. But it turned out that Jahwe gave that word as wide a meaning as he had given the word adultery and that he meant by it all sorts of things, so that 'murder' and 'killing' began with almost any transgression of the code. Almost every wound which one man inflicted upon another, whether through deceit or through fraud (and almost all of the people hankered a little after deceit and fraud), Jahwe considered bloodshed. They should not deal falsely with one another nor bear false witness against their neighbours, and they should use just weights, and just measures. It was to the highest degree unnatural, and for the time being it was only the natural fear of punishment which gave an aspect of naturalness to all this bidding and forbidding.

That one should honour one's father and mother as Moses demanded, that also had a wider meaning, wider than one suspected at first blush. Whosoever raised his hand against his progenitor and cursed him, well, yes, he should be done away with. But that respect should also be extended to those who merely could be your progenitors. Ye shall arise before a grey head. Ye shall cross your arms and incline your stupid head. Do ye understand me? Thus demands the decency of God. The only consolation was that since your neighbour was not permitted to kill you, you had a reasonable prospect of becoming yourself old and grey, so that the others would have to arise before you.

Finally, it appeared that old age was a symbol of what was old in general, everything which did not happen from today to tomorrow but which came from long ago: the piously traditional, the custom of the fathers. To that one had to pay the tribute of honour and awe in God. Ye shall keep my sabbaths, the day on which I led you out of Egypt, the day of the unleavened bread, and the day when I rested from the labours of my creation. Ye shall not defile my day with the sweat of your brow: I forbid it. For I have led thee out of the Egyptian house of bondage with mighty hand and with outstretched arm, where thou wert a slave and a work animal. And my day shall be the day of thy freedom, which thou shalt keep holy. Six days shalt thou be a tiller or a plough-maker or a potter or a coppersmith or a joiner. But on my day shalt thou put on clean garments and thou shalt be nothing, nothing but a human being who raises his eyes to the Invisible.

Though wert an oppressed servant in the land of Egypt. Think of that in your behaviour towards those who are strangers among you: for example, the children of Amalek, whom God gave into your hands. Do not oppress them. Look on them as ye look on yourself and give them equal rights, or I shall crash down upon you. For they too stand under the protection of Jahwe. In short, do not make such a stupid, arrogant distinction between thyself and the others, so that thou thinkest that thou alone art real and thou alone countest while the others are only a semblance. Ye both have life in common, and it is only an accident that thou art not he. Therefore do not love thyself alone but love him in the same way, and do unto him as thou desirest that he do unto you. Be gracious with one another and kiss the tips of your fingers when ye pass each other and bow with civility and speak the greeting, 'Be hale and healthy'. For it is quite as important that he be healthy as that thou be healthy. And even if it is only formal civility that ye do thus and kiss your fingertips, the gesture does leave something in your heart of that which should be there of your neighbour. To that say ye Amen!

And they all said Amen.

16

Actually, that Amen did not mean very much. They only said it because Moses was the man who had led them successfully out of Egypt, who had drowned Pharaoh's chariots, and had won

the battle of Kadesh. It took a long time before what he had
taught them, what he enjoined upon them – all those barriers,
laws, and prohibitions – sank into their flesh and blood. It was a
mighty piece of work which he had undertaken, the work of
changing the rabble into a people dedicated to the Lord, and to
a clean image which could pass muster before the Invisible. In
the sweat of his brow he worked in his workplace, Kadesh. He
kept his wide-set eyes on all. He chiselled, blasted, formed, and
smoothed the unwilling stone with a tenacious patience, with
repeated forbearance and frequent forgiving, and also with
flaming anger and chastising sternness. Yet often did he almost
despair when once again the flesh relapsed into stubbornness
and forgetfulness, when once again the people failed to use the
scoop, when they ate blindworms, slept with their sisters or
their animals, painted marks upon themselves, crouched with
fortune-tellers, slunk towards theft, and killed each other. 'O
rabble,' said he to them, 'ye shall see. The Lord shall appear
above you and devour you.' But to the Lord himself he said,
'What shall I do with this flesh and why have you withdrawn
your graces from me, that you burden me with a thing I cannot
bear? I would rather clean a stable untouched for years by water
or spade, I would rather clear a thicket with my bare hands, and
turn it into a garden, than try to form for you a clean image out
of them. Wherefore must I carry these people in my arms as if I
had given them birth? I am but half related to them from my
father's side; therefore I pray you let me enjoy my life and free
me from this task. Or else strangle me rather!'

But God answered Moses out of his inner consciousness with
so clear a voice that he could hear it with his ears and he fell
upon his face:

'Just because you are only half related to them from the side
of the buried one are you the man to form them for me and to
raise them to a holy people. For if you were wholly and only
one of them, then you could not see them as they are nor work
upon them. Anyway, that you complain to me and wish to
excuse yourself from your work is pure affectation. For you
know quite well that your work is beginning to take effect. You
know that you have already given them a conscience so that

279

they are ill at ease when they do ill. Therefore do not pretend to me that you do not desire your travail. It is my desire, God's desire, which you have, and lacking it you would sicken of life as our people sickened of manna after a few days. Of course, if I decided to strangle you, then yes, then would you be rid of that desire.'

The much-troubled Moses understood this, nodded his head at Jahwe's words as he lay there, and stood up once again to his travail. But now he had problems, not only in his capacity as a sculptor of the people; trouble and grief began to creep into his family life. Anger, envy, and bickering arose around him and there was no peace in his hut. Perhaps it was his own fault, the fault of his senses. For his senses, stirred up by overwork, hung on a Negro girl, the well-known Negro girl.

One knows that at this time he lived with an Ethiopian girl as well as with his wife Zipporah, the mother of his sons. She was a wench from the land of Kush who as a child had arrived in Egypt, had lived among the Hebrew tribes in Goshen, and had joined the exodus. Undoubtedly she had known many a man, yet Moses now chose her as the companion of his bed. She was a magnificent specimen of her type, with erect breasts, with rolling eyes, thick deep lips, to sink into which may well have been an adventure, and a skin redolent of spice. Moses doted on her mightily; she was his recreation, and he would not let go of her, though he drew upon himself the enmity of his whole house. Not only his Midianite wife and her sons looked askance at the affair, but also and especially his half-sister Miriam and his half-brother Aaron. Zipporah, who possessed much of the even worldliness of her brother Jethro, got along tolerably well with her rival, particularly since the Ethiopian girl knew how to hide her feminine triumph and conducted herself most subserviently towards her. Zipporah treated the Ethiopian girl more with mockery than hate, and adopted towards Moses a light tone of irony which hid the jealousy she felt. Her sons, Gershom and Eliezer, members of Joshua's dashing troop, possessed too much sense of discipline to revolt openly against their father; yet they let it be known unmistakably that they were angry and that they were ashamed of him.

Matters stood yet differently with Miriam the prophetess and Aaron the unctuous. Their hatred towards the Ethiopian mistress was more venomous than that of the others, because that hatred was the expression of a deeper and more general grudge which united them against Moses. For a long time now had they envied Moses his intimate relation with God and his spiritual master. That he felt himself to be God's elect worker they thought was largely conceit; they deemed themselves just as good as he, perhaps better. To each other they said, 'Does the Lord talk only through Moses? Does he not also talk through us? Who is this man Moses? that he has exalted himself above us?' That then was the real cause of the indignation which they manifested towards this affair with the Ethiopian. And every time they noisily reproached their unfortunate brother with the passion of his nights, they soon departed into more general complaints. Soon they would be harping on the injustice which was their fate because of Moses's elevation.

Once as the day was drawing towards an end, they were in his hut, and harassed him in a way I said they were wont to harass him: the Ethiopian here and the Ethiopian there, and that he was thinking of nothing but her black breasts, and what a scandal it was, what a disgrace to his wife Zipporah, and what exposure for himself who claimed to be a prince of God and Jahwe's sole mouthpiece on earth . . .

'Claimed?' said he. 'What God has commanded me to be I am. How ugly of you, how very ugly, that you envy my pleasure and my relaxation on the breasts of the Ethiopian. For it is no sin before God, and there is no prohibition among all the prohibitions which he gave me which says that one may not lie with an Ethiopian. Not that I know of.'

But they answered that he chose his own prohibitions according to his own tastes, and quite possibly he would soon preach that it was compulsory to lie with Ethiopians. For did he not consider himself Jahwe's sole mouthpiece? The truth was that they, Miriam and Aaron, were the proper children of Amram and the grandchildren of Levi, while he, when all was said and done, was only a foundling from the bulrushes; he might learn a little humility and not insist quite so much on his Ethiopian nor ignore their displeasure quite so offhandedly. Such behaviour was proof of his pride and his conceit.

'Who can help it that he is called?' answered he. 'Can any man help it if he comes upon the burning thorn bush? Miriam, I have always thought highly of your prophetic gifts and never denied your accomplishments on the timbrel . . .'

'Then why did you disallow my hymn "Steed and Man" and why did you prohibit me from leading the round dance of the women? You pretended that God forbade his flock to triumph over the downfall of the Egyptians. That was abominable of you.'

'And you, Aaron,' continued the hard-pressed Moses, 'you I have employed as the high priest in the tabernacle, and I have entrusted the Chest, the Ephod, and the Brass Serpent unto your care. Thus do I value you.'

'That was the least that you could have done,' answered Aaron. 'For without my eloquence could you never have persuaded the people to the cause of Jahwe, nor won them for the exodus. Consider how awkward is your mouth! But now you call yourself the man who has led us out of Egypt! If you really valued us, if you really did not exalt yourself so arrogantly over your blood relatives, then why do you not pay heed to our words? Why do you remain deaf to our admonition that you imperil our whole tribe with your black paramour? To Zipporah, your Midianite wife, she is draught as bitter as gall, and you offend all of Midian with your action, so that Jethro your brother-in-law might soon declare war on us – all for the sake of your coloured caprice.'

'Jethro,' said Moses with restraint, 'is an even man of the world who well understands that Zipporah – praised be her name! – no longer can offer the necessary recreation to a highly overworked and heavily burdened man. But the skin of my Ethiopian is like cinnamon and perfumed of carnation in my nostrils; all my senses long for her, and therefore I beg of you, my good friends, grant her to me.'

But that they did not want to do. They screeched and demanded not only that he should part from the Ethiopian and forbid her his bed, but also that he drive her into the desert without water.

Thereupon veins of anger rose on his forehead and terribly did his fists begin to tremble. But before he could open his mouth to respond, a very different trembling began – Jahwe interposed and set his visage against the hard-hearted brother and sister, and came to his servant's aid in a way they never forgot. Something frightful, something never before seen, now happened.

17

The foundations trembled. The earth shook, shivered, and swayed under their feet so that they could not stand but tottered to and fro in the hut, whose posts seemed to be shaken by giant fists. What had been firm began to waver, not only in one direction but in crooked and dizzying gyrations. It was horrible. At the same time there occurred a subterranean growling and rumbling and a sound from above and from outside like the blare of a great trumpet, followed by a droning, a thundering, and a rustling. It is very strange and peculiarly embarrassing if you are on the point of breaking out into a rage and the Lord takes the words out of your mouth and himself breaks out much more mightily than you yourself could have done it, and shakes the world where you could only have shaken your fists.

Moses was the least pale with fright, for at all times he was prepared for God. With Aaron and Miriam, who were deathly pale, he rushed out of the house. Then they saw that the earth had opened its jaws and that a great gap yawned right next to their hut. Obviously this rent had been destined for Miriam and Aaron, and had missed them only by a few yards. And they looked towards the mountain in the east behind the desert, Horeb and Sinai – but what was happening on Horeb, what was taking place on Sinai? It stood there enveloped from foot to summit in smoke and flames, and threw glowing crumbs towards heaven, with a far-off sound of fearful crackling. Streams of fire ran down its sides. Its vapour, crossed by lightning, obscured the stars above the desert, and slowly a rain of ashes began to descend upon the oasis Kadesh.

283

Aaron and Miriam fell upon their foreheads; the cleft destined for them had filled them with terror. This revelation of Jahwe showed them that they had gone too far and had spoken foolishly. Aaron exclaimed:

'O my master, this woman my sister has jabbered ugly words. Accept my prayer and let not the sin remain upon her, the sin with which she sinned against the man anointed by the Lord.'

Miriam also screamed to Moses and spoke: 'Master, it is impossible to speak more foolishly than spoke my brother Aaron. Forgive him and let not the sin remain upon him, so that God may not devour him just because he has twitted you a little about the Ethiopian.'

Moses was not quite certain if Jahwe's revelation was really meant for his brother and sister and their lack of love, or if it was the call meant for him, the call for which he had waited hourly, the call that summoned him to commune with God about his people and the work of their education. But he let them suppose what they supposed and answered:

'There, you see. But take courage, children of Amram. I shall put forth a good word for you up there with God on the mountain, whither he calls me. For now you shall see, and all the people shall see, whether your brother has become unmanned by his black infatuation or if the courage of God still dwells in his heart stronger than in other hearts. To the fiery mountain shall I go, quite alone, upward to God, to hear his thoughts and to deal without fear with the fearful one, on familiar terms, far from the people, but in their cause. For a long time have I known that he wishes to write down all that I have taught you for your salvation into binding words, into an eternal condensation, that I might carry it back to you from his mountain, and that the people may possess it in the tabernacle together with the Chest, the Ephod, and the Brass Serpent. Farewell. I may perish in God's tumult, in the fire of the mountain; I have to reckon with that. But should I return, then shall I bring out of his thunder the eternal word, God's law.'

Such was his firm resolve; whether for life or death, that had he decided. For in order to root the obdurate, always backsliding rabble in God's morality, in order to make them fear his laws, nothing was more effective than that he, bare and alone, should dare to climb up to Jahwe's terror, up the spewing mountain, and thence carry down the dictates. Then, thought he, would they observe the laws.

When the people came running from all sides to his hut, trembling at the knees, frightened by the signs and by the terrible undulations of the earth, which occurred once and twice again, though weaker, Moses forbade them their commonplace quaking and admonished them to decent composure. God called him, said he, for their sake, and he was to climb up to Jahwe, up to the summit of the mountain, and bring something back for them, with God's will. They, however, should return to their homes and should prepare for a pilgrimage. They should hold themselves clean and wash their garments and abstain from their wives, and tomorrow they should wander out from Kadesh into the desert near the mountain. There should they encamp and wait for him until he returned from the fearful interview, perhaps bringing something back for them.

And thus it happened, or at least almost thus. Moses in his fashion had only remembered to tell them to wash their garments and to abstain from their wives. Joshua, the strategic youth, had remembered what else was necessary for such an excursion; with his troop he provided the proper quantities of water and nourishment needful to the thousands in the desert. And he also established a line of communication between Kadesh and the encampment near the mountain. He left Caleb his lieutenant in Kadesh with a police detail to supervise those who could not or would not come along. When the third day had dawned and all preparations had been made, all the others set out with their carts and their slaughter animals. They journeyed towards the mountain, a journey of a day and still a half. There, at a respectable distance from Jahwe's fuming dwelling, Joshua erected an enclosure. He enjoined the people most strictly, and in Moses's name, not to think of climbing that mountain nor even to set foot upon it. The master alone was privileged to approach so near to God. Moreover, it was highly dangerous, and whoever touched the mountain should be stoned or pierced with the arrow. They took this command in their stride, for rabble has no desire whatever to come all too near to God. To the common man the mountain did not in the least look inviting, neither by day, when Jahwe stood upon it in a thick cloud crossed by lightning, nor certainly by night, when the cloud and the entire summit glowed.

Joshua was extremely proud of the courage of his master, who the very first day and before all the people set out on his way to the mountain, alone and on foot with his pilgrim's staff, provided only with an earthen flask, a few crusts, and some tools, an axe, a chisel, a spade and a stylus. Very proud was the youth, and pleased at the impression which such holy intrepidity would surely make on the multitude. But anxious was he too about the man he worshipped, and he implored him not to approach too near to Jahwe and to be careful of the hot molten streams which ran down the sides of the mountain. Also, said he, he would visit Moses once or twice and look after him, so that the master would not in God's wilderness lack the simplest necessities.

18

Moses, leaning on his staff, traversed the desert, his wide-set eyes fixed on God's mountain, which was smoking like an oven and spewed forth many times. The mountain was of peculiar shape: it had fissures and veins which seemed to divide it into terraces and which looked like upward-leading paths, though they were not paths, but simply gradations of yellow walls. On the third day, after climbing several foothills, God's delegate arrived at the bare foot of the mountain. Then he began to ascend, his fist grasping the pilgrim's staff which he set before him. He climbed without path or track many an hour, step by step, higher, always higher, towards God's nearness. He climbed as far as a human being could, for by and by the sulphurous fumes which smelled of hot metals and which filled the air choked him, and he began to cough. He arrived at the topmost fissure and terrace right underneath the summit, where he could have a wide view of the bald and wild mountain ranges on both sides, and out over the desert as far as Kadesh. Closer by he could see the people in their enclosure, far below and small.

Here the coughing Moses found a cave in the mountain wall, a cave with a projecting roof of rock which could protect him from the falling stones and the flowing broth. There he took up his abode and arranged himself to start, after a short breathing spell, the work which God had ordered from him. Under the difficult circumstances – for the metal vapours lay heavily on his breast and made even the water taste of sulphur – this work held him fast up there not less than forty days and forty nights.

But why so long? Idle question! The eternal had to be recorded, the binding word had to be briefed, God's terse moral law had to be captured and graved into the stone of the mountain, so that Moses might bring it down to the vacillating mob, to the blood of his buried father, down into the encampment where they were waiting. There it was to stand from generation to generation, unbreakable, graved also into their minds and into their flesh and blood, the quintessence of human decency.

From his inner consciousness God directed him to hew two tablets from the rock and to write upon them his dictate, five words on the one and five words on the other, together ten words. It was no easy task to build the two tablets, to smooth them and to shape them into fit receptacles of eternal brevity. For a lone man, even if he had drunk the milk of a mason's daughter, even if he had broad wrists, it was a piece of work subject to many a mishap. Of the forty days it took a quarter. But the actual writing down was a problem the solution of which could well have prolonged the number of Moses's mountain days far over forty.

For in what manner should he write? In the academy of Thebes he had learned the decorative picture writing of Egypt with all its current amendments. He had also learned the stiffly formal arrow script of Euphrates, in which the kings of the world were wont to exchange their thoughts on fragments of clay. In Midian he had become acquainted with still a third magic method of capturing meaning. This one consisted of eyes, crosses, insets, circles, and variously formed serpentine lines. It was a method used in Sinai which had been copied with desert awkwardness from the Egyptians. Its marks, however, did not represent whole words or word pictures, but only their parts. They denoted syllables which were to be read together.

None of these three methods of fastening thought satisfied him, for the simple reason that each of them was linked to a particular language and was indigenous to that language. Moses realized perfectly well that it would never under any conditions be possible for him to set upon the stone the dictate of ten words either in Babylonian or in Egyptian language, nor yet in the jargon of the Sinai Bedouins. The words on the stone could be only in the language of his father's blood, the very dialect which they spoke and which he himself employed in his teachings. It did not matter whether they would be able to read it or not. In fact, how could they be expected to read a language which no one could as yet write? There was no magic symbol at hand to represent and hold fast their speech.

With all his soul Moses wished that there existed such a symbol, one which they could learn to read quickly, very quickly; one which children, such as they were, could learn in a few days. It followed, then, that somebody could think up and invent such a symbol in a few days, with the help of God's nearness. Yet, because it did not exist, somebody had to think up and invent this new method of writing.

What a pressing and precious task! He had not considered it in advance, had simply thought of 'writing' and had not taken into account that one could not write just like that! Fired by his fervent search for symbols his people could understand, his head glowed and smoked like an oven and like the summit of the mountain. It seemed to him as if rays emerged from his head, as if horns sprang from his forehead, so great was his wishing exertion. And then a simple, illuminating idea came to him. True, he could not invent signs for all the words used by his kin, nor for the syllables from which they formed their words. Even if the vocabulary of those down in the enclosure was paltry, yet would it have required too many marks for him to build in the span of his mountain days and also for the others to learn to read quickly. Therefore he thought of something else, and horns stood upon his forehead out of pride over the flash of God's inspiration. He gathered the sounds of the language, those formed by the lips, by the tongue, by the palate, and by the throat; he put to one side the few open sounds which occurred every so often within the words, which in fact were framed by the others into words. He found that there were not too many of these framing sonant sounds – hardly twenty. If one ascribed definite signs to them, signs which everybody could alike aspirate and respirate, mumble and rumble, gabble and babble, then one could combine these signs into words and word pictures, leaving out the open sounds which followed by themselves. Thus one could form any word one liked, any word which existed, not only in the language of his father's kin, but in all languages – yes, with these signs one could even write Egyptian or Babylonian.

A flash from God. An idea with horns. An idea such as could be expected from the Invisible and the spiritual one, him to whom the world belonged, him who, though he had chosen those down below as his people, was yet the Lord of all the earth. It was an idea also which was eminently fitting to the next and most pressing purpose for which and out of which it was created: the text of the tables, the binding briefed text. This text was to be coined first and specifically for the tribe which Moses had led out of Egypt because God and he were inclined towards them. But just as with a handful of these signs all the words of all the languages of all the people could, if need be, be written, just as Jahwe was the God of all the world, so was what Moses meant to brief and write of such a nature that it could serve as fundamental precept, as the rock of human decency, to all the peoples of the earth.

Moses with his fiery head now experimented with signs loosely related to the marks of the Sinai people as he remembered them. On the wall of the mountain he graved with his stylus the lisping, popping, and smacking, the hissing, and swishing, the humming and murmuring sounds. And when he had all the signs together and could distinguish them with a certain amount of assurance, lo! with them one could write the whole world, all that which occupied space and all that which occupied no space, all that was fashioned and all that was thought. In short, all.

He wrote. That is to say, he jabbed, chiselled, and hacked at the brittle stone of the tablets, those tablets which he had hewn laboriously and whose creation went hand in hand with the creation of the letters. No wonder that it took him forty days!

Joshua, his youth, came to see him several times. He brought him water and crusts, without precisely telling the people of his visits. The people thought that Moses lived up there in God's proximity and communed with him quite alone. And Joshua deemed it best to let them believe this. Therefore his visits were short and made by night.

From the dawn of the light of day above Edom to its extinction, Moses sat behind the desert and worked. One has to imagine him as he sat up there with bare shoulders, his breast covered with hair, with his powerful arms which he may have inherited from his ill-used father, with his eyes set far apart, with his flattened nose, with the divided now greying beard – chewing his crust, now and then coughing from the metal vapours of the mountain, hammering, scraping, and polishing his tablets in the sweat of his brow. He crouched before the tablets propped against the rocky wall, and painstakingly carved the crow's-feet, then traced them with his stylus, and finally graved the omnipotent runes deep into the flatness of the stone.

On one tablet he wrote:

> I, Jahwe, am thy God; thou shalt have
> no other gods before me.
> Thou shalt not make unto thee any
> image.
> Thou shalt not take my name in vain.
> Remember my day, to keep it holy.
> Honour thy father and thy mother.

And on the other tablet he wrote:

> Thou shalt not murder.
> Thou shalt not commit adultery.
> Thou shalt not steal.

Thou shalt not harm thy neighbour by
false witness.
Thou shalt not cast a covetous eye on
the possessions of thy neighbour.

That is what he wrote, omitting the open sounds which formed themselves. And always it seemed to him as if rays like two horns stood out from the locks of his forehead.

When Joshua came for the last time to the mountain, he remained a little longer, two whole days. For Moses was not finished with his work and they wanted to descend together. The youth admired whole-heartedly what his master had accomplished. He comforted him because a few letters were cracked and unrecognizable in spite of all the love and care which Moses had expended. Joshua assured him that this did no harm to the total impression.

The last thing that Moses did while Joshua looked on was to paint the sunken letters with his blood so that they would stand out better. No other pigment was at hand. Therefore he cut his strong arm with his stylus and smeared the trickling blood into the letters so that they glowed rosily in the stone. When the writing had dried, Moses took one tablet under each arm, gave his pilgrim's staff, with which he had ascended, to the youth, and thus they wandered down from the seat of God towards the encampment of the people near the mountain in the desert.

19

When they had arrived at a certain distance from the encampment, just within hearing distance, a noise penetrated to them, a hollow screeching. They could not account for it. It was Moses who heard it first and Joshua who mentioned it first.

'Do you hear this peculiar clatter,' he asked, 'this tumult, this uproar? There is something doing, I think, a brawl, a bout, or I am much mistaken. And it must be violent and general, that we hear it as far as this. If it is what I think it is, then it is good that we come.'

'That we come,' answered Moses, 'is good in any case. But as far as I can make out, this is no scuffle and no tussle, but something like a feasting or a dance of triumph. Do you not hear the high-pitched jubilation and clash of timbrels? Joshua, how is it that they celebrate without my permission? Joshua, what has got into them? Let us hurry.'

He grasped his two tablets higher under his arms and strode faster with the puzzled Joshua.

'A dance of triumph ... a dance of triumph,' he repeated uneasily and finally in open terror. For it appeared all too clearly that this was not an ordinary brawl in which one person lay on top and the other below; this was a general united carousal. And now it was only a question of what kind of unity it was in which they thus revelled.

Even that question answered itself too soon, if indeed it need ever have been asked. The mess was horrible. As Moses and Joshua passed the high posts of the encampment they saw it in shameless unequivocalness. The people had broken loose. They had thrown off everything that Moses had laid upon them in holiness, all the morality of God. They wallowed in relapse.

Directly behind the portals was a free space which was the assembly place. There things were happening, there they were carrying on, there they wallowed, there they celebrated their miserable liberty. Before the dance they had all stuffed themselves full. One could see that at first glance. Everywhere the place showed the traces of slaughtering and gluttony. And in whose honour had they sacrificed, slaughtered, and stuffed themselves? There it stood. In the midst of barrenness, set on a stone, set on an altar pedestal, an image, a thing made by their hands, an idolatrous mischief, a golden calf.

It was no calf, it was a bull, the real, ordinary stud bull of all the peoples of the world. A calf it is called only because it was no more than medium size, in fact rather less, and also misshapen and ludicrously fashioned; an awkward abomination, yet all too recognizable as a bull.

Around this thing a multitudinous round dance was in progress, a dozen circles of men and women, hand in hand, accompanied by timbrels and by cymbals. Heads were thrown far back, rolling eyes were upturned, knees jerked towards chins; they screeched and they roared and made crass obeisance.

In different directions did the dance turn, one shameful circle turning towards the right, another towards the left. In the very centre of the whirlpool, near the calf, Aaron could be seen hopping around in his long-sleeved garment which he used to wear as the guardian of the tabernacle, and which he had gathered high so that he could jig with his long, hairy legs. And Miriam led the women with her timbrel.

But this was only the round dance near the calf. Farther on what was to be expected was taking place. It is difficult to confess how far the people debased themselves. Some ate blindworms, others lay with their sisters and that publicly, in the calf's honour. Others simply squatted and emptied themselves, forgetting the scoop. Men offered their force to the calf. Somewhere someone was cuffing his own mother.

At these gruesome sights, the veins of anger swelled to bursting on Moses's forehead. His face flaming red, he cut his way through the circles of the dancers – straight to the calf, the seed, the fountain, the womb of the crime. Recognizing the master, they gaped with embarrassed grins. High up he lifted one of the tablets of the law with mighty arms, and smashed it down on the ridiculous beast, so that its legs crumbled. Once again did he strike, and with such rage that though the tablet broke into pieces, nothing but a formless mass remained of the thing. Then he swung the second tablet and gave the abomination a final blow, grinding it completely to dust. And because the second tablet remained still intact, he shattered it with a blow on the pedestal. Then he stood with trembling fists, and deeply from his breast he groaned. 'Ye rabble, ye Godforsaken! There lies what I have carried down from God, what he has written for you with his finger as your talisman against the misery of ignorance. There it lies in ruins near the fragments of your idol. And what shall I now tell my Lord so that he will not devour you?'

He saw Aaron the jumper standing near with downcast eyes, and with oily locks at the nape of his neck; he stood silent and stupid. Moses seized him by his garment, shook him, and spoke: 'Where did the golden Belial come from, this excrescence, and what did the people do to you that you push them to their destruction while I am up on the mountain? Why do you yourself bray before them in their dance of debauchery?'

And Aaron answered, 'O my master, let not your anger be heaped on me and on my sister. We had to give in. You know that the people are evil. They forced us. You were away so long, you remained an eternity on the mountain, so that we all thought that you would never return. Then the people gathered against me and screamed, "Nobody knows what has become of that man Moses, who has led us out of Egypt. He shall not return. Probably the spewing mouth of the mountain has swallowed him. Arise, make us gods which shall go before us when Amalek comes. We are a people like other peoples, and want to carouse before gods which are like the gods of other peoples!" Thus they spoke, master, for if you pardon me, they thought they were rid of you. But now tell me what I could have done when they banded together against me. I asked them to break off the golden earrings from their ears. These I melted in the fire and made a form, and cast the calf as their god.'

'It is not even a good likeness of a calf,' interposed Moses contemptuously.

'They were in such a hurry,' answered Aaron. 'The very next day, that is, today, they wanted to hold their revels in honour of the sympathetic gods. Therefore I handed over to them the image as it was, a piece of work to which you ought not deny a certain amount of verisimilitude. And they rejoiced and spoke, "These are your gods, Israel, which have led you out of Egypt." And we built an altar and they offered burnt sacrifices and thank offerings and ate, and after that they played and danced a little.'

Moses let him stand there and made his way back to the portal through the scattered circles of dancers. There with Joshua he placed himself beneath the birchen crossbeam and called with all his might:

'Who is on the Lord's side, let him come unto me.'

Many came, those who were of sound heart and had not willingly joined the revels. Joshua's armed troop assembled around him.

'Ye unfortunate people,' said Moses, 'what have ye done, and how shall I now atone for you before Jahwe, that he shall not

294

blot you out as an incorrigibly stiff-necked people and shall not devour you? As soon as I turn my back, ye make yourselves a golden Belial. Shame on you and on me! Do ye see these ruins – I do not mean those of the calf, let the pest take them! – I mean the others? That is the gift which I had promised you and which I have brought down to you, the eternal condensation, the rock of decency, the ten words which I, in God's nearness, wrote down in your language and wrote with my blood, with the blood of my father; with your blood did I write them. Now lies the gift in fragments.'

Then many who heard this wept and there was a great crying in the encampment.

'Perhaps it will be possible to replace them,' said Moses. 'For the Lord is patient and of infinite mercy, and forgives missteps and trespasses. But' – he thundered of a sudden, while his blood rose to his head and his veins swelled to bursting – 'he lets no one go unpunished. For, says the Lord, I visit the iniquity of the fathers upon the children unto the third and fourth generation as the jealous God that I am. We shall hold court here,' exclaimed Moses, 'and shall order a bloody cleansing. It shall be determined who were the ringleaders who first screamed for golden gods and insolently asserted that the calf has led you out of Egypt, where I alone have done it, says the Lord. They shall all have to deal with the destroying angels, regardless of their rank or person. To death shall they be stoned and shot by the arrow, even if there are three hundred of them. And the others shall strip off their ornaments and mourn until I return – for I shall again ascend the mountain of God, and shall see what in any case I can do for you, ye stiff-necked people.'

20

Moses did not attend the executions which the golden calf had made necessary. That was the business of the dashing Joshua. Moses himself was once again up on the mountain in his cave underneath the rumbling summit. While the people mourned he again remained forty days and forty nights alone among the vapours. But why so long? The answer is thus: not only because

Jahwe directed him to form the tablets anew and to write down the dictate afresh – that task went more quickly because he had acquired practice and knew how to write – but also because he had to fight a long fight with the Lord before he would permit the renewal. It was a wrestling in which anger and mercy, fatigue over the work and love for the undertaking, were in turn victorious. Moses had to use much power of persuasion and many clever appeals to prevent God from declaring the covenant broken. For almost did God cast himself loose from the stiff-necked rabble, almost did he smash them as Moses in flaming anger had smashed the first tablets of the law.

'I shall not go before them,' said God, 'to lead them into the land of their fathers. Do not ask this of me – I cannot depend upon my patience. I am a jealous God and I flame up, and you shall see one day I shall forget myself and I shall devour them altogether.'

And he proposed to Moses that he would annihilate these people, who were as miscast as the golden calf and as incorrigible. It would be impossible, said he, to raise them into a holy people, and there was nothing left but to consume Israel and rot it out. But of him, Moses, he would make a great nation and live with him in covenant. But this Moses did not want, and he said to him, 'No, Lord,' said he, 'forgive them their sins; if not, then blot me out of the book also, for I do not wish to survive them. For my part, I wish for no other holy people but them.'

And he appealed to the Lord's sense of honour and spoke: 'Imagine, holy one, what is going to happen. If you kill these people as one man, then the heathen who shall hear their screams will say, "Bah! The Lord was not able to bring the people into the land which he had promised them. He was not powerful enough. Therefore did he slaughter them in the wilderness." Do you want that said of you by all the peoples of the world? Therefore let the power of the Lord appear great, and be lenient with the missteps of your children according to your mercy.'

It was this last argument which won God and decided him towards forgiveness. With the restriction, however, that of this generation none except Joshua and Caleb should ever see the promised land. 'Your children,' decided the Lord, 'I shall lead there. But all those who are above twenty in their age, they shall never see the land. Their bodies shall fall in the desert.'

'It is well, Lord, all shall be well,' answered Moses. 'We shall leave it at that.' For because this decision agreed with his and Joshua's purposes, he argued against it no longer. 'Now let me renew the tablets,' said he, 'that I may take your brevity down to the human beings. After all, perhaps it was just as well that I smashed the first in my anger. There were a few misshaped letters in them. I shall now confess to you that I fleetingly thought of this when I dashed the tablets to pieces.'

And again he sat, secretly nourished and succoured by Joshua, and he jabbed and he chiselled, he scraped and he smoothed. Wiping his brow from time to time with the back of his hand, he wrote, hacking and graving the letters into the tablets. They came out a good deal better than the first time. Then again he painted the letters with his blood and descended, the law under his arms.

It was announced to Israel that the mourning had come to an end, and that they again might put on their ornaments, except of course the earrings: these had been used up to bad purpose. And all the people came before Moses that he might hand them what he had brought down, the message of Jahwe from the mountain, the tablets with the ten words.

'Take them, blood of our fathers,' said he, 'and hold them sacred in the tent of God. But what they tell ye, that hold sacred in your actions. For here is briefed what shall bind you; here is the divine condensation; here is the alpha and omega of human behaviour; here is the rock of decency, which God has inscribed in lapidary writing, using my stylus. In your language did he write, but in symbols in which if need be all the languages of all peoples could be written. For he is the Lord of all, and therefore is the Lord of ABC, and his speech, addressed to you, Israel, is at the same time a speech for all.

'Into the stone of the mountain did I grave the ABC of human behaviour, but it must be graved also into your flesh and blood, Israel. So that he who breaks but one word of the ten commandments shall tremble before his own self and before

297

God and an icy finger shall be laid on his heart, because he has stepped out of God's confines. I know well and God knows in advance that his commandments will not be obeyed, and they will be transgressed at all times and everywhere. But at least the heart of anyone who breaks them shall turn icy, for the words are written in every man's flesh and blood and deep within himself he knows that the words are all-valid.

'But woe to the man who shall arise and speak: "They are no longer valid." Woe to him who teaches you: "Arise and get rid of them! Lie, murder, rob, whore, rape, and deliver your father and mother to the knife. For this is the natural behaviour of human beings and you shall praise my name because I proclaim natural licence." Woe to him who erects a calf and speaks: "This is your god. In his honour do all of this, and whirl around the image I have fashioned in a round dance of debauchery." He shall be mighty and powerful, he shall sit upon a golden throne, and he shall be looked up to as the wisest of all. For he knows that the inclination of the human heart is evil, even in youth. But that is about all that he will know, and he who knows only that is as stupid as the night and it would be better for him never to have been born. For he knows nothing of the covenant between God and man, a covenant that none may break, neither man nor God, for it is unbreakable. Blood shall flow in torrents because of his black stupidity, so much blood that the redness shall vanish from the cheeks of mankind. But then the people shall hew down the monster – inevitably; for they can do naught else. And the Lord says, I shall raise my foot and shall trample him into the mire, to the bottom of the earth shall I cast the blasphemer, one hundred and twelve fathoms deep. And man and beast shall describe an arc around the spot into which I have cast him; and the birds of the heavens, high in their flight, shall shun the place so that they need not fly over it. And he who shall speak his name, he shall spit towards the four corners of the earth and shall wipe his mouth and say, "Forfend!" That the earth may again be the earth, a vale of want, yes, but not a sty of depravity. To that say ye Amen!'

And all the people said Amen.

THE BLACK SWAN
(1953)

IN the twenties of our century a certain Frau Rosalie von
Tümmler, a widow for over a decade, was living in Düsseldorf on
the Rhine, with her daughter Anna and her son Eduard, in comfortable if not luxurious circumstances. Her husband, Lieutenant-
Colonel von Tümmler, had lost his life at the very beginning
of the war, not in battle, but in a perfectly senseless automobile
accident, yet still, one could say, 'on the field of honour' – a
hard blow, borne with patriotic resignation by his wife, who,
then just turned forty, was deprived not only of a father for her
children, but, for herself, of a cheerful husband, whose rather
frequent strayings from the strict code of conjugal fidelity had
been only the symptom of a superabundant vitality.

A Rhinelander by ancestry and in dialect, Rosalie had spent
the twenty years of her marriage in the busy industrial city of
Duisburg, where von Tümmler was stationed; but after the loss
of her husband she had moved, with her eighteen-year-old
daughter and her little son, who was some twelve years younger
than his sister, to Düsseldorf, partly for the sake of the beautiful
parks that are such a feature of the city (for Frau von Tümmler
was a great lover of Nature), partly because Anna, a serious girl,
had a bent for painting and wanted to attend the celebrated
Academy of Art. For the past ten years, then, the little family
had lived in a quiet linden-bordered street of villas, named after
Peter von Cornelius, where they occupied the modest house
which, surrounded by a garden and equipped with rather outmoded but comfortable furniture dating from the time of
Rosalie's marriage, was often hospitably opened to a small circle
of relatives and friends – among them professors from the
Academies of Art and Medicine, together with a married couple
or two from the world of industry – for evening gatherings

which, though always decorous in their merriment, tended, as the Rhineland custom is, to be a little bibulous.

Frau von Tümmler was sociable by nature. She loved to go out and, within the limits possible to her, to keep open house. Her simplicity and cheerfulness, her warm heart, of which her love for Nature was an expression, made her generally liked. Small in stature, but with a well-preserved figure, with hair which, though now decidedly grey, was abundant and wavy, with delicate if somewhat ageing hands, the backs of which the passage of years had discoloured with freckle-like spots that were far too many and far too large (a symptom to counteract which no medication has yet been discovered), she produced an impression of youth by virtue of a pair of fine, animated brown eyes, precisely the colour of husked chestnuts, which shone out of a womanly and winning face composed of the most pleasant features. Her nose had a slight tendency to redden, especially in company, when she grew animated; but this she tried to correct by a touch of powder – unnecessarily, for the general opinion held that it became her charmingly.

Born in the spring, a child of May, Rosalie had celebrated her fiftieth birthday, with her children and ten or twelve friends of the house, both ladies and gentlemen, at a flower-strewn table in an inn garden, under the parti-coloured light of Chinese lanterns and to the chime of glasses raised in fervent or playful toasts, and had been gay with the general gaiety – not quite without effort: for some time now, and notably on that evening, her health had been affected by certain critical organic phenomena of her time of life, the extinction of her physical womanhood, to whose spasmodic progress she responded with repeated psychological resistance. It induced states of anxiety, emotional unrest, headaches, days of depression, and an irritability which, even on that festive evening, had made some of the humorous discourses that the gentlemen had delivered in her honour seem insufferably stupid. She had exchanged glances tinged with desperation with her daughter, who, as she knew, required no predisposition beyond her habitual intolerance to find this sort of punch-inspired humour imbecilic.

She was on extremely affectionate and confidential terms with this daughter, who, so much older than her son, had become a friend with whom she maintained no taciturn reserve even in regard to the symptoms of her state of transition. Anna, now twenty-nine and soon to be thirty, had remained unmarried, a situation which was not unwelcome to Rosalie, for, on purely selfish grounds, she preferred keeping her daughter as her household companion and the partner of her life to resigning her to a husband. Taller than her mother, Fräulein von Tümmler had the same chestnut-coloured eyes – and yet not the same, for they lacked the naïve animation of her mother's, their expression being more thoughtful and cool. Anna had been born with a club-foot, which, after an operation in her childhood that produced no permanent improvement, had always excluded her from dancing and sports and indeed from all participation in the activities and life of the young. An unusual intelligence, a native endowment fortified by her deformity, had to compensate for what she was obliged to forgo. With only two or three hours of private tutoring a day, she had easily got through school and passed her final examinations, but had then ceased to pursue any branch of academic learning, turning instead to the fine arts, first to sculpture, then to painting, in which, even as a student, she had struck out on a course of the most extreme intellectualism, which, disdaining mere imitation of nature, transfigured sensory content into the strictly cerebral, the abstractly symbolical, often into the cubistically mathematical. It was with dismayed respect that Frau von Tümmler looked at her daughter's paintings, in which the highly civilized joined with the primitive, the decorative with profound intellection, an extremely subtle feeling for colour combinations with a sparse asceticism of style.

'Significant, undoubtedly significant, my dear child,' she said. 'Professor Zumsteg will think highly of it. He has confirmed you in this style of painting and he has the eye and the understanding for it. One has to have the eye and the understanding for it. What do you call it?'

'Trees in Evening Wind.'

'Ah, that gives a hint of what you were intending. Are those cones and circles against the greyish-yellow background meant to represent trees – and that peculiar spiralling line the wind? Interesting, Anna, interesting. But, heavens above, child, adorable Nature – what you do to her! If only you would let your art offer something to the emotions just once – paint something for the heart, a beautiful floral still life, a fresh spray of lilac, so true to life that one would think one smelt its ravishing perfume, and a pair of delicate Meissen porcelain figures beside the vase, a gentleman blowing kisses to a lady, and with everything reflected in the gleaming, polished table-top...'

'Stop, stop, Mama! You certainly have an extravagant imagination. But no one can paint like that any more!'

'Anna, you don't mean to tell me that, with your talent, you can't paint something like that, something to refresh the heart!'

'You misunderstand me, Mama! It's not a question of whether I can. Nobody can. The state of the times and of art no longer permits it.'

'So much the more regrettable for the times and art! No, forgive me, child, I did not mean to say quite that. If it is life and progress that make it impossible, there is no room for regret. On the contrary, it would be regrettable to fall behind. I understand that perfectly. And I understand too that it takes genius to conceive such an expressive line as this one of yours. It doesn't express anything to me, but I can see beyond doubt that it is extremely expressive.'

Anna kissed her mother, holding her palette and wet brush well away from her. And Rosalie kissed her too, glad in her heart that her daughter found in her work – which, if abstract and, as it seemed to her, deadening, was still an active handicraft – found in her artist's smock comfort and compensation for much that she was forced to renounce.

How greatly a limping gait curtails any sensual appreciation, on the part of the opposite sex, for a girl as such, Fräulein von Tümmler had learned early, and had armed herself against the fact with a pride which (in turn, as these things go), in cases where a young man was prepared despite her deformity to harbour an inclination towards her, discouraged it through coldly aloof disbelief and nipped it in the bud. Once, just after

their change of residence, she had loved – and had been grievously ashamed of her passion, for its object had been the physical
beauty of the young man, a chemist by training, who, considering it wise to turn science into money as rapidly as possible,
had, soon after attaining his doctorate, manoeuvred himself into
an important and lucrative position in a Düsseldorf chemical
factory. His swarthy, masculine handsomeness, together with an
openness of nature which appealed to men too, and the pro-
ficiency and application which he had demonstrated, aroused
the enthusiasm of all the girls and matrons in Düsseldorf
society, the young and the old being equally in raptures over
him; and it had been Anna's contemptible fate to languish
where all languished, to find herself condemned by her senses to
a universal feeling, confronted with whose depth she struggled in
vain to keep her self-respect.

Dr Brünner (such was the paragon's name), precisely because
he knew himself to be practical and ambitious, entertained a
certain corrective inclination towards higher and more recondite
things, and for a time openly sought out Fräulein von Tümmler, talked with her, when they met in society, of literature and
art, tuned his insinuating voice to a whisper to make mockingly
derogatory remarks to her concerning one or another of his
adorers, and seemed to want to conclude an alliance with her
against the mediocrities, who, refined by no deformity, impor-
tuned him with improper advances. What her own state was,
and what an agonizing happiness he aroused in her by his
mockery of other women – of that he seemed to have no inkling,
but only to be seeking and finding protection, in her intelligent
companionship, from the hardships of the amorous persecution
whose victim he was, and to be courting her esteem just because
he valued it. The temptation to accord it to him had been
strong and profound for Anna, though she knew that, if she
did, it would only be in attempt to extenuate her weakness for
his masculine attraction. To her sweet terror, his assiduity had
begun to resemble a real wooing, a choice, and a proposal; and
even now Anna could not but admit that she would helplessly
have married him if he had ever come to the point of speaking
out. But the decisive word was never uttered. His ambition for

higher things had not sufficed to make him disregard her physical defect nor yet her modest dowry. He had soon detached himself from her and married the wealthy daughter of a manufacturer, to whose native city of Bochum, and to a position in her father's chemical enterprise there, he had then betaken himself, to the sorrow of the female society of Düsseldorf and to Anna's relief.

Rosalie knew of her daughter's painful experience, and would have known of it even if the latter, at the time, in a moment of uncontrollable effusion, had not wept bitter tears on her mother's bosom over what she called her shame. Frau von Tümmler, though not particularly clever in other respects, had an unusually acute perception, not malicious but purely a matter of sympathy, in respect to everything that makes up the existence of a woman, psychologically and physiologically, to all that Nature has inflicted upon woman; so that in her circle hardly an event or circumstance in this category escaped her. From a supposedly unnoticed and private smile, a blush, or a brightening of the eyes, she knew what girl was captivated by what young man, and she confided her discoveries to her daughter, who was quite unaware of such things and had very little wish to be made aware of them. Instinctively, now to her pleasure, now to her regret, Rosalie knew whether a woman found satisfaction in her marriage or failed to find it. She infallibly diagnosed a pregnancy in its very earliest stage, and on these occasions, doubtless because she was concerned with something so joyously natural, she would drop into dialect – 'Da is wat am kommen,' she would say, meaning 'something's on the way.' It pleased her to see that Anna ungrudgingly helped her younger brother, who was well along in secondary school, with his homework; for, by virtue of a psychological shrewdness as naïve as it was keen, she divined the satisfaction that the superiority implied by this service to the male sex brought to the jilted girl.

It cannot be said that Rosalie took any particular interest in her son, a tall, lanky redheaded boy, who looked like his dead father and who, furthermore, seemed to have little talent for humanistic studies, but instead dreamed of building bridges and

highways and wanted to be an engineer. A cool friendllness, expressed only perfunctorily, and principally for form's sake, was
all that she offered him. But she clung to her daughter, her only
real friend. In view of Anna's reserve, the relation of confidence
between them might have been described as one-sided, were it
not that the mother simply knew everything about her repressed
child's emotional life, had known the proud and bitter resignation her soul harboured, and from that knowledge had derived
the right and the duty to communicate herself with equal
openness.

In so doing, she accepted, with imperturbable good humour,
many a fondly indulgent or sadly ironical or even somewhat
pained smile from her daughter and confidante, and, herself
kindly, was glad when she was kindly treated, ready to laugh at
her own simple-heartedness, convinced that it was happy and
right – so that, if she laughed at herself, she laughed too at
Anna's wry expression. It happened quite often – especially
when she gave full rein to her fervour for Nature, to which she
was for ever trying to win over the intellectual girl. Words cannot express how she loved the spring, *her* season, in which she
had been born, and which, she insisted, had always brought her,
in a quite personal way, mysterious currents of health, of joy in
life. When birds called in the new mild air, her face became
radiant. In the garden, the first crocus and daffodil, the hya-
cinths and tulips sprouting and flaunting in the beds around the
house, rejoiced the good soul to tears. The darling violets along
country roads, the gold of flowering broom and forsythia, the
red and the white may trees – above all, the lilac, and the way
the chestnuts lighted their candles, white and red – her daughter had to admire it all with her and share her ecstasy. Rosalie
fetched her from the north room that had been made into a
studio for her, dragged her from her abstract handicraft; and
with a willing smile Anna took off her smock and accompanied
her mother for hours together; for she was a surprisingly good
walker and if in company she concealed her limp by the utmost
possible economy of movement, when she was free and could
stump along as she pleased, her endurance was remarkable.

The season of flowering trees, when the roads became poetic, when the dear familiar landscape of their walks clothed itself in charming, white and rosy promise of fruit – what a bewitching time! From the flower catkins of the tall white poplars bordering the watercourse along which they often strolled, pollen sifted down on them like snow, drove with the breeze, covered the ground; and Rosalie, in raptures again, knew enough botany to tell her daughter that poplars are 'dioecious', each plant bearing only flowers of one sex, some male, others female. She discoursed happily on wind pollination – or, rather, on Zephyrus' loving service to the children of Flora, his obliging conveyance of pollen to the chastely awaiting female stigma – a method of fertilization which she considered particularly charming.

The rose season was utter bliss to her. She raised the Queen of Flowers on standards in her garden, solicitously protected it, by the indicated means, from devouring insects; and always, as long as the glory endured, bunches of duly refreshed roses stood on the whatnots and little tables in her boudoir – budding, half-blown, full-blown – especially red roses (she did not favour the white), of her own raising or attentive gifts from visitors of her own sex who were aware of her passion. She could bury her face, eyes closed, in such a bunch of roses and, when after a long time she raised it again, she would swear that it was the perfume of the gods; when Psyche bent, lamp in hand, over sleeping Cupid, surely his breath, his curls and cheeks, had filled her sweet little nose with this scent; it was the aroma of heaven, and she had no doubt that, as blessed spirits there above, we should breathe the odour of roses for all eternity. Then we shall very soon, was Anna's sceptical comment, grow so used to it that we simply shan't smell it any more. But Frau von Tümmler reprimanded her for assuming a wisdom beyond her years: if one was bent on scoffing, such an argument could apply to the whole state of beatitude, but joy was none the less joy for being unconscious. This was one of the occasions on which Anna gave her mother a kiss of tender indulgence and reconciliation, and then they laughed together.

Rosalie never used manufactured scents or perfumes, with the single exception of a touch of Eau de Cologne from C. M. Farina in the Jülichsplatz. But whatever Nature offers to gratify

our sense of smell – sweetness, aromatic bitterness, even heady
and oppressive scents – she loved beyond measure, and absorbed
it deeply, thankfully, with the most sensual fervour. On one of
their walks there was a declivity, a long depression in the
ground, a shallow gorge, the bottom of which was thickly
overgrown with jasmine and alder bushes, from which, on
warm, humid days in June with a threat of thunder showers,
fuming clouds of heated odour welled up almost stupefyingly.
Anna, though it was likely to give her a headache, had to
accompany her mother there time and again. Rosalie breathed in
the heavy, surging vapour with delighted relish, stopped,
walked on, lingered again, bent over the slope, and sighed:
'Child, child, how wonderful! It is the breath of nature – it is!
– her sweet, living breath, sun-warmed and drenched with moisture, deliciously wafted to us from her breast. Let us enjoy it
with reverence, for we too are her children.'

'At least you are, Mama,' said Anna, taking the enthusiast's
arm and drawing her along at her limping pace. 'She's not so
fond of me, and she gives me this pressure in my temples with
her concoction of odours.'

'Yes, because you are against her,' answered Rosalie, 'and pay
no homage to her with your talent, but want to set yourself
above her through it, turn her into a mere theme for the intellect, as you pride yourself on doing, and transpose your sense
perceptions into heaven knows what – into frigidity. I respect it,
Anna; but if I were in Mother Nature's place, I should be as
offended with all of you young painters for it as she is.' And she
seriously proposed to her that if she was set upon transposition
and absolutely must be abstract, she should try, at least once, to
express odours in colour.

This idea came to her late in June, when the lindens were in
flower – again for her the one lovely time of year, when for a
week or two the avenues of trees outside filled the whole house,
through the open windows, with the indescribably pure and
mild, enchanting odour of their late bloom, and the smile of
rapture never faded from Rosalie's lips. It was then that she
said: 'That is what you painters should paint, try your artistry
on that! You don't want to banish Nature from art entirely;

actually, you always start from her in your abstractions, and
you need something sensory in order to intellectualize it. Now,
odour, if I may say so, is sensory and abstract at the same time,
we don't see it, it speaks to us ethereally. And it ought to fascin-
ate you to convey an invisible felicity to the sense of sight, on
which, after all, the art of painting rests. Try it! What do you
painters have palettes for? Mix bliss on them and put it on
canvas as chromatic joy, and then label it "Odour of Lindens",
so that people who look at it will know what you were trying to
do.'

'Dearest Mama, you are astonishing!' Fräulein von Tümmler
answered. 'You think up problems that no painting teacher
would ever dream of! But don't you realize that you are an
incorrigible romanticist with your synaesthetic mixture of the
senses and your mystical transformation of odours into colours?'

'I know – I deserve your erudite mockery.'

'No, you don't – not any kind of mockery,' said Anna fervently.

Yet on a walk they took one afternoon in mid-August, on a
very hot day, something strange befell them, something that had
a suggestion of mockery. Strolling along between fields and the
edge of a wood, they suddenly noticed an odour of musk, at first
almost imperceptibly faint, then stronger. It was Rosalie who
first sniffed it and expressed her awareness by an 'Oh! Where
does that come from?' but her daughter soon had to concur:
Yes, there was some sort of odour, and, yes, it did seem to be
definable as musky – there was not doubt about it. Two steps
sufficed to bring them within sight of its source, which was
repellent. It was there by the roadside, seething in the sun, with
blowflies covering it and flying all around it – a little mound of
excrement, which they preferred not to investigate more closely.
The small area represented a meeting-ground of animal, or perhaps human faeces with some sort of putrid vegetation, and the
greatly decomposed body of some small woodland creature
seemed to be present too. In short, nothing could be nastier than
the teeming little mound; but its evil effluvium, which drew the
blowflies by hundreds, was, in its ambivalence, no longer to be

called a stench but must undoubtedly be pronounced the odour of musk.

'Let us go,' the ladies said simultaneously, and Anna, dragging her foot along all the more vigorously as they started off, clung to her mother's arm. For a time they were silent, as if each had to digest the strange impression for herself. Then Rosalie said:

'That explains it – I never did like musk, and I don't understand how anyone can use it as a perfume. Civet, I think, is in the same category. Flowers never smell like that, but in natural-history class we were taught that many animals secrete it from certain glands – rats, cats, the civet-cat, the musk-deer. In Schiller's *Kabale und Liebe* – I'm sure you must remember it – there's a little fellow, some sort of a toady, an absolute fool, and the stage direction says that he comes on screeching and spreads an odour of musk through the whole parterre. How that passage always made me laugh!'

And they brightened up. Rosalie was still capable of the old warm laughter that came bubbling from her heart – even at this period when the difficult organic adjustments of her time of life, the spasmodic withering and disintegration of her womanhood, were troubling her physically and psychologically. Nature had given her a friend in those days, quite close to home, in a corner of the Palace Garden ('Paintbox' Street was the way there). It was an old, solitary oak tree, gnarled and stunted, with its roots partly exposed, and a squat trunk, divided at a moderate height into thick knotty branches, which themselves ramified into knotty offshoots. The trunk was hollow here and there and had been filled with cement – the Park Department did something for the gallant centenarian; but many of the branches had died and, no longer producing leaves, clawed, crooked and bare, into the sky; others, only a scattered few but on up to the crown, still broke into verdure each spring with the jaggedly lobed leaves, which have always been considered sacred and from which the victor's crown is twined. Rosalie was only too pleased to see it – about the time of her birthday she followed the budding, sprouting, and unfolding of the oak's foliage on those of its branches and twigs to which life still forced its way, her sympathetic interest continuing from day to day. Quite close to the tree, on the edge of the lawn in which it stood, there was a bench; Rosalie sat down on it with Anna, and said:

'Good old fellow! Can you look at him without being touched, Anna – the way he stands there and keeps it up? Look at those roots, woody, and thick as your arm, how broadly they clasp the earth and anchor themselves in the nourishing soil. He has weathered many a storm and will survive many more. No danger of his falling down! Hollow, cemented, no longer able to produce a full crown of leaves – but when his time comes, the sap still rises in him – not everywhere, but he manages to display a little green, and people respect it and indulge him for his courage. Do you see that thin little shoot up there with its leafbuds nodding in the wind? All around it things haven't gone as they should, but the little twig saves the day.'

'Indeed, Mama, it gives cause for respect, as you say,' answered Anna. 'But if you don't mind, I'd rather go home now. I am having pains.'

'Pains? Is it your – but of course, dear child, how could I have forgotten! I reproach myself for having brought you with me. Here I am staring at the old tree and not worrying about your sitting there bent over. Forgive me. Take my arm and we will go.'

From the first, Fräulein von Tümmler had suffered severe abdominal pains in advance of her periods – it was nothing in itself, it was merely, as even the doctors had put it, a constitutional infliction that had to be accepted. Hence, on the short walk home, her mother could talk about it to the suffering girl soothingly and comfortingly, with well-intentioned cheerfulness, and indeed – and particularly – with envy.

'Do you remember,' she said, 'it was like this the very first time, when you were still just a young thing and it happened to you and you were so frightened but I explained to you that it was only natural and necessary and something to be glad over and that it was really a sort of day of glory because it showed that you had finally ripened into a woman? You have pains beforehand – it's a trial, I know, and not strictly necessary, I never had any; but it happens; aside from you, I know of two

or three cases where there are pains, and I think to myself:
Pains, *à la bonne heure*! – for us women, pains are something
different from what they are elsewhere in Nature and for men;
they don't have any, except when they're sick, and then they
carry on terribly; even Tümmler did that, your father, as soon
as he had a pain anywhere, even though he was an officer and
died the death of a hero. Our sex behaves differently about it; it
takes pain more patiently, we are the long-suffering, born for
pain, so to speak. Because, above all, we know the natural and
healthy pain, the God-ordained and sacred pain of childbirth,
which is something absolutely peculiar to woman, something
men are spared, or denied. Men – the fools! – are horrified, to
be sure, by our half-unconscious screaming, and reproach themselves and clasp their heads in their hands; and, for all that we
scream, we are really laughing at them. When I brought you
into the world, Anna, it was very bad. From the first pain it
lasted thirty-six hours, and Tümmler ran around the apartment
the whole time with his head in his hands, but despite everything it was a great festival of life, and I wasn't screaming
myself, *it* was screaming, it was a sacred ecstasy of pain. With
Eduard, later, it wasn't half so bad, but it would still have been
more than enough for a man – our lords and masters would
certainly want no part in it. Pains, you see, are usually the
danger-signals by which Nature, always benignant, warns that a
disease is developing in the body – look sharp there, it means,
something's wrong, do something about it quick, not so much
against the pain as against what the pain indicates. With us it
can be like that too, and have that meaning, of course. But, as
you know yourself, your abdominal pain before your periods
doesn't have that meaning, it doesn't warn you of anything. It's
a sport among the species of women's pains and as such it is
honourable, that is how you must take it, as a vital function in
the life of a woman. Always, so long as we are that – a woman,
no longer a child and not yet an incapacitated old crone – always,
over and over, there is an intensified welling up of the blood of
life in our organ of motherhood, by which precious Nature
prepares it to receive the fertilized egg, and if one is present, as,
after all, even in my long life, was the case only twice and with a

long interval between, then our monthly doesn't come, and we are pregnant. Heavens, what a joyous surprise when it stopped the first time for me, thirty years ago! It was you, my dear child, with whom I was blessed, and I still remember how I confided it to Tümmler and, blushing, laid my face against his and said, very softly: "Robert, it's happened, all the signs point that way, and it's my turn now, *da is wat am kommen* . . ." '

'Dearest Mama, please just do me the favour of not using dialect, it irritates me at the moment.'

'Oh, forgive me, darling – to irritate you now is the last thing I meant to do. It's only that, in my blissful confusion, I really did say that to Tümmler. And then – we are talking about natural things, aren't we? – and, to my mind, Nature and dialect go together somehow, as Nature and the people go together – if I'm talking nonsense, correct me, you are so much cleverer than I am. Yes, you are clever, and, as an artist, you are not on the best of terms with Nature but insist on transposing her into concepts, into cubes and spirals, and, since we're speaking of things going together, I rather wonder if they don't go together too, your proud, intellectual attitude towards Nature, and the way she singles you out and sends you pains at your periods.'

'But, Mama,' said Anna, and could not help laughing, 'you scold me for being intellectual, and then propound absolutely unwarrantable intellectual theories yourself!'

'If I can divert you a little with it, child, the most naïve theory is good enough for me. But what I was saying about women's natural pains I mean perfectly seriously, it should comfort you. Simply be happy and proud that, at thirty, you are in the full power of your blood. Believe me, I would gladly put up with any kind of abdominal pains if it were still with me as it is with you. But unfortunately that is over for me, it has been growing more and more scanty and irregular, and for the last two months it hasn't happened at all. Ah, it has ceased to be with me after the manner of women, as the Bible says, in reference to Sarah, I think – yes, it was Sarah, and then a miracle of fruitfulness was worked in her, but that's only one of those edifying stories, I suppose – that sort of thing doesn't happen any more today. When it has ceased to be with us after the manner of women, we are no longer women at all, but only the dried-up husk of a woman, worn out, useless, cast out of nature. My dear child, it is very bitter. With men, I believe, it usually doesn't stop as long as they are alive. I know some who at eighty still can't let a woman alone, and Tümmler, your father, was like that too – how I had to pretend not to see things even when he was a lieutenant-colonel! What is fifty for a man? Provided he has a little temperament, fifty comes nowhere near stopping him from playing the lover, and many a man with greying temples still makes conquests even among young girls. But we, take it all in all, are given just thirty-five years to be women in our life and our blood, to be complete human beings, and when we are fifty, we are superannuated, our capacity to breed expires, and, in Nature's eyes, we are nothing but old rubbish!'

To these bitter words of acquiescence in the ways of Nature, Anna did not answer as many women would doubtless, and justifiably, have answered. She said:

'How you talk, Mama, and how you revile and seem to want to reject the dignity that falls to the elderly woman when she has fulfilled her life, and Nature, which you love after all, translates her to a new, mellow condition, an honourable and more lovable condition, in which she still can give and be so much, both to her family and to those less close to her. You say you envy men because their sex life is less strictly limited than a woman's. But I doubt if that is really anything to be respected, if it is a reason for envying them; and in any case all civilized peoples have always rendered the most exquisite honours to the matron, have even regarded her as sacred – and we mean to regard you as sacred in the dignity of your dear and charming old age.'

'Darling' – and Rosalie drew her daughter close as they walked along – 'you speak so beautifully and intelligently and well, despite your pains, for which I was trying to comfort you, and now you are comforting your foolish mother in her unworthy tribulations. But the dignity, and the resignation, are very hard, my dear child, it is very hard even for the body to find itself in its new situation, that alone is torment enough.

And when there are heart and mind besides, which would still rather not hear too much of dignity and the honourable estate of a matron, and rebel against the drying up of the body – that is when it really begins to be hard. The soul's adjustment to the new constitution of the body is the hardest thing of all.'

'Of course, Mama, I understand that very well. But consider: body and soul are one; the psychological is no less a part of Nature than the physical; Nature takes in the psychological too, and you needn't be afraid that your psyche can long remain out of harmony with the natural change in your body. You must regard the psychological as only an emanation of the physical; and if the poor soul thinks that she is saddled with the all too difficult task of adjusting herself to the body's changed life, she will soon see that she really has nothing to do but let the body have its way and do its work on herself too. For it is the body that moulds the soul, in accordance with its own conditions.'

Fräulein von Tümmler had her reasons for saying this, because, about the time that her mother made the above confidence to her, a new face, an additional face, was very often to be seen at home, and the potentially embarrassing developments which were under way had not escaped Anna's silent, apprehensive observation.

The new face – which Anna found distressingly commonplace, anything but distinguished by intelligence – belonged to a young man named Ken Keaton, an American of about twenty-four whom the war had brought over and who had been staying in the city for some time, giving English lessons in one household or another or simply commandeered for English conversation (in exchange for a suitable fee) by the wives of rich industrialists. Eduard had heard of these activities towards Easter of his last year in school and had earnestly begged his mother to have Mr Keaton teach him the rudiments of English a few afternoons a week. For though his school offered him a quantity of Greek and Latin, and fortunately a sufficiency of mathematics as well, it offered no English, which, after all, seemed highly important for his future goal. As soon as, one way or another, he had got through all those boring humanities, he

wanted to attend the Polytechnic Institute and after that, so he
planned, go to England for further study or perhaps straight to
the El Dorado of technology, the United States. So he was
happy and grateful when, respecting his clarity and firmness of
purpose, his mother readily acceded to his wish; and his work
with Keaton, Mondays, Wednesdays, and Saturdays, gave him
great satisfaction – because it served his purpose, of course, but
then too because it was fun to learn a new language right from
the rudiments, like an abecedarian, beginning with a little
primer: words, their often outlandish orthography, their most
extraordinary pronunciation, which Ken, forming his l's even
deeper down in his throat than the Rhinelanders and letting his
r's sound from his gums unrolled, would illustrate with such
drawn-out exaggeration that he seemed to be trying to make fun
of his own mother tongue. 'Scrr-ew the top on!' he said. 'I
sllept like a top.' 'Alfred is a tennis play-err. His shoulders are
thirty inches brr-oaoadd.' Eduard could laugh, through the
whole hour and a half of the lesson, at Alfred, the broad-
shouldered tennis player, in whose praise so much was said
with the greatest possible use of 'though' and 'thought' and
'taught' and 'tough', but he made very good progress, just because Ken, not being a learned pedagogue, used a free and easy
method – in other words, improvised on whatever the moment
brought and hammering away regardless, through patter, slang,
and nonsense, initiated his willing pupil into his easy-going,
humorous, efficient vernacular.

Frau von Tümmler, attracted by the jollity that pervaded
Eduard's room, sometimes looked in on the young people and
took some part in their profitable fun, laughed heartily with them
over 'Alfred, the tennis play-err', and found a certain resemblance between him and her son's young tutor, particularly in the
matter of his shoulders, for Ken's too were splendidly broad. He
had, moreover, thick blond hair, a not particularly handsome
though not unpleasant, guilelessly friendly boyish face, to which
in these surroundings, however, a slight Anglo-Saxon cast of
features lent a touch of the unusual; that he was remarkably
well built was apparent despite his loose, rather full clothes;
with his long legs and narrow hips, he produced an impression

of youthful strength. He had very nice hands, too, with a not too elaborate ring on the left. His simple, perfectly unconstrained yet not rude manner, his comical German, which became as undeniably English-sounding in his mouth as the scraps of French and Italian that he knew (for he had visited several European countries) – all this Rosalie found very pleasant; his great naturalness in particular prepossessed her in his favour; and now and again, and finally almost regularly, she invited him to stay for dinner after Eduard's lesson, whether she had been present at it or not. In part her interest in him was due to her having heard that he was very successful with women. With this in mind, she studied him and found the rumour not incomprehensible, though it was not quite to her taste when, having to eructate a little at table, he would put his hand over his mouth and say 'Pardon me!' – which was meant for good manners, but which, after all, drew attention to the occurrence quite unnecessarily.

Ken, as he told them over dinner, had been born in a small town in one of the Eastern states, where his father had followed various occupations – broker, manager of a gas station – from time to time too he had made some money in the real-estate business. Ken had attended high school, where, if he was to be believed, one learned nothing at all – 'by European standards', as he respectfully added – after which, without giving the matter much thought, but merely with the idea of learning something more, he had entered a college in Detroit, Michigan, where he had earned his tuition by the work of his hands, as dishwasher, cook, waiter, campus gardener. Frau von Tümmler asked him how, through all that, he had managed to keep such white, one might say aristocratic hands, and he answered that, when doing rough work, he had always worn gloves – only a short-sleeved polo shirt, or nothing at all from the waist up, but always gloves. Most workmen, or at least many of them – construction workers, for example – did that back home, to avoid getting horny proletarian hands, and they had hands like a lawyer's clerk, with a ring.

Rosalie praised the custom, but Keaton differed. Custom? The word was too good for it, you couldn't call it a 'custom', in the sense of the old European folk customs (he habitually said 'Continental' for 'European'). Such an old German folk custom, for example, as the 'rod of life' – village lads gathering fresh birch and willow rods at Christmas or Easter and striking ('peppering' or 'slashing', they called it) the girls, and sometimes cattle and trees, with them to bring health and fertility – that was a 'custom', an age-old one, and it delighted him. When the peppering or slashing took place in spring, it was called 'Smack Easter'.

The Tümmlers had never heard of Smack Easter and were surprised at Ken's knowledge of folklore. Eduard laughed at the 'rod of life', Anna made a face, and only Rosalie, in perfect agreement with their guest, showed herself delighted. Anyhow, he said, it was something very different from wearing gloves at work, and you could look a long time before you found anything of the sort in America, if only because there were no villages there and the farmers were not farmers at all but entrepreneurs like everyone else and had no 'customs'. In general, despite being so unmistakably American in his entire manner and attitude, he displayed very little attachment to his great country. He 'didn't care for America'; indeed, with its pursuit of the dollar and insensate church-going, its worship of success and its colossal mediocrity, but, above all, its lack of historical atmosphere, he found it really appalling. Of course, it had a history, but that wasn't 'history', it was simply a short, boring 'success story'. Certainly, aside from its enormous deserts, it had beautiful and magnificent landscapes, but there was 'nothing behind them', while in Europe there was so much behind everything, particularly behind the cities, with their deep historical perspectives. American cities – he 'didn't care for them'. They were put up yesterday and might just as well be taken away tomorrow. The small ones were stupid holes, one looking exactly like another, and the big ones were horrible, inflated monstrosities, with museums full of bought-up European cultural treasures. Bought, of course, was better than stolen, but not *much* better, for, in certain places things dating from A.D. 1400 and 1200 were as good as stolen.

Ken's irreverent chatter aroused laughter; they took him to

task for it too, but he answered that what made him speak as he did was precisely reverence, specifically a respect for perspective and atmosphere. Very early dates, A.D. 1100, 700, were his passion and his hobby, and at college he had always been best at history – at history and at athletics. He had long been drawn to Europe, where early dates were at home, and certainly, even without the war, he would have worked his way across, as a sailor or dishwasher, simply to breathe historical air. But the war had come at just the right moment for him; in 1917 he had immediately enlisted in the army, and all through his training he had been afraid that the war might end before it brought him across to Europe. But he had made it – almost at the last minute he had sailed to France, jammed into a troop transport, and had even got into some real fighting, near Compiègne, from which he had carried away a wound, and not a light one, so that he had had to lie in hospital for weeks. It had been a kidney wound, and only one of his kidneys really worked now, but that was quite enough. However, he said, smiling, he was, in a manner of speaking, disabled, and he drew a small disability pension, which was worth more to him than the lost kidney.

There was certainly nothing of the disabled veteran about him, Frau von Tümmler observed, and he answered: 'No, thank heaven, only a little cash!'

On his release from the hospital, he had left the service, had been 'honourably discharged' with a medal for bravery, and had stayed on for an indefinite time in Europe, which he found 'wonderful' and where he revelled in early dates. The French cathedrals, the Italian campaniles, *palazzi*, and galleries, the Swiss villages, a place like Stein am Rhein – all that was 'most delightful indeed'. And the wine everywhere, the *bistros* in France, the *trattorie* in Italy, the cosy *Wirtshäuser* in Switzerland and Germany, 'at the sign of the Ox', 'of the Moor', 'of the Star' – where was there anything like that in America? There was no wine there – just 'drinks', whisky and rum, and no cool pints of Elässer or Tiroler or Johannisberger at an oak table in a historical taproom or a honeysuckle arbour. Good heavens! People in America simply didn't know how to live.

Germany! That was the country he loved, though he really

had explored it very little and in fact knew only the places on the Bodensee, and of course – but that he knew really well – the Rhineland. The Rhineland, with its charming, gay people, so amiable, especially when they were a bit 'high'; with its venerable cities, full of atmosphere. Trier, Aachen, Coblenz, 'Holy' Cologne – just try calling an American city 'holy' – 'Holy Kansas City', ha-ha! The golden treasure, guarded by the nixies of the Missouri River – ha-ha-ha – 'Pardon me!' Of Düsseldorf and its long history from Merovingian days, he knew more than Rosalie and her children put together, and he spoke of Pepin the Short, of Barbarossa, who built the Imperial Palace at Rindhusen, and of the Salian Church at Kaiserswerth, where Henry IV was crowned King as a child, of Albert of Berg and John William of the Palatinate, and of many other things and people, like a professor.

Rosalie said that he could teach history too, just as well as English. There was too little demand, he replied. Oh, not at all, she protested. She herself, for instance, whom he had made keenly aware of how little she knew, would begin taking lessons from him at once. He would be 'a little shy' about it, he confessed; in answer she expressed something that she had feelingly observed: It was strange and to a certain degree painful that in life shyness was the rule between youth and age. Youth was reserved in the presence of age because it expected no understanding of its green time of life from age's dignity, and age feared youth because, though admiring it whole-heartedly, simply as youth, age considered it due to its dignity to conceal its admiration under mockery and assumed condescension.

Ken laughed, pleased and approving. Eduard remarked that Mama really talked like a book, and Anna looked searchingly at her mother. She was decidedly vivacious in Mr Keaton's presence, unfortunately even a little affected at times; she invited him frequently, and looked at him, even when he said 'Pardon me' behind his hand, with an expression of motherly compassion which to Anna – who, despite the young man's enthusiasm for Europe, his passion for dates like 700, and his knowledge of all the time-honoured pothouses in Düsseldorf, found him totally uninteresting – appeared somewhat questionable in point of motherliness and made her not a little uncomfortable. Too often, when Mr Keaton was to be present, her mother asked, with nervous apprehension, if her nose was flushed. It was, though Anna soothingly denied it. And if it wasn't before he arrived, it flushed with unwonted violence when she was in the young man's company. But then her mother seemed to have forgotten all about it.

Anna saw rightly: Rosalie had begun to lose her heart to her son's young tutor, without offering any resistance to the rapid budding of her feeling, perhaps without being really aware of it, and in any case without making any particular effort to keep it a secret. Symptoms that in another woman could not have escaped her feminine observation (a cooing and exaggeratedly delighted laughter at Ken's chatter, a soulful look followed by a curtaining of the brightened eyes), she seemed to consider imperceptible in herself – if she was not boasting of her feeling, was not too proud of it to conceal it.

The situation became perfectly clear to the suffering Anna one very summery, warm September evening, when Ken had stayed for dinner and Eduard, after the soup, had asked permission, on account of the heat, to take off his jacket. The young men, was the answer, must feel no constraint; and so Ken followed his pupil's example. He was not in the least concerned that, whereas Eduard was wearing a coloured shirt with long sleeves, he had merely put on his jacket over his sleeveless white jersey and hence now displayed his bare arms – very handsome, round, strong, white young arms, which made it perfectly comprehensible that he had been as good at athletics in college as at history. The agitation which the sight of them caused in the lady of the house, he was certainly far from noticing, nor did Eduard have any eyes for it. But Anna observed it with pain and pity. Rosalie, talking and laughing feverishly, looked alternately as if she had been drenched with blood and frighteningly pale, and after every escape her fleeing eyes returned, under an irresistible attraction, to the young man's arms and then, for rapt seconds, lingered on them with an expression of deep and sensual sadness.

Anna, bitterly resentful of Ken's primitive guilelessness, which, however, she did not entirely trust, drew attention, as soon as she found even a shred of an excuse, to the evening coolness, which was just beginning to penetrate through the open French window, and suggested, with a warning against catching cold, that the jackets be put on again. But Frau von Tümmler terminated her evening almost immediately after dinner. Pretending a headache, she took a hurried leave of her guest and retired to her bedroom. There she lay stretched on her couch, with her face hidden in her hands and buried in the pillow, and, overwhelmed with shame, terror, and bliss, confessed her passion to herself.

'Good God, I love him, yes, love him, as I have never loved, is it possible? Here I am, retired from active service, translated by Nature to the calm, dignified estate of matronhood. Is it not grotesque that I should still give myself up to lust, as I do in my frightened, blissful thoughts at the sight of him, at the sight of his godlike arms, by which I insanely long to be embraced, at the sight of his magnificent chest, which, in wretchedness and rapture, I saw outlined under his jersey? Am I a shameless old woman? No, not shameless, for I am ashamed in his presence, in the presence of his youth, and I do not know how I ought to meet him and look him in the eyes, the ingenuous, friendly boy's eyes, which expect no burning emotion from me. But it is I who have been struck by the rod of life, he himself, all unknowing, has slashed me and peppered me with it, he has given me my Smack Easter! Why did he have to tell us of it, in his youthful enthusiasm for old folk customs? Now the thought of the awakening stroke of his rod leaves my inmost being drenched, inundated with shameful sweetness. I desire him – have I ever desired before? Tümmler desired me, when I was young, and I consented, acquiesced in his wooing, took him in marriage in his commanding manhood, and we gave ourselves up to lust when he desired. This time it is I who desire, of my own will and motion, and I have cast my eyes on him as a man casts his eyes on the young woman of his choice – this is what the years do, it is my age that does it and his youth. Youth is feminine, and age's relationship to it is masculine, but age is not happy and

321

confident in its desire, it is full of shame and fear before youth and before all Nature, because of its unfitness. Oh, there is much sorrow in prospect for me, for how can I hope that he will be pleased by my desire, and, if pleased, that he will consent to my wooing, as I did to Tümmler's. He is no girl, with his firm arms, not he – far from it, he is a young man, who wants to desire for himself and who, they say, is very successful in that way with women. He has as many women as he wants, right here in town. My soul writhes and screams with jealousy at the thought. He gives lessons in English conversation to Louise Pfingsten in Pempelforter Strasse and to Amélie Lützenkirchen, whose husband, the pottery-manufacturer, is fat, short-winded, and lazy. Louise is too tall and has a bad hairline, but she is only just thirty-eight and knows how to give melting looks. Amélie is only a little older, and pretty, unfortunately she is pretty, and that fat husband of hers gives her every liberty. Is it possible that they lie in his arms, or at least one of them does, probably Amélie, but it might be that stick of a Louise at the same time – in those arms for whose embrace I long with fervour that their stupid souls could never muster? That they enjoy his hot breath, his lips, his hands that caress their bodies? My teeth, still so good, and which have needed so little attention – my teeth gnash, I gnash them, when I think of it. My figure too is better than theirs, worthier than theirs to be caressed by his hands, and what tenderness I should offer him, what inexpressible devotion! But they are flowing springs, and I am dried up, not worth being jealous of any more. Jealousy, torturing, tearing, crushing jealousy! That garden party at the Rollwagens' – the machine-factory Rollwagen and his wife – where he was invited too – wasn't it there that with my own eyes, which see everything, I saw him and Amélie exchange a look and a smile that almost certainly pointed to some secret between them? Even then my heart contracted with choking pain, but I did not understand it, I did not think it was jealousy because I no longer supposed myself capable of jealousy. But I am, I understand that now, and I do not try to deny it, no, I rejoice in my torments – there they are, in marvellous disaccord with the physical change in me. The psychological only an emanation of the physical, says Anna, and the body moulds the soul after its own condition? Anna knows a lot, Anna knows nothing. No, I will not say that she knows nothing. She has suffered, loved senselessly and suffered shamefully, and so she knows a great deal. But that soul and body are translated together to the mild, honourable estate of matronhood – there she is all wrong, for she does not believe in miracles, does not know that Nature can make the soul flower miraculously, when it is late, even too late – flower in love, desire, and jealousy, as I am experiencing in blissful torment. Sarah, the old grey crone, heard from behind the tent door what was still appointed for her, and she laughed. And God was angry with her and said: Wherefore did Sarah laugh? I – I will not have laughed. I will believe in the miracle of my soul and my senses, I will revere the miracle Nature has wrought in me, this agonizing shy spring in my soul, and I will be shamefaced only before the blessing of this late visitation . . .'

Thus Rosalie, communing with herself, on that evening. After a night of violent restlessness and a few hours of deep morning sleep, her first thought on waking was of the passion that had smitten her, blessed her, and to deny which, to reject it on moral grounds, simply did not enter her head. The poor woman was enraptured with the survival in her soul of the ability to bloom in sweet pain. She was not particularly pious, and she left the Lord God out of the picture. Her piety was for Nature, and it made her admire and prize what Nature, as it were against herself, had worked in her. Yes, it was contrary to natural seemliness, this flowering of her soul and senses; though it made her happy, it did not encourage her, it was something to be concealed, kept secret from all the world, even from her trusted daughter, but especially from him, her beloved, who suspected nothing and must suspect nothing – for how dared she boldly raise her eyes to his youth?

Thus into her relationship to Keaton there entered a certain submissiveness and humility which were completely absurd socially, yet which Rosalie, despite her pride in her feeling, was unable to banish from it, and which, on any clear-sighted observer – and so on Anna – produced a more painful effect than all the vivacity and excessive gaiety of her behaviour in the beginning. Finally even Eduard noticed it, and there were moments when brother and sister, bowed over their plates, bit their lips, while Ken, uncomprehendingly aware of the embarrassed silence, looked questioningly from one to another. Seeking counsel and enlightenment, Eduard took an opportunity to question his sister.

'What's happening to Mama?' he asked. 'Doesn't she like Keaton any more?' And as Anna said nothing, the young man, making a wry face, added: 'Or does she like him too much?'

'What are you thinking of?' was the reproving answer. 'Such things are no concern of yours, at your age. Mind your manners, and do not permit yourself to make unsuitable observations!' But she went on: he might reverently remind himself that his mother, as all women eventually must, was having to go through a period of difficulties prejudicial to her health and wellbeing.

'Very new and instructive for me!' said the senior in school ironically; but the explanation was too general to suit him. Their mother was suffering from something more specific, and even she, his highly respected sister, was visibly suffering – to say nothing of his young and stupid self. But perhaps, young and stupid as he was, he could make himself useful by proposing the dismissal of his too attractive tutor. He had, he could tell his mother, got enough out of Keaton; it was time for him to be 'honourably discharged' again.

'Do so, dear Eduard,' said Anna, and he did.

'Mama,' he said, 'I think we might stop my English lessons, and the constant expense I have put you to for them. Thanks to your generosity, I have laid a good foundation, with Mr Keaton's help; and by doing some reading by myself I can see to it that it will not be lost. Anyway, no one ever really learns a foreign language at home, outside of the country where everybody speaks it and where one is entirely dependent on it. Once I am in England or America, after the start you have generously given me, the rest will come easily. As you know, my final examinations are approaching, and there is none in English. Instead I must see to it that I don't flunk the classical lan-

guages, and that requires concentration. So the time has come –
don't you think? – to thank Keaton cordially for his trouble
and in the most friendly way possible to dispense with his
services.'

'But Eduard,' Frau von Tümmler answered at once, and indeed at first with a certain haste, 'what you say surprises me,
and I cannot say that I approve of it. Certainly, it shows great
delicacy of feeling in you to wish to spare me further expendi-
ture for this purpose. But the purpose is a good one, it is important for your future, as you now see it, and our situation is
not such that we cannot meet the expenses of language lessons
for you, quite as well as we were able to meet those of Anna's
studies at the Academy. I do not understand why you want to
stop halfway in your project to gain a mastery of the English
language. It could be said, dear boy – please don't take it in bad
part – that you would be making me an ill return for the will-
ingness with which I met your proposal. Your final examinations – to be sure, they are a serious matter, and I understand
that you will have to buckle down to your classical languages,
which come hard to you. But your English lessons, a few times
a week – you don't mean to tell me that they wouldn't be more
of a recreation, a healthy distraction for you, than an additional
strain. Besides – and now let me pass to the personal and human
side of the matter – the relationship between Ken, as he is
called, or rather Mr Keaton, and our family has long since
ceased to be such that we could say to him: "You're no longer
needed", and simply give him his marching orders. Simply
announce: "Sirrah, you may withdraw." He has become a
friend, almost a member of the family, and he would quite
rightly be offended at such a dismissal. We should all feel his
absence – Anna especially, I think, would be upset if he no
longer came and enlivened our table with his intimate knowledge of the history of Düsseldorf, stopped telling us all about
the quarrel over right of succession between the duchies of
Jülich and Cleves, and about Elector John William on his
pedestal in the market place. You would miss him too, and so,
in fact, should I. In short, Eduard, your proposal is well meant,

but it is neither necessary nor, indeed, really possible. We had better leave things as they are.'

'Whatever you think best, Mama,' said Eduard, and reported his ill success to his sister, who answered:

'I expected as much, my boy. After all, Mama has described the situation quite correctly, and I saw much the same objections to your plan when you announced it to me. In any case, she is perfectly right in saying that Keaton is pleasant company and that we should all regret his absence. So just go on with him.'

As she spoke, Eduard looked her in the face, which remained impassive; he shrugged his shoulders and left. Ken was waiting for him in his room, read a few pages of Emerson or Macaulay with him, then an American mystery story, which gave them something to talk about for the last half hour, and stayed for dinner, to which he had long since ceased to be expressly invited. His staying on after lessons had become a standing arrangement; and Rosalie, on the recurring days of her untoward and timorous, shame-clouded joy, consulted with Babette, the housekeeper, over the menu, ordered a choice repast, provided a full-bodied Pfälzer or Rüdesheimer, over which they would linger in the living-room for an hour after dinner, and to which she applied herself beyond her wont, so that she could look with better courage at the object of her unreasonable love. But often too the wine made her tired and desperate; and then whether she should stay and suffer in his sight or retire and weep over him in solitude became a battle which she fought with varying results.

October having brought the beginning of the social season, she also saw Keaton elsewhere than in her own house – at the Pfingstens' in Pempelforter Strasse, at the Lützenkirchens', at big receptions at Chief Engineer Rollwagen's. On these occasions she sought and shunned him, fled the group he had joined, waited in another, talking mechanically, for him to come and bestow some notice on her, knew at any moment where he was, listened for his voice amid the buzz of voices, and suffered horribly when she thought she saw signs of a secret understanding between him and Louise Pfingsten or Amélie Lützenkirchen. Although the young man had nothing in particular to offer except his fine physique, his complete naturalness and friendly simplicity, he was liked and sought out in this circle, contentedly profited by the German weakness for everything foreign, and knew very well that his pronunciation of German, the childish turns of phrase he used in speaking it, made a great hit. Then, too, people were glad to speak English with him. He could dress as he pleased. He had no evening clothes; social usages, however, had for many years been less strict, a dinner jacket was no longer absolutely obligatory in a box at the theatre or at an evening party, and even on occasions where the majority of the gentlemen present wore evening dress, Keaton was welcome in ordinary street clothes, his loose, comfortable apparel, the belted brown trousers, brown shoes, and grey woollen jacket.

Thus unceremoniously he moved through drawing-rooms, made himself agreeable to the ladies to whom he gave English lessons, as well as to those by whom he would gladly have been prevailed upon to do the same – at table first cut a piece of his meat, then laid his knife diagonally across the rim of his plate, let his left arm hang, and, managing his fork with the right, ate what he had made ready. He adhered to this custom because he saw that the ladies on either side of him and the gentleman opposite observed it with such great interest.

He was always glad to chat with Rosalie, whether in company or *tête-à-tête* – not only because she was one of his sources of income but from a genuine attraction. For whereas her daughter's cool intelligence and intellectual pretensions inspired fear in him, the mother's true-hearted womanliness impressed him sympathetically, and, without correctly reading her feelings (it did not occur to him to do that), he allowed himself to bask in the warmth that radiated from her to him, took pleasure in it, and felt little concern over certain concomitant signs of tension, oppression, and confusion, which he interpreted as expressions of European nervousness and therefore held in high regard. In addition, for all her suffering, her appearance at this time acquired a conspicuous new bloom, a rejuvenescence, upon which she received many compliments. Her figure had always preserved its youthfulness, but what was so striking now was the light in her beautiful brown eyes – a light which, if there was something feverish about it, nevertheless added to her charm – was her heightened colouring, quick to return after occasional moments of pallor, the mobility of feature that characterized her face (it had become a little fuller) in conversations that inclined to gaiety and hence always enabled her to correct any involuntary expression by a laugh. A good deal of loud laughter was the rule at these convivial gatherings, for all partook liberally of the wine and punch, and what might have seemed eccentric in Rosalie's manner was submerged in the general atmosphere of relaxation, in which nothing caused much surprise. But how happy she was when it happened that one of the women said to her, in Ken's presence: 'Darling, you are astonishing! How ravishing you look this evening! You eclipse the girls of twenty. Do tell me, what fountain of youth have you discovered?' And even more when her beloved corroborated: 'Right you are! Frau von Tümmler is perfectly delightful tonight.' She laughed, and her deep blush could be attributed to her pleasure in the flattery. She looked away from him, but she thought of his arms, and again she felt the same prodigious sweetness drenching, inundating her inmost being – it had been a frequent sensation these days, and other women, she thought, when they found her young, when they found her charming, must surely be aware of it.

It was on one of these evenings, after the gathering had broken up, that she failed in her resolve to keep the secret of her heart, the illicit and painful but fascinating psychological miracle that had befallen her, wholly to herself and not to reveal it even to Anna's friendship. An irresistible need for communication forced her to break the promise she had made to herself and to confide in her brilliant daughter, not only because she yearned for understanding sympathy but also from a wish that what Nature was bringing to pass in her should be understood and honoured as the remarkable human phenomenon that it was.

A wet snow was falling; the two ladies had driven home through it in a taxicab about midnight. Rosalie was shivering.

'Allow me, dear child,' she said, 'to sit up another half-hour with you in your cosy bedroom. I am freezing, but my head is on fire, and sleep, I fear, is out of the question for some time. If you would make tea for us, to end the evening, it wouldn't be a bad idea. That punch of the Rollwagens' is hard on one. Rollwagen mixes it himself, but he hasn't the happiest knack of it, pours a questionable orange cordial into the Moselle and then adds domestic champagne. Tomorrow we shall have terrible headaches again, a bad "hangover". Not you, that is. You are sensible and don't drink much. But I forget myself, chattering away, and don't notice that they keep filling my glass and think it is still the first. Yes, make tea for us, it's just the thing, Tea stimulates, but it soothes at the same time, and a cup of hot tea, taken at the right moment, wards off a cold. The rooms were far too hot at the Rollwagens' – at least, I thought so – and then the foul weather outdoors. Does it mean spring already? At noon today in the park I thought I really sniffed spring. But your silly mother always does that as soon as the shortest day has passed and the light increases again. A good idea, turning on the electric heater; there's not much heat left here at this hour. My dear child, you know how to make us comfortable and create just the right intimate atmosphere for a little *tête-à-tête* before we go to bed. You see, Anna, I have long wanted to have a talk with you, and – you are quite right – you have never denied me the opportunity. But there are things, child, to express which, to discuss which, requires a particularly intimate atmosphere, a favourable hour, which loosens one's tongue ...'

'What sort of things, Mama? I haven't any cream to offer you. Will you take a little lemon?'

'Things of the heart, child, things of Nature, wonderful, mysterious, omnipotent Nature, who sometimes does such strange, contradictory, indeed incomprehensible things to us. You know it too. Recently, my dear Anna, I have found myself thinking a great deal about your old – forgive me for referring to it – your *affaire de cœur* with Brünner, about what you went through then, the suffering of which you complained to me in an hour not unlike this, and which, in bitter self-reproach, you even called a shame, because, that is, of the shameful conflict in which your reason, your judgement, was engaged with your heart, or, if you prefer, with your senses.'

'You are quite right to change the word, Mama. "Heart" is sentimental nonsense. It is inadmissible to say "heart" for something that is entirely different. Our heart speaks truly only with the consent of our judgement and reason.'

'You may well say so. For you have always been on the side of unity and insisted that Nature, simply of herself, creates harmony between soul and body. But that you were in a state of disharmony then – that is, between your wishes and your judgement – you cannot deny. You were very young at the time, and your desire had no reason to be ashamed in Nature's eyes, only in the eyes of your judgement, which called it debasing. It did not pass the test of your judgement, and that was your shame and your suffering. For you are proud, Anna, very proud; and that there might be a pride in feeling alone, a pride of feeling which denies that it has to pass the test of anything and be responsible to anything – judgement and reason and even Nature herself – that you will not admit, and in that we differ. For to me the heart is supreme, and if Nature inspires feelings in it which no longer become it, and seems to create a contradiction between the heart and herself – certainly it is painful and shameful, but the shame is only for one's unworthiness and, at bottom, is sweet amazement, is reverence, before Nature and before the life that it pleases her to create in one whose life is done.'

'My dear Mama,' replied Anna, 'let me first of all decline the honour that you accord to my pride and my reason. At the time, they would have miserably succumbed to what you poetically call my heart if a merciful fate had not intervened; and when I think where my heart would have led me, I cannot but thank God that I did not follow its desires. I am the last who would dare to cast a stone. However, we are not talking of me, but of you, and I will not decline the honour you accord me in wishing to confide in me. For that is what you wish to do, is it not? What you say indicates it, only you have spoken in such generalities that everything remains dark, show me, please, how I am to refer them to you and how I am to understand them!'

'What should you say, Anna, if your mother, in her old age,

were seized by an ardent feeling such as rightfully belongs only to potent youth, to maturity, and not to a withered woman-hood?'

'Why the conditional, Mama? It is quite obvious that you are in the state you describe. You're in love?'

'The way you say that, my sweet child! How freely and bravely and openly you speak the words which would not easily come to my lips, and which I have locked up in me so long, together with all the shameful joy and grief that they imply – have kept secret from everyone, even from you, so closely that you really used to be startled out of your dream, the dream of your belief in your mother's matronly dignity! Yes, I'm in love, I love with ardour and desire and bliss and torment, as you once loved in your youth. My feeling can as little stand the test of reason as yours could, and if I am even proud of the spring with which Nature has made my soul flower, which she has miracu-lously bestowed upon me, I yet suffer, as you once suffered, and I have been irresistibly driven to tell you all.'

'My dear, darling Mama! Then do tell me! When it is so hard to speak, questions help. Who is it?'

'It cannot but be a shattering surprise to you, my child. The young friend of the house. Your brother's tutor.'

'Ken Keaton?'

'Yes.'

'Ken Keaton. So that is it. You needn't fear, Mother, that I shall begin exclaiming "Incomprehensible!" – though most people would. It is so easy and so stupid to call a feeling incomp-rehensible if one cannot imagine oneself having it. And yet – much as I want to avoid hurting you – forgive my anxious sympathy for asking a question. You speak of an emotion inappropriate to your years, complain of entertaining feelings of which you are no longer worthy. Have you ever asked yourself if he, this young man, is worthy of your feelings?'

'He – worthy? I hardly understand what you mean. I love, Anna. Of all the young men I have ever seen, Ken is the most magnificent.'

'And that is why you love him. Shall we try reversing the positions of cause and effect and perhaps get them in their proper places by doing so? May it not be that he only seems so magnificent to you because you are ... because you love him?'

'Oh, my child, you separate what is inseparable. Here in my heart my love and his magnificence are one.'

'But you are suffering, dearest, best Mama, and I should be so infinitely glad if I could help you. Could you not try, for a moment – just a moment of trying it might do you good – not to see him in the transfiguring light of your love, but by plain daylight, in his reality, as the nice, attractive – that I will grant you! – attractive lad he is, but who, such as he is, in and for himself, has so little to inspire passion and suffering on his account?'

'You mean well, Anna, I know. You would like to help me, I am sure of it. But it cannot be accomplished at his expense, by your doing him an injustice. And you do him injustice with your "daylight", which is such a false, misleading light. You say that he is nice, even attractive, and you mean by it that he is an average human being with nothing unusual about him. But I tell you he is an absolutely exceptional human being, with a life that touches one's heart. Think of his simple background – how, with iron strength of will, he worked his way through college, and excelled all his fellow students in history and athletics, and how he then hastened to his country's call and behaved so well as a soldier that he was finally "honourably discharged" ...'

'Excuse me, Mama, but that is the routine procedure for everyone who doesn't actually do something dishonourable.'

'Everyone. You keep harping on his averageness, and, in doing so, by calling him, if not directly, then by implication, a simple-minded ingenuous youngster, you mean to talk me out of him. But you forget that ingenuousness can be something noble and victorious, and that the background of his ingenuousness is the great democratic spirit of his immense country ...'

'He doesn't like his country in the least.'

'And for that very reason he is a true son of it; and if he loves Europe for its historical perspectives and its old folk customs, that does him honour too, and sets him apart from the majority. And he gave his blood for his country. Every soldier, you say, is "honourably discharged". But is every soldier given a medal for bravery, a Purple Heart, to show that the heroism with which he flung himself on the enemy cost him a wound, perhaps a serious one?'

'My dear Mama, in war, I think, one man catches it and another doesn't, one falls and another escapes, without its having much to do with whether he is brave or not. If somebody has a leg blown off or a kidney shot to pieces, a medal is a sop, a small compensation for his misfortune, but in general it is no indication of any particular bravery.'

'In any case, he sacrificed one of his kidneys on the altar of his fatherland!'

'Yes, he had that misfortune. And, thank heaven, one can at a pinch make do with only one kidney. But only at a pinch, and it *is* a lack, a defect, the thought of it does rather detract from the magnificence of his youth, and in the common light of day, by which he ought to be seen, does show him up, despite his good – or let us say normal – appearance, as not really complete, as disabled, as a man no longer perfectly whole.'

'Good God – Ken no longer complete, Ken not a whole man! My poor child, he is complete to the point of magnificence and can laugh at the lack of a kidney – not only in his own opinion, but in everyone's – that is, in the opinion of all the women who are after him, and in whose company he seems to find his pleasure! My dear, good, clever Anna, don't you know why, above all other reasons, I have confided in you, why I began this conversation? Because I wished to ask you – and I want your honest opinion – if, from your observation, you believe that he is having an affair with Louise Pfingsten, or with Amélie Lützenkirchen, or perhaps with both of them – for which, I assure you, he is quite complete enough! That is what keeps me suspended in the most agonizing doubt, and I hope very much that I shall get the truth from you, for you can look at things more calmly, by daylight so to speak ...'

'Poor, darling Mama, how you torture yourself, how you suffer! It makes me so unhappy. But, to answer you: I don't think so – of course, I know very little about his life and have not felt called upon to investigate it – but I don't think so, and I have never heard anyone say that he has the sort of relationship you suspect, either with Frau Pfingsten or Frau Lützenkirchen. So please be reassured, I beg of you!'

'God grant, dear child, that you are not simply saying it to comfort me and pour balm on my wound, out of pity! But pity, don't you see, even though perhaps I am seeking it from you, is not in place at all, for I am happy in my torment and shame and filled with pride in the flowering spring of pain in my soul – remember that, child, even if I seem to be begging for pity!' -

'I don't feel that you are begging. But in such a case the happiness and pride are so closely allied with the suffering that, indeed, they are identical with it, and even if you looked for no pity, it would be your due from those who love you and who wish for you that you would take pity on yourself and try to free yourself from this absurd enchantment ... Forgive my words; they are the wrong ones, of course, but I cannot be concerned over words. It is you, darling, for whom I am concerned and not only since today, not only since your confession, for which I am grateful to you. You have kept your secret locked within you with great self-control; but that there has been some secret, that, for months now, you have been in some peculiar and crucial situation, could not escape those who love you, and they have seen it with mixed feelings.'

'To whom do you refer by your "they"?'

'I am speaking of myself. You have changed strikingly in these last weeks, Mama – I mean, not changed, I'm not putting it right, you are still the same, and if I say "changed", I mean that a sort of rejuvenescence has come over you – but that too isn't the right word, for naturally it can't be a matter of any actual, demonstrable rejuvenescence in your charming person. But to my eyes, at moments, and in a certain phantasmagoric fashion, it has been as if suddenly, out of your dear matronly self, stepped the Mama of twenty years ago, as I knew her when I was a girl – and even that was not all, I suddenly thought I saw you as I had never seen you, as you must have looked, that is, when you were a girl yourself. And this hallucination – if it was a mere hallucination, but there was something real about it too – should have delighted me, should have made my heart leap with pleasure, should it not? But it didn't, it only made my heart heavy, and at those very moments when you grew young before my eyes, I pitied you terribly. For at the same time I saw that you were suffering, and that the phantasmagoria to which I refer not only had to do with your suffering but was actually the expression of it, its manifestation, a "flowering spring of pain", as you just expressed it. Dear Mama, how did you happen to use such an expression? It is not natural to you. You are a simple being, worthy of all love; you have sound, clear eyes, you let them look into Nature and the world, not into books – you have never read much. Never before have you used expressions such as poets create, such lugubrious, sickly expressions, and if you do it now, it has a tinge of –'

'Of what, Anna? If poets use such expressions it is because they *need* them, because emotion and experience force them out of them, and so it is, surely, with me, though you think them unbecoming in me. You are wrong. They are becoming to whoever needs them, and he has no fear of them, because they are forced out of him. But your hallucination, or phantasmagoria – whatever it was that you thought you saw in me – I can and will explain to you. It was the work of *his* youth. It was my soul's struggle to match his youth, so that it need not perish before him in shame and disgrace.'

Anna wept. They put their arms around each other, and their tears mingled.

'That too,' said the lame girl with an effort, 'what you have just said, dear heart, that too is of a piece with the strange expression you used, and, like that, coming from your lips, it has a ring of destruction. This accursed seizure is destroying you, I see it with my eyes, I hear it in your speech. We must check it, put a stop to it, save you from it, at any cost. One forgets, Mama, what is out of one's sight. All that is needed is a decision, a saving decision. The young man must not come here any longer, we must dismiss him. That is not enough. You see him elsewhere when you go out. Very well, we must prevail upon him to leave the city. I will take it upon myself to persuade him. I will talk to him in a friendly way, point out to him that he is wasting his time and himself here, that he has long since exhausted Düsseldorf and should not hang around here for

ever, that Düsseldorf is not Germany, of which he must
see more, get to know it better, that Munich, Hamburg, Berlin
are there for him to sample, that he must not let himself be tied
down, must live in one place for a time, then in another, until,
as is his natural duty, he returns to his own country and takes
up a regular profession, instead of playing the invalid language-
teacher here in Europe. I'll soon impress it upon him. And if he
declines and insists on sticking to Düsseldorf, where, after all,
he has connections, we will go away ourselves. We will give up
our house here and move to Cologne or Frankfurt or to some
lovely place in the Taunus, and you will leave here behind you
what has been torturing you and trying to destroy you, and
with the help of "out of sight", you will forget. Out of sight – it
is all that is needed, it is an infallible remedy, for there is no
such thing as not being able to forget. You may say it is a
disgrace to forget, but people do forget, depend upon it. And in
the Taunus you will enjoy your beloved Nature and you will be
our old darling Mama again.'

Thus Anna, with great earnestness, but how unavailingly!

'Stop, stop, Anna, no more of this, I cannot listen to what
you are saying! You weep with me, and your concern is affectionate indeed, but what you say, your proposals, are impossible
and shocking to me. Drive him away? Leave here ourselves?
How far your solicitude has led you astray! You speak of
Nature, but you strike her in the face with your demands, you
want me to strike her in the face, by stifling the spring of pain
with which she has miraculously blest my soul! What a sin that
would be, what ingratitude, what disloyalty to her, to Nature,
and what a denial of my faith in her beneficent omnipotence!
You remember how Sarah sinned? She laughed to herself behind the door and said: "After I am waxed old shall I have
pleasure, my lord being old also?" But the Lord God was angry
and said: "Wherefore did Sarah laugh?" In my opinion, she
laughed less on account of her own withered old age than because her lord, Abraham, was likewise so old and stricken in
years, already ninety-nine. And what woman could not but
laugh at the thought of indulging in lust with a ninety-nine-
year-old man, for all that a man's love life is less strictly limited

than a woman's. But my lord is young, is youth itself, and how
much more easily and temptingly must the thought come to me
– Oh, Anna, my loyal child, I indulge in lust, shameful and
grievous lust, in my blood, in my wishes, and I cannot give it
up, cannot flee to the Taunus, and if you persuade Ken to go –
I believe I should hate you to my dying day!'

Great was the sorrow with which Anna listened to these unrestrained, frenzied words.

'Dearest Mama,' said she in a strained voice, 'you are greatly
excited. What you need now is rest and sleep. Take twenty
drops of valerian in water, or even twenty-five. It is a harmless
remedy and often very helpful. And rest assured that, for my
part, I will undertake nothing that is opposed to your feeling.
May this assurance help to bring you the peace of mind which,
above all things, I desire for you! If I spoke slightingly of
Keaton, whom I respect as the object of your affection, though
I cannot but curse him as the cause of your suffering, you will
understand that I was only trying to see if it would not restore
your peace of mind. I am infinitely grateful for your confidence,
and I hope, indeed I am sure, that by talking to me you have
somewhat lightened your heart. Perhaps this conversation was
the prerequisite for your recovery – I mean, for your restored
peace of mind. Your sweet, happy heart, so dear to us all, will
find itself again. It loves in pain. Do you not think that – let us
say, in time – it could learn to love without pain and in accordance with reason? Love, don't you see? –' (Anna said this as she
solicitously led her mother to her bedroom, so that she could
herself drop the valerian into her glass) 'love – how many things
it is, what a variety of feelings are included in the word, and yet
how strangely it is always love! A mother's love for her son, for
instance – I know that Eduard is not particularly close to you –
but that love can be very heartfelt, very passionate, it can be
subtly yet clearly distinguished from her love for a child of her
own sex, and yet not for an instant pass the bounds of mother
love. How would it be if you were to take advantage of the fact
that Ken could be your son, to make the tenderness you feel for
him maternal, let it find a permanent place, to your own benefit
as mother love?'

Rosalie smiled through her tears.

'And thus establish the proper understanding between body and soul, I take it?' she jested sadly. 'My dear child, the demands that I make on your intelligence! How I exhaust it and misuse it! It is wrong of me, for I trouble you to no purpose. Mother love – it is something like the Taunus all over again .., Perhaps I'm not expressing myself quite clearly now? I *am* dead tired, you are right about that. Thank you, darling, for your patience, your sympathy! Thank you too for respecting Ken for the sake of what you call my affection. And don't hate him at the same time, as I should have to hate you if you drove him away! He is Nature's means of working her miracle in my soul.'

Anna left her. A week passed, during which Ken Keaton twice dined at the Tümmlers'. The first time, an elderly couple from Duisburg were present, relatives of Rosalie's; the woman was a cousin of hers. Anna, who well knew that certain relationships and emotional tensions inevitably emanate an aura that is obvious, particularly to those who are in no way involved, observed the guests keenly. Once or twice she saw Rosalie's cousin look wonderingly first at Keaton, then at the hostess; once she even detected a smile under the husband's moustache. That evening she also observed a difference in Ken's behaviour towards her mother, a quizzical change and readjustment in his reactions, observed too that he would not let it pass when, laboriously enough, she pretended not to be taking any particular notice of him, but forced her to direct her attention to him. On the second occasion no one else was present. Frau von Tümmler indulged in a scurrilous performance, directed at her daughter and inspired by her recent conversation with her, in which she mocked at certain of Anna's counsels and at the same time turned the travesty to her own advantage. It had come out that Ken had been very much on the town the previous night – with a few of his cronies, an art-school student and two sons of manufacturers, he had gone on a pub-crawl that had lasted until morning, and, as might have been expected, had arrived at the Tümmlers' with a 'first-class hangover' as Eduard, who was the one to let out the story, expressed it. At the end of the evening, when the good nights were being said, Rosalie gave her daughter a look that was at once excited and crafty – indeed, kept her eyes fixed on her for a moment as she held the young man by the lobe of his ear and said:

'And you, son, take a serious word of reproof from Mama Rosalie and understand hereafter that her house is open only to people of decent behaviour and not to night-owls and disabled beer-swillers who are hardly up to speaking German or even to keeping their eyes open! Did you hear me, you good-for-nothing? Mend your ways! If bad boys tempt you, don't listen to them, and from now on stop playing so fast and loose with your health! Will you mend your ways, will you?' As she spoke, she kept tugging at his ear, and Ken yielded to the slight pull in an exaggerated way, pretended that the punishment was extraordinarily painful, and writhed under her hand with a most pitiable grimace, which showed his fine white teeth. His face was near to hers, and speaking directly into it, in all its nearness, she went on:

'Because if you do it again and don't mend your ways, you naughty boy, I'll banish you from the city – do you know that? I'll send you to some quiet place in the Taunus where, though Nature is very beautiful, there are no temptations and you can teach the farmers' children English. This time, go and sleep it off, you scamp!' And she let go of his ear, took leave of the nearness of his face, gave Anna one more pale, crafty look, and left.

A week later something extraordinary happened, which astonished, touched, and perplexed Anna von Tümmler in the highest degree – perplexed her because, though she rejoiced in it for her mother's sake, she did not know whether to regard it as fortunate or unfortunate. About ten o'clock in the morning the chambermaid brought a message asking her to see the mistress in her bedroom. Since the little family breakfasted separately – Eduard first, then Anna, the lady of the house last – she had not yet seen her mother that day. Rosalie was lying on the chaise-longue in her bedroom, covered with a light cashmere shawl, a little pale, but with her nose flushed. With a smile of rather studied languor, she nodded to her daughter as she came stumping in, but said nothing, so that Anna was forced to ask:

'What is it, Mama? You aren't ill, are you?'

'Oh no, my child, don't be alarmed, I'm not ill at all. I was very much tempted, instead of sending for you, to go to you myself and greet you. But I am a little in need of coddling, rest seems to be indicated, as it sometimes is for us women.'

'Mama! What do you mean?'

Then Rosalie sat up, flung her arms around her daughter's neck, drew her down beside her onto the edge of the chaise-longue, and, cheek to cheek with her, whispered in her ear, quickly, blissfully, all in a breath:

'Victory, Anna, victory, it has come back to me, come back to me after such a long interruption, absolutely naturally and just as it should be for a mature, vigorous woman! Dear child, what a miracle! What a miracle great, beneficent Nature has wrought in me, how she has blessed my faith! For I believed, Anna, and did not laugh, and so now kind Nature rewards me and takes back what she seemed to have done to my body, she proves that it was a mistake and re-establishes harmony between soul and body, but not in the way that you wished it to happen. Not with the soul obediently letting the body act upon it and translate it to the dignified estate of matronhood, but the other way around, the other way around, dear child, with the soul proving herself mistress over the body. Congratulate me, darling, there is reason for it! I am a woman again, a whole human being again, a functioning female, I can feel worthy of the youthful manhood that has bewitched me, and no longer need lower my eyes before it with a feeling of impotence. The rod of life with which it struck me has reached not my soul alone but my body too and has made it a flowing fountain again. Kiss me, my darling child, call me blessed, as blessed I am, and, with me, praise the miraculous power of great, beneficent Nature!'

She sank back, closed her eyes, and smiled contentedly, her nose very red.

'Dear, sweet Mama,' said Anna, willing enough to rejoice with her, yet sick at heart, 'this is truly a great, a moving event, it testifies to the richness of your nature, which was already evident in the freshness of your feeling and now gives that feeling such power over your bodily functions. As you see, I am entirely of your opinion – that what has happened to you physically is psychological in origin, is the product of your youthfully strong feeling. Whatever I may at times have said about such things, you must not think me such a Philistine that I deny the psychological any power over the physical and hold that the latter has the last word in the relationship between them. Each is dependent upon the other – that much even I know about Nature and its unity. However much the soul may be subject to the body's circumstances – what the soul, for its part, can do to the body often verges on the miraculous, and your case is one of the most splendid examples of it. Yet, permit me to say that this beautiful, animating event, of which you are so proud – and rightly, you may certainly be proud of it – on me, constituted as I am, it does not make the same sort of impression that it makes on you. In my opinion, it does not change things much, my best of mothers, and it does not appreciably increase my admiration for your nature – or for Nature in general. Club-footed, ageing spinster that I am, I have every reason not to attach much importance to the physical. Your freshness of feeling, precisely in contrast to your physical age, seemed to me splendid enough, enough of a triumph – it almost seemed to me a purer victory of the soul than what has happened now, than this transformation of the indestructible youth of your heart into an organic phenomenon.'

'Say no more, my poor child! What you call my freshness of feeling, and now insist that you enjoyed, you represented to me, more or less bluntly, as sheer folly, through which I was making myself ridiculous, and you advised me to retreat into a motherly dowagerhood, to make my feeling maternal. Well, it would have been a little too early for that, don't you think so now, my pet? Nature has made her voice heard against it. She has made my feeling her concern and has unmistakably shown me that it need not be ashamed before her nor before the blooming young manhood which is its object. And do you really mean to say that does not change things much?'

'What I mean, my dear, wonderful Mama, is certainly not that I did not respect Nature's voice. Nor, above all things, do I wish to spoil your joy in her decree. You cannot think that of me. When I said that what had happened did not change things much, I was referring to outward realities, to the practical aspects of the situation, so to speak. When I advised you – when I fondly wished that you might conquer yourself, that it might not even be hard for you to confine your feeling for the young man – forgive me for speaking of him so coolly – for our friend Keaton, rather, to maternal love, my hope was based on the fact that he could be your son. That fact, you will agree, has not changed, and it cannot but determine the relationship between you on either side, on your side and on his too.'

'And on his too. You speak of two sides, but you mean only his. You do not believe that he could love me except, at best, as a son?'

'I will not say that, dearest and best Mama.'

'And how could you say it, Anna, my true-hearted child! Remember, you have no right to, you have not the necessary authority to judge in matters of love. You have little perception in that realm, because you gave up early, dear heart, and turned your eyes away from such things. Intellect offered you a substitute for Nature – good for you, that is all very fine! But how can you undertake to judge and to condemn me to hopelessness? You have no power of observation and do not see what I see, do not perceive the signs which indicate to me that his feeling is ready to respond to mine. Do you mean to say that at such moments he is only trifling with me? Would you rather consider him insolent and heartless than to grant me the hope that his feeling may correspond to mine? What would be so extraordinary in that? For all your aloofness from love, you cannot be unaware that a young man very often prefers a mature woman to an inexperienced girl, to a silly little goose. Naturally, a nostalgia for his mother may enter in – as, on the other hand, maternal feelings may play a part in an elder woman's passion for a young man. But why say this to you? I have a distinct impression that you recently said something very like it to me.'

'Really? In any case, you are right, Mama, I agree with you completely in what you say.'

'Then you must not call me past hope, especially today, when Nature has recognized my feeling. You must not, despite my grey hair, at which, so it seems to me, you are looking. Yes, unfortunately I am quite grey. It was a mistake that I didn't begin dyeing my hair long ago. I can't suddenly start now, though Nature has to a certain extent authorized me to. But I can do something for my face, not only by massage, but also by using a little rouge. I don't suppose you children would be shocked?'

'Of course not, Mama! Eduard will never notice, if you go about it a little discreetly. And I ... though I think that artificiality will not go too well with your deep feeling for Nature, why, it is certainly no sin against Nature to help her out a little in such an accepted fashion.'

'So you agree with me? After all, the thing is to prevent a fondness for being mothered from playing too large a part, from predominating, in Ken's feeling. That would be contrary to my hopes. Yes, dear, loyal child, this heart – I know that you do not like talking and hearing about the "heart" – but my heart is swollen with pride and joy, with the thought of how very differently I shall meet his youth, with what a different self-confidence. Your mother's heart is swollen with happiness and life!'

'How beautiful, dearest Mama! And how charming of you to let me share in your great happiness! I share it, share it from my heart, you cannot doubt it, even if I say that a certain concern intrudes even as I rejoice with you – that is very like me, isn't it? – certain scruples – *practical* scruples, to use the word which, for want of a better, I used before. You speak of your hope, and of all that justifies you in entertaining it – in my opinion, what justifies it above all is simply your own lovable self. But you fail to define your hope more precisely, to tell me what its goal is, what expression it expects to find in the reality of life. Is it your intention to marry again? To make Ken Keaton our stepfather? To stand before the altar with him? It may be cowardly of me, but as the difference in your ages is equivalent to that between a mother and her son, I am a little afraid of the astonishment which such a step would arouse.'

Frau von Tümmler stared at her daughter.

'No,' she answered, 'the idea is new to me, and if it will calm your apprehensions, I can assure you that I do not entertain it. No. Anna, you silly thing, I have no intention of giving you and Eduard a twenty-four-year-old stepfather. How odd of you to speak so stiffly and piously of "standing before the altar"!'

Anna remained silent; her eyelids lowered a little, she gazed past her mother into space.

'Hope –' said her mother, 'who can define it, as you want me to? Hope is hope – how can you expect that it will inquire into practical goals, as you put it? What Nature has granted me is so beautiful that I can only expect something beautiful from it, but I cannot tell you how I think that it will come, how it will be realized, and where it will lead. That is what hope is like. It simply doesn't think – least of all about "standing before the altar".'

Anna's lips were slightly twisted. Between them she spoke softly, as if involuntarily and despite herself:

'That would be a comparatively reasonable idea.'

Frau von Tümmler stared in bewilderment at her crippled daughter – who did not look at her – and tried to read her expression.

'Anna!' she cried softly. 'What are you thinking, what does this behaviour mean? Allow me to say that I simply don't recognize you! Which of us, I ask you, is the artist – I or you? I should never have thought that you could be so far behind your mother in broad-mindedness – and not only behind her, but behind the times and its freer manners! In your art you are so advanced and profess the very latest thing, so that a simple person like myself can scarcely follow you. But morally you seem to be living God knows when, in the old days, before the war. After all, we have the republic now, we have freedom, and ideas have changed very much, towards informality, towards laxity, it is apparent everywhere, even in the smallest things. For example, nowadays young men consider it good form to let their handkerchiefs, of which you used to see only a little corner protruding from the breast pocket, hang far out – why, they let them hang out like flags, half the handkerchief; it is clearly a sign, even a conscious declaration, of a republican relaxation of manners. Eduard lets his handkerchief hang out too, in the way that is the fashion, and I see it with a certain satisfaction.'

'Your observation is very fine, Mama. But I think that, in Eduard's case, your handkerchief symbol is not to be taken too personally. You yourself often say that the young man – for such by this time he has really become – is a good deal like our father, the lieutenant-colonel. Perhaps it is not quite tactful of me to bring Papa into our conversation and our thoughts at the moment. And yet –'

'Anna, your father was an excellent officer and he fell on the field of honour, but he was a rake and a Don Juan to the very end, the most striking example of the elastic limits of a man's sexual life, and I constantly had to shut both eyes on his account. So I cannot consider it particularly tactless that you should refer to him.'

'All the better, Mama – if I may say so. But Papa was a gentleman and an officer, and he lived, despite all that you call his rakishness, according to certain concepts of honour, which mean very little to me, but many of which Eduard, I believe, has inherited. He not only resembles his father outwardly, in figure and features. In certain circumstances, he will involuntarily react in his father's fashion.'

'Which means – in what circumstances?'

'Dear Mama, let me be perfectly frank, as we have always been with each other! It is certainly conceivable that a relationship such as you vaguely anticipate between Ken Keaton and yourself could remain completely concealed and unknown to society. However, what with your delightful impulsiveness and your charming inability to dissimulate and bury the secrets of your heart, I have my doubts as to how well it could be carried off. Let some young whipper-snapper make mocking allusions to our Eduard, give him to understand that it is known that his mother is – how do people put it? – leading a loose life, and he would strike him, he would box the fellow's ears, and who knows what dangerous kind of official nonsense might result from his chivalry?'

'For heaven's sake, Anna! What things you imagine! You are excruciating. I know you are doing it out of solicitude, but it is cruel, your solicitude, as cruel as small children condemning their mother . . .'

Rosalie cried a little. Anna helped her to dry her tears, affectionately guiding the hand in which she held her handkerchief.

'Dearest, best Mama, forgive me! How reluctant I am to hurt you! But you – don't talk of children condemning! Do you think I would not look – no, not tolerantly, that sounds too supercilious – but reverently, and with the tenderest concern, on what you are determined to consider your happiness? And Eduard – I hardly know how I happened to speak of him – it was just because of his republican handkerchief. It is not a question of us, nor only of people in general. It is a question of you, Mama. Now, you said that you were broad-minded. But are you, really? We were speaking of Papa and of certain traditional concepts by which he lived, and which, as he saw them, were not infringed by the infidelities to upset you with. That you forgave him for them again and again was because, fundamentally, as you must realize, you were of the same opinion – you were, in other words, conscious that they had nothing to do with real debauchery. He was not born for that, he was no libertine at heart. No more are you. I, at most, as an artist, have deviated from type in that respect, but then again, in another way, I am unfitted to make any use of my emancipation, of my being morally *déclassée*.'

'My poor child,' Frau von Tümmler interrupted her, 'don't speak of yourself so gloomily!'

'As if I were speaking of myself at all!' answered Anna. 'I am speaking of you, of you, it is for you that I am so deeply concerned. Because, for you, it would really be debauchery to do what, for Papa, the man about town, was simply dissipation, doing violence neither to himself nor to the judgement of society. Harmony between body and soul is certainly a good and necessary thing, and you are proud and happy because Nature, your beloved Nature, has granted it to you in a way that is almost miraculous. But harmony between one's life and one's innate moral convictions is, in the end, even more necessary, and where it is disrupted the only result can be emotional disruption, and that means unhappiness. Don't you feel that this is true? That you would be living in opposition to yourself if you made a reality out of what you now dream? Fundamentally, you are just as much bound as Papa was to certain concepts, and the destruction of that allegiance would be no less than the destruction of your own self ... I say it as I feel it – with anxiety. Why does that word come to my lips again – "destruction"? I know that I have used it once before, in anguish, and I have had the sensation more than once. Why must I keep feeling as if this whole visitation, whose happy victim you are, had something to do with destruction? I will confess something to you. Recently, just a few weeks ago, after our talk when we drank tea late that night in my room and you were so excited, I was tempted to go to Dr Oberloskamp, who took care of Eduard when he had jaundice, and of me once, when I had laryngitis and couldn't swallow – you never need a doctor; I was tempted, I say, to talk to him about you and about what you had confided to me, simply for the sake of setting my mind at rest on your account. But I rejected the idea, I rejected it almost at once, out of pride, Mama, out of pride in you and for you, and because it seemed to me degrading to turn your experience over to a medical man who, with the help of God, is competent for jaundice and laryngitis, but not for deep human ills. In my opinion, there are sicknesses that are too good for the doctor.'

'I am grateful to you for both, my dear child,' said Rosalie, 'for the concern which impelled you to talk with Oberloskamp about me, and for your having repressed the impulse. But then what can induce you to make the slightest connection between what you call my visitation – this Easter of my womanhood, what the soul has done to my body – and the concept of sickness? Is happiness – sickness? Certainly, it is not light-mindedness either, it is living, living in joy and sorrow, and to live is to hope – the hope for which I can give no explanation to your reason.'

347

'I do not ask for any explanation from you, dearest Mama.'

'Then go now, child. Let me rest. As you know, a little quiet seclusion is indicated for us women on such crowning days.'

Anna kissed her mother and stumped out of the bedroom. Once separated, the two women reflected on the conversation they had just held. Anna had neither said, nor been able to say, all that was on her mind. How long, she wondered, would what her mother called 'the Easter of her womanhood', this touching revivification, endure in her? And Ken, if, as was perfectly plausible, he succumbed to her – how long would *that* last? How constantly her mother, in her late love, would be cast into trepidation by every younger woman, would have to tremble from the very first day, for his faithfulness, even his respect! At least it was to the good that she did not conceive of happiness simply as pleasure and joy but as life with its suffering. For Anna uneasily foresaw much suffering in what her mother dreamed.

For her part, Frau Rosalie was more deeply impressed by her daughter's remonstrances than she had allowed to appear. It was not so much the thought that, under certain circumstances, Eduard might have to risk his young life for her honour – the romantic idea, though she had wept over it, really made her heart beat with pride. But Anna's doubts of her 'broad-mindedness', what she had said about debauchery and the necessary harmony between one's life and one's moral convictions, preoccupied the good soul all through her day of rest and she could not but admit that her daughter's doubts were justified, that her views contained a good part of truth. Neither, to be sure, could she suppress her most heartfelt joy at the thought of meeting her young beloved again under such new circumstances. But what her shrewd daughter had said about 'living in contradiction to herself', she remembered and pondered over, and she strove in her soul to associate the idea of renunciation with the idea of happiness. Yes, could not renunciation itself be happiness, if it were not a miserable necessity but were practised in freedom and in conscious equality? Rosalie reached the conclusion that it could be.

Ken presented himself at the Tümmlers' three days after Rosalie's great physiological reassurance, read and spoke English with Eduard, and stayed for dinner. Her happiness at the sight of his pleasant, boyish face, his fine teeth, his broad shoulders and narrow hips, shone from her sweet eyes, and their sparkling animation justified, one might say, the touch of artificial red which heightened her cheeks and without which, indeed, the pallor of her face would have been in contradiction to that joyous fire. This time, and thereafter every time Ken came, she had a way, each week, of taking his hand when she greeted him and drawing his body close to hers, at the same time looking earnestly, luminously, and significantly into his eyes, so that Anna had the impression that she very much wished, and indeed was going, to tell the young man of the experience her nature had undergone. Absurd apprehension! Of course nothing of that sort occurred, and all through the rest of the evening the attitude of the lady of the house towards her young guest was a serene and settled kindliness from which both the affected motherliness with which she had once teased her daughter, as well as any bashfulness and nervousness, any painful humility, were gratifyingly absent.

Keaton, who to his satisfaction had long been aware that, even such as he was, he had made a conquest of this grey-haired but charming European woman, hardly knew what to make of the change in her behaviour. His respect for her had, quite understandably, diminished when he became aware of her weakness; the latter, on the other hand, had in turn attracted and excited his masculinity; his simple nature felt sympathetically drawn to hers, and he considered that such beautiful eyes, with their youthful penetrating gaze, quite made up for fifty years and ageing hands. The idea of entering into an affair with her, such as he had been carrying on for some time – not, as it happened, with Amélie Lützenkirchen or Louise Pfingsten, but with another woman of the same set, whom Rosalie had never thought of – was by no means new to him, and, as Anna observed, he had begun, at least now and again, to change his manner towards his pupil's mother, to speak to her in a tone that was provocatively flirtatious.

This, the good fellow soon found, no longer seemed quite to come off. Despite the handclasp by which, at the beginning of each meeting, she drew him close to her, so that their bodies almost touched, and despite her intimate, searching gaze into his eyes, his experiments in this direction encountered a friendly but firm dignity which put him in his place, forbade any establishment of what he wished to establish, and, instantly dispelling his pretensions, reduced his attitude to one of submission. The meaning of the repeated experience escaped him. 'Is she in love with me or not?' he asked himself, and blamed her repulses and her reprobation on the presence of her children, the lame girl and the schoolboy. But his experience was no different when it happened that he was alone with her for a time in a drawing-room corner – and no different when he changed the character of his little advances, abandoning all quizzicalness and giving them a seriously tender, a pressing, almost passionate tone. Once, using the unrolled palatal 'r' which so delighted everyone, he tried calling her 'Rosalie' in a warm voice – which, simply as a form of address, was, in his American view, not even a particular liberty. But, though for an instant she had blushed hotly, she had almost immediately risen and left him, and had given him neither a word nor a look during the rest of that evening.

The winter, which had proved to be mild, bringing hardly any cold weather and snow, but all the more rain instead, also ended early that year. Even in February there were warm, sunny days redolent of spring. Tiny leaf buds ventured out on branches here and there. Rosalie, who had lovingly greeted the snowdrops in her garden, could rejoice far earlier than usual, almost prematurely, in the daffodils – and, very soon after, in the short-stemmed crocuses too, which sprouted everywhere in the front gardens of villas and in the Palace Garden, and before which passers-by halted to point them out to one another and to feast on their particoloured profusion.

'Isn't it remarkable,' said Frau von Tümmler to her daughter, 'how much they resemble the autumn colchicum? It's practically the same flower! End and beginning – one could mistake them for each other, they are so alike – one could think one was back in autumn in the presence of a crocus, and believe in spring when one saw the last flower of the year.'

'Yes, a slight confusion,' answered Anna. 'Your old friend Mother Nature has a charming propensity for the equivocal and for mystification in general.'

'You are always quick to speak against her, you naughty child, and where I succumb to wonder, you mock. Let well enough alone; you cannot laugh me out of my tender feeling for her, for my beloved Nature, least of all now, when she is just bringing in my season – I call it mine because the season in which we were born is peculiarly akin to us, and we to it. You are an Advent child, and you can truly say that you arrived under a good sign – almost under the dear sign of Christmas. You must feel a pleasant affinity between yourself and that season, which, even though cold, makes us think of joy and warmth. For really, in my experience, there is a sympathetic relation between ourselves and the season that produced us. Its return brings something that confirms and strengthens, that renews our lives, just as spring has always done for me – not because it is spring, or the prime of the year, as the poets call it, a season everyone loves, but because I personally belong to it, and I feel that it smiles at me quite personally.'

'It does indeed, dearest Mama,' answered the child of winter. 'And rest assured that I shan't speak a single word against it!'

But it must be said that the buoyancy of life which Rosalie was accustomed – or believed she was accustomed – to receive from the approach and unfolding of 'her' season was not, even as she spoke of it, manifesting itself quite as usual. It was almost as if the moral resolutions which her conversation with her daughter had inspired in her, and to which she so steadfastly adhered, went against her nature, as if, despite them, or indeed because of them, she were 'living in contradiction to herself'. This was precisely the impression that Anna received, and the limping girl reproached herself for having persuaded her mother to a continence which her own liberal view of life in no sense demanded but which had seemed requisite to her only for the dear woman's peace of mind. What was more, she suspected herself of unacknowledged evil motives. She asked herself if she, who had once grievously longed for sensual pleasure, but had never experienced it, had not secretly begrudged it to her mother and hence had exhorted her to chastity by all sorts of trumped-up arguments. No, she could not believe it of herself, and yet what she saw troubled and burdened her conscience.

She saw that Rosalie, setting out on one of the walks she so loved, quickly grew tired, and that it was she who, inventing some household task that must be done, insisted on turning home after only half an hour or even sooner. She rested a great deal, yet despite this limitation of her physical activity, she lost weight, and Anna noticed with concern the thinness of her forearms when she happened to see them exposed. People no longer asked her at what fountain of youth she had been drinking. There was an ominous, tired-looking blueness under her eyes, and the rouge which, in honour of the young man and of her recovery of full womanhood, she put on her cheeks created no very effective illusion against the yellowish pallor of her complexion. But as she dismissed any inquiries as to how she felt with a cheerful, 'I feel quite well – why should you think otherwise?' Fräulein von Tümmler gave up the idea of asking Dr Oberloskamp to investigate her mother's failing health. It was not only a feeling of guilt which led her to this decision; piety too played a part – the same piety that she had expressed when she said that there were sicknesses which were too good to be taken to a doctor.

So Anna was all the more delighted by the enterprise and confidence in her strength which Rosalie exhibited in connection with a little plan that was agreed on between herself, her children, and Ken Keaton, who happened to be present one evening as they lingered over their wine. A month had not yet passed since the morning Anna had been called to her mother's bedroom to hear the wonderful news. Rosalie was as charming and gay as in the old days that evening, and she could have been considered the prime mover of the excursion on which they had agreed – unless Ken Keaton was to be given the credit, for it was his historical chatter that had led to the idea. He had talked about various castles and strongholds he had visited in the Duchy of Berg – of the Castle on the Wupper, of Bensberg, Ehreshoven, Gimhorn, Homburg, and Krottorf; and from these he went on to the Elector Carl Theodore, who, in the eighteenth century, had moved his court from Düsseldorf, first to Schwetzingen and then to Munich – but that had not prevented his Statthalter, a certain Count Grottstein, from embarking on all sorts of important architectural and horticultural projects here: it was under him that the Electoral Academy of Art was conceived, the Palace Garden was first laid out, and Jägerhof Castle was built – and, Eduard added, in the same year, so far as he knew, Holterhof Castle too, a little to the south of the city, near the village of the same name. Of course, Holterhof too, Keaton confirmèd, and then, to his own amazement, was obliged to admit that he had never laid eyes on that creation of the late Rococo nor even visited its park, celebrated as it was, which extended all the way to the Rhine. Frau von Tümmler and Anna had, of course, taken the air there once or twice, but they had never succeeded in viewing the interior of the charmingly situated castle, nor had Eduard.

'*Wat et nit all jibt!*' said the lady of the house, using, in jocular disapproval, the local equivalent of 'Will wonders never cease!' It was always an indication of good spirits when she dropped into dialect. 'Fine Düsseldorfers you are,' she added, 'the lot of you!' One had never been there at all, and the others had not seen the interior of the jewel of a castle which every tourist made it a point to be shown through! 'Children,' she cried, 'this has gone on too long, we must not allow it. An excursion to Holterhof – for the four of us! And we will make it within the next few days! It is so beautiful now, the season is so enchanting and the barometer is steady. The buds will be opening in the park, it may well be pleasanter in its spring array than in the heat of summer, when Anna and I went walking there. Suddenly I feel a positive nostalgia for the black swans which – you remember, Anna – glided over the moats in such melancholy pride with their red bills and oar-feet. How they disguised their appetite in condescension when we fed them! We must take along some bread for them ... Let's see, today is

Friday – we will go Sunday, is that settled? Only Sunday would do for Eduard, and for Mr Keaton too, I imagine. Of course there will be a crowd out on Sunday, but that means nothing to me, I like mixing with people in their Sunday best, I share in their enjoyment, I like being where there's "something doing" – at the outdoor carnivals at Oberkassel, when it smells of fried food and the children are licking away at red sugar-sticks and, in front of the circus tent, such fantastically vulgar people are tinkling and tootling and shouting. I find it marvellous. Anna thinks otherwise. She finds it sad. Yes you do, Anna – and you prefer the aristocratic sadness of the pair of black swans in the moat ... I have an inspiration, children – we'll go by water! The trip by land on the street railway is simply boring. Not a scrap of woods and hardly an open field. It's much more amusing by water, Father Rhine shall convey us. Eduard, will you see to getting the steamer timetable? Or, just a moment, if we want to be really luxurious, we'll indulge ourselves and hire a private motor-boat for the trip up the Rhine. Then we'll be quite by ourselves, like the black swans ... All that remains to be settled is whether we want to set sail in the morning or the afternoon.'

The consensus was in favour of the morning. Eduard thought that, in any case, he had heard that the castle was open to visitors only into the early hours of the afternoon. It should be Sunday morning, then. Under Rosalie's energetic urging, the arrangements were soon made and agreed on. It was Keaton who was designated to charter the motor-boat. They would meet again at the point of departure, the Rathaus quay, by the Water-gauge Clock, the day after tomorrow at nine.

And so they did. It was a sunny and rather windy morning. The quay was jammed with a crowd of pushing people who, with their children and their bicycles, were waiting to go aboard one of the white steamers of the Cologne-Düsseldorf Navigation Company. The chartered motor-boat lay ready for the Tümmlers and their companion. Its master, a man with rings in his ear-lobes, clean-shaven upper lip, and a reddish mariner's beard under his chin, helped the ladies aboard. The party had hardly seated themselves on the curved bench under the awning, which was supported by stanchions, before he got under way. The boat made good time against the current of the broad river, whose banks, incidentally, were utterly prosaic. The old castle tower, the crooked tower of the Lambertuskirche, the harbour installations, were left behind. More of the same sort of thing appeared beyond the next bend in the river – warehouses, factory buildings. Little by little, behind the stone jetties which extended from the shore into the river, the country became more rural. Hamlets, old fishing villages – whose names Eduard, and Keaton too, knew – lay, protected by dykes, before a flat landscape of meadows, fields, willow-bushes, and pools. So it would be, however many windings the river made, for a good hour and a half, until they reached their destination. But how right they had been, Rosalie exclaimed, to decide on the boat instead of covering the distance in a fraction of the time by the horrible route through the suburbs! She seemed to be heartily enjoying the elemental charm of the journey by water. Her eyes closed, she sang a snatch of some happy tune into the wind, which at moments was almost stormy: 'O water-wind, I love thee; lovest thou me, O water-wind?' Her face, which had grown thinner, looked very appealing under the little felt hat with the feather, and the grey-and-red-checked coat she had on – of light woollen material with a turn-down collar – was very becoming to her. Anna and Eduard had also worn coats for the voyage, and only Keaton, who sat between mother and daughter, contented himself with a grey sweater under his tweed jacket. His handkerchief hung out, and, suddenly opening her eyes and turning, Rosalie stuffed it deep into his breast pocket.

'Propriety, propriety, young man!' she said, shaking her head in decorous reproof.

He smiled: 'Thank you,' and then wanted to know what song it was she had just been singing.

'Song?' she asked. 'Was I singing? That was only singsong, not a song.' And she closed her eyes again and hummed, her lips scarcely moving: 'How I love thee, O water-wind!'

Then she began chattering through the noise of the motor, and – often having to hold on to her hat, which the wind was trying to tear from her still abundant, wavy grey hair – expatiated on how it would be possible to extend the Rhine trip beyond Holterhof, to Leverkusen and Cologne, and from there on past Bonn to Godesberg and Bad Honnef at the foot of the Siebengebirge. It was beautiful there, the trim watering-place on the Rhine, amid vineyards and orchards, and it had an alkaline mineral spring that was very good for rheumatism. Anna looked at her; she knew that her mother now suffered intermittently from lumbago, and had once or twice considered going to Godesberg or Honnef with her in the early summer, to take the waters. There was something almost involuntary in the way she chattered on about the beneficial spring, catching her breath as she spoke into the wind; it made Anna think that her mother was even now not free from the shooting pains that characterize the disease.

After an hour they breakfasted on a few ham sandwiches and washed them down with port from little travelling-cups. It was half past eleven when the boat made fast to a flimsy landing-stage, inadequate for larger vessels, which was built out into the river near the castle and the park. Rosalie paid off the boatman, as they had decided that it would after all be easier to make the return journey by land, on the street railway. The park did not extend quite to the river. They had to follow a rather damp footpath across a meadow, before a venerable, seigniorial landscape, well cared for and well clipped, received them. From an elevated circular terrace, with benches in yew arbours, avenues of magnificent trees, most of them already in bud, though many shoots were still hidden under their shiny brown covers, led in various directions – finely gravelled promenades, often arched over by meeting branches, between rows, and sometimes double rows, of beeches, yews, lindens, horse chestnuts, tall elms. Rare and curious trees, brought from distant countries, were also to be seen, planted singly on stretches of lawn – strange conifers, fern-leafed beeches, and Keaton recognized the Californian sequoia and the swamp cypress with its supplementary breathtaking-roots.

Rosalie took no interest in these curiosities. Nature, she considered, must be familiar, or it did not speak to the heart. But the beauty of the park did not seem to hold much charm for her. Scarcely glancing up now and again at the proud tree-trunks, she walked silently on, with Eduard at her side, behind his young tutor and the hobbling Anna – who, however, soon hit on a manoeuvre to change the arrangement. She stopped and summoned her brother to tell her the names of the avenue they were following and of the winding footpath that crossed it just there. For all these paths and avenues had old, traditional names, such as 'Fan Avenue', 'Trumpet Avenue', and so on. Then, as they moved on, Anna kept Eduard beside her and left Ken behind with Rosalie. He carried her coat, which she had taken off, for not a breath of wind stirred in the park and it was much warmer than it had been on the water. The spring sun shone gently through the high branches, dappled the roads, and played on the faces of the four, making them blink. In her finely tailored brown suit, which closely sheathed her slight, youthful figure, Frau von Tümmler walked at Ken's side, now and again casting a veiled, smiling look at her coat as it hung over his arm. 'There they are!' she cried, and pointed to the pair of black swans; for they were now walking along the poplar-bordered moat, and the birds, aware of the approaching visitors, were gliding nearer, at a stately pace, across the slightly scummy water. 'How beautiful they are! Anna, do you recognize them? How majestically they carry their necks! Where is the bread for them?' Keaton pulled it out of his pocket, wrapped in newspaper, and handed it to her. It was warm from his body, and she took some of the bread and began to eat it.

'But it's stale and hard,' he cried, with a gesture that came too late to stop her.

'I have good teeth,' she answered.

One of the swans, however, pushing close against the bank, spread its dark wings and beat the air with them, stretching out its neck and hissing angrily up at her. They laughed at its jealousy, but at the same time felt a little afraid. Then the birds received their rightful due. Rosalie threw them the stale bread, piece after piece, and, swimming slowly back and forth, they accepted it with imperturbable dignity.

'Yet I fear,' said Anna as they walked on, 'that the old devil

357

won't soon forget your robbing him of his food. He displayed a well-bred pique the whole time.'

'Not at all,' answered Rosalie. 'He was only afraid for a moment that I would eat it all and leave none for him. After that, he must have relished it all the more, since I relished it.'

They came to the castle, to the smooth circular pond which mirrored it and in which, to one side, lay a miniature island bearing a solitary poplar. On the expanse of gravel before the flight of steps leading to the gracefully winged structure, whose considerable dimensions its extreme daintiness seemed to efface, and whose pink façade was crumbling a little, stood a number of people who, as they waited for the eleven o'clock conducted tour, were passing the time by examining the armorial pediment with its figures, the clock, heedless of time and supported by an angel, which surmounted it, the stone wreaths above the tall white portals, and comparing them with the descriptions in their guidebooks. Our friends joined them, and, like them, looked at the charmingly decorated feudal architecture, up to the *œils-de-bœuf* in the slate-coloured garret storey. Figures clad with mythological scantiness, Pan and his nymphs, stood on pedestals beside the long windows, flaking away like the four sandstone lions which, with sullen expressions, their paws crossed, flanked the steps and the ramp.

Keaton was enthusiastic over so much history. He found everything 'splendid' and 'excitingly continental'. Oh dear, to think of his own prosaic country across the Atlantic! There was none of this sort of crumbling aristocratic grace over there, for there had been no Electors and Landgraves, able, in absolute sovereignty, to indulge their passion for magnificence, to their own honour and to the honour of culture. However, his attitude towards the culture which, in its dignity, had not moved on with time, was not so reverent but that, to the amusement of the waiting crowd, he impudently seated himself astride the back of one of the sentinel lions, though it was equipped with a sharp spike, like certain toy horses whose rider can be removed. He clasped the spike in front of him with both hands, pretended, with cries of 'Hi!' and 'Giddap!', that he was giving the beast the spurs, and really could not have presented a more attractive picture of youthful high spirits. Anna and Eduard avoided looking at their mother.

Then bolts creaked, and Keaton hastened to dismount from his steed, for the caretaker, a man wearing military breeches and with his left sleeve empty and rolled up – to all appearances a retired non-commissioned officer whose service injury had been compensated by this quiet post – swung open the central portal and admitted the visitors. He stationed himself in the lofty doorway and, letting them file past him, not only distributed entrance tickets from a small pad, but managed too, with his one hand, to tear them half across. Meanwhile, he had already begun to talk; speaking out of his crooked mouth in a hoarse, gravelly voice, he rattled off the information which he had learned by rote and repeated a thousand times: that the sculptured decoration on the façade was by an artist ·whom the Elector had summoned for the purpose from Rome; that the castle and the park were the work of a French architect; and that the structure was the most important example of Rococo on the Rhine, though it exhibited traces of the transition to the Louis Seize style; that the castle contained fifty-five rooms and had cost eight hundred thousand taler – and so on.

The vestibule exhaled a musty chill. Here, standing ready in rows, were large boat-shaped felt slippers, into which, amid much snickering from the ladies, the party were obliged to step for the protection of the precious parquets, which were, indeed, almost the chief objects of interest in the apartments dedicated to pleasure, through which, awkwardly shuffling and sliding, the party followed their droning one-armed guide. Of different patterns in the various rooms, the central intarsias represented all sorts of star shapes and floral fantasies. Their gleaming surfaces received the reflections of the visitors, of the cambered state furniture, while tall mirrors, set between gilded pillars wreathed in garlands and tapestry fields of flowered silk framed in gilded listels, repeatedly interchanged the images of the crystal chandeliers, the amorous ceiling paintings, the medallions and emblems of the hunt and music over the doors, and, despite a great many blind-spots, still succeeded in evoking the illusion of rooms opening into one another as far as the eye could see. Unbridled luxuriousness, unqualified insistence on gratification, were to be read in the cascades of elegant ornamentation, of gilded scrollwork, restricted only by the inviolable style and taste of the period that had produced them. In the round banquet room, around which, in niches, stood Apollo and the Muses, the inlaid woodwork of the floor gave place to marble, like that which sheathed the walls. Rosy *putti* drew back a painted drapery from the pierced cupola, through which the daylight fell, and from the galleries, as the caretaker said, music had once floated down to the banqueters below.

Ken Keaton was walking beside Frau von Tümmler, with his hand under her elbow. Every American takes his lady across the street in this fashion. Separated from Anna and Eduard, among strangers, they followed close behind the caretaker, who hoarsely, in stilted textbook phrases, unreeled his text and told the party what they were seeing. They were not, he informed them, seeing everything that was to be seen. Of the castle's fifty-five rooms, he went on – and, following his routine, dropped for a moment into vapid insinuation, though his face, with its crooked mouth, remained wholly aloof from the playfulness of his words – not all were simply open without further ado. The gentry of those days had a great taste for jokes and secrets and mysteries, for hiding-places in the background, retreats that, offering opportunities, were accessible through mechanical tricks – such as this one here, for example. And he stopped beside a pier glass, which, in response to his pressing upon a spring, slid aside, surprising the sightseers by a view of a narrow circular staircase with delicately latticed banisters. Immediately to the left, on a pedestal at its foot, stood an armless three-quarters torso of a man with a wreath of berries in his hair and kirtled with a spurious festoon of leaves; leaning back a little, he smiled down into space over his goat's beard, priapic and welcoming. There were ah's and oh's. 'And so on,' said the guide, as he said each time, and returned the trick mirror to its place. 'And so too,' he said, walking on; and made a tapestry panel, which had nothing to distinguish it from the others, open as a secret door and disclose a passageway leading into darkness and exhaling an odour of mould. 'That's the sort of thing they liked,' said the one-armed caretaker. 'Other times, other manners,' he added, with sententious stupidity, and continued the tour.

The felt boats were not easy to keep on one's feet. Frau von Tümmler lost one of hers; it slid some distance away over the smooth floor, and while Keaton laughingly retrieved it and, kneeling, put it on her foot again, they were overtaken by the party of sightseers. Again he put his hand under her elbow, but, with a dreamy smile, she remained standing where she was, looking after the party as it disappeared into further rooms; then, still supported by his hand, she turned and hurriedly ran her fingers over the tapestry, where it had opened.

'You aren't doing it right,' he whispered, 'Let me. It was here.' He found the spring, the door responded, and the mouldy air of the secret passageway enveloped them as they advanced a few steps. It was dark around them. With a sigh drawn from the uttermost depths of her being Rosalie flung her arms around the young man's neck; and he too happily embraced her trembling form. 'Ken, Ken,' she stammered, her face against his throat, 'I love you, I love you, and you know it, I haven't been able to hide it from you completely, and you, and you, do you love me too, a little, only a little, tell me, can you love me with your youth, as Nature has bestowed it on me to love you in my grey age? Yes? Yes? Your mouth then, oh, at last, your young mouth, for which I have hungered, your dear lips, like this, like this – Can I kiss? Tell me, can I, my sweet awakener? I can do everything, as you can. Ken, love is strong, a miracle, so it comes and works great miracles. Kiss me, darling! I have hungered for your lips, oh how much, for I must tell you that my poor head slipped into all sorts of sophistries, like thinking that broad-mindedness and libertinism were not for me, and that the contradiction between my way of life and my innate convictions threatened to destroy me. Oh, Ken, it was the sophistries that almost destroyed me, and my hunger for you ... It is you, it is you at last, this is your hair, this is your mouth, this breath comes from your nostrils, the arms that I know are around me, this is your body's warmth, that I relished and the swan was angry...'

A little more, and she would have sunk to the ground before him. But he held her, and drew her along the passage, which grew a little lighter. Steps descended to the open round arch of a door, behind which murky light fell from above on an alcove whose tapestries were worked with billing pairs of doves. In the alcove stood a sort of causeuse beside which a carved Cupid with blindfolded eyes held a thing like a torch. There, in the musty dampness, they sat down.

'Ugh, it smells of death,' Rosalie shuddered against his shoulder. 'How sad, Ken my darling, that we have to be here amid this decay. It was in kind Nature's lap, fanned by her airs, in the sweet breath of jasmines and alders, that I dreamed it should be, it was there that I should have kissed you for the first time, and not in this grave! Go away, stop it, you devil, I will be yours, but not in this mould. I will come to you tomorrow, in your room, tomorrow morning, perhaps even tonight. I'll arrange it, I'll play a trick on my would-be-wise Anna ...' He made her promise. And indeed they felt too that they must rejoin the others, either by going on or by retracing their steps. Keaton decided in favour of going on. They left the dead pleasure chamber by another door, again there was a dark passageway, it turned, mounted, and they came to a rusty gate, which, in response to Ken's strenuous pushing and tugging, shakily gave way and which was so overgrown outside with leathery vines and creepers that they could hardly force their way through. The open air received them. There was a plash of waters; cascades flowed down behind broad beds set with flowers of the early year, yellow narcissi. It was the back garden of the castle. The group of visitors was just approaching from the right; the caretaker had left them; Anna and her brother were bringing up the rear. The pair mingled with the foremost, who were beginning to scatter towards the fountains and in the direction of the wooded park. It was natural to stand there, look around, and go to meet the brother and sister. 'Where in the world have you been?' And: 'That's just what we want to ask *you*!' And: 'How could we possibly lose sight of one another so?' Anna and Eduard had even, they said, turned back to look for the lost couple, but in vain. 'After all, you

couldn't have vanished from the face of the earth,' said Anna.
'No more than you,' Rosalie answered. None of them looked at
the others.

Walking between rhododendrons, they circled the wing of the
castle and arrived at the pond in front of it, which was quite
close to the street-railway stop. If the boat trip upstream,
following the windings of the Rhine, had been long, the return
journey on the tram, speeding noisily through industrial districts and past colonies of workmen's houses, was correspon-
dingly swift. The brother and sister now and again exchanged a
word with each other or with their mother, whose hand Anna
held for a while because she had seen her trembling. The party
broke up in the city, near the Königsallee.

Frau von Tümmler did not go to Ken Keaton. That night,
towards morning, a severe indisposition attacked her and
alarmed the household. What, on its first return, had made her
so proud, so happy, what she had extolled as a miracle of
Nature and the sublime work of feeling, reappeared calamitously.
She had had the strength to ring, but when her daughter and
the maid came hurrying in, they found her lying in a faint in
her blood.

The physician, Dr Oberloskamp, was soon on the spot. Reviving under his ministrations, she appeared astonished at his
presence.

'What, Doctor, you here?' she said. 'I suppose Anna must
have troubled you to come? But it is only "after the manner of
women" with me.'

'At times, my dear Frau von Tümmler, these functions re-
quire a certain supervision,' the grey-haired doctor answered.
To her daughter he declared categorically that the patient must
be brought, preferably by ambulance, to the gynaecological hospital. The case demanded the most thorough examination –
which, he added, might show that it was not dangerous. Certainly, the metrorrhagias – the first one, of which he had only
now heard, and this alarming recurrence – might well be caused
by a myoma, which could easily be removed by an operation. In
the hands of the director and chief surgeon of the hospital,

Professor Muthesius, her dear mother would receive the most trustworthy care.

His recommendations were followed – without resistance on Frau von Tümmler's part, to Anna's silent amazement. Through it all, her mother only stared into the distance with her eyes very wide open.

The bimanual examination, performed by Muthesius, revealed a uterus far too large for the patient's age, abnormally thickened tissue in the tube, and, instead of an ovary already greatly reduced in size, a huge tumour. The curettage showed carcinoma cells, some of them characteristically ovarian; but others left no doubt that cancer cells were entering into full development in the uterus itself. All the malignancy showed signs of rapid growth.

The professor, a man with a double chin, a very red complexion, and water-blue eyes into which tears came easily – their presence having nothing whatever to do with the state of his emotions – raised his head from the microscope.

'Condition extensive, if you ask me,' he said to his assistant, whose name was Dr Knepperges. 'However, we will operate, Knepperges. Total extirpation, down to the last connective tissue in the true pelvis and to all lymphatic tissue, can in any case prolong life.'

But the picture that the opening of the abdominal cavity revealed, in the white light of the arc-lamps, to the doctors and nurses, was too terrible to permit any hope even of a temporary improvement. The time for that was long since past. Not only were all the pelvic organs already involved; the peritoneum too showed, to the naked eye alone, the murderous cell groups, all the glands of the lymphatic system were carcinomatously thickened, and there was no doubt that there were also foci of cancer cells in the liver.

'Just take a look at this mess, Knepperges,' said Muthesius. 'Presumably it exceeds your expectations.' That it also exceeded his own, he gave no sign. 'Ours is a noble art,' he added, his eyes filling with tears that meant nothing, 'but this is expecting a little too much of it. We can't cut all that away. If you think that you observe metastasis in both ureters, you observe correctly.

Uremia cannot but soon set in. Mind you, I don't deny that the uterus itself is producing the voracious brood. Yet I advise you to adopt my opinion, which is that the whole story started from the ovary – that is, from immature ovarian cells which often remain there from birth and which, after the menopause, through heaven knows what process of stimulation, begin to develop malignantly. And then the organism, *post festum*, if you like, is shot through, drenched, inundated, with estrogen hormones, which leads to hormonal hyperplasia of the uteral mucous membrane, with concomitant haemorrhages.'

Knepperges, a thin, ambitiously conceited man, made a brief, covertly ironical bow of thanks for the lecture.

'Well, let's get on with it, *ut aliquid fieri videatur*,' said the professor. 'We must leave her what is essential for life, however steeped in melancholy the word is in this instance.'

Anna was waiting upstairs in the hospital room when her mother, who had been brought up by the elevator, returned on her stretcher and was put to bed by the nurses. During the process she awoke from her post-narcotic sleep and said indistinctly:

'Anna, my child, he hissed at me.'

'Who, dearest Mama?'

'The black swan.'

She was already asleep again. But she often remembered the swan during the next few weeks, his blood-red bill, the black beating of his wings. Her suffering was brief. Uremic coma soon plunged her into profound unconsciousness, and, double pneumonia developing, her exhausted heart could only hold out for a matter of days.

Just before the end, when it was but a few hours away, her mind cleared again. She raised her eyes to her daughter, who sat at her bedside, holding her hand.

'Anna,' she said, and was able to push the upper part of her body a little towards the edge of the bed, closer to her confidante, 'do you hear me?'

'Certainly I hear you, dear, dear Mama.'

'Anna, never say that Nature deceived me, that she is sardonic and cruel. Do not rail at her, as I do not. I am loth to go away – from you all, from life with its spring. But how should there be spring without death? Indeed, death is a great instrument of life, and if for me it borrowed the guise of resurrection, of the joy of love, that was not a lie, but goodness and mercy.'

Another little push, closer to her daughter, and a failing whisper:

'Nature – I have always loved her, and she – has been loving to her child.'

Rosalie died a gentle death, regretted by all who knew her.

FOR THE BEST IN PAPERBACKS, LOOK FOR THE

In every corner of the world, on every subject under the sun, Penguin represents quality and variety – the very best in publishing today.

For complete information about books available from Penguin – including Pelicans, Puffins, Peregrines and Penguin Classics – and how to order them, write to us at the appropriate address below. Please note that for copyright reasons the selection of books varies from country to country.

In the United Kingdom: For a complete list of books available from Penguin in the U.K., please write to *Dept E.P., Penguin Books Ltd, Harmondsworth, Middlesex, UB7 0DA*

In the United States: For a complete list of books available from Penguin in the U.S., please write to *Dept BA, Penguin, 299 Murray Hill Parkway, East Rutherford, New Jersey 07073*

In Canada: For a complete list of books available from Penguin in Canada, please write to *Penguin Books Canada Ltd, 2801 John Street, Markham, Ontario L3R 1B4*

In Australia: For a complete list of books available from Penguin in Australia, please write to the *Marketing Department, Penguin Books Australia Ltd, P.O. Box 257, Ringwood, Victoria 3134*

In New Zealand: For a complete list of books available from Penguin in New Zealand, please write to the *Marketing Department, Penguin Books (NZ) Ltd, Private Bag, Takapuna, Auckland 9*

In India: For a complete list of books available from Penguin, please write to *Penguin Overseas Ltd, 706 Eros Apartments, 56 Nehru Place, New Delhi, 110019*

In Holland: For a complete list of books available from Penguin in Holland, please write to *Penguin Books Nederland B.V., Postbus 195, NL–1380AD Weesp, Netherlands*

In Germany: For a complete list of books available from Penguin, please write to *Penguin Books Ltd, Friedrichstrasse 10 – 12, D–6000 Frankfurt Main 1, Federal Republic of Germany*

In Spain: For a complete list of books available from Penguin in Spain, please write to *Longman Penguin España, Calle San Nicolas 15, E–28013 Madrid, Spain*

Thomas Mann

DEATH IN VENICE · TRISTAN
TONIO KRÖGER

'Death in Venice' tells how Gustave von Aschenbach, a writer utterly absorbed in his work, arrives in Venice as the result of a 'youthfully ardent thirst for distant scenes', and meets there a young boy by whose beauty he becomes obsessed. His pitiful pursuit of the object of his affection and inevitable and pathetic climax is told here with the particular skill the author has for this shorter form of fiction. The same skill is evident in 'Tristan' and 'Tonio Kröger'. The action of 'Tristan' takes place in a sanatorium, and, as he did in his long novel, *The Magic Mountain*, the author brilliantly portrays the uncertain emotions of people who are forced to live in such places. The theme of 'Tonio Kröger' is that of the artist striving to conform to the pattern of everyday existence.

The pathos of the human condition is a recurring theme with Thomas Mann, but it is a measure of his greatness as a writer that he causes the idea of despair to be surpassed by establishing a sense of spiritual tranquillity.

Also published
THE HOLY SINNER
LITTLE HERR FRIEDEMANN AND OTHER STORIES
THE MAGIC MOUNTAIN
BUDDENBROOKS
CONFESSIONS OF FELIX KRULL, CONFIDENCE MAN
DOCTOR FAUSTUS